THE NEW REPUBLIC

ALSO BY LIONEL SHRIVER

So Much for That
The Post-Birthday World
We Need to Talk About Kevin
Double Fault
A Perfectly Good Family
Game Control
Ordinary Decent Criminals
Checker and the Derailleurs
The Female of the Species

LIONEL SHRIVER

THE NEW REPUBLIC

HarperCollins*Publishers*

HarperCollins*Publishers*
77–85 Fulham Palace Road,
Hammersmith, London W6 8JB

www.harpercollins.co.uk

Published by HarperCollins*Publishers* 2012
1

First published in Great Britain by
HarperCollins*Publishers* 2012

A catalogue record for this book
is available from the British Library

ISBN: 978 0 00 745980 3

Printed and bound in Great Britain by
Clays Ltd, St Ives plc

To Sarowitz, of course—
a solo dedication being long overdue

My experiences with journalists authorize me to record that a very large number of them are ignorant, lazy, opinionated, intellectually dishonest, and inadequately supervised . . . They have huge power, and many of them are extremely reckless.

—CONRAD BLACK

Political language . . . is designed to make lies sound truthful and murder respectable, and to give an appearance of solidity to pure wind.

—GEORGE ORWELL

CONTENTS

ATLANTIC
OCEAN
Porto
PORTUGAL
Madrid
Lisbon
SPAIN
Seville
BARBA
GULF
of
BARBA
Cinzeiro
MEDITERRANEAN SEA
MOROCCO

THE NEW REPUBLIC

CHAPTER 1
Honorable Mention

WHISKING INTO HIS apartment house on West Eighty-Ninth Street, Edgar Kellogg skulked, eager to avoid eye contact with a doorman who at least got a regular paycheck. His steps were quick and tight, his shoulders rounded. Unable to cover next month's rent, he peered anxiously at the elevator indication light stuck on twelve, as if any moment he might be arrested. Maxing out the credit cards came next. This place used to give him such a kick. Now that he couldn't afford it, the kick was in the teeth, and tapping cordovans literally down at the heel, he calculated morosely that for every day in this fatuous dive he was out ninety bucks. Waiting on a $175 check from the *Amoco Traveler* was like trying to bail out a rowboat with an eyedropper while the cold, briny deep gushed through a hole the size of a rubber boot.

Up on the nineteenth floor, Edgar shot a look around at what, underneath it all, was a plushly appointed one-bedroom, but the management's cleaning service had been one of the first luxuries to go. At only ten a.m., Edgar found himself already eyeing the Doritos on the counter. One thing he hadn't anticipated about the "home office" was Snack Syndrome; lately his mental energies divided evenly between his new calling (worrying about money, which substituted neatly for earning it) and not stuffing his face. God, he was turning into a girl, and in no time would find himself helplessly contriving sassy Ryvita open-faces with cherry tomatoes (only twenty-five calories!). The thought came at him with a thud: *This isn't working out.* Quick on its heels, *I've made a terrible mistake.* And, since Edgar was never one to put too fine a point on it, *I'm an ass.*

This was not the positive thinking that the how-tos commended in the run-up to a job interview, in preparation for which Edgar cleared off the beer cans and spread out the *National Record*. Hours in advance, his concentration was already shaky. Picking out single words in strobe, his eyes skittered across an article about terrorism: these days it was news that there wasn't any. Further down: some correspondent had gone missing three months ago. The gist: he was still missing. If it weren't a reporter who'd vanished, this "story" would never have run, much less on the front page. After all, if Edgar Kellogg disappeared tomorrow, the *Record* was unlikely to run frantic updates on the ongoing search for a prematurely retired attorney turned nobody freelancer. In the argot of his new trade, "freelance" was apparently insider jargon for "unemployed," and when he mumbled the word to acquaintances they smirked.

Yet instead of getting up to speed on current events, Edgar found himself once again compulsively scanning for a Tobias Falconer byline. Funny thing was, when he found one, he wouldn't read the article. And this was typical. For years he'd snagged this oppressively earnest, tiny-print newspaper—one of the last austere holdouts that refused to go color—solely to locate Falconer's pieces, but he could seldom submit to reading them. Edgar had never tried to identify what he feared.

Collapsing into the deep corduroy sofa, Edgar surrendered to the free-floating reflection that ten frenzied years on Wall Street had so mercifully forestalled. For all that time, Toby Falconer's supercharged byline had given Edgar a jolt, its alternating current of envy and wistfulness confusing but addictive. These little zaps made his scalp tingle, but reading whole features would be like sticking his fingers into a light socket. In that event, why buy the paper at all? Why monitor the career of a man whom Edgar hadn't seen in twenty years, and of a traitor to boot, whose very surname made him wince?

But then, Falconer's fortunes had been easy to follow. A foreign correspondent first for *U.S. News and World Report*, then, seminally, for the *National Record*, he filed peripatetically from Beirut to Belfast to Sarajevo. More than once he'd won a prize for covering a story that was especially risky or previously neglected, and these awards filled Edgar with a baffling mixture of irritation and pride. Of course, Edgar had chosen the far more lucrative occupation. Yet he'd learned to his despair how little money was worth if it couldn't buy you out of slogging at seven a.m. into a law firm you reviled. "Well compensated" was an apt turn of phrase, though in the end he couldn't imagine any sum so vast that it could truly offset flushing twelve, thirteen hours of every waking day down the toilet.

When Edgar ditched his "promising" career in corporate law (though what it promised, of course, was more corporate law) in order to try his hand at journalism six months ago, he'd been reluctant to examine in what measure this impetuous and financially suicidal reinvention might have been influenced by his old high school running buddy—who, having always obtained the funnier friends, the prettier girls, and the sexier summer jobs, had naturally secured the jazzier vocation. If Toby Falconer and Edgar Kellogg were both drawn to journalism in the fullness of time, maybe the convergence merely indicated that the two boys had had more in common at Yardley Prep than Edgar had ever dared believe as a kid.

Dream on. To imagine that he bore any resemblance to Falconer in adolescence was so vain as to be fanciful. Toby Falconer was a specimen. No doubt every high school had one, though the singular was incongruous as a type; presumably there was no one else like him.

A Falconer was the kind of guy about whom other people couldn't stop talking. He managed to be the center of attention when he wasn't even there. He always got girls, but more to the point he got *the* girl. Whichever dish you yourself envisioned with the bathroom door closed, she'd be smitten with our hero instead. Some cachet would rub off, of course, but if you hung with a Falconer you'd spend most of your dates fielding questions about his troubled childhood. A Falconer's liberty was almost perfectly unfettered, because he was never punished for his sins. Anyway, a Falconer's sins wouldn't seem depraved but merely naughty, waggish, or rather enchanting really, part of the package without which a Falconer wouldn't be the endearing rogue whom we know and love and infinitely forgive. Besides, who would risk his displeasure by bringing him to book? He did everything with flair, not only because he was socially adroit, but because the definition of flair in his circle was however the Falconer did whatever the Falconer did. To what extent a Falconer's magnetism could be ascribed to physical beauty was impossible to determine. Good looks couldn't have hurt; still, if a Falconer had any deviant feature—a lumpy nose, or a single continuous eyebrow—that feature would simply serve to reconfigure the beautiful as archetype. A Falconer set the standard, so by his very nature could not appear unattractive, make a plainly stupid remark, or do anything awkward at which others would laugh, save in an ardent, collusive, or sycophantic spirit.

Hitherto Edgar had been the Falconer's counterpart, that symbiotic creature without which a Falconer could not exist. The much admired required the admirer, and to his own dismay Edgar had more than once applied for the position. While he'd have far preferred the role of BMOC if the post were going begging, he was eternally trapped by a Catch-22: in yearning to be admired himself, he was bound to admire other people who were admirable. Which made him, necessarily, a fan.

To date, the only weapon that had overthrown a Falconer's tyranny was cruel, disciplined disillusionment. Sometimes a Falconer turned out to be a fraud. Lo and behold, he could be clumsy, if you kept watch. At length it proved thoroughly possible, if you forced yourself, to laugh at his foibles in a fashion that was less than flattering. Wising up was painful at first, but a relief, and when all was said and done Edgar would be lonely but free. Yet taking the anointed down a peg or two was a puzzling, even depressing exercise, in consequence of which he reserved his most scathing denunciations for the very people with whom he had once been most powerfully entranced.

Edgar's public manner—gruff, tough, wary, and deadpan—was wildly discrepant with his secret weakness for becoming captivated by passing Falconers, and he worried privately that the whole purpose of his crusty exterior was to contain an inside full of goo. He couldn't bear to conceive of himself as a sidekick. Having ever been slavishly enthralled to an idol of any sort shamed him almost as much as having once been fat. Hence of Edgar's several ambitions at thirty-seven the most dominant was never to succumb to the enchantment of a Falconer again.

It was in the grip of precisely this resolution that Edgar Kellogg had marched out of Lee & Thole six months ago, determined to cast off the dreary Burberry of the overpaid schmo. At last he would grow into the grander mantle of standard-bearer, trendsetter, and cultural icon. It was in the grip of this same resolution that Edgar set off for his four p.m. job interview with the *National Record*. He'd had it with being The Fan. He wanted to be The Man.

CHAPTER 2
Saddling Up

"WIN, THAT YOU? Guy Wallasek at the *Record.* I know it's been three months, so this is a formality—I'm way past the mother-hen stage. But Saddler hasn't *deigned* to show his face in Barba, has he? . . . Here? At this point, he wouldn't dare . . . I stand corrected. Whatever Saddler lacks in consideration, he makes up in gall." The lardy editor covered the receiver's mouthpiece and murmured to his four p.m. appointment, "Be right with you."

Edgar squinted at framed Pulitzers, nodding, pretending to be impressed. These props exhausted, from the lamp table he picked up a rectangular coaster, laminated with a reduced front page from the *National Record*, **RED ARMY OVERTHROWS GORBACHEV GOVERNMENT**. The byline, hard to make out, began with a B. He'd change places with that reporter in a New York minute. Chasing tanks with a microcassette beat the dickens out of filing another prospectus for public offering. The window behind Guy Wallasek afforded an uninspiring view of solid green glass; soon Edgar would run out of ostensible fascinations. He didn't want to seem to lose himself in the copy of today's *Record*, implying that he hadn't read it.

The desk chair squealed as Wallasek leaned back. "I'd sure like to give him a piece of my . . ." The big man chuckled. "Yeah, I'm kidding myself. I'd probably fix our prodigal a cup of tea. I'm *only* his boss, right? . . . Me? At first I assumed it was a stunt. Another one. But what would Saddler do with more attention? Keep it in jars? And that peninsula of yours is such a snake pit . . ."

Edgar's face was stiff from keeping an unnaturally pleasant

I'm-in-no-hurry expression in place for ten minutes. Wallasek could easily have made this call before their appointment. And why bother with the power play? Edgar would have stripped to his boxers and danced the cha-cha for a chance to write for Wallasek's foreign desk.

The editor guffawed, shooting Edgar a glance to make sure he felt left out of the joke. "You do see him," Wallasek went on, "tell Barrington next time he takes a vacation maybe he could send a postcard. Lucky for the *Record* the story's gone into deep freeze. The SOB hasn't claimed so much as a faulty Chinese firework since Saddler went AWOL, right?

" . . . Rich, isn't it? That bastard has drawn slack-jawed adulation by the drool bucket—not to mention apoplectic rage. But *worry* is new. Must be the odd champagne glass raised in his absence, yeah? . . . *Cer-ve-ja de puka pera?*" Wallasek pronounced with difficulty. "Sounds revolting. Thank the Lord for you brave foreign correspondents and your sacrifice for the world's hungry need to know . . . Sarcastic, *moi*?" Chortle-chortle. "Yeah, they don't make nemeses like they used to, Win. Ciao."

Edgar's amiable grin had, he feared, slid to a grimace. His girlfriend Angela always ragged on him for slouching, and his erect I'm-just-the-man-you're-looking-for posture in the director's chair was hurting his back. Meanwhile, Wallasek fussed with papers on a desk that was every job applicant's nightmare: crumpled piles doubtless dating back two presidential administrations, grease-stained with Danish crumbs. You'd never get away with a desk like that at Lee & Thole.

"So!" Wallasek exhaled, locating Edgar's clips and CV. Their binder was missing, the photocopies disheveled. An uncomprehending gaze betrayed that Wallasek hadn't read a paragraph of Edgar's articles. Next time he wouldn't bother with the color photocopying, which looked nifty but cost a buck a page. Edgar squirmed. Maybe clued-up hacks never sent color clips. The bright borders beaming from the editor's hands looked overeager. Edgar welcomed the common charge that he was a wiseass—rude, surly, and insubordinate—but the prospect of appearing a rookie was mortifying.

He slouched.

"Mr.—Kellogg!" Wallasek exclaimed, with the same sense of discovery with which he'd looked up to find that a stranger had been sitting in his office for the last fifteen minutes. "No trouble finding the place?"

"The Equitable Building is bigger than a breadbox." Edgar chafed at pre-interview chitchat and its artifice of relax-we-haven't-started-yet, when empty schmooze was really one more test to pass. He had to stop himself from fast-forwarding, this summer has sure been a hot one and that's a *mighty fine* wife in your desk photo there and you don't have to ask where I live since the address is on my résumé and no I don't want a cup of coffee.

"Can I get you—?"

"Nothing, thanks." To encourage a cut to the chase, Edgar shot a pointed glance at his chunky gold-plated diving watch. In the context of Edgar's current average income of $300/month, its gratuitous dials spun with a dizzying exorbitance that until this spring he'd taken for granted.

"Second in your class," Wallasek muttered, running a finger down the CV. "Vice president . . . Honorable mention . . . Salutatorian . . . Second prize . . . Second-chair . . . Say, you've *almost* snagged a lot of things."

"I'm one of life's runners-up." Having failed to keep the edge from his voice, Edgar moderated pleasantly, "We try harder."

Wallasek pulled back the arm on a pair of nail clippers and stuck the end in his ear, digging for wax. "A book review for *Newsday*," he ruminated, spreading the photocopies. "The *Village Voice*—that's a freebie now, isn't it?"

"Yes, sir," Edgar said stonily.

"*Washington Times* . . . The Moonie paper."

Since the early eighties the *Washington Times* had been owned by a fat Korean evangelist. "The staff does maintain independent editorial control."

"Yes—or so they claim. Still, it's not the *Post*, is it?"

"No, sirree," Edgar agreed, clicking his eyeteeth, "it ain't the *Washington Post*."

"*Columbia Alumni Magazine*, *Amtrak Express*." Examining his nail clipper arm, the editor removed a sulfurous chunk from its tip before returning to Edgar's fledgling journalism, none of which seemed to generate the intense fascination of the gunk from Wallasek's ear.

"And the *New Republic*," Edgar pointed out.

"The rest of these seem to be law review. How much do you know about the *National Record*?"

"I'm a regular reader," Edgar lied; once he'd scanned for Falconer's byline he generally tossed the rag, since its sports section sucked. "I appreciate that the *Record* filled a void. For this country's only national newspaper to have remained *USA Today* would have been a scandal."

Wallasek still looked expectant; Edgar hadn't yet laid it on thick enough. "The *Record* also embraces America's post–Cold War global leadership. Your international coverage is at least as thorough as the *New York Times*. In assuming that readers care about the rest of the world, you don't condescend to your subscribers." Edgar had to stop; his inflection had developed the lilt of implausible enthusiasm employed to retail panty shields.

"Of course we condescend to our subscribers," Wallasek dismissed with a wave. "International coverage is a sop to their vanity. Only a handful read that stuff. With one exception: when our American everyman tucks the *Record* under one arm and trundles into a seven-forty-seven and one of those filthy little foreigners blows it up. Those articles get read, my friend. Every column inch."

Edgar found railing against terrorists the height of tedium. The issue invited over-obvious moralizing, since who's going to contend that wasting those two kids with a trashcan bomb in a D.C. shopping mall in April was a profound political statement? Presumably Edgar was now obliged to chime in with hearty indignation over the *Soldatsies Oozhatsies*, or whatever those sorry-ass crackpots called themselves, clenching his fist in we-shall-not-be-moved solidarity with his fellow Americans, who will *never capitulate to terrorism*. Or maybe he should small-talk about how amazing it was that the FBI hadn't collared a single one of these dirtbags, to demonstrate that he was on top of the story. But this interview wasn't going well, the application had been a long shot to begin with, and Edgar passed.

"You aware of how the *Record* managed to establish a reputation for quality journalism in so few years?" asked Wallasek.

"Astute editing, a clearly defined remit—"

"Balls," Wallasek cut him off. "By paying better than any paper in the country."

Edgar smiled despite himself. "I know."

"What I'm getting at here is that, well, you've got a few nice clips—"

"Those are only samples, of course."

They both knew that Edgar had furnished every semicolon he'd ever published.

"Still, Mr. Kellogg, aren't you aiming a little high?"

"I explained in my cover letter—"

"Yes—you 'quit the law to become a freelance journalist.' That caught my eye."

"I left a top Wall Street firm where I was about to make partner," said Edgar. "Until a few months ago I was making two hundred grand a year and rising. The *Record* may pay well, but that well? Seems to me that, however you slice it, I'm not 'aiming high,' but asking for a whopping cut in salary."

"So I should hire you because you're nuts?"

Edgar laughed. "Or what's the latest prissy buzz phrase? *Learning-delayed.*"

Wallasek squinted. "What possessed you?"

Edgar paused. He'd rehearsed his explanation in the taxi on the way here, the cab itself an extravagance left over from the Lee & Thole days—a habit he'd have to break. Despite his designer slouch, Edgar must have been nervous; the glib rationale fled. Only overwrought snippets from college D. H. Lawrence classes flitted back to him, like "inchoate yearning." He could not emote to some bovine newspaperman about "inchoate yearning" any more than he could assert to Toby's own boss that he was driven to become "a Falconer."

Lately he'd had to wonder, *was* he crazy? Papaya King again for lunch, when six months ago he might have dined on a client's tab at The Cub Room. Had he been asked to go to Syracuse on short notice, he could have charged the firm for a new shirt and sent a messenger to pick it up. If he stayed past 7:30 p.m. (like, until 7:31), a Dial-car would drive him home. How could he ever explain to Guy Wallasek that privilege might have enticed an overworked paralegal, but that when Edgar was finally able to overbill clients himself the practice had seemed abruptly low-rent? Or that for no self-evident reason Edgar was meant for something finer than drafting turgid briefs? Or that he wanted to "say something," when the very ache to say "something" and not something in particular must have put Edgar in the same boat as every other flailing schmuck in the country?

"I got bored," Edgar telescoped lamely.

"Writing for *Amtrak Express* amuses you more?"

"Gotta start somewhere. And the law felt, I don't know, passive. We're parasites."

"Journalists are parasites," Wallasek countered, "on everyone else's events. Plenty of scribblers spend their workdays merely recording what you just walked away from: mergers and acquisitions, transfers of money and power. The worst thing that can happen to a correspondent is to start thinking of himself as a player. The hack who fancies himself a mover-and-shaker gets slipshod—thinks he's covering his own story. Reporting is a humble profession, Mr. Kellogg. Journalists—" Wallasek shrugged—"are History's secretaries."

"Better History's secretary than Philip Morris's lawyer," Edgar ventured. "At least hacks get bylines. Law's an anonymous profession, behind the scenes. Attorneys are paid so much because the work is drab and thankless. A predictable calling for runners-up. But I don't want honorable mentions anymore, Mr. Wallasek. I'd like to distinguish myself."

"You want to see your name in print," said Wallasek skeptically.

"I want to see anything in print that isn't solely composed to help some suit who already has more money than he knows what to do with make a little more." Edgar pressed on with a willful geekiness refreshingly unlike him, "I want to get at the truth."

"The 'truth' most reporters get at is pretty pedestrian: the secretary of state left the White House at five forty p.m. and not at six o'clock. As for the big-picture sort . . ." Wallasek seemed to take a moment to reflect, and ran a dirty nail along the stitching of his jacket. "I didn't used to camp behind a desk, Mr. Kellogg. Funny, I don't miss pounding the pavement much as I might have expected. I cut my teeth in Vietnam, hung up my hat after Grenada. I can't say for sure if I've a better understanding, of anything, than the folks who stayed in bed. Damnedest thing, but you can be right there in the middle, two armies tearing each other apart, and afterwards have not one thing to say about it. Not one thing. Way it should be. A reporter's not supposed to chip in his two cents. But this—failure to achieve perspective. It can be personally discouraging. There's no overarching 'truth' out there. Only a bunch of menial, dissociated little facts. And the facts don't often add up to much. Lotta trees; not much forest. Oh, once in a rare while you trip over an *All the President's Men*, and get to play the hero. But for the most part you just find out what happened, and what happened is depressing."

"No more depressing than Lee & Thole."

"I only wonder if your expectations aren't a mite steep. Not only of getting a staff job at this newspaper, but of what the job would entail if I were rash enough to offer a post to an inexperienced, middle-aged cub."

Edgar could skip the fatherly advice, as well as being classed at only thirty-seven as "middle-aged." Before he could stop it, his hand was tracing his forehead, as if his hairline might have receded another half-inch since he checked it this morning. On the way back to his lap, Edgar's fingertips traced the deep V-shaped runnels of a scowl so habitual that Angela claimed he frowned in his sleep.

"You're the one who asked me for an interview," Edgar grunted. "You could've flipped my CV in the trash." Edgar reached for his briefcase.

Wallasek raised his palm. "Hold your horses. Toby Falconer recommended you, and he's the most solid, levelheaded staffer here. Toby said you were 'persevering, thorough, and single-minded' once you'd set your sights on something."

Edgar was quietly embarrassed. Making last month's tremulous phone call to Falconer (to whom the adjectives "solid" and "levelheaded" would never have been applied at Yardley) had been so difficult that it made him physically ill. Although Falconer had been dumbfoundingly decent, Edgar had a queasy feeling that on his end the call hadn't gone well. He'd felt ashamed of himself—tapping Toby for connections, after all those years without so much as a how-do-you-do. Chagrin had made him resentful, maybe even truculent. This was hardly the circumstance in which he'd fantasized about contacting the guy, and he'd never have pushed his luck like that if his level of desperation hadn't gone through the roof. But by then, the night sweats had begun. In his dreams, Edgar implored Richard Stokes Thole to take him back without health coverage while wearing nothing but lime-green socks; the imposing senior partner scolded that the firm had gone casual on Fridays but it was Thursday and his socks ought really to be brown or black.

As for that "single-minded" jazz? Edgar's shedding a hundred pounds in his junior year at Yardley must have left a lasting impression.

"Toby figured your law skills would transfer to journalism: interviewing, library research, writing up cases. Besides," Wallasek got to the point at last, "I have a problem."

Edgar's eyebrows shot up before they plowed into a more agreeable scowl. Once resumed, his slouch cut a jauntier slant.

"You up to speed on the Barban conflict?" asked Wallasek.

Though Edgar had scanned his share of headlines (who could miss them when they were two inches high?), the SOB's cause had sounded so tiresome when the fringe group surfaced a few years ago that Edgar had happily added Barba to the growing list of too-complicated-and-who-gives-a-fuck shit holes about which Edgar refused to read—along with Bosnia, Angola, Algeria, and Azerbaijan. Before cramming current events to prepare for this interview, Edgar couldn't have pinpointed the jerkwater within a thousand miles on a map.

"Never been there," said Edgar. "But of course I've followed the story closely."

"Wouldn't speak any Portuguese, would you?"

"I went to prep school in Stonington, Connecticut, settled by Portuguese immigrants. I'm not fluent, but I get by." In truth, his total Portuguese vocabulary came down to three words, *filho da puta*, and "son of a whore" had limited application. Still, something was opening up here, and Edgar had no desire to go home and draft a proposal for American's in-flight magazine.

Wallasek rose and stretched; his thigh splayed as he perched chummily on the desk. "The SOB has been lying low, and the story may be played out. But some folks are convinced that this is an undeclared cessation not because they're giving up, but because they're gearing up for something big. Thomas Friedman wrote in the *Times* last week that canny terrorists vary the pace of their campaign. For a while there, the Sobs were blowing up a subway or an airplane like clockwork, every six weeks or so. People can get used to anything. Pretty soon, you've got these miscreants going to all that trouble blowing stuff up, only to maintain the impression that nothing's new. Tom was ostensibly urging we not get complacent about security, but I wasn't sure about that column myself. Almost like Friedman giving those maniacs good tactical advice."

It was Pavlovian: Wallasek mentions Barba, and Edgar's mind wanders. In fact, Edgar had been musing how when the "SOB" first emerged in the news everyone had thought the name of the group was a laugh. Nowadays even management types like Wallasek here cited the acronym with a straight face. You actually had to remind yourself that in olden times it meant son of a bitch.

"Point is," Wallasek continued, "any day now we could have another horror show splattered across the front page, and the *Record* could be caught with its pants down."

"How's that?"

Wallasek sucked his cheeks between his molars and chewed. He stood up. He jammed his hands in his pockets and jingled his keys. He glowered piercingly at his toes, as if trying to burn extra holes in his wingtips.

"Barrington Saddler."

He didn't ask, "Have you heard of—?" or introduce, "There's this fellow called—" The editor simply plunked the name in the room like a heavy object he'd been lugging around and was relieved to chuck on the floor. Wallasek himself gazed at a midpoint in the office as if some large physical presence would manifest itself.

Sure, Edgar had caught references to some bombastic-sounding buffoon while he was waiting for Wallasek to get off the phone. But that didn't altogether explain Edgar's nagging impression of having heard the name before.

In any event, the name put Edgar off from the start. The "Barrington" bit was overblown and beefy, and anyone who didn't have the wit to shorten the pretentious appellation down to "Barry" was a pompous ass. The tag evoked adjectives like over*bear*ing and un*bear*able, and New Englanders would experience an irksome impulse to place the word "Great" in front of it.

"Barrington Saddler was sent to earth to try my personal patience," Wallasek had resumed. "Maybe it's because I'm still trying valiantly to pass God's test of my character that I haven't fired the man. That and because Saddler is supposedly one of our star reporters. I'll spare you the nitty-gritty unless someday you appear in need of a cautionary tale, but Barrington was posted to Russia, where Barrington was bad. I could've axed him then, but his boosters would've put up a stink, and I do have this indefensible fondness for the lout.

"So I decided to exile him instead. I spread out a map of Europe and located the most far-flung, poorest, *dullest* corner of the Continent. This worthless jut of Portugal hadn't rated passing mention in the American press for two hundred years. I figured, here was the perfect place for Saddler to contemplate the error of his ways. Here was the one place he'd never draw a crowd—another protective, gossipy clique that goads him into mischief. Because *no one went there.* No tourists, no expats, much less any of his journo buddies on assignment, because there was jack to cover, just a bunch of Iberian crackers babbling a language he'd be too lazy to learn and good Catholic girls who'd keep their bodices buttoned. I'd keep him on salary until he'd learned his lesson, and he'd come back from this sandbox having got nothing in the paper all year, suitably chastened and ready to play by the rules as one more humble steno in History's secretarial pool.

"And *where* is this Podunk across the pond?" Wallasek charged ferociously.

"Barba," Edgar guessed.

"BARBA! Which within months of Saddler's arrival sprouts the single most lethal terrorist organization of the twentieth century. Ever, I reckon. And there's Saddler, happy as a pig in shit, in the very center of the story, firing off front-page leads on the ultimatums of the SOB. A predictable cadre descends on the dump—the *Times*, the *Post*, and the *Guardian* now have permanent staffers in the provincial capital, Cinzeiro. Even the London *Independent*, which is terminally broke, keeps a string. Presto, Saddler's leading a hack pack again. I'd say the man is charmed, except that lately I've wondered if this cat is finally on life number ten."

"Saddler's in trouble?" Once again, Edgar felt a weird familiarity with this preposterous character, a shared exasperation.

"Maybe he cozied up to those murderous douchebags too close, I don't know. He's reckless; he thinks danger is funny. Anyway, three months ago he disappeared. Vanished, poof, gone. Practically left his coffee cooling and his Camel burning. Which is where you come in."

"I was a lawyer, not a PI."

"I don't expect you to look for him. That's the cops' job, which they've already done, badly if you ask me. This Cinzeiro police chief Lieutenant Car-ho-ho, or whoever, *claims* to have left no stone unturned. He's one of those parochial rubes crazed with petty power who's very possessive about his patch. I've talked to him. Try to suggest maybe he hasn't tried all the angles, and he gets snippy and defensive and patriotic on you. You'll see—Barbans are all like that. Touchy. And all roads lead to their cloverleaf politics. Mention the flipping weather—which I gather stinks—and you've insulted their precious national pride. Anyway, the guy came up with diddly. No leads. Left me to believe Saddler must have been abducted by aliens or something."

"So what's the gig?" Edgar pressed, forcing his leg to stop jittering.

Wallasek clapped his hands. "I need a correspondent in Barba. I've given up waiting for Saddler to send flowers. So I'm offering you a string. There is a retainer, which technically makes you a 'super-stringer,' but don't let the heroic title go to your head; our monthly gratuity will keep your tape recorder in fresh batteries, and that's about it. Flat-rate four hundred bucks an article, plus expenses, but only for the pieces we print. We'll pay your initial freight. No benefits. You can set yourself up in Barrington's digs; I gather he even left his car.

"But this arrangement would be provisional," Wallasek barreled on before Edgar had a chance to say yes or no. "Barrington's been on board this paper from its inception. He's an institution, if you like. If he shows up with an explanation I can even pretend to swallow, the posting's his again. He knows this story, been on it from the ground up. So Saddler shows up next week, your string is for one week."

"The retainer, how much . . . ?"

"You're embarrassing me," Wallasek cut him off. "Three-fifty a month, which is as appalling as it is nonnegotiable. Furthermore, you gotta be prepared for plenty of computer solitaire. It's possible the SOB has called it quits, or maybe they've clawed each other's eyes out; these hot-blooded paramilitary outfits often self-destruct. In that case, the story's dead, and you're on your own. I can't guarantee another posting, either. This is a one-time offer. On the other hand, the story heats up, Saddler's still among the disappeared? You could spin this into a big break. Think you could handle that?" In brandishing disclaimers, the editor clearly read Edgar as so hard-up that he couldn't afford to be choosy. Wallasek was right.

This was indeed a big break, so Edgar's hesitation was absurd. The offer far exceeded his expectations, the very expectations that Wallasek had mocked for being set so high. Edgar had figured that at best he'd get the go-ahead to submit a feature on spec, or a promise to keep his CV "on file"—that is, incinerated only after he walked out and not before his eyes. This "super-string" paid peanuts, but had a spicy *ring* to it, and was a foot in the door. Maybe sometime soon 245 civilians would make him a lucky man: **DEATH TOLL IN HUNDREDS AS SOB CLAIMS SABOTAGE OF UNITED FLIGHT 169**, *by Edgar Kellogg, Barba Correspondent.*

Still, something in the setup oppressed him. Whoever Saddler was, sight-unseen the guy clearly belonged to the elite Exception to Every Rule Club, whose members cast the sort of shadow in which Edgar had lived all his life: the eponymous Falconer, of course, but Edgar's super-jock older brother as well; the suffocatingly august Richard Stokes Thole; Angela's affected ex-lover on whom she was secretly still stuck; all those valedictorians, first-chairs, first-prize winners, and presidents.

Furthermore, Edgar was leery of substituting for a minor-league celeb who could show up unannounced any time to reclaim his home, his car, his beat, his half-smoked Camel, and his cold coffee. The very name "Saddler" sounded burdensome. Edgar imagined himself trudging a bleak landscape mounded with his predecessor's baggage, like a loose burro too dumb and biddable to buck the chattel off his back.

"I guess I'm game," said Edgar uncertainly. "How soon should I go?"

"ASAP. And here . . ." Wallasek scribbled an address, which he apparently knew by heart. "Saddler's digs." He held out a sheet of paper, adding obscurely, "You won't suffer."

Edgar accepted the paper. "So how do I . . . ?"

"Book a flight, submit a receipt, we'll reimburse," Wallasek yadda-yadda-ed. "Oh, and one more thing." The editor thumbed a furry leather contact book on his desk, then snatched the paper back to scrawl a number. "You might get a key to the house from Nicola." Returning the page with a teasing shimmy, Wallasek leered. "One of Saddler's *friends*. His very best *friend*, from all reports. I've never met her, but it's funny how often Saddler's numerous *friends* turn out to be good-looking women."

A red flag went up: after spending ten seconds on the logistics of Edgar's whole new life and forty-five minutes on this feckless cad playing hooky, *Wallasek still couldn't stop talking about Saddler.*

Edgar folded the paper, stalling. He was sure there were dozens of questions he should be asking, equally sure that they wouldn't occur to him until he was on the plane. "So, um. What's my first assignment?"

"The strange and terrible fate of Barrington Saddler, what else?"

CHAPTER 3
Long Time, No See

IT MAY HAVE been almost twenty years since they'd nodded stiffly at each other across a throng of parents at Yardley's graduation, but Edgar didn't anticipate having any trouble recognizing Toby Falconer when they met for a post-interview drink. Toby was one of those golden boys. His hair was so blond it was almost white, confirming for Edgar, whose own mop was mouse-brown, that the chosen people weren't self-made but genetically marked. Vertical as a mast, Toby's Nordic frame and sea-green eyes called out for bearskins and a javelin. It was unlikely he'd kept that smooth, narrow chest into manhood, but Falconer was vain enough by sixteen that he'd probably become one of those Nautilus obsessives who poured rice milk on his muesli. Besides, Edgar's paltry efforts to update his mental mock-up of Toby Falconer—to bulge the muscular wavelets of his stomach into a paunchy swell, to dull the sublime adolescent promise of that platinum blond down to pewter—felt juvenile, like drawing zits on a *GQ* model with a ballpoint.

He was a little surprised that Falconer's choice of venue didn't show more panache. The Red Shoe had once been a chic Flatiron watering hole, but that was years back. Since, the crimson velvet cushions had faded to sickly pink, their plush nap flattened like a cat's fur in the sink. The varnish on the dark banquettes had worn to expose stained pine. Its waiters were old enough to no longer describe their shifts as "day jobs." Even Wall Street knew The Red Shoe was déclassé. Maybe it was sufficiently out of fashion to qualify for a tongue-in-cheek reprise, and Toby, as usual, was setting the pace.

Edgar paused in The Red Shoe's foyer, preparing himself for his old friend—or whatever it was that Toby had become by senior year. After mussing his hair, releasing his top shirt button, and yanking the Windsor knot to the side the way he once wrenched his school tie, Edgar ditched his suit jacket on the coat rack. Edgar's image at Yardley had been hostile, unkempt, and seditious; an intact chalk-stripe might give Falconer a shock.

Edgar turned and heard a plop. The hanger arm had flipped upside-down and dumped his jacket on the floor. Stripped screw. Flustered, Edgar scooped up the jacket, hastily brushing the lapels. Damn. Especially in these in-between moments—tossing a coat on a rack, swinging from a bucket seat—Toby Falconer had been infuriatingly graceful.

Inhaling, Edgar launched through the double doors, his coat hooked over a shoulder. He was flattering himself to picture his old buddy, waiting expectantly in a corner by himself. Falconer was always mobbed. Forget homing in on the beacon of hair. Just locate the social goat-fuck in the very center of this dive, its biggest table, the one crammed with extra chairs—one more of which Edgar would be obliged to fetch and wedge in somewhere. Falconer would be braying, those mighty fluoride-fortified teeth arrayed to the smoky tin ceiling, arms spread and palms lifted like Jesus, the rest of the rabble wheezing, flopping, wiping tears.

But the bar was quiet. Edgar scanned the large round middle tables: one subdued party, workmates, glancing at watches, looking for an excuse to scram. A couple of loners sagging in booths—one wrung-out dishrag, quietly sobbing (that made three weeping women that he'd happened across today; the daily New York average was five or six), and some balding nondescript.

But then, why would Toby Falconer be prompt? Edgar would stew here for an hour, knocking back beers and refurbishing a resentment that two decades had failed to anodize into indifference. Finally, when Edgar was requesting his check, Toby would sashay in, double doors swinging with his dozen disciples, all drunk, loud, and dashingly dressed, infusing this old-man's-bathrobe of a bar with its original camp, smoking-jacket flash. For now refusing to consider the higher likelihood that Falconer had blown off their appointment altogether, Edgar assumed a chair at the center-most table and signaled for a waiter.

"Edgar?"

Edgar twisted at the finger on his arm, and experienced one of those blank moments induced by headlines about Barba or Montenegro. It was the balding nondescript. His eyes were mild and dilute, their lids puffy; his face was broad and bland, his figure padded. The man's skin was pallid, in contrast to the lustrous walnut glow of a thrill-seeker who hot-dogged the winter slopes and sailed at the head of his regatta. But between the gray straggles across his scalp gleamed a few nostalgic streaks of platinum.

"Falconer!" Edgar pumped the stranger's hand.

"I don't know what football team you're expecting. Let's sit over here. Listen, I'm sorry about The Red Shoe. Last time I was here it was hopping, but I don't get out much. Christ, you look the same! A little more pissed off, maybe . . . If that's possible. But you sure kept that weight off."

"You, too, you look—terrific!"

Falconer guffawed, a more muffled version of the old clarion bray, recognizable but rounder, less piercing. "Never thought I'd see the day Edgar Kellogg was polite. I look like dog shit! Dog shit with three hyperactive kids and a depressive wife. What'll you have?"

Edgar liked to think of himself as a Wild Turkey man. "Amstel Light."

"Never lose *the fear*, do you?" Falconer smiled, his teeth no longer blinding, though that was unfair; everybody's teeth yellowed a bit with age. But the smile also seemed physically smaller, and that was impossible.

"Not quite," Edgar admitted, telling himself not to stare. "Inside this runt there's always a fat slob struggling to get out."

"A lot of Yardley's a blur now, but one thing I remember clear as a *Dialing for Dollars* rerun is our very own Incredible Shrinking Man: Edgar Kellogg, dropping a size a week. I could track the calendar by the notches cinched on your belt. Night after night in the dining hall, chomping through a barricade of celery sticks. Amazing."

"I'd read somewhere that you burn more energy eating celery than you ingest. Still, I don't remember inspiring much amazement. More like hilarity."

"Only for the first fifty pounds."

"Fifty pounds' worth of ridicule could last a lifetime."

"Seems so. Look at you. You're still mad!"

Edgar emitted a derisive *puh* and looked away, signaling once more, fruitlessly, for the waiter. He cracked a half-smile, and tore at a cuticle. "Maybe."

Toby biffed him softly on the arm. "You knocked my socks off. Never seen such determination, before or since."

"Yeah, I did get the feeling at the time that's what earned me—"

"Earned you what?"

"Admission. To your—" it was hard to put this tactfully—"demanding circle."

"I don't remember *admitting* you to anything," Toby dismissed. "You just stopped keeping to yourself for a while. A short while, come to think of it. Hey, service stinks here. Better get us drinks from the bar."

Edgar welcomed the interruption, since Falconer's rewrite of history was outlandish.

Accepting the Amstel, he tried to restore an easy humor. "I order this cow piss compulsively. But I've no idea how I'll ever get to be a larger-than-life character drinking candy-ass beer."

"You're a character." Falconer reared back in the booth with some of his Yardley authority and took a slug of his microbrew draft. "That's enough. No such thing as larger-than-life, Kellogg. There's only life-size, and any magnification is just other people's bullshit. So how'd the interview go?"

Dazed by his good fortune, Edgar was only beginning to apprehend that the interview had gone staggeringly well. Much as he might have liked to conclude that he'd cut an impressive figure, chances were that Falconer had given him a recommendation far more enthusiastic than Edgar's virtual-stranger status merited, and that Falconer had stroke.

"Swell, I guess. Wallasek gave me a super-string. In Barba."

Toby made a face. "I should have warned you that's what he had in mind. Better than nothing, I hope. But I've done a couple of features out of there. It ain't Club Med."

"You think it's dangerous?" asked Edgar hopefully.

"Well, as you know the Sobs have never set off anything in their own territory. I guess the logic runs, don't shit in your own bed. But that could change. And what makes for a dangerous place is dangerous people. Or that's the line Saddler used to squeeze a hardship allowance out of Wallasek. I don't know why his lordship bothered to be so creative. Wallasek would have handed Saddler his firstborn son swaddled in C-notes, no questions asked."

Already any reference to Barrington Saddler threw Edgar lurching nauseously between opposing inclinations, as if he were careering up switchbacks in a bus. He both longed to discuss this preposterous fellow and to avoid all mention of the man with the same degree of urgency. When he gave in and pursued the subject, he instantly regretted it, the way you curse yourself for having picked a scab. "*What* is so wonderful about the little prick?"

"Saddler's not little. I've only met him a handful of times. Bit scary, frankly."

Even in this bewilderingly modest an incarnation, Edgar couldn't fathom Tobias Falconer being frightened by anybody.

"That name for starters. What kind of a blowhard goes by 'Barrington'?"

"You obviously haven't met the guy. Weird, but it suits him. He's English, you know. And large. He almost requires three syllables."

"So he's *fat*," Edgar pounced upon victoriously.

Falconer frowned. "Nnno-o. Just big. Big, big, big. In every sense."

"Why's he scary? I get the impression you don't like the guy much."

"That's just it: I shouldn't. He's got my own editor wrapped around his pinky. He gets away with murder—like, for .01 percent of the shit he's pulled any mere mortal would have been canned. He has this tut-tut, frightfully-frightfully accent that makes Americans feel crass and Coca-Cola by comparison. So whenever I've thought about it—and I've thought about it, which is one thing that's scary—everything about the man grates. But Saddler only gets on my nerves when he's not there. He never rubs me the wrong way in person. Face-to-face Barrington Saddler is inexpressibly charming, and I spend the entire time frantically trying to get *him* to like *me*."

"*That* is scary," said Edgar, thinking: money down, no one had ever described Edgar Kellogg behind his back as "inexpressibly charming."

"How'd you find Wallasek?" Falconer asked.

"Paternalistic for my taste." Absent any encouragement in Toby's expression, Edgar exercised his proclivity for putting his foot in it. "And awfully *in the know*. Wallasek thinks he has a window into the mind of the SOB because of Saddler—when what are the chances that both of them know dick?

"Also," Edgar plunged recklessly on, "Wallasek talks a humble line, about 'history's secretaries,' but you can tell he thinks journalism is a lofty calling fraught with daunting tests of fire. As opposed to being mostly about the ability to write a sentence. Which I can, but I don't think he was impressed by my clips. I've only been at this a few months, and Wallasek didn't care what the articles said—typical name-brand mentality. I didn't walk in with the *New York Times* and *The Atlantic* plastered to my forehead . . . What's so funny?"

"You really haven't changed, have you?"

"How's that?" asked Edgar warily.

"Guy Wallasek gave you an interview on the basis of a pretty slight clip file, and what's more gave you a *job*. Which, though Barba's not Hawaii, I assume you want. Doesn't that make you grateful?"

Edgar folded his arms and bunched into the corner, scowling to beat the band. It was a hatches-battened position he'd often assumed when he was fat. "Wallasek offered me a temporary post that could be ripped out from under me by your *big, big, big* friend any time he cares to show his face, an arrangement that would be intolerable to staffers. A string will pay squat. I was a sharp lawyer and I can write. I'll do an ace job, and he's getting a bargain. Why should I be grateful?"

Falconer shook his head. "So hard on people, Kellogg. You that hard on yourself?"

An honest answer was too complicated: that he hacked on other people as a substitute for hacking on himself, and it didn't work. That he rushed to dislike others before they could dislike him; that Edgar's hasty dislike veritably ensured they would indeed dislike him; that, alas, beating acquaintances to the antagonistic punch had never protected him from the ensuing sense of injury that he had apparently brought on himself. A simpler answer—that Edgar perceived himself as an island of underrated promise in a sea of undeserving incompetence—would sound iffy in the open air. "I call them as I see them. You said yourself that Wallasek's relationship to this Barrington guy is fucked up."

"I didn't say that. Wallasek's a good editor, and a decent man. He claims he doesn't, but he misses the fray—being so smack in the middle when some corner of the world goes up in flames that the hairs singe off your arm. So he has a weakness for the inside track; any journalist does. As for Saddler? Wallasek nine-to-fives it, he's bored, feels left out. Saddler blasts into town and they go out until all hours and get slammed and meet kooky people and get kicked out of bars and Wallasek feels plugged in again. A minor failing, if it's a failing at all. Why not give him a chance? It's not a bad policy. You're a smart guy, Kellogg, but you can be so—*savage*."

Edgar felt chastened. He didn't like feeling chastened. "Good God, Falconer. You've gone and got sincere on me."

Toby was rolling the bottom of his empty beer mug in contemplative circles. "I was actually surprised to hear from you. Not sorry, mind you. But surprised."

Edgar wasn't about to admit that he rang Falconer over his own dead body. "It had been a long time," he submitted neutrally.

Falconer laughed. "It's been nineteen years! And when I finally hear from you, it's not because you want to invite me to your wedding, or talk about old times. You want a favor! That takes balls, boyo."

To Edgar's undying relief the gamble had paid off in spades, but the odds had been a hundred-to-one that Falconer would put in a good word for him. Most hacks would see Edgar as a wet-nosed neophyte, his designs on their vocation impertinent. The uncanny cordiality should have been a red flag: this was not the Toby Falconer of yore.

"Didn't beat around the bush, either," Falconer recalled wryly. "No small-talk."

Edgar squirmed. "I hate that how're-the-kids shit. No offense, but why should I care if your youngest is in the choir? You'd figure out that I was hitting you up for a contact soon enough."

"Since Yardley, I haven't even been on your Christmas card list. Weren't you worried I'd brush you off?"

"Worried? I expected it. But I figured, what's to lose? A little pride. Maybe when I was still raking in the bucks at Lee & Thole, losing face would have seemed like a big deal. In my newly influential career as a commentator on world affairs, I've sold my car, let my health-club membership lapse, and forgone the firm's box at Yankee Stadium. What's next? Among a host of other luxuries, dignity is expendable."

Falconer shot a wry glance at Edgar's wrist. "I see you'll sell off your dignity before you'll pawn your watch."

Parting with the $1,500 diving watch would have amounted to the ultimate admission of defeat. "A present for passing the bar, from my mother. Call me a sap."

"Sentimentality from you, Kellogg, is a relief."

Pushing himself, Edgar opened his mouth, and it gaped before the words came out—if strangely difficult to say, wildly important, and he was mortified that he'd almost skipped them altogether: "Anyway, um. Thanks. Thanks a lot."

"I'd never have given you the thumbs-up with Wallasek if I didn't expect you were capable," Falconer said good-naturedly. "The one thing I never doubted at Yardley was that you were smart, even if I wasn't always too thrilled about what you applied your intelligence to—like, to locating people's weak spots. Besides, I admit I had an agenda. I've got some rusty curiosity to satisfy. If I snagged you an interview with my editor, even the surly Edgar Kellogg might feel beholden enough to have this drink."

Edgar sat up in surprise. "I wasn't sure you'd remember me."

"How could I forget? Some of the things you said about me senior year. They got back. Maybe they were meant to."

Edgar had contempt for New Age confessionalism, and wasn't going to enjoy this. He shrugged. "Kids can be mean."

"You're not a kid. You're still—"

"You think I'm mean? That's rich."

They looked at one another squarely for a beat. "I don't get it," said Falconer.

"How do you think *I* was treated, as a two-hundred-forty-pound punching bag?"

"You ever going to let that go? I thought junior year at least we treated you all right."

"Like with Wallasek. I'm supposed to be grateful."

Falconer threw up his hands. "It's just—what happened? One minute you were hanging out with us twenty-four-seven, and the next, bang, opposite side of the dining room. You passed me in the hall like a parking sign. And then all this stuff starts filtering back, that I'm on a 'power-trip,' that I'm a fag, that I get other guys to write my papers—"

"You did—"

"We all did! And that I *dyed my hair.*"

"I never said that."

"You might as well have! What got into you?"

"I liked you," Edgar said with difficulty. "I was disappointed."

"I don't—"

"I overheard you, okay?" Edgar's raised voice carried over the dead bar and drew a glance from the sniffling Miss Loneliheart, who looked relieved that other people had troubles, too. "I overheard you," he continued quietly. "In the locker room, you and that crowd, you didn't realize I was in the shower. I turned off the water and stayed behind the wall. I hadn't been aware that my nickname was 'Special K'—"

"Come on, we were always razzing somebody—"

"This was different! You mimicked me, like, 'Oh, no, I can't have that chocolate chip, it has a whole eleven calories! A moment on the lips, a lifetime on the hips!'" Edgar twisted in his seat. "And you made fun of my stretch marks."

"Edgar, if anything, a little teasing only meant you were

included. It was the zeros we *didn't* talk about you should have felt sorry for."

Edgar looked up sharply; this was the Toby Falconer he remembered. "It got worse. You said I was always hanging around you with goo-goo eyes. That it was like having some girl on your hands, or a lost puppy. That every time you turned around I was yapping at your heels—wanting to know where you were going so I could go, too, or what club you were joining so I could join, too, and what albums you liked so I could go out and buy them. You all cackled at how I'd started wearing a red baseball jacket just like yours, and how I'd applied to switch into your English section. *Clingy*. You used the word *clingy*. So I let go."

Thumbs pressed into his temples, Falconer kneaded his forehead with his fingertips, eyes closed. "God, Kellogg, I'm so sorry. I promise, it wasn't you, or only you. It was all of them. I was tired. I was only seventeen years old, and I was already tired."

Having held in that story for two decades like a breath, now that he'd exhaled it Edgar relaxed, looking on his companion with uncharacteristic tenderness. "Hey, water under the bridge. Anyway, you've changed. I mean, you've grown up and all, and you seem a lot more—forgiving." Edgar thought that was a nicer way of putting the fact that Falconer had no edge anymore and had turned into a soft touch for the likes of Wallasek. "But there's something else. Something, I don't know—missing."

Falconer didn't take offense, but smiled wanly and smoothed his palms down his face to rest them flat on the table. "You mean I'm not surrounded by adoring fans? I'm not tap-dancing on the ceiling with a hat rack?"

Edgar tore a wet shred slowly off his Amstel label. "Whatever."

"Senior year—you heard my father died?"

"Secondhand."

"You weren't speaking to me at the time. Anyway, it hit me hard. All the gang were consoling, for about five minutes. Maybe that made me lucky. Maybe less, well, less prominent kids whose parents died got consoled for only two or three minutes. But after my five minutes were over I was supposed to go back to thinking up pranks to play on our Spanish teacher, leading sneaks off campus after curfew, and inventing new ways to propel our pineapple upside-down cake at lunch. I couldn't do it. I had more 'friends' than anyone at Yardley and I was so lonely I could scream. They all wanted their emcee back, but meanwhile, who was going to lighten things up for me?

"So my mom was a mess without my dad, and I felt bad for being away at school. My sister had started sleeping around at the age of twelve. You were spreading rumors that I led circle-jerks, and I was badgered by volunteers who wanted to join in. I was depressed and couldn't concentrate on exams. All I got from my buddies was *snap out of it*. I was sick of the phone ringing in my hall and it was always for me. I was sick of people whispering and all their little theories about what made me tick. I was sick of brown-nosers who liked me a lot more than I liked them.

"This is going to sound a little out there, so cut me some slack. That 'something missing' you mentioned: it was all that crew wanted and it had nothing to do with me. It was some weird power that wasn't to my credit because I didn't invent it, and it was totally beyond my comprehension. I had no idea why if I said jump in the lake, you guys would jump in the lake. If you told *me* to jump, *I* wouldn't do it. And I looked at myself, I saw a regular high school senior with problems, and you people saw, what—truth is, I have no idea what you saw. This gift, it was like a magic lantern. But it was also a curse.

"So I tossed it. I didn't apply to Yale or Harvard, but Haverford. And at college I wore pastel button-downs and plain slacks. I didn't talk in class and I didn't go to keg parties. I stayed in my dorm room and studied. I was a bore and nobody ever talked about me behind my back any more than they'd mention the wallpaper."

"And then you lost your hair." Edgar was being undiplomatic again, but he almost wondered if Toby's metallic locks had been yanked as punishment. The notion of willingly giving up whatever it was that Falconer had in high school was reprehensible.

"Like Samson." Toby grinned. "I wonder if it's just as well. Maybe it all came down to my hair to begin with, huh? My sister has the same coloring, and I swear that half her admirers only wanted to sink their fingers into that waist-long corn silk. Deborah got so pissed off with one guy that she cut it off and gave it to him in a box."

"It wasn't the hair."

"I don't even care. Whatever you guys were so hot for, I couldn't see it myself. I'm sorry I called you 'clingy.' I don't remember saying it, but I'm not surprised I did. Honestly, Kellogg, you did get to be a pain. You were always dogging me, but never wanted to really talk. That part of you that I was drawn to, that lost a hundred pounds in six months? That part never seemed to speak up. And on the one hand you acted so hard-ass, but on the other, you, I don't know, seemed to idolize me or something. Made me feel creepy, like a fake. I'd no idea what you saw in me, what about me was so great."

"I guess I did try to impress you," Edgar admitted. "Maybe I tried too hard. But you had such style, Falconer." Edgar couldn't help the past tense. "It's rare."

"I may be kidding myself that I gave it up," Toby mused. "It could have just got away from me."

"I've watched out for your byline for years: from Belfast, Somalia, the Gulf War. I always pictured your life as exotic, edgy. One reason I quit law. Thought I'd join you."

The confidence got out before Edgar realized that it sounded like more of the same: searching a dozen vintage clothing shops for a fifties baseball jacket, and the one that fit the best and had the coolest logo on the back just happened to be the same cardinal-red as Toby Falconer's. Edgar's biggest concern about his own character was that he wasn't original. He didn't know how to become original except by imitating other people who were.

"I do my job, and pretty well," said Falconer. "It's more ordinary than it seems, though. Like you said, to do with sentences—plodding, workaday. I am, anyway. I'm quiet. I've got to the point I don't much like being on the road, and I've encouraged Guy to give the firefighting assignments to younger reporters who're still hot to trot. I like going home to Linda, sourdough pretzels, and the Mets on TV. You put your finger on it: I'm sincere. I don't have a lot of friends, but they're real."

Edgar raised his empty Amstel and clinked it against Falconer's mug. "Just got yourself one more, then." Edgar's inability to complete the toast with a swig seemed apt. If idolatry made a poor basis for a friendship, pity wasn't much of an improvement. Falconer seemed like a dead nice guy, and Edgar felt robbed.

"When you off to Barba?"

"Soon as I can pack."

"Good luck with Saddler, anyway."

"I don't expect to have good or bad luck with Saddler," Edgar protested. "He disappeared, remember? Abracadabra. Hell, the guy probably just fell in a ditch."

"The likes of Saddler don't just fall in ditches. Or if they do, there's plenty more to the story, and nine times out of ten they crawl out again. I got a gut sense says the legendary Barrington belongs in your life."

Edgar found himself obscurely cheered up. Much as he might resist the prospect of some bombastic and unaccountably fawned-over scoundrel bursting unannounced through his front door, suddenly he felt he had a future, and its vista widened into the *big, big, big*—big as life; bigger, even. As Falconer settled the bill at the bar, having waved off a half-heartedly proffered ten-spot, Edgar studied the plain, kindly face, searching its prematurely haggard lines scored by "three hyperactive kids and a depressive wife," too many red-eyes out of Addis and tight connections in Rome. Though he thought he was scanning for some flicker of the sly, playful Adonis at whom he'd marveled at Yardley, Edgar recognized in his failure to see any resemblance at all that he didn't want to see a resemblance.

Out on the street, they shook hands. Edgar clapped Toby's shoulder for good measure. Neither made a feint toward meeting again. "Take care of yourself, Falconer."

"You know, there didn't used to be an airport in Cinzeiro, only a bus from Lisbon. Now there are two planes a day. Presumably to make it that much easier for the SOB to blow them up. Watch your back, Kellogg."

Instead Edgar watched Toby Falconer's. In no time the beige knit shirt and gray slacks blended with the bland attire of other pedestrians, helping to form the backdrop against which strange or striking New Yorkers would stand out.

CHAPTER 4
Inversion 101

HANGING ON THE subway strap, Edgar considered Toby Falconer, Joe Average. Certainly senior year at Yardley Edgar had caught a harried look in Falconer's eyes, the submerged panic of a boy who couldn't swim sinking below the surface. Edgar had worked hard at the time at foreshortening his former icon into another small-pond egotist.

From a distance, Edgar had discovered everything that had captivated him about Falconer could be slyly inverted: confidence transposed to arrogance, grace to effeminacy, popularity to shallowness. That famous sense of humor upended into flippancy, powers of persuasion into slimier powers of manipulation. Apparently the most sterling quality could be turned upside-down, like a reversible placemat. Courage flipped to irresponsibility, passion to mawkishness. The self-sacrificial were dupes, and the loyal? Were *clingy*. Now Falconer had gone and inverted himself. It should have been satisfying.

Childhood obesity having put his own flaws on such flagrant display, in self-defense Edgar had developed an eagle eye for the faults of other people. Though the facility gave him a deadliness it didn't make him happy and it probably didn't make him attractive. Nor did it save him from practicing the craft of inversion on himself. Resigning from Lee & Thole, for instance: heads, the move was bold. Tails? It was retarded.

Fearing a failure of nerve, Edgar had rung the Portuguese airline TAP from a pay phone in front of The Red Shoe to make a reservation for Barba via Lisbon three days hence. That would give him just enough time to wrap up loose ends—like Angela—and not enough time to back out.

The process of inverting Angela was almost complete. He had yet to get over wanting to fuck her, but everything else that had first drawn him to her had capsized. Her far-flung general knowledge, for instance, translated neatly into superficiality: she could discuss anything for five minutes and nothing for half an hour. When she professed strong views about new Freud biographies at parties, she'd only read the reviews. She subscribed to all the right magazines but only skimmed the pull-quotes, and in movies concentrated primarily on the credits. That she remembered names, exact addresses, and which restaurants had changed hands had once made her repartee seem zippy, but nowadays when Edgar pictured her mind all he saw was the Yellow Pages.

More to the heart of the matter, that enigmatic quality of hers had revealed itself in time as garden-variety duplicity. For everything Angela said there was something else she omitted. At first the gaps had been scintillating. But after living with her for two years Edgar put his gift of inversion to proper use for once and concluded that Angela wasn't *elusive*. She was a *liar*. She wasn't *mysterious* or *complicated*. She was, and always had been, in love with someone else.

As Edgar slipped his key in the apartment door, he could hear Angela chattering on the phone, and before he'd pushed inside he knew she'd be on her feet.

Pacing, fidgeting from one piece of furniture to another, sure enough Angela was picking and poking at faxes and fountain pens; she couldn't stand still. Edgar's entrance earned him a distracted nod. As usual, she'd wedged the receiver between her ear and shoulder so that she could use her hands when she talked. He used to find it charming.

Now Edgar could only picture what Angela doubtless looked like when she was talking on the phone to him. Perhaps she languished on the sofa with her eyes shut, the cord slack, one arm tossed limply midair. In any event, she definitely didn't use this voice—plosives pipping, aspirates rushing, and fricatives fizzing with the effervescence of Perrier:

"You should have seen him—that's exactly! Then naturally after—HAH! ha-ha-ha-hahhhhhh . . ."

As for content, there wouldn't be any that was discernible on this end. He'd heard her go on like this for an hour without planting enough substantive key words in a row for him to determine whether the conversation was about toenail fungus or Senate hearings on the Waco siege. Of only one thing could Edgar be certain: she was talking to *Jamesie*—an affectionate private nickname that Edgar had only recently started using aloud.

This glib, gray-templed geeze in his fifties had kept Angela on the side for years. James pre-dated Edgar, who had come to suspect that he wasn't the first to fill in for James when the old fart was nailing someone else. Angela was forthright about having once been gaga for this big-spending silk importer, but that was all over and now, officially, James and Angela were just "veryveryveryvery good friends." After two patient years of observation, Edgar had concluded that those two should probably spring for an extra *very*.

Edgar's initial tolerance of this "friendship" had won him credit with Angela for being a sophisticated man who realized that all adults in their thirties had pasts. Edgar didn't go funny when she announced that she was meeting James for dinner, and he didn't wait up. He didn't replay Angela's messages, rifle her mail, or sniff her panties; he didn't third-degree and he didn't stage scenes. All of which made him a *secure, mature, respectful* partner, a.k.a.—Inversion 101—a *chump*.

"Bye—I can't now, you know why—later! Bye-bye." She hung up tenderly. "You wouldn't believe what—oh, I forgot." Angela's bubbly cadence sloshed a bit and then went stagnant. "No more stories about James. You've got touchy."

"Just bored."

"You were sent some more rejections. They're on the counter."

The flaps were sealed. "How can you be sure they're rejections?"

Angela tossed her hair impatiently, and Edgar finally noticed that it was the same color as the adolescent Toby Falconer's. "These days, only bad news comes in the mail. That's what it's for: to blow you off with as little personal contact as possible. Good news comes in phone calls, or for the last year or two e-mail, if the opposite party is the slightest bit hip. Christ, they should start dyeing all envelopes black."

"You sure seem torn up about my disappointments."

"I don't mean to sound callous, Edgar, but if I stroked your head every time one of those letters arrived, you'd go bald. This journalism gambit sounded good at first, 'cause I thought we'd go somewhere exciting. Even James—" her spine straightened in a refusal to apologize—"James travels everywhere, like, China, Hong Kong. So far your 'freelancing' has landed us mostly in this apartment. Night after night, I might add."

"I'm happy as a clam to eat out," Edgar said flintily. "You just have to pay for it."

"I'm a publicist, for Christ's sake. The Garden swamps me with comps but they pay crumbs, and you can't satisfy AmEx with free tickets." She flounced theatrically into the kitchen, to retrieve a lone can of Bartlett pears.

Edgar's heart wasn't in an argument, and he cast his eye around his living room with the generosity of nostalgia. Even quotidian quarters achieved an Edward Hopper glow when you were leaving them forever. So did women. Contemplating his girlfriend—her lithe legs, impetuous gold hair, and close breasts that didn't need a bra but still had an alluring quiver—Edgar despaired that there was one attribute he had never successfully inverted. Good taste boomeranged to snobbery, self-respect to self-regard. But he was at a loss to hold against any woman the fact that she was beautiful.

"Have you ever considered how it might go, living with *Jamesie*?" Throwing Angela on her new future felt almost as delicious as embracing his own.

"Certainly not, not for years," she growled, managing to make opening that can look like hard work. "We're just—"

"Friends," Edgar completed with a smile; funny, all the old sourness had fled. "You might think twice. Shadowy characters don't always function in the foreground. If nothing else, *Jamesie* needs me around to make himself look good."

"Honestly, Edgar, you're getting to be impossible!"

Edgar collapsed onto the corduroy sofa with his feet up, feeling dozy, relaxed. You couldn't say that he didn't warn her.

Three days later, Edgar withdrew his key from the same lock, and for good measure worked the key off its ring to slip it through the letterbox. He didn't want to be misunderstood. Shouldering his baggage, Edgar turned his back on the apartment that Angela couldn't afford, either.

At the elevator, however, he felt a twinge of loss. It wasn't Angela. It was stuff. All the furniture was his, and he'd not stinted. His suitcase had been too small to accommodate most of his favorite shirts, a closetful of costly suits, or his extensive collection of grunge CDs. He would need, he thought wryly, Replacements.

But then, the alternative course entailed all the recriminatory scenes he'd so elegantly finessed: a tawdry separation of Angela's Alanis Morissette from his Gin Blossoms, hiring movers and renting storage and breaking the lease—all odious and time-consuming and totally lacking in class. Style required sacrifice. So in lieu of a hasty note, he'd left a cup of coffee cooling and a Camel burning. Leave Angela disconcerted, Edgar figured. He didn't smoke.

Stashing his boarding card, Edgar flopped into a seat at his Kennedy gate and discarded the unread *Wall Street Journal* that he'd snagged out of reflex. Though almost as expensive as a round-trip, the one-way ticket tucked in his battered leather bomber jacket had a more intrepid touch and feel.

Repudiation seemed to agree with him. Why, he could acquire a taste for renouncing entire lives like this, and for the present viewed the acquisition of new ones—new friends, new jobs, new lovers—as merely a laborious prerequisite to gleefully forsaking the works. The airport itself, in its all-white nowhere-in-particular-ness, its duty-free replication of dozens of like non-places, offered up a seductive vision of pure departure, a cleanly and permanently wiped slate.

Yet once the flight was called and the plane penetrated the enveloping black vacuum, Edgar's stomach lurched with the dread certainty that there was only one perfectly negative experience in life, and you got to pull that number only once. Unless he was rescued by an SOB bomb in the cargo hold, the thrill of departure would be inevitably corrupted by arrival somewhere else.

Worse, arrival in a country about which Edgar knew zip, whose politics were notoriously tortuous, where he was supposed to be a reporter. Edgar didn't know how to be a reporter. Hazily he pictured a journalist dialing up "contacts," but he'd no idea whom he was meant to phone or what he should ask. In a moment of weakness, Edgar wished faintly that the *big, big, big* bag of hot air would indeed show up and take his beat back.

The flight attendant was a cow, and her cart was out of light beer. Defiantly, Edgar ordered bourbon, and wolfed down his smoked almonds.

Groping into his carry-on, Edgar lugged out his portable library. The previous afternoon he had ravaged Barnes & Noble's burgeoning Barba section, scarfing up academic analyses (*The Moorish Presence in Barba After the Siege of Lisbon*), the odd political treatise (*When Democratic Protest Fails: Resort to International Incident as a Consciousness-Raising Tool*), recent histories (*The Evolution of SOB Strategy and the Rise of O Creme de Barbear*), special-interest titles (*An Ill Wind: The Role of Weather in Social Defiance*), and sensationalist paperbacks (*I Was an SOB!*—an anonymous memoir by a "reformed Barban bomber" whose authenticity had been hotly contested). His checked bags were lined with general texts on terrorism, most of which said it was bad.

Between sips of JD, Edgar plowed into the book on top, whose first iteration of *the right to national self-determination* was more soporific than his drink. The author had heavily quoted Tomás Verdade, president of the SOB's reputed political wing, O Creme de Barbear. Verdade's verbiage was long-winded and dry, laden with references to dead Barban heroes like Duarte o Estupendo and Teodósso o Terrível, dense with insistence on "defending the integrity of the predominant indigenous culture and the rights of the operative majority within the context of respect for the multiple traditions on a richly varied peninsula"—which, when Edgar applied himself, reduced to xenophobic claptrap.

Three pages and ten *national self-determinations* later Edgar was ready for another JD. *What had he done?* The narcolepsy that this Iberian slagheap had always induced in Edgar wasn't letting up but was growing more intense. In comparison to Tomás Verdade's prolix *patriotismo*, briefs on whether water company mergers violated antitrust laws ranked with *Sports Illustrated*'s swimsuit issue. The only bearable aspect of this story was violent boy-stuff. Over dinner Edgar put aside *The Barban Peninsula: A Test Case in Immigration Saturation* and devoured *Forced Landing!*, a breathless account of British Airways' infamous Flight 321 that bulged with gory photographs.

Meanwhile, the cabin hummed with the susurrant murmur of what Edgar could only assume was Portuguese. Though a soothing drone, it raised a light sweat across the back of his neck. *Zhshchaoshzhgoshshdgeshzhye* . . . He'd hoped a year of high school Spanish would help, but this mishmash of consonant blends sounded more like Russian.

"You are a glutton for punishment."

Edgar glanced over at the bearded, fifty-ish man in the window seat. "You mean, eating airline fettuccini?"

The man chuckled. "The books. Not by any chance headed for beautiful Barba, are you?" he asked sardonically, in-joke.

"I'm covering the province for the *National Record*." The claim sounded convincing; at least Edgar's seatmate didn't laugh.

Rather, the man's eyes lit like Christmas. "Why, I'm not graced by the presence of *Barrington Saddler*, am I? I'd read, to my dismay, that for a time you went missing!" Before Edgar could correct him, the fusty-looking character had wiped his hand on a napkin before extending it across the empty middle seat. "Dr. Ansel P. Henwood, delighted!"

Edgar didn't know what else to do but to take Henwood's hand. "Edgar Kellogg."

Henwood's fierce clasp went limp.

"Saddler's still taking his impromptu sabbatical," Edgar explained.

"My mistake." Henwood drew back and distractedly wiped his hand on the napkin again. "I'd presumed that such a prominent man of letters must have turned back up, or the mystery of his tragic disappearance would have dominated the news. How quickly we forget! True, I haven't seen his byline for a while, but then Barba's been quiet—ominously so, some might say. I'm sure you'll do a fine job—sir."

Dr. Henwood seemed already to have forgotten Edgar's name. Between withering glances thrown Edgar's way, the man's expression warped from crestfallen to victorious. He should have known, spoke the scornful gaze. Five-eight and dressed with festive slovenliness, Edgar mustn't have conformed to Henwood's preconception of his imposing predecessor.

"Fascinating assignment, of course," Henwood allowed. "Been there yourself?"

"First time."

Pushing back his tray, the man reared in his seat, adjusting his tweed lapels. Lacking a pipe and snifter, Henwood settled for brandy in a plastic glass. "This is my third trip. Very difficult place to come to grips with. Hard nut to crack."

Apparently Edgar's stony silence was misread as encouragement.

"I'm director of the University of Texas Conflict Studies Department," Henwood preened. "We're establishing a PhD program that focuses on Cinzeiro, among other trouble spots. Of course, in Austin we're confronting a lot of the same complicated issues entailed in massive Mexican immigration, so there's, shall we say—" a puckish grin—"generous grant money at hand."

"In the last five years the SOB has killed over two thousand civilians. So they're assholes. What's so complicated?"

"Of course, no one endorses their methods—"

"You say that as if being cutthroat is incidental."

"It can be a distraction. After all, throughout human history numerous causes have merited resort to violence—"

"So if you don't give me more leg room—" Edgar gestured to a bawling infant in the middle seats—"I shoot the kid."

"That's oversimplifying—"

"It's simplifying," Edgar differed, noting that Henwood had instinctively pulled his knees back. "Hell of a way to run your affairs, isn't it?"

"You'll have to develop a little more sophistication for the likes of the *National Record*," the academic declared haughtily. "Your predecessor has an unparalleled sensitivity to the nuances—"

"No one ever warned me when I took this job that I'd have to write horseshit."

"A lucid argument can be made that the distinction between state and extra-state violence is artificial," Henwood lectured, unwrapping his dinner mint. "Especially in the creation of new states. Most nations come into being through what could be perceived at the time, from an establishmentarian's outlook, as 'atrocities'—including our own US of A. Once a nation is founded, the violence of nation-building is elevated to heroism. The 'terrorists' of today are the town-square monuments of tomorrow."

Edgar had finished off two wine miniatures with dinner, on top of the JDs. His speech was unimpaired, but then he was usually alerted to a growing buzz by the fact that he'd become obnoxious. "So the assholes have always won, the assholes are still winning, and you'd like to see the assholes keep coming out on top."

"That's just the sort of reductionist demonization of one party in a divided conflict that only forestalls reconciliation," the professor chided. "The Barban situation is sufficiently polarized that it's hardly helpful to heap on more hatred."

Edgar pressed a button for the flight attendant; this conversation was going to require a lot more booze. "I don't recall trying to be *helpful*."

"To contribute to debate, a journalist is obliged to appreciate the legitimacy of more than one point of view. O C-r-r-reme de Bar-r-rbear-r-r," Henwood rolled the Rs, "is justifiably alarmed that Barba's predominantly Catholic culture is being engulfed by container ships full of Muslims emigrating from North Africa. Now, Lisbon's budget for immigration enforcement is indeed puny, and the government's approach to this ethnically and religiously charged matter is look-the-other-way. So Verdade makes a credible case that Barba can only get control of its borders through sovereignty."

"You don't say," said Edgar sourly. Even for his own C-minus grasp of the subject, this lowdown was condescending.

"Of course, the logic runs that if the SOB makes life unpleasant enough for Lisbon's allies and neighbors, powerful friends like the U.S.—with no strategic investment in the integrity of Portugal—will persuade Lisbon to jettison the Barban peninsula.

So understandably, Lisbon is torn. Portugal is loath to encourage terrorism. Moreover, the Moroccan and Algerian immigrants, if they're not fleeing persecution, are simply seeking to better themselves, and there is some reason to worry about mass expulsions and widespread human rights abuses should Barbans be given free rein in their own state—which, unless it applied for admission separately, would also lie outside the mollifying influences of the EU. Yet Portugal is under enormous international pressure to halt the SOB campaign, and the most obvious expedient is to grant Barban independence—"

"How do you 'contribute to debate' by getting so lost in mushy sympathy for every side that you sacrifice any perspective whatsoever?" Edgar intruded, reminded once again why as a rule he kept his trap shut on airplanes.

"In turn," the professor barreled on as if hugging a podium, "opinion polls in Barba do not document majority support for independence—"

"Back up," Edgar cut him off. "*National self-determination* for Barba not only has zero support in Portugal as a whole, but minority backing in Barba? So the SOB is bombing the fuck out of the whole world to win independence for a people that don't want it."

"Once again, you oversimplify. Amongst native Barban Latinos, there's a broad-based sympathy with the SOB cause, but discomfort with the armed struggle dilutes—"

"So the fact that the poor fucks don't even want independence is another *distraction*, just like the fact that SOB guerrillas are murdering scumbags?"

Other passengers trying to sleep glared over their blankets.

"You have a great deal of reading to do before you're ready to assume the mantle of someone of Mr. Saddler's stature. Perhaps I should leave you to it." Henwood pointed. "May I suggest you begin with that one. I use it in my introductory courses. It's only a crude overview. But crudeness might appeal to your sensibility at that." Henwood raised the book in his lap, *Comparative Demographic Projections of Citizenship With and Without the Grandfather Clause in Barba*, so that the hardback blocked his face.

The prof had gestured to *Out of Impasse*, authored by, lo and behold, Dr. Ansel P. Henwood. The picture on the back was twenty years old if a day, the weak chin revealing why Henwood had grown a beard. The text did prove useful. Edgar was desperate to grab some shut-eye, and required only three or four lines to fall fast asleep.

CHAPTER 5
Security Theater

THANKS TO THE edifications of Dr. Henwood, Edgar copped only a few Zs. Bleariness sapped any incipient curiosity about Portugal. Drained and weaving, Edgar was at a loss as to why anyone ever went anywhere besides to bed. He was equally at a loss to explain the purpose of sending passengers through a security check right off the plane, when they'd been through security right before boarding. What were they frisking for, stolen headsets?

At immigration, the dark, petite woman at the desk was brisk but polite, affording Edgar a flickered smile. But once she'd examined his ticket, her cordiality iced over. "You are flying on to *Barb*-a?" she asked frostily, planting a hook in the word.

Edgar nodded feebly. Immigration always made him feel sneaky.

She stabbed at her computer, attacking keys as if mashing an invasion of ants. "What is the purpose of your visit, please?"

"I'm covering Barba for the *National Record*." Hitherto Edgar had enjoyed repeating this assertion in the hopes that it would begin to resonate plausibly to himself, but just now it sounded like a transparent cover for unspeakable wickedness.

"You have documents of this position?"

Edgar rubbed his moist forehead. "I—might, my assignment was last-minute, just—let me check." Stooping, Edgar scrambled through his carry-on. He should have asked Wallasek for a letter of introduction. Maybe Guy had at least scrawled Saddler's address on letterhead stationery. Meanwhile, at the next desk, Henwood was flourishing such a snowstorm of papers that the immigration clerk raised a hand to make him stop.

"What is so interesting to Americans about *Barb*-a?" Edgar's inquisitor asked stiffly as he splayed books with incriminating titles on the floor. "Much of Portugal is beautiful—Lisboa, O Porto, Algarve. Your newspapers never send reporters to these places. *Barb*-a is ugly and poor and the people are ungrateful . . . *ressentidos*."

Edgar found the paper; no letterhead. "What can I say? Americans like to read about folks who are—" frantic to ingratiate himself, Edgar grabbed the dictionary from the floor—"*mau.*"

She didn't seem impressed with his Portuguese. "You have no documents? Wait one moment, please." The woman marched off behind a partition, heels hitting the polished floor as if shooting rivets, her ass switching the tight navy skirt. By the time she returned he'd at least scrounged a copy of his prized *New Republic* article.

"See?" Edgar fingered the byline. "That's me."

She squinted. "This is not about *Barb*-a."

"I've never written about Barba in my life."

She melted a degree, but rejoined, "Then why you start now?"

"This was the only job I could get!"

Barba-as-desperation-move won him one degree more, but the slight thaw only loosened a floe of tremulous emotion. "I would not put my foot in that *efluentes* for the last job on earth!"

Passengers in line grumbled; only three stations were open.

Recovering herself, the official grilled Edgar about where he planned to reside, entering his new address on Rua da Evaporação into the computer, but making no move to stamp his passport. You have friends in Cinzeiro? You have contacts in the SOB? Edgar fell all over himself denying any such unpalatable acquaintances, adding gratuitously, "Creeps. Dirtbags. No sympathy whatsoever." The lady eyed him with jaundice; terrorists probably shoveled this shit all the time.

"How long you are planning to stay, *Senhor*—" she checked his passport—"Kellogg?" Nobody ever seemed to remember Edgar's name.

"I can't say. I'm filling in for someone else. He disappeared. He might come back. Barrington Saddler."

Bingo. Thus far Edgar had been flicking a Bic at this woman's glacial demeanor, and finally he'd blasted her with a blowtorch. Her eyes went gooey, her head assumed a fetching tilt, and her smile was positively human.

"You know—*Barrington*?"

"Yes," said Edgar. "Yes, indeed. Bear and I go way back. Whenever he's in New York, we do the town. 'Til five a.m., getting kicked out of bars. We're thick as thieves. Couldn't be tighter. See?" He shoved the scrap scribbled with *Saddler* forward. "Bear's address."

The functionary touched the paper with a kleptomaniacal expression, as if having to restrain herself from jotting down the phone number. "Disappeared . . . Is true, I hear something of this months ago." Her olive brow rumpled; her lips pouted with worry. The woman's transformation recalled the sitcom spinster who unpins her hair and removes her horn-rims: voilà, a pretty dishy broad. "I am concern. Barrington come through here many times. Sometimes," she admitted shyly, "he let others go first so he pass through my station. We always have joke. I hope nothing bad happen to him, *sim*?"

"That's my first assignment: find out what happened to our friend Barrington. Make sure he's all right."

Bam. The stamp.

"*Adeus.* You find Barrington, tell him Isobel say *hallo*. Be very careful, *senhor*." She even waved.

Because he'd been headed for Barba, Edgar hadn't been allowed to check his luggage through to his destination, unlike passengers headed anywhere else in continental Europe. Immigration had taken so long that at least his bag was already bumping around the belt, but re-entry into the airport after customs mandated another security check, and yet another at the entrance to Departures. X-rays, hand-frisk, ticket-check, every time.

At the gate itself, Edgar was consternated to confront *another* queue for *another* security check. This time, they took his luggage apart piece by piece—riffling every book, unwinding ten feet of dental floss, squeezing the toothpaste up and down and insisting he dab Cool Mint Crest on his tongue. They depressed the PLAY button on his microcassette, and Edgar's test recording echoed down the corridor: "This is Edgar Kellogg, your caped correspondent in Big Bad Barba, interviewing yet another SOB freedom-fighter in shit-hot shades." Oh, swell.

After that, they were naturally suspicious when his portable printer wouldn't light up, and just try explaining that an appliance doesn't have a battery and needs a converter to work on European current to troglodytes whose entire English vocabulary comprised "open please" and "turn on." By the time he'd hooked up the converter with lots of hand-signals, the security staff had poked and pried at his Bubblejet until they broke the tabs off his paper feeder.

His flight was already boarding, and all his remaining worldly possessions were spread out over three square yards of table. Stuffing and muttering, Edgar didn't have time for all the ingenious wedging that had taken him an hour on West Eighty-Ninth Street, and he had to ask for a plastic bag for the overflow.

Beyond security, another interview: had he accepted any packages, had his luggage been out of his sight at any time, did he pack his own bag? Edgar had answered these same questions half a dozen times already and his replies were getting testy. Any minute boarding would close. Meanwhile the same cautions about tending to your luggage crackled incessantly over the intercom. Posters plastered around the gate gaily advertised the *Telefone Confidencial*, just in case en route to Cinzeiro after peanuts you had a larkish impulse to rat out your SOB buddies on the credit-card phone.

But when Edgar wheeled from the desk to board he couldn't stop himself from shrieking, "You *cannot* be *serious*!" Right before the Jetway was another security check.

Edgar hurled his carry-on, laptop, and plastic bag onto the belt.

"Turn on, please."

"Look!" Edgar shouted. "I have booted up my computer ten times on this trip and the goddamned battery's running out! Now just shove the fucking stuff through, because my fucking plane is taking off!"

Another official oozed up from the shadows, and his better English was ominous. "There is some problem, sir?"

"Fuck yeah, there's a problem!" Edgar knew he shouldn't curse, but toadying at immigration had left him determined to reestablish his manhood. "You *just searched* my luggage down to the skid marks on my boxers. What's next, a particle separator? How could I possibly have slipped a Stinger missile in my carry-on in the last *twenty feet*?"

"Sir, you have just threatened the airline. You will have to come this way, please."

They did a full body-cavity search, and he missed the plane.

One of Edgar's contacts at US Air, a Lee & Thole client, had shared confidentially that much of modern airline security was theater, often a front for jaw-dropping laxity behind the scenes. They made you sample your toothpaste with everyone watching, but postal freight was routinely loaded unscreened. Despite showy pawing of passengers' Tampax and Trojans, any sleazebag with the wit to wear a brown technician's coverall could waltz on and off airplanes as he pleased, and most security violations were arranged through corrupt caterers or bribable baggage handlers. Trying to think with the nimble opportunism of his new occupation, Edgar wondered if he might get an exposé out of today's fiasco.

For now this wasn't good copy but bad life, though the two seemed often to go hand in hand. Edgar had nine hours to kill before the evening flight, and sitting was uncomfortable; his asshole was sore. Edgar hoped idly that staging scenes in airports signaled that his apprenticeship to the larger-than-life was getting off to a smashing start. Yet a little voice murmured in the back of Edgar's head that Barrington Saddler would never have arranged matters so that some sadistic joker was shoving a Latexed index finger up his backside. More likely that crowd would be refolding Saddler's slacks so the creases aligned while scrambling to arrange his free upgrade to first class.

That little voice. It had a British accent.

CHAPTER 6
Only Edgar

GRATEFUL FOR A task with so much time to kill in the Lisbon airport, Edgar cashed a traveler's check and got change for the pay phone. To smooth logistics, he really should have contacted this Nicola person from New York, but he'd put the call off. It was a bit embarrassing, acting on Wallasek's assumption that she must have a key to Saddler's house because she was one of his known floozies.

"I see," said the woman, once Edgar had haltingly explained his business; her accent vaguely English, at least it wasn't the ram-it-down-your-throat variety. "So you're Barrington's *replacement*." She sounded both mournful and bemused.

"I'm supposed to move into—" Edgar scrambled to avoid Saddler's name, whose mention from the first had seemed to constitute a torment—"the house on Rua da Evaporação. No one at the *Record* had a key. I can always stay in a hotel tonight and bring in a locksmith tomorrow. But my editor thought maybe . . ."

"I do have a key," she admitted gravely. "When do you arrive?"

"Tennish, tonight."

"Oh, I'm so sorry," she said, and she did sound incredibly sorry, though perhaps most of all that the phone had rung and it was just another visiting journalist. Nicola had answered, *Hello?* with breathy anticipation; her subsequent downshift of timbre recalled Angela's, on realizing it was *only* Edgar. "I'd have liked to have met your plane. But a few odds and sods are coming over this evening, and leaving my guests would be rude. Not that I won't be tempted." A small laugh, minor key. "After all, the members of our incestuous set run into each other every day—"

The call was interrupted by an unintelligible recording. Edgar felt an irrational urgency to keep this melodious voice on the phone, and shoveled more escudos in the slot. "Please," he pressed. "You were saying?"

"It's just the local hacks. But this is the first time we've gathered socially since Barrington left." She said the name firmly, as if granting Edgar permission to employ it at will. Equally firm was the word *left*—not *vanished*, not *was kidnapped*, not even *fled*, much less *was assassinated*. The verb wasn't merely descriptive; it was a verdict. "You'd be welcome to join us, Mr. Kellogg."

She remembered his name! "Edgar," he corrected. "I wouldn't presume—"

"Please, you'd not impose. Everyone will be terribly interested to meet you." She refrained from asserting that her guests would be *glad* to meet him, but the interest might be real enough.

"I'm afraid I'll be just off the plane—"

"We'll try not to detain you. And I'll make every allowance for the fact that you're exhausted." After dictating her address, Nicola reduced her volume another notch. "There's only one thing, Edgar. That I have that key? If you'd please not call it to anyone's attention. Simply say you're calling by to meet your new colleagues. Which you will be."

"I'll be discreet," Edgar promised.

"God knows what you must think of me," Nicola whispered.

"Hey, it's none of my business," Edgar protested.

"You can't think any worse than I think of myself." Without saying good-bye, she hung up.

Innocently whitewashed and cheerfully lit, the tiny square building of the Aeroporto Internacional de Cinzeiro was roofed in scalloped terra-cotta like an Arizona community center. While VÓS AGORA ENTRAS NA BARBA OCUPADA! was boldly spray-painted across an outside wall, the graffiti's red lettering was neatly outlined in green, the second B painstakingly extended to make it as tall as the first, its exclamation mark dotted with a daisy. The slogan less resembled the threatening defacement of a terrorist insurgency than a day-camp crafts project.

Deplaning onto the tarmac struck Edgar as quaintly retro-chic until he emerged from the cabin to be broadsided, *foom*, by a gale wind, which threw him so violently against the portable staircase rail that he nearly pitched over it. As another gust slapped his face in reproof that he'd ever considered air the same as nothing, Edgar clutched the railing hand-over-hand to the runway—skin tightening, eyes tearing, ears roaring. Once he exited through baggage claim's revolving door, whose flaps swish-swished without aid of electricity, he was again blindsided by a solid atmospheric wall. After stumbling to the taxi stand, using his bags as ballast, Edgar clutched a post while the cabby loaded the trunk. Eyes shielded by protective plastic goggles, the heavyset cabby hunched with a widely planted stance, tilting into the wind and lifting his feet as little as possible. The maneuver looked practiced.

Edgar slumped into the rattletrap taxi, glad that darkness spared him gaping out the window. He didn't have the energy to be fascinated, and wanted to appraise his new home with a fresh eye. Edgar had already formed a nascent affection for Barba, if only because Lisboners seemed to hate it so much. A kicked cur as a kid, Edgar identified with outcasts more than most of his countrymen, whose reputation for sympathy with underdogs was in his view highly exaggerated.

Such a piercing whistle sang through window cracks that Edgar's headache was immediate. As the hump-fendered sedan galumphed down the road, it swayed in and out of lane, though the driver wrestled manfully with the wheel. Now and again a thud sounded against the doors as if a linebacker had assaulted the cab with a running tackle.

"Is it always this *windy*?" Edgar shouted over the teakettle shrill.

"Windy? Is no so windy," the cabby yelled cheerfully back.

Fighting nausea as the taxi threw him from door to door, Edgar kicked himself for promising to stop by Nicola's little soirée tonight. Better to have picked up the key tomorrow and sprung for a hotel. He vowed to get in, then get out. So far his "fellow" journalists had hardly constituted a mutually supportive intellectual fraternity, and one carelessly ignorant remark about the SOB could take him months to live down; Edgar admonished himself, *Keep your pie hole shut*. This Nicola broad sounded all right, but Edgar had minimal taste for socializing at the best of times. The truth was he didn't like people much, even if he was never sure whether a misanthrope was allowed to deduct himself, like taking a standard personal exemption on a 1040.

Most of all, after a half day in Portugal he'd already had it up to the eyeballs with Barrington Fucking Saddler. Edgar had to write that mop-up article on what might have befallen his predecessor, bringing the story, for the paper, to a close. But the last thing he planned to blather in his free time was, "Gee whiz, guys, whadda ya think mighta happened to lovable old Bear?" Were Edgar to solicit any more gushy hog slop about Saddler, he would have to be paid.

The taxi drew up to a villa whose flat left-hand side loomed three stories high, unperforated by a single window. From this sheer blank edifice, a frivolous hodgepodge of turrets, porticos, and balconies with curlicued grillwork tumbled off to the right. From its fanciful leeward end, the villa resembled a set for *Carmen*; from the windward side, a nuclear power plant.

Foom. Edgar had trouble getting the taxi door shut. Doubled over, he dragged his luggage toward the entrance, his heavy leather bomber jacket flying horizontally to the right. Grains of sand stung his left cheek like acupuncture. Once he lunged onto the porch and tucked behind that mammoth wall, the roar ceased, the jacket dropped, and Edgar staggered from no longer having to lean into the squall to stay upright. Leonard Cohen dirged from inside.

The door opened only wide enough for Edgar to see in the porch light that the young man's face presented the same impenetrable façade of the villa's windbreak.

"Barrington the Second, right?" the boyish-looking Englishman said joylessly. "Surprised they sent someone else. Thought we'd all spend the rest of our poxy lives moping about and waiting for stigmata proof that Our Redeemer liveth."

This was well too much for two hours' sleep and a six-hour time difference. "I was looking for Nicola—"

"Naturally," said the young man savagely.

"Henry, please," whispered from inside. "If you have to, take it out on me. That poor bloke never did a thing to you."

"In your version, you done bugger-all to me yourself, remember? I'm 'paranoid,' so I'm acting my part." Henry turned heel, and retreated.

"Edgar! Do come in."

Edgar thunked his luggage in the candlelit foyer. The taxi was still within hailing distance; after Henry's warm reception, Edgar was considering a curt request for the key, so he could scram right away. But that was before he got a good look at Nicola.

She was a pre-Raphaelite vision. Tall, narrow, and delicate, the woman's figure echoed the precision of her speech, the sharply articulated wrists, clavicle, and cheekbones as exactingly wrought as haiku. Tressing in wavelets to her waist, her hair reflected a range of hues from blond to red. She was draped in an assemblage of scarves and shawls that Edgar would have found cockamamie on most women, but Nicola could get away with as much flourish as she liked. She belonged in a tower, weaving by a shattered looking-glass, or banished eternally from Camelot in a longboat drifting downstream.

The crimsons and cobalts of her fabrics set off a shocking pallor. Nicola's pained expression captured the very *inchoate yearning* that Edgar had been too embarrassed to express to Wallasek, and echoed the ruinous cycle of desire and disappointment tyrannizing his own life. How many times had Edgar confronted the mirror ball of a sparkling new acquaintance, only to reach for the facets and cut his hand—to complete another soul-sickening *inversion* as in the cold light of day the bauble revealed itself as a cheap disco trick? How many times had he met the likes of Nicola and vowed to see through the gaudy gypsy get-up as tacky theatrics, to remember that behind every pretty face lurked yet another grasping, lying, scheming, petty, faithless shrew? And how many times had these warnings to himself successfully protected him from heartbreak?

Not once. Taking the slim white hand, Edgar had to stop himself from kissing it.

"Nicola Tremaine."

Edgar burst out, "That sounds like a movie star!"

She must have thought him a complete rube. "Thanks. I've felt selfish keeping the *Tremaine*, but *Nicola Durham* simply sounded too prosaic. I'm afraid Henry was rather offended."

"You're an aesthete," said Edgar, hoping that in candlelight it wasn't too obvious his countenance was crestfallen.

"Almost nothing but," she confessed easily, leading him around a bend and down a few stone steps. "I care mostly about names with a ring, juniper berries in jasmine rice, or soup bowls and dinner plates from different sets that uncannily go together. Grace, taste, appearances. You'll soon learn that I'm a shamefully superficial person."

Edgar reflected that if his own surfaces were as pleasing as hers he'd have no motivation to probe beneath them himself, but didn't know how to say as much without sounding oily. So he trotted after her fringed train as it shivered down the stairs, mouth open like a dog's. God-fucking-damn it. She would have to be married.

The moment Edgar entered Nicola's living room he felt the collective resentment of her guests so forcefully that he came physically to a halt. It wasn't as if he had gatecrashed a genuine ho-down; a mere desultory murmur ceased when he walked in. Yet the dozen people scattered around the room turned to greet the *National Record*'s fill-in stringer with one long synchronized sneer. Meanwhile, "Famous Blue Raincoat" droned its tuneless, depressive best: *Yes, and Jane came by with a lock of your hair . . .* Real party music.

Nicola's eyes darted the room; if she was deciding to whom it was safest to introduce him, she was having a hard time. Stranded by the table of booze and eats—intricate open-faced sandwiches, individually assembled into one-of-a-kind Miros—Edgar was keenly aware that his shirt was crumpled, his jeans smelled stale, his teeth were furry, and the gale had tossed his hair to salad.

"You can always go local." A rangy fellow gestured at the bottles, having eased off his stool and gimped to Edgar's side.

"What constitutes going local?" asked Edgar warily.

"Try it," the weathered American dared him, uncapping a brown bottle labeled CHOQUE.

Though alerted by a sadistic twitch in the older man's face, Edgar felt eyes on him and swigged. Before the beer was down his gullet, Edgar's oral membrane had constricted into a dry pucker, like mouth eczema. Slamming down the bottle, he scrubbed his lips with a napkin, then stuffed down a sandwich. Edgar was reminded of the time he sneaked into his parents' bathroom to swill what he thought was codeine-laced cough syrup, and instead chugged his father's prescription anesthetic for rectal itch.

"Cerveja de pera peluda," the man explained. "*Choque* means what it sounds like, 'shock,' but you get used to it."

"What the hell's a *putrid pera*?" Edgar gasped, still scouring his lips.

"Barba's only thriving native fruit: the hairy pear," said his new acquaintance. "It grows in such abundance that it would provide a cash crop, only no one else wants it—so they export terrorism instead. There's more of a market. Meanwhile, they put *peras peludas* in everything. The fruit ferments like a bastard. Some of us old-timers have acquired a sick addiction to hairy-pear beer. Speaking of which—Durham! Did the *Independent* run your fluff piece?"

"They spiked it," said Henry. "With Barba dropped out of the news and that, the foreign desk didn't think a feature was timely."

"Curious," the tough old hand observed, "the way Saddler took the party with him—like the Grinch that stole Christmas. Not an incident since he dearly departed. Hardly thoughtful. The rest of us have to make a living. Reuters just e-mailed that they'll close the bureau in three months if nothing blows up."

"I thought Henry's feature was better than fluff," Nicola intervened. "Barbans' taste for *peras peludas* made a trenchant metaphor. The way a bitterness runs in their blood—"

"Nick, nobody gives a rat's ass about the cultural niceties of this toilet bowl if the *Soldados Ousados* aren't releasing nerve gas in Paris metros," the Reuters man overrode. "If the Sobs slaughter enough innocents, Henry can sell a feature on how Barbans tweeze their nose hairs."

"I thought the piece provided good color," Nicola maintained staunchly.

"So your husband doesn't get his hundred quid," the leathery wire-service man noted with a cynical squint. "The rent will be late?"

Nicola hung her head. Henry's face remained impassive. Whatever this razzing was about, Henry was used to it.

"Win Pyre." The man extended a hand, its palm callused,

his veined metacarpus tinged the gray-brown of a cancerous tan. "Where you last posted, Kellogg?"

"The States—freelancing." *Freelancing* prompted the usual smirk. Not wanting to be taken for a complete loser, Edgar added, "I'm a lawyer. Or was a lawyer. Actually, I'm still a lawyer." Made a hash of that bio. But *is, was*—tense was tricky. The fact that Edgar remained a member of the New York bar in good standing was surprisingly important to him.

"Criminal law?" Pyre fished.

"Corporate," said Edgar defiantly.

"I see." The smirk curled into a pitying simper. "So you're taking a break from the drones to see the world."

If Edgar had just branded himself an unimaginative robot, that's just how Edgar perceived his own legal persona by the time he quit. Still the dismissal smarted, just as any outsider would raise hackles criticizing a family that you yourself detest. Besides, suits in high-rises ran "the world" that Pyre seemed to think Edgar was glimpsing for the first time; they paid this cowboy's salary. The footfall of the financial colossus shook the ground a reporter walked, and if Pyre discounted the fee-fi-fo-fum of corporate giants as humdrum, then Pyre was incompetent, and Pyre was the one to be pitied.

"How enterprising," Pyre added archly. He meant how *impudent*. He meant, *I can't wait to watch you fall flat on your face, you presumptuous dullard.* He meant, *You may be accustomed to throwing wads around with your drab business cronies, but around here all that counts is copy and you just demoted yourself to boot camp, buddy.*

Edgar buried his right fist in his left palm, and changed the subject. "So is the wind often this howling? In ten seconds off the plane, it had ripped open my nostrils, torn down my throat, and whistled out my ass. Free rolphing."

"You're on your maiden assignment to a notorious cradle of

international terrorism," Pyre said incredulously, "and you want to talk about the *weather*?"

"Why not?" said Nicola. "Gauging *o vento insano* is a local preoccupation. There's an unstable high-to-low-pressure interface between the Med and the Atlantic that creates a near-permanent sirocco across the Barban peninsula. And no, it's not always this bad, Edgar; it's generally much worse. Some days advisories are issued not to leave your house. Most natives learn to protect themselves, but others give over. There's a certain stupefied idiocy you'll find around here that results from gross exposure to the atmosphere. *Vento*-heads extend their arms to let the gale keep them aloft. Their eyes glaze and dry out. Sometimes they fall asleep, since the wind props them up. *O vento insano* can get into your head. Like tinnitus."

"Or like Creamie propaganda," said Pyre. "It's incessant, it never varies except in decibel level, and subjection to enough of it turns you into a moron."

"Sweetheart?" Nicola looked about rapidly, her long hair flailing, before she located her husband. It wasn't such a large room that she should worry about losing him, physically at least. "Would you like another Diamond White?"

Henry ignored her, and collapsed indolently into an armchair. Surprisingly, on close examination Nicola's husband was probably about thirty-five. Slight and gangly with a cowlick and freckles, in charitable light Henry might have passed for a kid, except for a telltale hardening of his adolescent features, as if a seventeen-year-old had been sculpted in wax. If he looked a little careworn, his *Happy Days* face appeared frozen in perpetual distress that he didn't have a prom date. By contrast, ever since the Celery Wars Edgar's brow had been plowed with mature furrows, the grooves from his nose to the corners of his mouth scored with the gravity of a stock-market crash.

One aspect of the Madame Tussauds teenager was intriguing.

Money has an eye for money, and Edgar not long ago had a lot of it. That watch on Henry's wrist was gold, and not plate. Clean lines, sweet dial: classy, and three thousand bucks if it was ten cents. Someone had taste, and Edgar bet it wasn't Henry. Yet the clasp was fastened carelessly loose, and the face dropped around his hand. Likewise that salmon raw-silk shirt was Yves Saint Laurent, the blond suede vest Gucci, but the sleeves were crudely bunched above his elbows, and the suede was filthy. Whoever had spent a lot of dough on that gear, it now roused only Henry's indifference.

"Henry? Sweetie? Let me get you a cold one." Nicola scurried to the kitchen.

Pyre tsked at her back. "Poor Nick and Henry. They used to be so repulsively happy. Now they just seem that way, like everyone else."

"What happened?" asked Edgar.

"With couples, it's more often *who*."

"Let me guess," said Edgar.

"You're quick," Pyre conceded. "You'll need to be. Those aren't easy boots to fill."

"Another devoted fan?" asked Edgar dryly.

"I deplore the man," said Pyre, and for the first time Edgar warmed to the veteran hack. "He's everything that gives journalists a bad name: arrogant, irresponsible, inaccurate. He thinks he's bigger than his story. Barba, well, he thinks he *owns* Barba, as if he made the place up. He's unserious. Saddler's seen a lot of the world, and at its worst. But I have, too—Lebanon, Somalia—and it's the dickens not to simply turn nasty. But Saddler, Saddler's reaction has been hysterical. I mean he finds everything funny. Me, I'm not amused. Saddler covers terrorist incidents as if they're practical jokes. But I've had one pulled on me." Pyre patted his bad leg. "In eighty-three, I was conducting an interview near that Marine barracks car bomb in Beirut. Though I got off light, I'll never play tennis again. Saddler thinks that's a hah-hah. But I liked playing tennis."

"You still talk about him in the present tense."

"Barrington Saddler would never submit to anything melodramatic without an audience. I doubt he takes a dump without someone watching."

"Even flamboyant fatheads get run over by buses," Edgar countered.

"Saddler would more likely run over the bus himself."

"He's that much of a load?"

"He's that determined that nothing get in his way. Now, can I introduce you to a few of your colleagues? Though don't expect overnight fast friends."

"How did I manage to step on toes from twenty feet?"

"By *not* being Merry Barry. Since Saddler jumped ship, the pulse of this town has slowed to hibernation levels. Truth is, I kinda miss hating the guy."

CHAPTER 7
Edgar Meets His New Little Friends

"ARE WE STILL playing, or not?" asked the blonde, whose face had that clear-eyed, clear-skinned symmetry used to sell moisturizing cream, but that for the life of him Edgar could never find sexy.

Win Pyre thumped his cane on the carpet and made introductions.

"Am I interrupting something?" asked Edgar.

"Yes, thank God. Party games." The reporter for the London *Guardian*, Roland Ordway, spewed a thin stream of smoke. His spiky black hair sprayed at the cleverly balanced Katzenjammer angles of a pricey designer cut. Young and sleazily good-looking, Ordway kept the arms of his sports jacket jammed above his elbows, and his jeans were ironed with a crease. As for the cowboy boots, Ordway was the sort of Brit who thought Americana was hip so long as Americans didn't come with it.

"What's the game?" Edgar bounced onto the balls of his feet, literally on his toes.

"To name the game is to lose it." Sucking his ciggie, Ordway pinched the butt from underneath.

"Let Trudy explain, then," said the frump on the loveseat, a correspondent for the *Washington Post* whose name was Martha Hulbert. "She adores losing."

Martha was one of those women who look terrible on purpose. Her shapeless dress was scalloped with chintzy gold-painted plastic chain at the waist, its fabric the corrupted green of aged broccoli florets; imagining any woman walking into a store and choosing this spoilage-colored sack boggled the mind. Martha might have looked presentable if she lost twenty pounds, but Edgar knew the sort: all her life she'd hug those twenty pounds like a kid with a stuffed bunny.

"We're timing ourselves," said Ordway. "To see how long we can go without mentioning He Who Is No Longer With Us. There. A black mark for me."

"It's a stupid game," said Trudy Sisson, the cover-girl blonde whom Pyre had introduced with a curdled lip as a "freelance photographer." In this case "freelance" appeared to mean "bankrolled by Daddy," and in Pyre's mind Trudy Sisson's bowling-pin calves and syrupy Southern accent must have dropped her IQ thirty points. Edgar had ridiculed his share of secretarial bimbos at the firm, but like the smell of your own armpits prejudice is less obnoxious when it's yours, and for the moment he felt sorry for her. He'd get over it.

"Leastways when Barrington comes up it's a little like he's still here," Trudy went on. "For a few seconds we have some energy. And I wanted to hear about the twins."

"I gather they're still not speaking," said Martha.

"Lucky us," said Ordway. "Remember what they *said*?"

"Sorry." Martha glanced dutifully at Edgar. "Bear had an affair—"

Ordway began to singsong, *"Bear had an affair with two twins—"*

"A team, once upon a time," Martha persevered.

"And shimmied all four shapely shins—"

"Roland, if you don't mind, I'm trying to be polite!" said Martha sharply. "They wrote and photographed for *Esquire*. Very successful duo—"

"'Til one bim said, 'Mister! You're shagging my sister! Confess your identical sins.'"

"Behold the Bard of Barba," said Martha, rolling her eyes. "Anyway, each found out about the other—how would they not?

And you've never seen such a falling out. It would have made more sense to turn on Barrington, but they went for each other instead. Operating on the ridiculous premise that the one who tore the most hair would win the two-timing trophy."

"I've never thought he cared fuck-all for either one of them," said Ordway. "He just wanted to watch the cat fight."

"It was malicious," said Martha primly. "He saw how close they were. Just like—" Martha glanced furtively around the room, then lowered her voice—"*you* know. Anyway, they wore each other's clothes, finished each other's sentences. Erin told me once that they sometimes had the same dreams. Now they despise each other, and Mary's defected to *Vanity Fair.* It was tragic and he did it on purpose. Emotional vandalism, if you ask me."

"Oh, don't be so moralistic," said Trudy. "Barrington got bored so Barrington slept around."

"You should know," said Ordway.

Trudy raised her chin. "But can you blame him? I wake up the day after he disappeared—or whatever, I'm too scared to think about it. I look around and think, I'm living in a dump. The food stinks, the beer stinks, you can't even lie on the beach 'cause it's too cold, not to mention the *wind.* I think, one more blast up my skirt, one more *whoosh* wrecking my hair and I'm booking for the States. Well, it didn't seem that way before. With Barrington, Barba was exciting. Y'all feel the same way but won't admit it."

"Another beer, Kellogg?" asked Pyre.

"You just want to watch me commit hairy-peary again," said Edgar.

The awful pun cast a pall.

"Barrington already used that line," said Trudy, glaring.

"Definitely going to need that beer," said Edgar, turning to fetch it himself. Jesus. Saddler had even beaten him to the jokes.

Edgar lingered by the drinks to look around. As if rendered freehand, everything in the room was subtly imperfect. The cushions' needlework was lumped with tufty bits. The throw rug beneath Edgar's feet included one aberrant purple stripe that, while it looked like a mistake, also electrified the pattern and was the sole reason the rug drew his eye. None of the picture frames was quite rectangular, and the original watercolors within were fraught with charming little errors in perspective. The ceramic tiles around the fireplace were crookedly inlaid. The pitcher on the drinks table canted to the left. Spearing a pickled onion, he noticed that the handles of the wooden hors d'oeuvre forks were whittled into animals, and it was impossible to tell if this one was a lion or a sheepdog.

At first Edgar assumed that Nicola was a boutiquey sort who shopped at import outlets, except these objects exhibited neither the soullessness of mass production nor the shoddiness of some arthritic Third Worlder hacking out cocktail forks for ten cents an hour. Rather, every curtain, upholstery job, and one-of-a-kind dessert plate bore the indelible imprimatur of the same gently perverse sensibility. Like Martha Hulbert's frumpiness, the living room's appointments were flawed on purpose.

When Nicola rearranged the sandwiches, Edgar commended, "You're quite a cook."

She sighed. "I'm afraid no one has much appetite tonight."

"So—you a journalist yourself?"

"Gracious, no. I'm a housewife." The admission was cheerful.

So rarely had Edgar met women in New York who confessed to doing nothing that he floundered for lack of follow-up. "To support you, and this house—which is big . . ."

"Not as big as yours."

"It's just, Henry must be doing okay."

"I wouldn't say that Henry's *okay*."

"Financially, I mean." Instead of nosing into their bank statement he should have asked if she had kids, but he too badly didn't want her to have any.

"Even financially," Nicola reflected, "I'd not describe Henry as *okay*. In fact, Henry's financial situation is woeful. That is, full of woe."

Edgar was determined not to drop another clangor like, *So you weave your own rugs because you can't afford commercial ones*. He held up the dog-lion end of his fork. "Is there anything in this house you didn't make?"

Nicola scrutinized the room. "Of course. The wine glasses—I haven't learned to blow glass yet, but I'd love to . . . And I didn't make nearly all the furniture, because Henry put his foot down. It takes too long, and he didn't want to eat off the floor."

"This handicrafting. It's some kind of policy, then?"

"I don't have policies. I have whims. I'm a total child, Edgar. All I do is play. In adult terms, I'm a dabbler. I can't explain, but there's something about scooping lettuce from a salad bowl that you carved yourself. Preferably lettuce from your own garden, but nothing grows in this godforsaken province other than *peras peludas*.

"In our case, these whims of mine have proved a funny antidote. Henry has a closetful of designer silk and Italian suede, but he's much safer walking around in hand-sewn cotton. If I had the time he'd wear cloth I wove as well—from thread I spun, from cotton I ginned, but obviously there are limits. A homemade shirt might not hang quite right, but it's a kind of protection." She hung her head. "The last few months he's gone back to the Calvin Kleins. I don't blame him, but I think it's dangerous."

"Why's that?" Edgar was completely out of his depth.

"I'm talking about the conservation of meaning," she said passionately. "When you're young, you take significance for granted. In childhood, every silly clockwork donkey, or your first garish pink lipstick, is important. Then the problem is the opposite: you're overpowered by meaning, drowning in it. But later . . . Well, I can't go *buy* Henry a present, can I?"

Edgar could only intuit vaguely that they had money troubles.

"Barrington understood," she added sadly. "But Barrington collected meaning like lint. Like that *Peanuts* character: it followed him in a cloud."

"You're the only one I've met so far who mentions him in the past tense."

"It's a discipline."

"I hope your, um, circumstances don't mean you'll have to clear out of this house," said Edgar. "It's cool."

"I'm sorry, I've misled you. You're new here, you must be knackered after your long journey, and here I'm being coy. Don't worry about our being evicted, Edgar. We own this house and five others all over Europe. But I'm a little tired myself. If you don't mind, we won't get into it now."

Dismissed and disconcerted, Edgar drifted back to the knot of gossips in the corner, his gate a bit unsteady. He'd switched to Heineken but eyed the brown bottles of Choque, curiously magnetic. The stuff was awful, punishing, but, much like the subject of Mr. Saddler, inexplicably difficult to leave alone.

At least when Edgar rejoined the group they'd moved on, which was probably the work of the visiting German from *Der Spiegel*. In his fidgety silence, Reinhold Glück had seemed impatient with ceaseless scuttlebutt on someone he didn't know. Serious and bespectacled, Glück was doing a feature comparing O Creme de Barbear with German neo-Nazis. Edgar recognized the tone before penetrating the German accent; liberal indignation whiffled with the same strident huffiness all over the world.

"It is nothing but racism!" said Glück.

"We're not talking about a handful of funny-sounding visitors," said Trudy, crossing her legs. "What about all those Turks in Germany? What if there were more Turks than Germans? If they could vote your prime minister out of office—"

"Chancellor," said Martha.

"Whatever. And you walk down the street and everyone's talking Turkish? And it's hard to find a Pilsner anymore, like, all you can find is, I don't know, mead, or whatever Turkish people drink. Know what a place like that's called? *Turkey.* There wouldn't even be a Germany anymore. Wouldn't that tee you off? Where's your national pride?"

"The whole world has suffered for Germany's national pride," said Glück. "I have a different kind of pride."

"Well, I have American pride," said Trudy. "Us Floridians have Cubans, Haitians, and Mexicans up the wazoo. When I grab a cab, if I don't know Spanish for 'airport' the cabby looks at me like *I'm* the nitwit. In Miami, I feel like a foreigner in my own country."

"In a truly pluralistic society, all people feel equally foreign and equally at home. You are not talking about being American, but about being white and in control. It is the same in Barba. The fascists in O Creme only want to stay in power—"

"I'm with you in theory, Reinhold," said Martha. "Still, nobody in crappy little Barba has power of any description to hang on to."

"They do now," said Ordway. "Whole bloody Western world is up in arms about immigration in *crappy little Barba*. That's power. Look at us: we live here, we file from here, we're consumed with local politics. And we'd never have considered so much as a bargain package holiday to this filthy bog five years ago."

"That impresses you?" said Edgar.

"It is impressive, innit?" Ordway's standard middle-class London accent was decorated with lowbrow touches. Translate: white geeks from Long Island lacing their conversation with *yo!* and *I hear dat!* like the brothers in the 'hood.

"The Sobs having murdered over two thousand people—that impresses you, too?" The journalistic penchant for calling members of the SOB *the Sobs* and their political counterparts in O

Creme de Barbear *Creamies* had first jarred as swaggeringly familiar, but Edgar got a charge out of tossing off the jargon himself.

"Kellogg, don't be so earnest!" said Ordway. "There must be some bloke side of you that fancies their flash. The Sobs have Interpol, the FBI, the CIA, the Portuguese Army, and the local coppers combing every *pera peluda* peel of Barban rubbish, and nobody can find a trace of them. Even Creamies keep their hands clean. They get lifted, but the next week they're back on the street when nothing sticks. Other than the author of that sodding autobiography, *I Was an SOB*—a load of bollocks, in my view—no one's dug up a single bona fide member of that lot in five years. That's impressive, mate."

"Only to little boys," said Martha.

"Already, half the schoolchildren in the States are Spanish-speaking," Trudy was preaching fervently to Reinhold. "And kids grow up. They're taking over!"

"Majority status is no people's right," Glück insisted. "It is an accident, a lucky advantage. Like any advantage you want to hold on to it. But it is typical reasoning of privileged people to assume that just because you have something, ipso facto you deserve it. In truth, this 'defense of borders' is naked defense of self-interest—not of justice."

"I still think Verdade has a point," said Trudy sulkily. "If I were Barban, I'd sure get peeved with hordes of North African Muslims overrunning my home. These immigrants don't have any money—"

"From what I have read, the Moroccans are much more industrious than the lazy native Iberians," said Glück. "And Moroccans don't blow up airplanes, either."

"Okay, the Creamies are extreme," said Trudy. Recrossing her legs, she added slyly, "But you gotta admit: Tomás Verdade is pretty sexy."

"Violence puts an issue on the map," Ordway was lecturing

Edgar. "Sob tactics may not be pretty, but they're sussed. No casualties, we're not even having this conversation."

"I'd concede that targeting world powers is smart," said Edgar, beginning to get in the swing. "Terrorizing has-been Portugal wouldn't work. No one would give a shit."

"Yes," Ordway droned wearily. "That observation has been made before."

Edgar flagged the jaded response. By nature he had both a good feel for the trite and a special aversion to it. He could pinpoint the exact instant when having a "bad hair day" was no longer funny.

"Anyway," said Ordway, "you'll soon clue that your new profession is dull as ditch water unless someone gets hurt. I covered the Quebec referendum on secession: few punch-ups, a bit o' shouting. Even my mum used the paper to line her kitty-litter box."

"News isn't entertainment," said Edgar.

"News is exclusively entertainment," said Martha, "according to Barrington."

"Ten minutes, girls and boyos!" Ordway exclaimed, checking his watch. "A record."

CHAPTER 8
Ninety-Nine Push-Ups and Cloudberry Shampoo

AT A PAT on his shoulder, Edgar jolted upright. Nicola laughed. "You look like a *vento* head!" she teased. "Can I drive you home?"

Unchivalrously, he accepted the lift. After Nicola went up to fetch her car keys, she met Edgar in the foyer with a significant glance. "Before I forget." From the folds of her cloak, she withdrew an oversize brass skeleton key, its head cast with runes, as if it might open a chest of gold doubloons or a secret medieval torture chamber. The key was heavy, with a smaller, modern key attached, and so made quite a clatter when she dropped it on the flagstones. As she dived to scoop it up, Henry was walking up the stairs.

"No, let me," said Edgar, lunging for the set. "My keys," he said to Henry, "from the *Record*. Dropped them. Clumsy of me. Must be tired."

Henry blinked. The key was distinctive. Something didn't quite compute. Still Nicola looked, though whiter by a shade, relieved.

"That was quick thinking, in the foyer," said Nicola, as they pulled off in her Land Rover. "Thanks."

"You may be a dandy rug weaver," said Edgar. "But when it comes to the art of deception, you suck."

She smiled, tightly. "I'm not sure if I should be offended by that, or not."

Edgar delivered a few slash-slash assessments of her other guests, but Nicola didn't pick up, and Edgar feared that he'd just queered the goodwill of one of those if-you-can't-say-anything-nice types.

"I'm sorry that your new home won't have been tidied," she said. "It was left more or less *au naturel.* Not that Barrington was a slob—I mean, he was, but after these big, impromptu dos of his a few guests were always eager to stay and clear up. Some nights—mornings, rather—they actually fought over the Hoover. I dare say there were certain young ladies who'd have scoured his toilet bowl with their own toothbrushes."

"No, the real test," Edgar mumbled, "is whether they'd use them after."

"Funny, some people go missing for weeks, and no one notices until a frightful smell starts leaking from their flats. But the alarm went out about Barrington in a matter of hours. He was meant to dine at Trudy's that night. She'd made beef Wellington, of all things, an all-day-in-the-kitchen affair that Barrington had once mentioned in passing that he fancied. Foie gras, wild mushrooms, goodness knows what else. She insisted on making the puff pastry from scratch; the leaves came out a bit thick. Me, I find it's often the simplest . . . Oh, never mind.

"He was always late, of course, but he'd usually make an appearance. I'm afraid that Trudy's having gone to so much bother would count for all too little, but there's not that much to do here, and the rest of us were all at Trudy's."

"More to the point, *you* were at Trudy's."

Nicola ignored the insinuation. "By two a.m. she was hysterical. We all thought she was overreacting, upset about having made rather a hash of the beef (not to be unkind, but it came out a tad well-done, and there was no disguising that cutting the crust was hard work). We thought she was hurt that after all her talking up the dish he'd made other plans. The dear girl has made great capital since from her intuition that something ghastly was wrong. How she felt 'a wash of cold air' and 'suddenly Cinzeiro felt empty.' She claims she'll never again eat beef Wellington—which she insists on calling 'beef Barrington' in tribute. Well. Not much danger, in Barba.

"I've only been back to Barrington's once," she continued.

"And please don't mention it to Henry. But I simply couldn't bear the idea of the police smashing that lovely cedar door with a battering ram. So when Barrington became an official missing person, I rang the chief inspector and arranged to let him in.

"The detectives went through everything," she explained. "All they found was some gibberish on Barrington's computer disks. Nonsense, according to Lieutenant de Carvalho. There was only one part of the house I steered the police away from. A small tower; they never noticed the door. You've the key to its padlock. But Barrington told me not to go up there. So I haven't."

"Even Bluebeard's wives didn't play along with that shit," Edgar slurred. "You always so obedient?"

"When I make a promise."

Including to your husband? "What do you think's up there, then? Bodies?"

"Maybe one. That's the only place we haven't checked for Barrington. But on the off chance . . . I guess I didn't want to know."

She pulled up to a long dark hulk and sat, with the Land Rover idling, hands in her lap. Though the villa was virtually invisible, she closed her eyes, as if for good measure. "It does light up," she said dismally, all but spelling out: Though only when a certain someone was inside.

Edgar fumbled his good-byes and trundled with his bags to the dim front porch. The lock responded gladly to his skeleton key. Pushed by the Barban gale, the thick cedar door opened by itself, as if Edgar were expected.

After groping for a light switch, he had a vague, cockeyed impression of having infiltrated a deserted sheikdom. He bumbled upstairs to a king-size four-poster. An ironing board would have sufficed. Having dragged off his clothes, he plunged into a small death.

Edgar woke between royal blue satin sheets, under billows of goose-down duvets. Pillows buttressed his every side, as if he were packed for overseas shipping. Opposite, lemony late-day sunlight filtered between shifting drapes of crimson velvet, and upper panes of leaded stained glass dolloped red and green lollipops onto the bed. A sole reminder of where he was, a high hissing whistle sang through the window cracks. Panes rattled as if *o vento insano* were rapping to get in, and a faint, low-pitched moan groaned outside.

According to his diving watch—in his freelance poverty so discordantly showy, yet in the context of his immediate surroundings a dime-store trinket—he'd slept fifteen hours.

Edgar propped on the springy pillows, which puffed cool air onto his cheek at every readjustment. This was indeed a *master* bedroom. Laid with overlapping Oriental carpets, the floor was elevated a step under the bed. Raising the four-poster into a throne of repose, the dais made fifteen hours' sleep seem his due. Edgar could easily see settling here for days at a time amid splayed half-read books, occasionally granting an audience or tinkling a clear brass bell for breakfast service. The image of broad trays (carved camphor wood, Edgar decided, with ivory handles) hovered over both tall side tables. Spread with embroidered cloths, they'd be littered with goblets of guava juice, crumbs of honeyed pastries, ornate cups of thick, sweet coffee, and filigreed silver spoons.

Disquieted, Edgar disentangled himself. He disapproved of sloth, and had a positive horror of honeyed pastries. The bedding was contaminated with another man's fantasy life.

Edgar padded gingerly around the room, as if afraid to wake someone up—like himself. More crimson velvet canopied the bed, and velvet drapes hung on rings from the frame's upper rail. The curtains could be pulled all the way around the mattress to make a private tent. The fragrant dark cherries and rosewoods of the massive furniture were carved into busty prows of women or tumbles of ripe fruit; the bureau shimmered with mother-of-pearl inlays. A mosaic of colored glass beads framing the mirror threw highlights on Edgar's naked figure, making his chest look more finely muscled than it was and his complexion lustier than he felt. The reflection likewise elongated his frame to tower beside the bedpost, and Edgar was only five-foot-eight. It was a mirror made for self-deceit. What it must have done for Saddler, a much larger man by all accounts, well—he must have looked leviathan.

Penetrating scents of cedar, sandalwood, and the residual haunt of a woman's perfume intoxicated Edgar with the giddy notion of going back to bed. Rubbing his eyes, he ambled to the cavernous en suite bath to splash his face in the black alabaster sink. Drying, he plunged into a white towel plush as rabbit's fur; the nap buried his fingers to the first knuckle. Scoping out the sunken tub—round, black marble, and wide enough for laps—he drew himself a bath.

Edgar treated himself to warm-up hot-water blasts and picked through an array of toiletries—saffron conditioner, mandarin-and-cloudberry shampoo, almond oil, truffle-and-musk mud-mask: effeminate frippery. Edgar inclined toward plain Ivory and timeless Head & Shoulders: man-stuff. Still. He tried the cloudberry shampoo.

The clothing he'd packed was clearly too summery, so Edgar was able to rationalize picking through rack upon rack of preposterous regalia in the walk-in closet: old-fashioned tails and cutaways, with magenta cummerbunds; kimonos whose dragons licked up the facing; quilted smoking jackets; flowing rayon shirts wide as kites, writhing with van Gogh sunflowers or flaming with foot-wide poinsettias; a charcoal woolen cape, lined with cream silk, fit for Bela Lugosi; some biblically voluminous caftans and togas; and a number of officers' uniforms from foreign military outfits, whose appearance of authenticity was all the more reason not to prance around in them. None of the outlandish glad rags suited a man for writing, only for being written about. Although a smattering of standard Anglo fare—Burberrys, camelhairs, and tweeds from the finest London tailors—bespoke a journalist who occasionally did his job, the suspenders (*braces*, a voice whispered) marched with toy soldiers, and there wasn't a tie to be found, just two dozen *ascots*.

Impetuously, Edgar slipped a dressing gown off its wooden hanger. The radiant golden robe faced with plum brocade might have costumed Apollo Creed.

Camp, sure. But somehow in their vastness all these garments stopped shy of kitsch. The lines of the finery were so drastic, their patterns so fantastic, their pretensions drafted on such a scale that they were rescued from ridiculousness by sheer audacity.

Except on Edgar. A foot too long, the nacreous dressing gown dragged like a wedding train. The shoulder pads drooped to his elbows, and the sleeves dangled inches beyond his fingertips. Even in the magic mirror, he looked like a Norman Rockwell: *Junior Wears Father's Bathrobe.*

Fuck it. Edgar gathered the train and swirled out of the bedroom with a little transvestite flounce, assured that you could get away with anything so long as you did it with conviction.

Nicola was right: the house was enormous. Edgar's disgust that the *National Record* would coddle any correspondent with such palatial accommodations failed to undermine exultation at his own good fortune. Aside from the one tiny round tower, the villa rose only two stories high, but spread across what must have amounted to half a New York City block. Its Moorish architecture expressed the clean, wide lines of Frank Lloyd Wright fare, without the iciness of modernity. Hanging tapestries and Oriental carpet softened the perpendiculars of mosaic tile and marble parquet. Downstairs was constructed on a variety of levels, the floors landscaped into benches cushioned with rotund pillows. The dining area's table, like the bath, was sunken.

Though the western windows looked frosted, their panes were

pitted irregularly: dulled by gale-borne sand. When the wind would *poom* a door against its frame, like a body slammed from the patio, it took practice not to jump.

Edgar's favorite room at ground level was the atrium: open and Romanesque, lit by skylights slit around the ceiling, and organized around a rectangular pool whose fountain still plashed in Saddler's absence. The atrium called out for scantily clad slave girls offering fleshy grapes, palm-leaf fans, and a flow of red wine as ceaseless as the fountain. While Edgar formed an instantaneous affection for the hall, it also made him nervous. Lassitude! Indiscipline! Sloth!

In fact, the entire villa was imbued with an indulgent sensibility to which Edgar was constitutionally hostile. The drinks cabinet clinked with a bonanza of top-shelf booze. Beckoning pillows plumping every room made Edgar's head list and his eyelids heavy. Numerous guest bedrooms invited all-night social excess. The pantry, chock-full of absurd gift tins and jars—hazelnuts in Cointreau, glacé cherries, pickled quail eggs, smoked baby oysters—enticed three a.m. binges when no one was watching. Though the airy kitchen was fitted with every convenience, Edgar couldn't picture Saddler chopping onions, and sure enough there was a Post-it note gummed to the *Silver Palate Cookbook*: "B, Could I leave this here for next time? See page 46—yum! —E."

Since Edgar could no more envision Saddler plowing through *The Peloponnesian Wars* in original Greek than slicing zucchini, the upstairs study's glassed-in leather-bound library—rows of erudite European histories and biographies in multiple languages from Flemish to Hungarian—was expensive paneling.

It was the study that showcased the got-the-T-shirt trinkets of a foreign correspondent, keepsakes that recalled the *We Were There* series that Edgar had devoured as a kid. In *We Were There at Pearl Harbor . . . at Appomattox . . . at the Boston Tea Party*, a pack of lucky brats always popped up at the right time and place. He should have told Wallasek that he quit being an attorney in order to jump between the covers of *We Were There* before it was too late, since no one was about to write a book about kids who serendipitously visit a corporate law firm in a season of hostile takeovers.

At any rate, *Barrington Was There*. The room overflowed with souvenir booty: a rifle slug, a rubber bullet, a melted metal bicycle pump, a human skull with a patch of scalp sun-dried to the bone. A U.S. Army C-ration kit gritty in the crevices may have commemorated the Gulf War or the invasion of Panama; a tin ladle cleverly fashioned from a can of potted beef, marked "Gift of Finland," must have been saved in fond remembrance of a famine.

On the wide, curly maple desk sat a clear, catering-size mayonnaise jar, the sort coveted in primary school for terrariums. It brimmed with coins, from rands to bahts, including currencies, like the Zaire, that had become so devalued that its silver was no longer minted. Next to this cosmopolitan piggybank lay an unopened letter from Amnesty International addressed to Mohamed Siad Barre, a Spider-Man comic book in Russian, and a sheet of ghoulish "AIDS Has No Cure" postage stamps from Kenya. The left-hand desk drawer was brimming with electoral buttons: Vote for Marcos, Mengistu, Mobutu, Duvalier, Rabin . . . Mostly demagogues, plus Rabin had been assassinated: quite a cynical tribute to democracy. One file opened on the desk appeared to include every SOB atrocity claim and policy statement ever issued; another drawer rattled with microfloppies alluringly labeled SOB STORIES. The floppies could save Edgar some work.

A set of three-ringed notebooks lined one bookshelf, and Edgar pulled the first volume: Saddler's clip files. Edgar scanned the initial feature, an impassioned exposé about Thai prostitution—the slave wages, diseases, indentured servitude. Touching, if overwritten. But reading is the ultimate submission. Edgar shoved the notebook back. Turning gruffly from his predecessor's accomplishments, Edgar started as a pair of eyes met his own.

Well, well. The *big, big, big* man in the foreground of that black-and-white enlargement had to be none other than Himself. Saddler was seated on the downstairs ottoman, bulwarked by pillows. His barrel-chest burst with such self-satisfaction that it strained the rhinestone buttons of the tuxedo shirt. His eyes sparked with the sinister twinkle of Santa Claus paging kiddy porn. And his right arm was hooked in a virtual headlock around *Nicola*.

Edgar was consternated. Sure, he'd caught the wink-and-nod in Wallasek's office, but that was before he'd met her and before he knew she was married. Edgar was mystified why such an elegant and estimable woman would muck in with a scumbag like Saddler.

Yet a second revelation rankled more considerably.

Edgar had verified in childhood what the New Testament only hints at. Yes, mobs will reprieve murderous hooligans before they acquit a babbling messianic head case; Barabbas was merely wicked, and Jesus was actually irritating. What the Bible failed to illustrate was Edgar's personal Apocrypha: that people will exonerate sadists, braggarts, liars, and even slack-jawed morons before they'll pardon eyesores. If you're attractive, people need a reason to dislike you; if you're ugly, people need a reason to like you. They don't usually find one. In his tubby school days, Edgar had learned the hard way that every vulgar slob on the block was an aesthete.

Now along comes this absentee paragon, about whom no one from New York to Cinzeiro can stop talking for more than ten minutes even using a stopwatch, and guess what? *Barrington Saddler wasn't even handsome.*

Saddler was built like a grain silo. Drawn practically into his lap, Nicola looked like a stick puppet in comparison. His eyelids were swollen, his cheeks loose; he had an infant double chin. Some great frames afforded no end of abuse, but in a few years' time the likes of that full back-up case of Beefeaters in the pantry would begin to show. His lips had a faintly feminine fullness, and his neck was thick. His features were pinched, gathered too closely into the middle of his face, as if someone had laced a drawstring around its perimeter and pulled. Though shaggy around the ears, in front his hair was thin. This was no Romeo, but a sybaritic lout well on his way to a stout and gouty middle age. *How did he do it?*

Defiantly, Edgar tossed the golden robe onto an overstuffed leather armchair. He began his daily one hundred push-ups, keeping his back perfectly straight, lowering his nose fully to the floor. From overhead, Saddler seemed to find the hale-and-hearty exhibition bemusing. For no reason that Edgar could fathom, he stopped at ninety-nine.

CHAPTER 9

G;p[[u Mpmdrmdr

EDGAR'S TOPSY-TURVY SCHEDULE gave the rest of the night the anarchic atmosphere of a school snow day, as the wind screamed *wheeeee!* like faraway kids on a sled. While the sun set through his own morning, Edgar discovered several bulbs out, maybe from having been left on when Barrington beat a hasty retreat. Vigorously finding spares and replacing the bulbs helped to offset the mesmerizing idleness that exuded from the plague of cushions. Unpacking took if anything too little time, though limping next to Saddler's thick, satinate wardrobe Edgar's wrinkled short-sleeves looked insipid.

Nicola's warnings were warranted; the place was pretty disheveled. Everything was dusty, and the fridge hadn't been cleaned for months. Inside, the smoked salmon was swimming, the caviar had hatched, and the liqueur-filled dark chocolates had turned fright-white. Numerous anonymous concoctions had grown branches of exotic molds the size of bonsais. Tautly cellophaned and lovingly garnished with desiccated sprigs, these rows of leftovers portrayed an unabating string of doting culinary benevolence.

Gagging, Edgar chucked the remnants of Saddler's tête-à-têtes and washed the reeking bowls. As reward, he sank at the kitchen's long middle table with a stiff shot of small-batch bourbon from his host's ample cabinet. Where were Edgar's adoring crumpets to scour the toilet bowls with their toothbrushes? The sensation might ebb, but for now he felt not only like a guest in what was presumably his own abode, but like the help. As if Barrington had suggested, be a good lad would you and do something about that dreadful ice box? Attaboy.

Edgar drained the shot resentfully and slammed down the glass, which rattled the lone cup of coffee and ashtray left at the far end. The black coffee had evaporated to leave a thin sediment of dried powder. The ashtray was a distinguished pewter affair, and offered up a single partially smoked cigarillo, which had burned half an inch of ash before extinguishing. Edgar reached for the butt, along with the classy brass lighter left graciously alongside. He tapped the ash, lit up, took a drag. The tobacco was stale, but underneath smoldered a more disturbing flavor—the tinge of a breath whose very foulness was arresting, like the unsettling allure of high French cheeses. The cigarillo was vile and Edgar didn't even smoke fresh ones, yet after a second furtive drag Edgar had to force himself to stub it out.

By now it was five forty-five a.m. Disorientation set in, and loneliness. Angela would have found this place a hoot. She'd have extended naked on the cold marble parquet by the fountain, her keen ribs flickering in the flames of sconces, and Edgar might have figured out what that room and all its pillows were good for. As it was, the villa's opulence mocked the paltriness of his imagination. Let loose in a palace, Edgar Kellogg dusted furniture and threw old salmon in the trash. This was a house you had to live not only in, but up to.

Scrounging for amusement worthy of his fanciful surroundings, Edgar returned to the study and stuck a SOB STORIES micro-floppy into his laptop. Though the computer seemed to recognize the program code, the files were nonsensically titled:

2" Er;vp,r yp yjr <pmlru Jpidr
3" Nsttomhypm'd Gotdy Sytpvoyu
4" Dpm pg Nsttomhypm Od Nptm
5" Yrttptod, <sfr Rsdu
6" Nstns :ppld S;obr

When Edgar loaded in *2" Er;vp,r yp yjr <pmlru Jpidr*, what came up on the screen was no more coherent:

> *Vpmhtsyi;syopmd@ Nu mpe upi ,idy jsbr dryy;rf om' O fp jp[r upi gomf yjr svvp,,pfsyopmd dioysn;r/ Niy im;rdd upi gp;;pe fotrvyopmd vstrgi;;u. mp mi,nrt pg syytsvyobr;u vtpvjryrf [o;;ped eo;; [tpyrvy upi gtp, yjr [ortvomh nptrfp, pg yjod fidy npe;. s diovofs;;u frno;oysyomh rmmio yjsy [rmrytsyrd upit rbrtu [ptr ;olr yjr htoy om yjsy dpffomh eomf/ Es;;sdrl vjpdr er;;/ Ypp er;;/ Jsf jr hobrm ,r sy ;rsdy s g;pert djpe pt yep yp vpbrt. O ,ohjym*
>
> *y jsbr nrrm gptvrf yp hrmrtsyr ,u pem mred/*
>
> *Yjod kpitms; esd nrhim gpt ,u pem rmyrtysom,rmy. niy upi eo;; gomf ,ptr yjsm rmpihj omgpt,syopm eoyjom oy yp vsttu pm ,u hppf eptl/ Yjrm. ,pdy kpitms;odyd str yo,of vtrsyitrd. ejp etoyr dyptord sd s dindyoyiyr gpt ;obomh yjr,. smf og upi str pmr pg yjsy ;py. upi ,su n;pe yjr ejody;r pm pit ;oyy;r drvtry og upi ;olr/ Ury s;trsfu O djpi;f estm upi" kidy ytu/*

Was Saddler out of his tree? Edgar and his brother Jeff had produced similar drivel playing with their father's typewriter as kids, but a grown man mashing mindlessly at keys for paragraphs on end was unnervingly reminiscent of *The Shining*. Edgar fiddled around a little more, testing to see if the computer was malfunctioning, and his own files loaded fine. Yet each floppy in the drawer was all *ypys; hpnn;rfuhppl* . . . The words didn't read backward, they suggested no simple pig-Latinate cognates and contained no systematically inserted syllables. Though a few shorter clumps were acronyms for real words, most of the longer ones were short of vowels.

Edgar wandered to the last part of the villa still unexplored. The entrance to the turret was on the second floor at the back, and Edgar found the little wooden door locked and thumbtacked with a printed sign that read, ABRAB WAS I ERE I SAW BARBA. *I don't know, buddy,* thought Edgar, *those files looked pretty* abrab *to me.*

He hesitated before fitting the smaller key into the padlock. Remembering Nicola's hushed caution that this was the one place no one had looked for the remains of the villa's master, he visualized a gaseous three-month-old corpse farting overhead. Twisting up the tight spiral staircase in the dark, Edgar gripped the cold railing, catching his breath on the landing before the final flight. Naturally he dreaded confrontation with a large-scale version of the salmon sliming in the fridge. But he was equally distressed by the prospect of Saddler's demise. When Edgar took on an antagonist, he wanted some fight left in the guy.

CHAPTER 10
The Empty Wingchair

ASIDE FROM BEING endearing—with little square windows at each point of the compass, a desk and lamp, even a separate computer printer—the tower was a disappointment at first. Yet after poking around (Edgar was a snoop), he found three things that he couldn't explain.

The first was a pile of stationery on the desktop, letterheaded with a variety of Barban hotels. But Edgar couldn't picture the extravagant lord of this manor snitching paper before checkout to scrimp, and the study exhibited a powerful prejudice toward souvenirs with patches of human hair.

Second, in the top desk drawer lay a six-inch-long, two-inch-wide metal pipe, with wax paper rubber-banded over one end and a single hole drilled through one side. While the gizmo looked crudely practical, it served no function that Edgar could fathom.

Third and most peculiar, in the bottom drawer sat a box of latex surgical gloves, once holding three hundred pairs and about half-full. Had Saddler been handling corrosive substances? Checking the advancement of an illness, like prostate cancer? Or might the new narcotic elite inject heroin with perfectly clean hands?

Edgar was puzzled, but in the absence of cadavers charmed by the private hideaway. It offered a cozy reprieve from the expanse of the lower two floors, which he couldn't begin to inhabit. Saddler's tower had the exclusive, barricaded aura of the tree houses into which neighborhood boys had never allowed him to clamber as a porky pariah. He'd break the ladder, they jeered. It was no big deal, but like most of his classmates' parents his own were divorced, and his father's uncomfortable, coffee-sipping visits were never long enough to help Edgar build a tree house of his own. Besides, his father had always seemed faintly disgusted. Edgar couldn't really blame him; the guy had never reckoned on having a fat kid.

After trotting down to retrieve his laptop and the bottle of bourbon, Edgar booted up in his new cylindrical retreat and started a letter to Angela. Breezily he informed her that he now had a full-time post in Barba, where fair enough it was dangerous, but she shouldn't worry, since worry never saved anyone from harm. He'd already made several sharp acquaintances, and the politics were fascinating . . .

After a little more bourbon, he cleared the screen and started again:

> *Dear Angela—I'm terribly lonely and wondering if I made a big mistake leaving you in the lurch so suddenly. I have no idea what I'm doing in Barba, and so far all these geeks can talk about is this annoying turd I'm standing in for. I miss you terribly—*

It wouldn't do to use "terribly" twice. After several more attempts, Edgar didn't print out a single version, much less post or e-mail one, though he did save the letters to his hard drive for archival purposes. Maybe later he'd find them funny.

By the following evening Edgar had grown so accustomed to the *vento* slamming doors against their jambs that at first he didn't recognize the knocker-pounding of a visible visitor at the front entrance. Dark cape whipping around a turtleneck, skirt, and stockings all in black, Nicola stood on the veranda, proffering a basket, like Little Red Riding Hood in mourning—for the wolf, presumably. Edgar wrestled the door shut behind her.

"I brought you a few leftovers from the party." She handed Edgar the basket, whose caning lurched with the signature skew of another homemade handicraft. "I thought maybe you'd not have managed to market, with your schedule unsettled."

Edgar peeked inside the cloth. "These aren't two-day-old sandwiches."

She blushed, throwing back the hood. "I added a few fresh bits."

"Are you always this considerate?" he asked, foraging a cheese twist. "Worrying about a stranger's jet lag, and baking welcome-wagon cookies?"

"Only when I feel guilty," she admitted, trailing him to the kitchen. "I hate you. And that's not fair."

"Funny way of showing it."

"Not you personally. You seem—"

"How do I seem?" Edgar took his hand out of the fish balls and raised his chin.

Flustered, she stared at the parquet. "To be honest, I haven't really noticed."

"*Not* like Barrington?" Edgar proposed.

At last Nicola looked up at him, truly looked. Hitherto she'd addressed this surrogate Saddler from an angle of ninety degrees, as if in the blur of her peripheral vision he might shimmer into the real thing.

She laughed. "I'm sorry. The robe . . ."

Edgar was wearing his own jeans and plaid flannel shirt underneath, but the golden dressing gown to keep off the chill. In private, the robe lent him a regal flourish, and while reading Edgar had spread its resplendent train across the pillows. "I wouldn't have pilfered the closet, except—"

"No, the robe's apt, in a way. You look lost."

"Swell," said Edgar, arranging hors d'oeuvres on a platter; no matter how many snacks he added, the finger food looked friendless. "I guess *Barrington* never looked lost."

"Barrington was at home everywhere." Discreetly, Nicola nudged a pickle this way, a kalamata that; she placed a cheese twist on the diagonal, and *voilà*: the food suddenly appeared convivial.

"Though there's a desolation to that, don't you think?" she supposed, licking her fingers. "Getting too comfortable? No longer finding any corner of the world strange? Here you're abruptly in a new country; you walk smack into a party of strangers; the guests are intent on making you feel like a wally because you don't know the niggly details of an arcane political movement . . . It's disorienting. But that's part of life. Barrington was left out of that. He was never at a loss for words; he never told jokes that went down like a dose of salts; he never felt small. You know the days you have nothing to say to anyone and you feel like, almost, a *tree*? Barrington never had those. Now that I think of it, Barrington couldn't have understood anyone else very well."

"Anyone like me? You just met me," said Edgar, leaving the platter to the expert. "How can you be sure that Saddler and I are so damned different?"

"Well, look at you," said Nicola. "Feet planted apart. Arms lifted at your sides, quick-draw. Hips thrown forward. Shoulders hunched, head down, jaw thrust. That's the same boxing stance you assumed on my front porch. As if someone's about to slug you."

Edgar tried to straighten gradually; he'd not snap to attention because some dame made fun of his posture. "Saddler's Napoleonic, while I'm a whipped puppy?" he snapped—having intended to keep his tone humorous, but Edgar wasn't really amused.

"I didn't mean you were cowering," she clarified politely, "but *hostile*."

"You're the one who said you hated me."

"You stand as if you expect me to hate you."

"Saddler expected everyone to fall in love?"

"They did," said Nicola.

"Win Pyre sure didn't," Edgar countered, picking up the platter and heading for the living room.

"Ever gone deep-sea fishing?" asked Nicola after him. "Some catches swim to the gunwale. Others thrash and run out the line. Win may have been a fighter, but he was still hooked." Reaching the foyer, she stopped.

"Listen, how about a drink? I've got a fire on."

"I can't stay."

"Why not?"

Nicola glanced beside the door, as if searching for a white lie left behind by a previous guest like an umbrella. Apparently she didn't find one. "Because Henry no longer trusts me."

"I'm flattered."

"Don't be. Distrust has become Henry's weapon of choice. He uses it quite indiscriminately." Nicola still hadn't moved toward the living room, though Edgar bet she knew where the fireplace was.

"*Please* stick around a few minutes," he pleaded in earnest. "This place is cavernous, and I've got nobody to talk to."

She melted, and handed him her cape with a killer smile. "Well, Henry's already so suspicious that a few minutes can't make him any more so."

Heading for the living room, Edgar began to wriggle surreptitiously from the robe.

"Don't take that off on my account," said Nicola. "I think you need it." She added hastily, "To keep warm, I mean."

Edgar led her to the flagging fire. Once Nicola pokered the logs, they burst to flame. She had that touch. After sliding the tray of eats onto the seaman's trunk, Edgar switched off the lamp and fetched drinks, refusing to panic that having arisen only two hours before he was effectively boozing in the morning. Instead he was suffused with joy. Bourbon for breakfast and a beautiful woman at his beck! Overlooking for the moment that this long-legged apparition had only materialized to haunt the home of another man, he decided to keep on the dressing gown. In this light he could almost forget that she was married. Barrington would.

"Where you from originally?" asked Edgar, delivering her brandy. Quietly, he slipped the Remy and Noah's Mill bottles from the crook of his arm; refills that required getting up were asking for *It's really time I . . .*

"I was born in Zambia, where my parents have a farm. University in Edinburgh, design. I did an au pair stint in Rhode Island—but the kids resented that I monopolized their toys, and the parents got frustrated that I wouldn't stop playing to come in for dinner. They hadn't planned on hiring a fourth child, so that didn't last. A spot of teaching and odd jobs in London; then I met Henry."

Edgar invited Nicola to have a seat on the ottoman, backless but buttressed on both ends and parallel to the fireplace. Edgar settled on the opposite end, rejecting the obvious alternative: a high-backed wingchair in emerald velveteen, with scrolled mahogany arms. True, the plush green armchair was too remote from his guest, wouldn't allow for the chance grazing of knees, and was positioned in such proximity to the fire as to seem piggy. But perplexingly, he avoided it because it didn't seem like *his* chair. As if the seat were taken, and were its tenant to return to find Edgar parked in it, embarrassment might ensue.

"I can't compete with that," said Edgar, toasting. "Born in Wilmington; Columbia No-I-Didn't-Get-into-Harvard undergrad, Boston University No-I-Didn't-Get-into-Harvard Law School; Wall Street until I lost my mind. I'd give my eyeteeth to have been born in Zambia."

"By the standards of your new colleagues, Zambia is one of the most pedestrian parts of East Africa to hail from. It's not very bloody. But then, I find the aggro they relish tedious myself. For the life of me I can't get excited about the SOB. The hacks like to think it's so complicated. I don't think so."

"You don't see the immigration issue as having more than one side?"

"Possibly. But as far as I can see, Barban immigration has nothing to do with blowing up airplanes. Which is awful, full stop. Roland calls me simplistic."

"Are you?" Come to think of it, there *was* something simple about Nicola. She'd run until she tired and eat until no longer hungry. She'd take concepts like good and evil at face value, and if she said she had a headache, she had a headache. Edgar wasn't sure if this made Nicola especially wonderful, or everyone else he knew especially fucked up.

"If considering terrorism wrong and ugly is simpleminded, I suppose I am. In fact, since I can't see two sides to it, the issue doesn't even engage me. Barrington thought terrorism was fun," she added forlornly. "He'd get into a particular ecstatic, hyperactive humor, and that's how I'd know there'd been another gory Amtrak derailment without having to tune into the World Service."

"Speaking of the Big B, I can set your mind at rest on the tower. No bodies."

"Pity," she said flippantly. "Mystery unsolved."

"He wasn't, I don't know, an IV drug-user, was he?" Edgar asked idly.

Nicola leaned forward and fixed Edgar with a disrobing stare. "Did you find something?"

"Not really," Edgar backed off. "Just curious." As if playing a rivalrous game of Clue, Edgar felt compelled to hoard the stationery, metal pipe, and rubber glove discoveries to himself.

Whatever secrets Nicola discerned in Edgar's face, they mustn't have amounted to much, and she sank back. "Drugs? He'd try anything once. For all I know, Barrington has shot up lemon meringue pie. He wasn't what you'd call health-conscious. But I don't think any substance ever took. Barrington's interest in chemistry was social. He loved dropping some new catalyst into a gathering to see what precipitated. He wasn't interested in the colors of his soul. He didn't need to be. Other people told him repeatedly what he was like."

"What do you think happened to him?" asked Edgar.

Nicola swirled her cognac, gazing into the snifter as if the Remy's long legs would sidle off in a telling direction. "He could be sulking. For that matter, he might still be holed up in Cinzeiro. Looking on, chuckling while the press corps gets overwrought. He's one of those attend-your-own-funeral types. If he has simply gone to ground, I may bear some of the blame."

"Why would Saddler sulk on your account?" Edgar noted tactfully, "I got the impression you were fond of him."

Nicola arched her eyebrows. "Oh, did you? I told you that Barrington treated the whole world like his own backyard. But he still wasn't satisfied. So I wasn't enough, either. Whatever else you hear, Barrington was a very greedy man. And childish."

In Edgar's experience, these were both qualities that women found universally irresistible. "You sound pissed off."

"I have reason to be." She mashed a half-eaten mushroom whatnot as if stubbing out a cigarette. "He ruined my marriage."

"You and Henry are still together, aren't you?"

"We still live in the same house." Nicola flounced back on the cushion and buried herself in hair. "Oh, who am I kidding? No one ruined my marriage but me. I just don't understand how it happened. Have you ever had a relationship that sang? Where you're like deliciously incestuous brother and sister? When every day is such an outrageous frolic that it feels illegal, and any minute you expect to be arrested?"

"If you put it that way," said Edgar glumly, "no."

"Well, that's what it used to be like, and *now* we *talk*."

"How terrible."

"I mean have regular conversations! With badly chosen words that we have to say we didn't mean, and then we have to find another word and see if that works better. It's Neanderthal. Like going back to hitting your clothes on a rock when you used to use a washer. God, these days Henry and I have to *tell* each other how we *feel*."

"All couples wax and wane," Edgar supplied lamely.

"I was never on my guard against being attracted to someone else, because I simply wasn't attracted to anyone else, ever. Henry knew I wasn't. I knew Henry wasn't. No one was on the lookout, don't you see? That's how it happened. I was unprotected because I thought I was impervious, and maybe that's the hubris I've been punished for. Daring to think that all those tawdry 'wandering eyes' and 'seven-year itches' and 'midlife crises' in magazines didn't apply to me. Still, how much safer could it get? We were a threesome. We did everything together! It seemed so innocent at first. And Henry *adored* Barrington."

"But not anymore."

"Of course he still does, that's half the problem. When you adore someone and then you think they've betrayed you, it's the fact that you continue to adore them that keeps the injury fresh. If Henry could dislike Barrington, he wouldn't keep feeling the knife twist. I'm sorry, I must be trying your patience."

"I don't mind." Edgar could listen to this woman describe how her marriage was "ruined" for hours.

"Then it's all right if I mention your predecessor from time to time?" She shot a glance at the green wingchair. "All the hacks are such gossips; I feel as if I've been holding my breath. Then Barrington absconds, and I can hardly confide in Henry."

Mention him? Wallasek onward, Edgar had heard nothing but wall-to-wall Saddler, and this broad took the prize. Edgar was of two minds about this familiar shoulder-to-cry-on role. Sometimes the jiltee patched things up with Mr. Right with the benefit of his excellent advice, and Edgar was left laundering hankies like a chump. The alternative brand of loneliheart dabbed her eyes, tilted her pretty cheeks a few degrees, and stuck her tongue down his throat.

"Better to talk about Saddler than around him," Edgar allowed. "According to the photo upstairs, that's a wide detour."

"You will keep my confidences to yourself?" pleaded Nicola, placing a hand on his knee. "Barrington always said there are two types of people: the sort who dispense information, and the sort who collect it. Just like money: you're a spender or a saver."

"Which are you?" Who cares? Just *don't move that hand.*

"By nature, prodigal. But I've had to become more calculating." As if to demonstrate, she withdrew from Edgar's knee.

"You're terrible at it," said Edgar. "Like, you've got no reason to trust me."

"No, but you have that tight-lipped, retentive look, as if you tear out pages of the encyclopedia and stuff them in your mattress."

"So Saddler and I do have something in common. No one would divide people into secret-tellers and secret-keepers and then pride himself on being one of the blabs."

"True. He was lavish with money, but stingy with facts."

"Everyone has been," said Edgar, folding his arms. "About Saddler anyway. You want to talk about him, then how about some brass tacks? Like, why was a Brit working for an American newspaper?"

"Mmm, I think Barrington was always angling for advantage. There's nothing special about being British in Britain, is there? While in America . . . Besides, he claimed he liked Americans. Because, he said, they're so 'obvious.'"

"Easy to manipulate," Edgar translated. "Brothers or sisters?"

"One of each. It's hard for them. They didn't get it, whatever *it* is, the gene, the spell cast over the crib? Mark is hardworking and very nice." The description was like a death sentence. "Lola is overweight and not very bright. She's besotted with Barrington, and in his absence has taken to ringing me up. I feel sorry for them both, but Lola's getting difficult. She wants to hire a detective, establish a search fund, run adverts in the *Sun*. There's nothing wrong with either of them; they're simply ordinary, and I think it must be a terrible cross to bear, having a brother who—" Nicola floundered—"takes up so much room."

"Where's Saddler from?"

"Some village in Yorkshire." She frowned.

Edgar rapped the trunk. "The town, the town!" His urgency was jarring, but he'd had his fill of enigma after Angela. Nothing demystified like particulars, e.g., *fact*: you've been fucking *Jamesie* every other Thursday for the last two years. Magically, the fog lifts.

Nicola shot Edgar a chary eye. "I'm not sure. Oddly, his accent is all very Earl Grey. But he attended university at LSE, and a Yorkshire accent's Midlands—hardly aristocratic. On the other hand, if the posh pronunciation is put on, I never heard it slip. And so many Eton types in England these days ape the working class that genteel pretensions have become almost refreshing. Barrington did mention his mother, a schizophrenic who walked around in nothing but men's Y-fronts and raised chickens in the house. Or something—it was more hilarious than that. But I never trusted Barrington's stories. They were too entertaining."

"Was he a liar?"

"Which kind? I dare say his mother *did* walk around in men's underdrawers, but maybe it wasn't funny. You know how draining it can be when people talk about their families, their childhoods? I try to make the effort, because sometimes the dullest details are the most telling. But Barrington was never boring. That's suspicious, isn't it? And a little sad. He didn't trust anyone enough to be dreary with them. I think that's the biggest favor you can grant anyone, don't you? Permission to be dull. I know Henry will sometimes say something so utterly uninteresting that I could faint. And that's when you know you're in love: the tedium isn't unbearable, it's lovely. Barrington never dared take that risk. I wonder what he thought might happen."

"Bullshit."

Nicola started. "Sorry?"

"Your partner's a yawn, you're *not* in love," Edgar contradicted brutally. "Or not anymore."

Nicola drew herself upright. "How can you—"

"I had a friend in prep school," Edgar cut her off, rising to mess with the fire. "He fascinated me. I swiped one of his bank statements once just to find out his middle name. *Mohr*, with an H: *Tobias Mohr Falconer*. I used to doodle his initials in the margins of my physics notes, and even today *TMF* has a *sound* to it. I took a train from Delaware over Christmas break to find his house in Greenwich. Not to visit; just to cruise by and check it out. I knew Falconer's hat size and he didn't even wear one. I knew the exact hour he was born and how rare he liked his steak. Everything about him seemed so cool: his Hush Puppies, his father's old Boy Scout knapsack. But Falconer could have come to class in a duck suit and that would have seemed cool, too." Having managed nearly to smother the flames altogether, Edgar twisted to face her. "And Nicola, *Toby Falconer never bored me, either*."

"So?" she asked dubiously.

"Saddler could have read you the obituaries from Lansing, Michigan, and you'd have been riveted!" Edgar exclaimed, waving the poker about. "This theory of yours that Saddler didn't *allow* himself to be dull because he didn't 'trust' people is nuts. You and his fan club set up the rules so that nothing Barrington Saddler said could be boring because Barrington Saddler said it. He sings 'Three Blind Mice,' isn't that cute! He refuses to say anything at all? Oh dear, Barrington is brooding, what could be the matter? Saddler pukes? All the girls rush to help clean up and pat his face. Next day, it's not an embarrassing display, but the stuff of myth! *Old Bear sure tied one on!* Believe me, Nicola, I know about these people. If they live in some dung heap like Cinzeiro, suddenly Nowheresville, Barba, more than Paris or Tuscany, is ultrachic. If they ever fall in love, you expect headlines and suicides, and for the lucky princess, some kind of coronation—that is, before she's assassinated."

Nicola laughed. "Why does Barrington rankle you so?"

"Because I don't understand it!" The poker hit the fireplace mosaic; a tile cracked. "I may not wear it on my sleeve, but I'm pretty motherfucking smart. My grades were good, I test high. I'm not witless; I can deliver punch lines. Women tell me I'm not bad-looking. I'm well-read; I keep up. Until recently, I even made money. But to my knowledge nobody has ever filched my bank statement to find out my middle name."

"Which is?"

"Earl. But you won't scribble *EEK* in your margins, and if *I* read the Lansing obits you'll snore. I want to know how they do it, what's the trick. Christ, why did you really come over here tonight? Not because you were smitten with me."

"I was being hospitable," she said, injured.

"Horseshit. You couldn't stay away from this house. You had to come sniffing around Saddler's digs for a whiff of the old bastard himself." Restive, Edgar noshed down a pastry. "UCH!" Edgar groped for a napkin and spit it out.

"Oh dear," said Nicola quietly.

"What *was* that?"

"I try to use local ingredients," she confessed.

"Not *hairy pears*?"

"*Torta de uvas peludas*: hairy-grape pie. Same fruit, immature—small and hard. Less gooshy, but more bitter. It's an acquired taste."

"So far, baby, this whole shtick is an acquired taste." Edgar drained his bourbon. "The wind, the beer, the peevish politics, *and* your friend Saddler."

"How can you be so envious of someone you've never met?" She poured Edgar another finger of Noah's Mill. "And despite that, obviously don't like?"

"I never said I was envious. Here." He handed Nicola the poker. "Do something. It's dark."

"But socially—you'd like to take Barrington's place?"

Edgar flopped onto the ottoman to assume his favorite slouch: feet-up, chin-on-chest, view-of-the-girl. His back ached from demonstrating that he didn't always assume the defensive stance of a besieged middleweight. "Only so long as I didn't have to become a total asshole. From what I've scoped so far, that's the price. To be everybody's favorite uncle you've apparently gotta be a complete jerk-off."

Flames once again shot passionately up the flue. Her profile lined in pumpkin, the black turtleneck warmed to brown, Nicola knelt on the hearth like an undiscovered Rembrandt. Most of the attractive women Edgar had dated all strode with the same look-at-me languor, high heels indolently clopping the pavement like drays on cobblestone. They posed statuesquely in chairs and cast frequent glances at their own legs, typically projecting a disconcerting blend of insecurity and contempt. It had taken him years to digest that at any given moment, even while Edgar discussed nuclear proliferation across the table, uppermost on the mind of your average fox was her own appearance. Ironically, it wasn't pretty. As a self-confessed aesthete, Nicola would have noticed her looks, but maybe only in passing. To inhabit beauty that entirely she had to be thinking about something else.

"Why *are* you poised at-the-ready?" Nicola wondered. "Dukes up? What you said about the press corps when I drove you here—I know they've their flaws. But you were scathing! Trudy was a 'bimbette'; Martha was a 'cow.' Win was a 'crusty know-it-all'; Reinhold, a 'sanctimonious killjoy.' And Roland? A 'jive-talking greaseball.' You were so tired you could barely talk, and you could still muster the energy for character assassination. What makes you so wary of people, so unsparing?"

Three thousand miles from home, Edgar had never been presented with a more sublime opportunity to repudiate his past; he could make up anything.

CHAPTER 11
The Celery Wars

"I WAS FAT," said Edgar.

"How fat?" asked Nicola.

"I think the medical term is 'morbidly obese.' Until I was sixteen. I lost the weight, but kept the attitude—since most people *are* about to slug you, given the chance."

"Do you," she hazarded, "really believe you're thin?"

Edgar half-smiled. He wasn't about to admit that, now that she mentioned it, a subtle bulge at the top of his thighs would never, no matter how he stinted on fried foods, melt away; nor would he confide that in an odd way he didn't want the bulges to retreat completely. Those residual swells were mementos of an era as instructive as it was painful, useful reminders that he should never get too trusting.

"Maybe not," said Edgar. "At least I always think that with one extra cheese twist it's back to taking up two seats on the bus. As a blimp, you learn stuff about people. Not some people. Everybody. Stuff you don't want to know."

"What made you decide to slim down?" Nicola asked, head cocked as if regarding him in a somewhat different light. "Anything in particular?"

Having inadvertently triggered a memory that Edgar conventionally kept from himself, Nicola looked up, all innocence. Helplessly, he suffered the old flecked footage as it came blazing at him, triple-X, wide-screen. July, back in Wilmington. Even blubber balls pass puberty, and Edgar routinely shut himself in the john when no one was home. Beforehand (so to speak), he always vowed privately that he'd merely unzip and be clinically efficient about meeting what even Yardley's Health Sciences teacher asserted was a *perfectly normal need*. And the procedure would save his sheets—though Edgar jerked off often enough, sometimes three or four times on the Saturdays his mother played golf, that nocturnal emissions were a theoretical complaint.

At any rate, the efficiency pledge never lasted, particularly if it was the first of the day, and Mom would be gone for hours. In fact, it took about sixty seconds for Edgar to turn that forbidden corner, beyond which he became—not quite himself. Keeping his right hand firmly and furiously on his dick, he worked with the left to tug his jeans down his thighs. The denim would puddle around his ankles. To Edgar's frustration, he could never get all his clothes off and hold on at the same time. Forcing himself to let go, he'd tear off his clinging shirt, kick off his splayed sneakers, disentangle the forty-two-inch-waist Levis from around his feet, and return to business—this time swiveling from the toilet to face the full-length mirror, hung like child abuse on the inside of the bathroom door.

Ordinarily, sitting on the can or dripping from the shower, Edgar averted his eyes from the obscenity of his own reflection, but on these Saturday afternoons that staggering expanse of fat was just what excited his fist to pummel faster. Standing close to the glass, he marveled at his own extent, punctuated midway by a little red finger pointing at the enormity of his accomplishment: 238 pounds by the age of fifteen. Both exhilarated and repulsed—the emotions mingled—Edgar would knead his pale, bloated flesh with his free hand, smearing the sweat beading between the rolls of his abdomen up over his full, effeminate breasts. At his peak, he'd press against the mirror and make love to his own mass, spraying the glass and rubbing his belly into the spatter to form a sticky emulsion.

Of course, like the promise to be "efficient," Edgar always made a pact with himself that he wouldn't do that, wouldn't actually come onto the mirror, even if in a shadowy part of his mind lurked the awful knowledge that he would. But the jizz made a god-awful mess, and the glass was murderous to clean, though he stashed a secret bottle of Windex under the sink for this purpose. Too often a haze remained behind even after this desperate squirting and wiping. The washcloth, still sharp with window cleaner and hung to dry, seemed telltale. Once his mother had commented on the film, feigning incomprehension or so he feared, and Edgar, heart whomping, had sneered sourly at the ineptitude of their black housekeeper.

The memory that Nicola had triggered was a generic Saturday afternoon porn flick, up to a point. If anything his performance before the mirror was more athletic than ever, and for inspiration his weight that summer was maxing out. Oh, his mother was golfing all right, but he'd forgotten that his older brother Jeff was due back from winch-grinding in the Caribbean. Mistaking the house as his for hours, Edgar hadn't locked the bathroom door. Just as he was about to shoot, the door flew open.

Stark-naked, left hand clutching his flushed right nipple, right hand shanking away, abruptly Edgar found himself staring not into his own friendly flab but the flabbergasted face of his evenly tanned, leanly muscled older brother. Edgar's hand sprang from his cock, but too late. A white dollop arced onto Jeff's freshly washed Izod shirt.

"Oh, *gross*!" Jeff screeched, gaping with horror from his shirt to Edgar's cock, which still poked ridiculously forward and bobbled against a shelf of gut. "I'm gonna hurl! Fat spurting spunk!"

As Jeff pushed past his stricken younger brother to get at a towel and wipe his shirt, Edgar vowed right then and there not to be "efficient" next time or to restrain himself from coming on the mirror, but to (A) lose one hundred pounds by Christmas, or (B) kill himself. For the next thudding minute, as he stuffed his pink sausage legs into their denim casing, Plan B was unquestionably the more appealing.

"I decided to swap disgust with myself for disgust with everybody else," Edgar telescoped to Nicola. Something about the long version wouldn't *tell well.*

"Now I understand that posture of yours. Bearing a grudge that size—it's surprising you don't lurch around like Quasimodo."

"Some things don't bear forgiving," said Edgar gruffly. "Not from other folks. Not from yourself."

"If you can commend self-reproach, you've never done anything all that dreadful."

Edgar parried, "In my neck of the woods, that's an insult."

Sitting on the floor, Nicola clasped Edgar's sock-covered toes. "Do you really think I don't love my husband?"

She must have already wearied of talk about Edgar, since the connection between his adolescent weight problem and Nicola's marriage eluded him. "How should I know?"

"I was a bit disingenuous, before." Nicola twisted a stray thread on his argyle while Edgar prayed his socks didn't stink. "About how happy we were. Oh, *we* were happy, I think. But Henry isn't, and hasn't been for years. I blame the lottery."

"Henry won the lottery?" Edgar asked absently, shutting his eyes. If he didn't seem to notice that she was fiddling with his feet, maybe she'd keep doing it.

"My euphemism of choice. But yes, he did win a morbid sort of lottery. Poor Henry is so sick of this story, and pained by it, that I'd not even tell you, except that anyone else around here is bound to. You remember British Airways' Flight 321?"

"Who could forget? Even read the book."

"Oh, that gruesome WHSmith-type thing. Henry hated it. He refused to cooperate with the authors."

"Cooperate—?"

"Both of Henry's parents, his older sister Ravenna, and his brother-in-law Aaron were all on that plane."

"Yikes," said Edgar, hastily knocking the pathos of juvenile overindulgence in frozen Mars Bars down a peg. "No survivors."

"Only one thing survived," said Nicola dolorously. "Money."

"There was a mass of lawsuits brought over that flight," Edgar recalled. "Security at Kennedy was lax. They allowed a bag to be checked without a passenger flying with it, right? The jury awards for relatives were gigantic."

"You're telling me," Nicola groaned. "And Henry cashed in—a phrase he's none too fond of—on three bereavements. He'd only the one sister, so he was the sole next-of-kin to collect compensation. Then medical records revealed that Ravenna was pregnant. The jury loved that. All told, Henry walked away with four million pounds."

"Holy shit!" For a former corporate lawyer, numbers still had the power to shock. Forgetting to leave Nicola his socks to play with, Edgar wheeled his feet to the floor.

"Please skip the standard, 'Well, knock me down with a feather!' I'm so tired of it. Besides," she added with dread, "there's more."

"More story, or more money?"

"More of both. You may have noticed from his accent: Henry's from Southampton. His roots aren't quite working-class, but close. Still, his father was enterprising, and on a visit to a cousin in New Jersey he took a shine to American bagels. You couldn't get bagels in England at the time. He researched the process, took out a small loan, started a shop . . . Bagels became the rage in Southampton, and soon he was able to open outlets from Portsmouth to Cornwall. My father-in-law made a packet. As his parents got better-heeled, a silver spoon left a bad taste in Henry's mouth. I guess the family was happier in the old days, when they were skint. Shortly before Flight 321, Henry's father sold The British Bagel for several million quid. And after Flight 321—"

"Henry inherited several million quid." Edgar whistled.

Massaging her temples in circles, Nicola spoke quickly, as if wanting to get the story over with. "It was like a macabre pyramid scheme. Next, Henry's brother-in-law, Aaron? His parents were bazillionaires. After the Second World War, Aaron's father bought up carpet-bombed property for spare change—then cleared the rubble, paved over the plots, and made a fortune from automated car parks. Three months before BA-321, Aaron's parents had been killed in a smash-up on the M-20 as they headed for the ferry to Calais. Aaron was an only child, and came into the lot. In fact, Henry's parents had invited Ravenna and her husband along to holiday in San Francisco partly to cheer Aaron up. It was on the last leg back to Heathrow that the plane exploded over Long Island. Aaron himself owned a computer-importing business. The couple didn't have any children, *yet* . . . You get the picture. It *all went to Henry*."

"I'm losing track of the arithmetic."

"I lost track some time ago. Fortunately, taxes helped prune the inheritance back. But you know dosh: in quantity, it grows like hogweed."

"Let me guess: Henry's loaded, thanks to calamity. Though he'd swap all his do-re-mi for his relatives' being alive and well, he's plagued by a guilty sense of having swapped his family for the high life. Only, some high life. If Henry's flush, what's he doing in *Barba*?"

Nicola shrugged. "Stringing for the *Independent*. Oh, there's a thin logic to it. The SOB blew up the plane, and even Henry got interested in the issues—if conceiving a personal hatred qualifies as interest. I'm sure there's an element of working off that guilt you picked up on. And Henry had toyed with the idea of becoming a journalist for a while; he'd already done a bit of subbing for the *Evening Standard*. So we thought, why not head here? The *Independent* was keen. Henry was in the news, he's so wealthy that he didn't ask for a retainer, and handing him the string gave the paper super publicity."

"Good angle," Edgar agreed.

"Yes, at first. But his editor's not into it any longer. They've made as much capital out of hiring Henry as they're going to, and with this drought of SOB operations he's getting bugger-all in the paper. Oh, and don't imagine his mission to 'expose the moral poverty of his family's killers'—that's the *Daily Mail*—has earned any points with the characters you met the other night. You know how the Sunday-school brigade is always promoting these wonderful things that money can't buy? High on the list is professional respect."

"Henry's story may be a tearjerker, but your pals here don't seem sentimental."

"Journalists pride themselves on being anything but," said Nicola. "And most aren't that well paid. Unlike Henry, they'd never use their expenses checks for coffee coasters. So they can be awfully condescending, which makes Henry mad. When we first met, he was just larking about. But between Flight 321 and this unwholesome windfall, my husband's been determined to get serious."

"Sounds tragic," said Edgar, regretting having withdrawn his feet.

"It is," Nicola concurred dolefully. "Henry used to be so laddish, so happy-go-lucky. When we moved to Barba, he started plunging himself in thought, and he's not cut out for it. Then we met Barrington. At last we started having a good time again. Henry sometimes reverted to his old self: whimsical, cheeky, spontaneous. I was relieved. But we grew dependent. You know how when you're in love, and your sweetie walks in the door, and suddenly the air is richer, food tastes better, colors flush, and you keep wanting to laugh for no reason? One day I noticed that's how we felt when Barrington walked in. When he walked out, Henry and I went flat. Food went to ash."

"Obviously the BA thing was a drag," said Edgar, conscious of gross understatement. "But couldn't the money be some compensation, as that jury intended? Instead of making things easier, a fortune seems like one more burden for you guys. Sure, there'd have been nicer ways to come by the cash. But it beats me why a mountain of payola would turn a cheerful wiseass into an earnest nerd."

"Then you've never thought very hard about winning lotteries, even the traditional kind. Most people haven't, which is why they buy tickets. But best you talk to Henry about all this." She stood up. "In fact, we hoped you might come round to dinner next week."

"Sure. Besides, I wanted to interview you both, for an article on what you think happened to Saddler. Wallasek is convinced that all his readers are busting to know."

"Keep me out of it. I suggest you kill a flock of gossipy birds with one stone and spend an evening at the Rat."

"Come again?"

"*O Rato que Late*—The Barking Rat. The bar where all your colleagues are wont to congregate. Rumor has it that's where the SOB recruits, though I've never seen any hooded thugs with AKs there myself. And Edgar?" She buttoned her cape. "Thanks for telling me. About having once been heavy."

"Fat," Edgar corrected.

"I can't explain it, but somehow that's the sweetest thing I've ever heard."

Go figure. "Anyway, sorry I'm a little sour about Saddler," Edgar grunted grudgingly in return. "I guess you miss him. It's just I'm kinda tired of constantly coming up against another bozo who 'takes up a lot of room.' Even after I lost that weight, some apple of everybody's eye has always made me look like a *hairy pear* in comparison. I'm trying to carve out a second career for myself here. It doesn't help to be told straight off the plane that I can't hope to measure up to the last guy. Someday I could stand to see other people trying to measure up to me."

"What is it you want, to be famous?" she asked gently.

Edgar answered only with a shrug. The truth was too embarrassing. Standard celebrity had in fact never attracted him. He couldn't see what Robert Redford got out of it if total strangers tacked posters of *The Sting* over their bedsteads. Edgar craved a more immediate renown, the kind that filled his incoming message tape, tiddled its nails on his door, and exploded in a squeal of delight that he'd decided to come for drinks after all. Edgar didn't want to be famous. He wanted to be popular.

CHAPTER 12

Edgar Meets Baby Serious and Debuts at the Barking Rat

AS BARRINGTON HAD obligingly left the keys to his black Saab 900 Turbo in his kitchen, Edgar forced himself to stay awake during daylight hours for a foray into Cinzeiro. Abrab Manor, as Edgar had affectionately nicknamed Saddler's villa, lay a few miles out of town, so he could scope out the local countryside on the way into the provincial capital.

Keeping the Saab on the road in the easterly *vento* took vigilance. Whenever the lane curved north or south the Saab's body went *foom*, and Edgar's adrenaline surged with fear that the coupe had been broadsided by a bus. Bleak and low-lying, the plain rumpled with not so much hills as lumps. The khaki grass was stubbled, its nap bent universally eastward like a fabric that smoothed in only one direction. Stunted olive trees hunkered in clumps, wider than they were high, their splayed branches reaching toward Spain, as if beseeching to be rescued from Barba. The muted green leaves, while glaucous and lackluster, still hit the brightest notes in the terrain, whose hues were otherwise restricted to dun, rust, and sulfur.

A few of the dwellings Edgar passed were roofed with distinctively Iberian terra-cotta tiles, but for the most part the squat, paranoid stucco cubes could double as bomb shelters. Like Nicola's villa, each house was built with one high, solid wall facing west; Abrab Manor's windowed western face defied local convention. Often the traditional windbreak extended to protect a rickety swing set, or a few plastic chairs with legs rammed optimistically into the lawn for garden parties, as if that foul-tasting beer would grow any more palatable mixed with sand.

The low moan that Edgar had noticed when he first awoke at Abrab Manor emitted from the birdhouse-like thingamabobs planted in every yard. Standard wind chimes of shells or shards of glass would shatter in gales, so the Barban variation was industrial-strength. Mounted on a thick post, a hollowed log was slit at an angle on one side; *o vento insano* tore through the opening. Engineered to accommodate the embouchure of the atmosphere itself, the wind whistles were all pitched at the deepest tones of a panpipe. The moans carried a remarkable distance, and together chorused like a boatload of seasick passengers. When a particularly bombastic blast of air advanced across the landscape, a groan rose over the fields as if the whole population were about to spew.

Meanwhile, splotches of purple goo pooped across the tarmac every few inches, some viscous patches of sufficient mass to send the Turbo into a skid. Even with the windows closed, the glop stank: gaggingly sweet, yet spiked with a sharp, malevolent undersmell.

It took Edgar a few miles to make the connection between the gelatinous blobs under his wheels and the midget baobabs that grew along the roadside. Their trunks were thick, with a diameter of three feet or more, but the stumpy trees grew only eight feet high. They looked beheaded. Wafting on their leeward side, fist-sized balls of brown fur dangled from sticks, like baby muskrats that had hanged themselves. Anything that looked that disgusting and smelled that disgusting surely tasted disgusting as well. *Peras peludas.*

Curiosity got the better of revulsion. Edgar pulled over and stepped from the car to pick a hairy pear. The testicular blob had the pulpy give of a fig, though the scraggly inch-long threads on its skin were coarse. It was something like a kiwi on testosterone, or Cousin Itt from *The Addams Family* reincarnated as a fruit. And with a little squeeze, the fucking thing exploded.

Edgar flung the scraps away, but sticky violet smoosh had got all over his hands. When he sponged at his shirt with a napkin from the glove compartment, he made one last discovery about the *pera peluda*: it stained.

As Edgar drew into Cinzeiro, the city proved so remarkably ugly that Edgar wanted to shake somebody's hand. There's not-giving-a-shit ugliness, not-knowing-any-better ugliness, nakedly-cheap ugliness, and worst of all intending-to-be-really-attractive ugliness, but Cinzeiro was the kind of ugly that took effort.

From what Edgar had read, Cinzeiro (Portuguese for "ashtray") must have suffered from the fact that its residents had slightly too much cash. Stark, bone-aching poverty is the best guarantor of historical preservation, since the destitute can't afford to give expression to their bad taste. Alas, Cinzeiro's local industry had put spare change into the pockets of its citizenry, who had promptly razed every structure within reach that predated the architecturally illustrious 1965.

This man-made catastrophe appeared far more devastating than the notorious earthquake that had leveled Lisbon two centuries earlier. According to Edgar's books, Cinzeiro was over two thousand years old. But forget the intricate iron grillwork, painted tiles, the fanciful plaster moldings of Lisbon's eighteenth-century revival—much less the residual Moorish influences reflected in Abrab Manor, remnants of 711 AD's original North African invasion of Portugal. And never mind the sturdy stone castles from medieval times that had once dotted the entire province remarkably intact. Downtown Cinzeiro was uncannily evocative of Lincoln, Nebraska.

Barbans had subscribed wholesale to the aesthetic tradition of the suburban bank. Materials ran to brown bricks, brown-tinted glass, and brown spray-painted aluminum. Façades were flat, windows undressed, forms rectangular. Presumably the point of all this fecal plainness was a statement of modernity, though an irony typical of such statements was their aura of the old hat.

Then again, the primary aim of savings-and-loan architecture was not to give offense, and you'd think the one advantage of setting your sights that low would be meeting your miserable target. Yet Edgar was plenty offended, especially when he considered how much marble mosaic must have been bulldozed in the last few decades to make way for linoleum, or how many ornamental banks of brightly tiled *solares* had been wrecking-balled to prepare for gray cement. So far the only patches of the city that showed signs of funk were Moroccan restaurants, or the pleasantly grungy immigrant districts flapping with colorful laundry. No wonder Barbans resented the encroachments of another culture. The North Africans had one.

Edgar prided himself on being streetwise, so it was curious that, no matter how dilapidated a residential neighborhood he steered into, his urban alarm bells never sounded. Much of the housing was run-down and like the central commercial sector sterile, but dusty children played in the street and waved at the black Saab, hair flying merrily eastward, cheap toys sailing midair on horizontal strings. The most threatening aspect of the adolescents huddled in doorways was their dress sense. Zigzagged polyester cardigans were all the rage, along with mid-calf bell-bottoms and canary-yellow or baby-blue knee-highs. Had locals menaced the rest of Europe with such fashions, they might have won Barban independence overnight.

Graffiti blazed everywhere, but its penmanship was tidy and obedient, like the "Aa Bb Cc" above primary school bulletin boards. Some of the vandals had used stencils; others had changed Es to Is, as if to avoid markdowns for misspelling. Many walls were simply branded SOB or PARA CIMA O CREME ("Up the Creme")—go-team! in Barba.

The racial slogans were almost polite: ADEUS NORTE AFRICANOS! or the yet more well-wishing SALVO-CONDUTO AOS TANGIER, OS ESTRANGEIROS—"Safe conduct to Tangier, foreigners." Edgar's favorite inscription not only demonstrated a good sense of musical history but obviated another scrounge through his dictionary with its broken English: DON'T YOU KNOW YOU RIDING ON MARRAKESH EXPRESS? WE TAKING YOU TO MARRAKESH! Sweet, but no match for the vulgar racial epithets scrawled in Wilmington and New York projects. The graffiti came across as conscientious exercises copied from *Insurgency for Beginners.*

"Senhor!" A raggedy little boy who'd been following Edgar's travails with the dictionary waved down the car. *"Americano?"* Edgar nodded. *"Você quer a minha fotografia?"* The urchin made a shutter-clicking motion. Shrugging, Edgar got out his camera.

The child scuttled in front of a spray-painted SOB, knelt, squinted, and sighted down his arm as if aiming an assault rifle. A little creepy, but Edgar snapped the shot to get rid of the kid.

The boy held out a hand, raising five fingers on the other. *"Quinhentos escudos."*

Rolling his eyes, Edgar fished out his wallet. The boy nimbly picked out a five-hundred-escudo note and ran away. Over three bucks! And chances were that picture had been published before.

The trouble with phrasebooks was that they were boffo at instructing how to *ask* for directions. That was quite another matter from *understanding* directions. In four different bodegas, *"Aonde é o Rato que Late, por favor?"* invited a gracious torrent of Slavic-sounding mush. Having kept his face in an attentive mask, he backed from each shop blithering, *"Obrigado! Muito obrigado!"* or: thanks for nothing.

Finally Edgar ran across *O Rato que Late* blinking in purple neon. In a crude latex-on-plywood painting by the entrance, a stumpy-legged albino creature with a pointed pink snout bared its teeth, the cartoon bubble overhead growling, URRRRF! Aside from the hairless tail, it was a passable representation of a bull terrier.

Edgar trotted down the gritty steps, only to come up short against the first thoroughly intimidating character he'd encountered in Barba. While the Portuguese bruiser who blocked the entranceway was wide as a Deluxe Frigidaire, it was neither the man's mass that was unnerving nor his encroachment on Edgar's *personal space*. It was the face. The mouth described an unsmiling straight line, as if typed with an em-dash. The eyes were bricked, like the windows of an abandoned house: no one was home. Perfectly round and obscenely smooth for a grown man's, the infantile countenance didn't flicker with the slightest visible intelligence. For one long moment Edgar stared into this huge, blank moon pie, in recognition that, on a sufficiently awesome scale, stupidity could be terrifying.

"Quem você," the strongarm droned. By comparison, the relentless *vento insano* roared with personality.

Edgar could only discern that he wasn't getting farther into the bar. "I, uh—" His phrasebook practice fled. *"Journalissimo!"* Wrong.

"Bebê!" Roland Ordway's voice oozed from the interior. *"Está bem! Apresento-lhe Senhor Kellogg, um amigo do Senhor Saddler!"*

After the usual open-sesame, the boulder rolled expressionlessly back, and Edgar proceeded to where the press corps had been enjoying his discomfort with the doorman. They were seated at a round table in the middle of the gloomy bar, much like the crowd of hangers-on that Edgar had expected to accompany Toby Falconer to The Red Shoe.

However, at a glance this Barban circle was clearly bereft of a center. Wistfully, Edgar wondered how Barrington must have felt sashaying into this bar—as heads swiveled in unison, eyes brightened, and boisterous gratitude rose above the quiet, gratifying gnash of Win Pyre's teeth.

"So is that the 'Barking Rat'?" Edgar asked the table at large, gesturing toward the doorman. "I've met floats at the Macy's Thanksgiving Day parade with higher IQs."

"That's Bebê Serio," explained Martha Hulbert, who had

exchanged her rotten-broccoli dress for a cheese-mold print. "Baby Serious, in English; no one knows his real name. And he's not employed to do calculus, Edgar. He's Tomás Verdade's muscle. Bodyguard, when Barba heats up. Meantime, he's the Rat's bouncer. Pull up a chair."

Edgar did so. "What's the point of vetting patrons in this dive?"

"The Rat's a Creamie bar."

"Is that something like a Fudgsicle?"

Martha paused politely. What, had Saddler patented this quip, too?

"The Creams like to keep tabs on who's where, especially foreigners," Ordway injected, collusively sotto voce. "I can't say if Bebê Serio has personally bombed any tube stations, but I wouldn't cross him. Bear's the only bloke I know who doesn't give the big yob wide berth. Word is that Bear actually got Serio to smile once, but that must be an urban myth, right, Marth? Even Bear had his limits."

"Limits?" asked Martha archly. "I've heard countless theories, but that one's new."

Edgar took orders, and the company was keen to stick the newcomer with a round of six drinks. After discreet consultation of his phrasebook, Edgar ordered *três vinhos do Porto* for the girls. Ordway and Pyre both wanted Choques; impulsively, Edgar made that three.

Waiting at the bar, he borrowed a damp towel to wipe the sticky *pera peluda* glop from between his fingers. The tea towel was embroidered with SUPORTE NOSSOS SOLDADOS OUSADOS in bright red. In fact, the whole dive was inundated with political ephemera. Bumper stickers plastered on the walls read, LIBERTA A BARBA OCUPADA, VIVA OS BARBEADORES, VOTE O CREME DE BARBEAR. SOB and Tomás Verdade lapel buttons were stuck around the cash register; pennants were festooned with rifle replicas and cherry bombs. Posters featured unfocused photos of goons in balaclavas and combat fatigues sighting down automatics, as the kid had mimed that afternoon. A gold-plated AK-47 lapel pin twinkled on the barkeep's apron. Under its gapping bib, the sullen publican's T-shirt declared, VIVEMOS LIVRES OU VOCÊ MORRER!

"Catch the shift in person," Ordway said quietly at Edgar's back, nodding at the T-shirt as he helped with the drinks. "'*We* live free or *you* die.' Barba has a wider streak of self-preservation than New Hampshire."

"I can understand the political gimcracks," said Edgar, collecting the port order. "But what's with all that kitsch on the top shelf?"

Serving no apparent ideological purpose, a line of misshapen plastic reproductions was arrayed over the booze: a rotund Statue of Liberty with the pop-eyed expression of John Belushi at a toga party, a lopsided Eiffel Tower and a Tower of Pisa that stood up straight, and a Baby Jesus sufficiently deformed to have played a bit part in *Alien 3*.

"Cinzeiro's main industry is the production of rinky-dink souvenirs," Ordway explained. "This burg earned its name from making millions of ashtrays. Barba supplies the kiosks around Buckingham Palace, Times Square, Bethlehem, and the Pyramids. The trinkets are grim enough when they come out properly, but the rejects are horror shows. Workers take them home. The Rat's a favorite repository. What's really class, though—" Ordway distributed the drinks—"is they're starting to manufacture bits and bobs for the SOB on the quiet. Lighters, coffee mugs. I've started a corking collection."

"Where do you pick them up?" Edgar asked casually.

"The Creams run a shop," said Ordway. "Raises dosh for the party. It's dead legit; O Creme's legal. Nothing criminal about advocating random murder, so long as no one catches you slitting someone's throat. Isn't democracy brilliant?"

"But you couldn't call Creamie propaganda slick, could you?" Edgar noted, taking a seat. "Those gun-toting poster boys look like Mr. Potato Head dolls."

"Watch what you say here," Ordway muttered. He swept his eyes significantly toward a well-populated corner, which seemed deliberately kept dark for the purpose of lurking. "Anywhere in Cinzeiro. Crap graphics maybe, but the Sobs aren't a joke. These wankers are deadly. The rest of this lot like to pretend that Bear sailed off on a magic carpet with some randy skirt to Bali. It's not just because they like him and don't want to see him hurt. They don't want to see themselves hurt. To bims like Trudy, Barba's just a titillating panto, a feather in her cap to tickle her mates in Florida. Martha imagines liberal platitudes and journalistic credentials offer some sort of protection. Pyre knows better, but he's too burnt-out to glance over his shoulder anymore. They're all too blasé. Don't follow their example."

Refusing to play to Roland's self-importance, Edgar asked full-voice, "So you think Saddler was murdered by the SOB?"

Not only the whole table but the rest of the Rat's patrons went quiet.

"Not exactly a fast learner, are you Kellogg?" said Ordway.

Edgar gestured to the posters. "Why should I tiptoe around losers with their heads in socks? And you didn't answer my question."

"Never overlook the obvious," Ordway croaked harshly under his breath. "Bear was covering a terrorist movement that's demonstrated a gleeful disregard for human life. His copy wasn't always flattering. One day, *poof,* he's gone. Doesn't take a brain surgeon. I hope I'm wrong. But Bear could be a warning to us all. So if you ever speak to me that loudly in public about a violent paramilitary organization with ears at the bar, I will not only avoid your company but I will personally coldcock you to keep those blighters off my back."

"Roland," said Win. "Laying it on a little thick?"

Ordway stood up. He continued in a hoarse stage whisper, "I've had it up to my eyes with gormless gits flying into this town, who don't have a political clue, and who can't even ask for the loo in Portuguese. I'm supposed to hold their hands and show them around the dodgy parts of town, while they broadcast self-righteous bromides about terrorism at the top of their lungs and might as well be painting a bull's-eye on my forehead. No, thank you."

Before marching out of the Rat, Ordway picked up his Choque and chugged the whole bottle straight—the first thing the *Guardian* reporter had done that Edgar found truly impressive.

CHAPTER 13
A Brief Apprenticeship as an Ignorant Dipshit

MARTHA PATTED EDGAR'S sticky hand. "Don't mind Roland. TV crews are always coming through here needing a tour guide, and he's tired of driving the bus. But he's right. We all get careless. Best keep your lip buttoned, and watch where you walk."

"I poked around the better part of Cinzeiro today," said Edgar, taking a slug of his beer and trying not to wince. "Didn't seem too ominous."

"Not *Terra do Cão*?" Martha asked in alarm, describing where Edgar had snapped the photo of that kid. "Don't go in there by yourself. Take a local, preferably a Cream."

"Excuse me," said Edgar, keeping his sarcasm to sociable levels. "I didn't know the rules."

"Roland shames everybody about not speaking Portuguese," said Trudy. "He's miffed 'cause the *Guardian* made him take a course? Nobody else had to. Like, Barrington hardly spoke a word."

"Why bother?" said Pyre. "With the faithful Roland Ordway to translate for him?"

"Barrington knew just enough Portuguese to make bilingual puns," said Martha. "He claimed that's all foreign languages were for."

Edgar reached covertly into a jacket pocket to switch on his microcassette. "So what's the consensus?" Begrudgingly, he kept his voice just low enough not to offend local toughs. "Did the Sobs whack Saddler?"

"Man gets in trouble," said Pyre, bending back his gnarled

fingers, "it's one of three things: money, women, or politics. Saddler had a taste for all three. I'd say it's even odds."

"Was Saddler's copy so righteous that they'd take him out?" Edgar asked. "I've read op-eds in practically every paper deploring the SOB."

"I don't think Barrington was critical *enough*," Martha snipped. "He gave the Creams scads of column inches and did exhaustive features explaining their point of view. The *Post* has been much harder on those cretins. If Barrington was punished for *his* politics, then I'd really better watch my back." She was clearly invigorated by the prospect of being pursued by anyone.

"No chance they went for him over negative coverage," said Pyre. "If anything, he got into something scuzzy over his head. Fact is, Saddler loved the SOB. By association, the Sobs made Saddler seem important. Anything less than adulatory that he said in print? A faint, unconvincing nod toward civilization for the sake of appearances."

"Y'all just never forgave him 'cause he wouldn't share his sources," said Trudy.

Pyre reared back with a sigh. "You'll see, Kellogg. Blow-ins from CNN, all they want to know is, *Do you have contacts in the SOB?* Pant-pant. Pretty unsavory. Like telling your host, 'I've heard there are unscrupulous scumbags in your town, can we have *those* miscreants to dinner?' Saddler was a tease. *Maybe I know some scumbags, maybe I don't*, wink-wink. But he never came across. With any of us. Meanwhile, his stuff's riddled with quotes 'not for attribution' or from 'sources in Terra do Cão.' "

"You guys are such suckers," said a schoolmarmish type standing behind Pyre. "You expect him to file, 'Here's what I like to think a terrorist would say if he were stupid enough to speak to me'?"

"Kellogg, you're blessed," said Pyre. "The *New York Times* correspondent her very self! Who has taken a few precious minutes away from fevering at the keyboard to have an itsy-bitsy drink. Edgar, Dame Alexis Collier."

"Charmed," Alexis said primly, sounding anything but. "Anyone for a refresher?" Though Alexis had only just arrived, she seemed in a hurry.

"Another Choque," said Edgar. The bitter brew was growing on him.

"Gone native, already?" Alexis asked archly, and whisked to the bar. Her bony butt cheeks were squeezed so tightly together that if she held a pencil between them she could sign her name. Her face was pinched, her manner officious, her haircut butch, and she was wearing a *pants suit*. When Alexis smiled at the bartender, she looked pained. The snap on her pocketbook reported smartly like a slap on the wrist.

"Hard to tell, of course," Martha determined, "but I *think* she's in a bad mood."

"Of course." Pyre smiled maliciously. "How's she going to win a Pulitzer writing unpublished features on Barban wind flutes? I may be twiddling my thumbs, but at least this news vacuum keeps Ms. Coldkeister out of the *paper of record*."

"You said Saddler had a lot of SOB contacts," Edgar pressed Pyre. "But he played those cards close to his chest. Still, would you know who any of them are?"

"Likely I know any number of Sobs," said Pyre slyly, and gestured at the barkeep. "But they don't wear T-shirts. That's what blow-ins don't get. They expect to waltz into Cinzeiro and find terrorists in the Yellow Pages, under T."

"The cops went after Barrington once," said Trudy. "After he published an interview? And they wanted his source? But he said the guy was wearing a balaclava—you know, a ski mask—and disguised his voice and everything. And stayed behind a sheet."

"That famous interview was probably with Verdade in Groucho glasses," said Pyre.

Edgar leaned forward. "Think Verdade would give *me* an interview?"

Win Pyre had perfected an expression that simultaneously conveyed boredom and antipathy; he was either about to take a swing at you or drop off to sleep. "Oh, Kellogg, not you, too." He sighed in fatherly disappointment. "Ordinarily, Verdade's audience is as hard to win as the Pope's. Lately, with nothing going blooey, he's less in demand. You might get lucky. If that's the word. I should warn you, he's trying. Not so much enraging as stultifying. There've been times I'd set off a bomb myself to get him to shut up."

"What's the difference between O Creme and the SOB? Are they really interchangeable?"

If Edgar sounded overeager, even rushed, the race was with his own temperament. He placed a premium on savvy. Yet since you could only obtain new information by admitting you didn't know it already, savvy required an apprenticeship as a naïve twit. You had to ask crude, obvious questions like, *What's the difference between O Creme and the SOB?* You had to sit still while worldly-wise warhorses like Win Pyre fired withering glances as if you were born yesterday.

Well, Edgar was born yesterday for the moment, although his tolerance for being treated like a simpleton was in short supply. He'd need to rattle off a multitude of stupid questions before he embraced his next incarnation as an insider. The trouble was that savvy coated your brain in plastic like a driver's license: nothing more could get in. Hence the point at which you decided you knew everything was exactly the point at which you became an ignorant dipshit. Nevertheless, Edgar knew his own weaknesses. He'd transform into an ignorant dipshit in a matter of weeks.

"They're ostensibly separate organizations, and the conceit has proved useful," said Alexis, setting the Choque before Edgar crisply. "If nothing else, as an allegedly harmless democratic party whose support for the 'armed struggle' is supposedly just impassioned speeches, O Creme de Barbear is legal; as a proscribed terrorist group, the SOB isn't. So whenever the SOB does anything unpopular—which is often—O Creme backs off. *It wasn't me, it was my imaginary friend*, etc. But Verdade needs the SOB's clout. Without wink-wink paramilitary connections, he's a no-account leader of a third-string political party in the back of beyond."

"Collier!" Pyre exclaimed. "Aren't you afraid Kellogg will steal your ideas?"

Pruning her lips at Win, Alexis situated her chair a bit outside the circle and clunked her Motorola International cellular phone conspicuously on the table, rubbing everyone's nose in the fact that only the *New York Times* could afford those things. "Whether O Creme is the SOB or is merely associated with the SOB has never been established. In any case, Verdade's running the only game in town that Lisbon can play. He's the one Barban extremist with a postal address, so he's the sole route to negotiating a ceasefire. Terrorist godfather or humble intermediary, Tomás Verdade is in the driver's seat either way."

"And you guys don't think Verdade is smart," said Trudy.

"I think he's cunning, which is more dangerous than smart," said Martha. "Anyway, Verdade and this press corps have something in common: we both need bombs. Without the SOB, we're *covering* the back of beyond."

"Oh, let's not have another guilt fest about how we're parasites on other people's suffering," Alexis dismissed. "I'm tired."

"From what?" asked Pyre.

"Doing nothing. If this news no-show carries on another month or two, I'm applying for Bosnia."

"You miss Barrington," Trudy wheedled.

"I don't, particularly," the *Times* reporter announced briskly. "He was an unprofessional influence. Guy Wallasek keeping him on after that atrocious business in Moscow was an outrage. Journalists like Barrington make us all look sloppy."

"What'd he do?" asked Edgar, as he was expected to.

"To keep it short, he made things up," said Alexis.

"I read some of those articles, and they were terrif!" said Trudy.

"Too 'terrif,'" said Pyre. "One of his sources in the Russian army was so eloquent, so hilarious, and so bare-all about the shabby state of the military that David Remnick came over to do a profile for *The New Yorker*. Wallasek ordered Saddler to cooperate. At length it came to light that there was no General Syedlo."

"Bear obviously took it too far," said Martha. "But Alexis, haven't you ever used a composite character for an interview?"

"I have never used a composite," said Alexis. "I quote verbatim. Factual veracity in journalism is sacred, and Barrington, regrettably, had only an acute sense of the profane."

"She's so full of it," Trudy muttered in Edgar's ear. "Alexis hung on Barrington's every word. *They* think she wanted to get in good with his contacts. But I bet the ice queen isn't as frigid as Win thinks."

"Nuts, the joke's on Wallasek," said Pyre. "Barba turned out to be some 'exile.' By sheer accident, he threw the bunny into the briar patch, and Saddler landed on the biggest story of the decade. Typical."

"You know, that happened everywhere Barrington went?" Martha marveled. "He goes to Haiti, Duvalier's overthrown. To Africa, bingo, Ethiopia obliges him a famine. He goes to Moscow, there's a military coup. He goes on *vacation* in Israel and bang, Rabin's assassinated. He had some unearthly karmic power. Honestly, that man could turn me mystic. There seem to be certain catalytic types around whom things just happen. That bastard had such a string of world-class events behind him that you had to start wondering if he made them happen. Barrington steps off a plane and suddenly some poor right-wing schmuck has an uncontrollable urge to shoot the prime minister."

"Did you like Saddler?" Edgar asked Martha point-blank.

She paused, as if never having answered the question to her own satisfaction. "I think—maybe I did. But I felt strongly that I shouldn't. Barrington Saddler was abusive, cocky, and unreliable. He hurt people's feelings, whether from malice or negligence I'm not sure it matters. But when he made an appearance, well—I didn't mind."

"Didn't *mind*?" exclaimed Trudy.

"Does that make sense?" asked Martha.

"Yeah," said Edgar, remembering Falconer's confession. "You could only dislike him when he was out of the room."

"Excellent," said Pyre. "He's out of the room, forever. Start practicing, Hulbert."

Since this crowd was sure to keep picking at the subject of Saddler like a hangnail, Edgar slipped off to the bar to order *carne de porco à alentejana*, commended in his guidebook as a national specialty. When he returned, whatever methodicalness he'd imposed on the discussion of Saddler's fate had given way to pandemonium.

"IN SUM," Edgar shouted, struggling to get the rabble under control, "none of you agree with Ordway, right? Saddler's copy was if anything sympathetic to the SOB, and there was no reason he should have been singled out as an example. Win, you said Saddler might have got in 'over his head.' How? Could he have run guns, sold information? Or did he just know too much?"

Pyre snorted. "That hotdog thought he wrote the book, but I doubt the Sobs saw him—"

"This is ridiculous speculation," said Martha. "Barrington was a user, and he was too charming for his own good, but I can't see him running guns. It would be too much trouble. He was the laziest man on God's green earth."

"Then let's move on," Edgar agreed readily, having grown attached to the idea that Saddler was a craven fake. "Win, you said there were three possibilities. Two: money. Could Saddler have been deeply in debt?"

"He was free with cash," said Alexis, "but he could afford to be. The weasel made a killing on exchange rates."

"How?"

"When you submit expenses to your paper, you cite the official exchange rate. If you're in Congo, say, the official rate is a fraction of the rate for dollars on the black market. Posted to enough Third World cesspits, you can make a fortune from the disparity."

"Alexis!" said Martha. "How would you know?"

"I've read about it," the *Times* reporter demurred.

"He didn't need to scam," said Pyre. "He would, since grifting was Saddler's idea of fun. But Wallasek paid him a fortune."

"That villa you're camped in, Edgar," said Alexis. "I think Barrington owns it."

"I'd like to know how the hell he got that house," said Pyre. "The rest of us live in run-down prefabs. Aside from Henry Durham's—and that squirt could buy Luxembourg if he wanted—Saddler's swank Moorish palace is the only decent architecture left in Barba. You're one lucky cuss, Kellogg."

"So just like Nicola," said Edgar, as his pork-with-clams arrived. "You hate me, too."

Pyre raised his eyebrows. "Touché. Nicola Tremaine doesn't waste hatred on many people."

Martha said sourly, "Nicola sees the good side of *everybody*."

"Even if Barrington did owe money," said Trudy, "*she'd* have given him, like, millions of dollars if he asked."

"My," said Alexis, nodding at Edgar's food. "Aren't you brave!"

The bartender was plunking dark nuggets into Edgar's bowl, along with a litter of stiff bits—clams? With a proud flourish, the barman ladled translucent yellow liquid over the meat, perhaps a broth. The dish wasn't very appealing—the tight brown lumps in a vast yellow pool had a sort of bathroom look—but Edgar was famished. At the risk of sounding earnest, before digging in he interjected loyally, "I like Nicola."

"Of course you do," Alexis purred. "I've never met a man who didn't. She's a wonderful cook, she knits adorably lumpy sweaters, she has no career, and she falls all over herself proclaiming her dearth of ambition in any sphere. Even Barrington fell for it. A sign of weakness, in my view. A strong man should want a strong partner."

Trudy rolled her eyes. "Gosh. Like who?"

"Alex, you're being unfair," said Pyre.

"Oh, we won't hear a harsh word against her," said Alexis. "I should warn you, Edgar. Ms. Tremaine comes on like Snow White, but she's a terrible flirt."

"Nicola is the only reason Durham ever got published," said Pyre. "She massaged his copy like nobody's business. Ever since Durham got a bug up his ass about Saddler, he hasn't let his wife near his articles. He's shown me a few: dog meat. The *Independent* has spiked every one."

"Durham's not your best pal?" Edgar finally gave up trying to cut the musket ball of pork in two, and popped it whole.

"Henry Durham is pathetic," Pyre announced while Edgar chewed. "Sure, it's a shame about his family. But hard luck doesn't make a journalist. I don't even know if it's still called hard luck when you get so much out of it. And sad sack or no, Durham's a dilettante. Worse, a dilettante with money. The *Independent* only keeps him on hand because he costs the paper jack. You were in law, Kellogg. How'd you feel if some lamebrain whose nearest-and-dearest took the wrong airplane bought into your firm with booty and bathos?"

"I got the impression—" the fried pork was so hard that Edgar's jaw ached—"that buy his way into journalism was exactly what Henry Durham couldn't do."

"Oh, the *Independent* brought him on board for his sappy novelty value," Pyre barreled on. "But those two aren't living on his day rates, are they? Your average wannabe couldn't afford to pitch a tent in a hotspot for long without redeeming himself in print. Henry Durham can import fine wines and diddle over his word processor forever. But being lousy rich doesn't mean you can write."

As the dry meat scraped down his gullet, Edgar reflected that little enough qualified these scribblers for their own jobs. Most hacks wrangled postings through sheer doggedness or serendipity. Which explained Pyre's bile: if there's one thing a dilettante hates, it's another dilettante.

"If Saddler was already loaded," Edgar proposed, sipping several spoonfuls of the yellow liquid to moisten his raw throat, "that leaves women."

"Barrington didn't need to cross the street for a girl," said Martha, arms bunched. "Why would he leave the country for one?"

"Or with one," Alexis supposed.

"And if he were going to leave *with* one," said Martha, "why is she still here?"

"Only because he never asked her," Trudy said significantly.

"I didn't mean *you*," said Martha.

"And why would *that* be so crazy?"

"I didn't want to tell you," said Martha, "but you know what he called you behind your back? *Truly Sissy*. Is that a nickname for the love of your life?"

"He had names for everybody. Including," Trudy threatened darkly, "you."

"Please," said Martha. "I've been called every name under—"

"Martha *Hugebutt*," spit Trudy.

"At least I don't go on and on about 'our relationship,'" said Martha, "on the basis of a one-night stand!"

"It was not a one-night stand!"

"You had a longer affair with Reinhold Glück!"

The yellow substance had left a disagreeable coating on Edgar's gums, and it was slippery. That wasn't chicken broth. In Barba, corn oil was a sauce.

"Reinhold was a drip," said Trudy. "I was trying to console myself, and it didn't work. If you wanna know the truth, Barrington was afraid of love. He was starving for it, but when he looked it in the face he ran a mile. He could seem so cocksure, but deep down he reckoned he was dirt. None of y'all understand him at all."

"What I do understand," said Martha, "is that Barrington always had something going on the side. Hell, he's probably been having an affair with Benazir Bhutto for ten years, and he's flown to Pakistan."

"It only seemed he had friends everywhere," said Trudy. "But they weren't real friends. Everyone expected him to be all funny and lively, and it was hard work! Real ironic and everything, but in private he admitted he was lonely—"

"Not this routine again," said Alexis.

"Alesbo!" said Trudy, wheeling. "That's what Barrington called *you*."

"Men often accuse women of being lesbians when they're intimidated," said Alexis coolly. "Personally, I'm convinced that Barrington had very little interest in sex, the act itself."

"That's what ladies always say when guys think they're dogs," Trudy muttered.

"He was interested in power," Alexis went on. "And he liked to play games. Often when a flirtation is consummated, the game is over. I think he liked to put off that closure as long as possible. Physical gratification was very low on his list. I think he found it embarrassing. Sexual congress is, after all, difficult to pull off with élan. And one shudders to contemplate Barrington in the buff. His soul is clad. He probably emerged from the birth canal in tails."

"Hell, I think the guy was a fag," Pyre intruded.

"Now, that's a stretch," said Alexis.

"Look at the women he went after with a vengeance," said

Pyre. "Nicola; *my wife*. It was their husbands he wanted to poke up the ass."

"But as FAR AS YOU ALL KNOW," Edgar raised his voice to overcome Trudy and Martha, who were arguing over Trudy's claim that Barrington suffered from an *unfillable hollow in his heart*, "Saddler had no big-deal relationship going elsewhere, aside from *Benazir*?"

They ignored him.

"You don't honestly think he was *happy*?" Trudy shouted.

"Who wouldn't be happy?" Martha shouted back. "With success, totally *unearned* adulation, and women galore—"

"Your version of happiness is sad, Martha!"

"You sound jealous," Alexis chided Pyre. "Did you want him to 'poke' you, too?"

"Nymphos, the theory goes, can't get satisfaction," said Pyre. "It's not that they're oversexed; they're frigid. Why should men be any different? Saddler's appetite for poontang was suspicious. I think he kept going back for more because he didn't like it the first time."

"Oh, that makes sense!" said Alexis.

"What he liked is sticking it to other men—"

"The only reason he chose Nicky is he couldn't have her!" Trudy screamed over Pyre. "And that's typical when you don't feel worthy—"

"Oh, puh-lease, he ran after Nicola so he could RUIN HER LIFE!" screamed Martha.

Discreetly, Edgar worked his chair from the circle, reached into his jacket, and switched off the tape. He had enough material. As he eased out of the Barking Rat, Edgar felt unnecessary. This crowd hardly required the prodding of an interviewer and a microcassette. In his very extraneousness Edgar felt a curious alliance with Saddler. Even vanished, Barrington was a franchise, in which other people enjoyed a controlling interest. Absent or dead, he'd left his investors with a toy version of himself—a bauble with which his acquaintances might endlessly fiddle, a puzzle to obsessively take apart and reconstruct. Like Falconer, Saddler was less man than notion, a glittering mirror ball in which his companions could see flashes of themselves or, more bitterly, glimpses of what they were not.

CHAPTER 14

No Trace Found of Reporter in Terrorist Stronghold

EDGAR KELLOGG, BARBA CORRESPONDENT

Cinzeiro—Neither his acquaintances nor Portuguese authorities have successfully shed light on the whereabouts of Barrington Saddler, who went missing in April this year. Until his disappearance, Mr. Saddler was the Barba correspondent for the National Record.

Cinzeiro is home to the headquarters of O Creme de Barbear, the political arm of Os Soldados Ousados de Barba (SOB). Pronounced "Osh Sol-DA-dosh Oo-ZHA-dos" and literally "The Daring Soldiers of Barba," the SOB has built a reputation for ruthlessness by sponsoring a series of devastating terrorist incidents abroad over the last five years. Some fear Mr. Saddler's unexplained absence might involve paramilitary foul play.

Were Mr. Saddler to have met misfortune at the hands of the SOB—determined to win Barba independence from Portugal—the move would mark an alarming shift in SOB strategy. Hitherto, the southern Portuguese militants have steered clear of journalists. Remaining correspondents in the province have grown uneasy.

O Creme de Barbear (Portuguese for "shaving cream," as the party hopes to shear Barba, the "beard" of the peninsula, from the mainland) is protective of its public image, and courts a friendly relationship with foreign reporters through regular press conferences. The party's president, Tomás Verdade (pronounced "Ver-DADZH"), could not be reached for comment. Other sources high up in O Creme deny any knowledge of the journalist's whereabouts.

Of all the correspondents posted to Cinzeiro, Mr. Saddler would make a curious target. The missing reporter's coverage was unusually sensitive to the SOB's outrage over high rates of illegal Muslim immigration. A deluge of both economic and political refugees from North Africa has been transforming the demographic make-up of the region.

Now forty-one, Mr. Saddler is originally from Yorkshire in the United Kingdom, but has worked for American newspapers most of his career. After leaving the Los Angeles Times under cloudy circumstances, Mr. Saddler joined the staff of the National Record at the paper's inception. Previous postings include Bangkok, Port-au-Prince, Nairobi, and Moscow.

Flamboyant and controversial—some would say notorious—Mr.

Saddler was a devotee of "new journalism," or what one anonymous source deemed "screaming fabrication." Certainly he bent the rules of his craft, as he likewise bent the rules of social life. A known womanizer who played fast and loose with both money and the truth, Mr. Saddler was renowned for his storytelling in every sense.

Theories about his truancy range from paramilitary assassination to an illicit *femme fatale* tryst, but common irresponsibility never features in popular versions of Mr. Saddler's fate. Few onlookers wish to believe that the vanishing of a local luminary could be explained by the lame misadventures that seem to befall mere mortals who fail to show up for work.

Yet do mythic characters always meet mythic ends? No SOB statement has taken credit for the reporter's disappearance. In times past, the organization has displayed a veritable eagerness to claim even the most heinous crimes.

The celebrated Barrington Saddler could well have slipped on a banana peel—or, in Barba, more likely an overripe *pera peluda*, or hairy pear—and tumbled haplessly into a ditch. But despite ostensible dedication to the straight scoop, his journalistic colleagues reject pedestrian hypotheses out of hand.

"News is entertainment," Mr. Saddler is reputed to have declared. He might be gratified to learn that as news he, too, is entertainment. Alive or dead, the reporter continues to thrive in the obsessive conjecture of his contemporaries. Another of Mr. Saddler's aphorisms apparently ran, "Never let the facts get in the way of a good story." They haven't.

"I loved your article," said Nicola on opening the door, confounding at the outset Edgar's vow to cleanse his conversation of you-know-who for her husband's sake.

Henry shouted from the living room, "Been nervous of ditches ever since!"

"First draft was snappier," Edgar allowed, delivering a bottle and a flat wrapped package. "But Wallasek wouldn't publish that his own reporter was a total fraud."

"Don't tell me." Nicola glanced at his gifts. "You had a dreadful time deciding what to bring. Lafite Rothschild? Fortunately for you, Cinzeiro off-licenses don't carry bottles worth more than a fiver. This is lovely port. Thank you." She kissed his cheek. "I'd tell you not to bother next time, except that no one ever brings us anything anymore. Honestly, I'd be delighted if you kept it up."

She tore at the ribbon with childlike impatience. "Now you

can appreciate how hard it is for me to be generous with Henry. The irony of wealth is that it becomes impossible to treat yourself. Oh, brilliant!"

"I'm afraid it's labeled, 'For ages four to seven,'" said Edgar of the little tin watercolor set. Maybe one viable alternative to exorbitance with the affluent was a gift exquisitely cheap.

"That's a little old for me, but I have my precocious moments. And what super colors! Come on in. Henry has promised to be more personable."

This time, down the stone steps and into the parlor Edgar did feel welcome. Almost too. Nicola was burbling with gratitude, and Henry's face relaxed in relief. Any guest apparently improved on just the two of them alone in the room.

"Edgar!" Henry roused himself from a sprawl to shake Edgar's hand. "Sorry I was shirty the other night, right? That lot can get up my nose."

The lanky clasp felt sincere, and a heaviness descended on Edgar for the duration. Damn it to hell. Henry Durham showed every sign of being a stand-up guy.

"Your article was, what do you Yanks say? A three-pointer."

"I wouldn't call it better than a solid bank shot," Edgar dismissed, though he'd pulled an all-nighter debating *celebrated* versus *fawned over*, *flamboyant* versus *garish*.

"A blinder." Henry plopped back to the sofa. The pillow he tucked behind his head was crocheted with the growling logo of the Barking Rat. "Still, you mustn't expect sweet nothings from the rest of that bunch. They don't like new boys. They don't like crack competition. They don't like the whole notion of Barrington being replaced. And they don't like being written up—accurate-like, right?—as gossipy old bints. I doubt Barrington slipped on a hairy pear, but I fancied the picture."

"Speaking of hairy pears, you should consider retooling that *pera peluda* piece for an American magazine," said Edgar, attempting a professional camaraderie thus far singularly lacking in Cinzeiro's press corps. "It's perfect for a 'Postcard from Barba' in *The New Republic*, but their rates are derisory. How about *Esquire*, or even one of those in-flight rags—*Sky*, *American Way*? Light on the prestige, but they pay great." Uncapping himself a Choque, Edgar felt his cheeks tingle. In his nervousness, he'd blanked on the fact that Henry had no need to swallow his pride for fifty cents a word.

Henry smiled grimly at Edgar's faux pas. "Cheers, mate. I'm chuffed. Don't think I don't appreciate the gesture. But it ain't necessary, right?"

"Yeah," Edgar scrambled, "I guess in your, you know, position, you should stick to the heavy hitters."

"Sorry, I meant it was dead decent of you to shift the subject right when you walked in. A soldierly effort, but doomed, mate. We've tried avoiding Barrington. It don't work. Becomes just another way of talking about the bloke. Reduces all other subjects to diversion, like. So now I push him right to the top of the agenda. That way there's some chance we can *wink-wink, nudge-nudge, know-what-I-mean* at something else. We haven't yet. But here's hoping." Henry clinked his Diamond White whimsically against Edgar's *cerveja*.

Curious about the down-market booze, Edgar said, "I noticed last time you're a Diamond White man, but I couldn't find any to bring. You import it yourself?"

"By the lorry-load. When you're flush, you sort out that you right fancy stuff that's dirt cheap. Like bangers and beans—which is yards better with mealy forty-nine-P sausages than the posh sort with walnuts."

"Yeah, simple pleasures," Edgar agreed, concluding after another slug of Choque that any brew that was 8 percent alcohol couldn't be all bad. "Hard to beat plain buttered toast."

"Or," said Henry as Nicola returned with snacks, "nipping

home to your wife dead confident that you're the apple of her bleeding eye."

Nicola's face turned aside as if she'd been slapped.

"So, Edgar," Henry proceeded, ignoring his wife. "Caught the Barrington bug yet? When he first got here, Reinhold Glück thought we was all barking—so much bother over one bloke. By the time he left, I'd to promise on a stack of Bibles to ring if Bear comes up for air. Glück's in a panic to interview our local Jack-the-lad for *Der Spiegel*."

"Hey, I'd love to talk about something else. No one will let me." Edgar perched on a stool whose three wooden legs supported a broad, springy leather bicycle seat. A multimillionaire, and Nicola cannibalizes her old Raleigh three-speed for furniture. "Including you."

"I'm getting the bastard out of my system." Henry chugged his cider, which didn't seem to be his first. "Trouble is, that's a crap substitute for getting him out of someone else's."

"I've the same problem as you, Edgar," said Nicola coldly. "It's like parting a dog from his bone. Henry won't let me bury it." Nicola raised her head in defiance, folding her legs into an armchair. Her knees were small and chiseled. Though she always seemed self-possessed, tonight she owned herself to excess, cocooning her shawl tightly around both arms.

Edgar gestured to the fringed shawl, whose vivid pink and yellow roses jumped from a black background. "That scarf's very striking."

Henry chuckled. "Nice try."

"Thank you," said Nicola calmly. "It was a present."

"So," said Edgar, "you *can* give nice gifts to the rich."

"It isn't from Henry," she said deadpan. "It's from Moscow."

"All roads lead." Henry thumped his Doc Martens on the coffee table.

"Henry insisted I wear it. Since I don't own a hair shirt."

"We're giving that wrap some air, right?" said Henry. "Letting the spell wear off, like you get rid of a smell."

"Forgive us, Edgar," said Nicola. "I'd thought we might talk about how you found Barba. Maybe explore what drove you to leave the law, which must have been lucrative, for the insecure life of a journalist. I thought that was an intriguing leap. Courageous, even. But I'm afraid that conversation will have to wait. My husband is only interested in discussing our old friend, Barrington Saddler. Henry misses Barrington, though he'll not tell you that, and if Henry wants to talk about Barrington, that's just what we'll do."

Nicola clasped her hands like a teacher at story time. "Henry claims that my shawl has a 'spell' cast on it. But as I recall, Edgar, you're the skeptical sort who can't bear to watch a magic show without finding out what the trick is—where's the false bottom, how do you palm the hard-cooked egg. Isn't that what you asked me last week? How did Barrington 'do it'? We've just watched a fabulous vanishing act; supposedly Barrington has 'disappeared.' So first and foremost, my husband owes you a credible explanation of how, for all practical purposes, Barrington is still here."

A gauntlet. Edgar was reminded of that old Psych 101 example of "positive punishment" in behaviorism. Some biddy in a loony bin has a towel fetish. She swipes them, hoards the suckers. The lady can't get enough—or thinks she can't. Until the staff is told to deliver the crackpot towels, in piles. Every day, more towels. The old bat's cramped little room towers with towels, and still more towels arrive, mounding outside her door, choking her cupboards, stacking in the shower. Finally, bang: the maids clear off all the linen. The biddy never steals a towel again.

"You want to know how Barrington did it?" said Henry. "I've made a study of it, friend." Having not, apparently, made a study of B. F. Skinner, Henry took up Nicola's challenge, as the fetish lady would have greedily squirreled away those first few extra towels delivered by the hospital staff.

"Lesson One." Henry raised a finger. "Barrington Goes to a Party. Of course, the hostess will be gutted if you don't show. So you'll be late, right? All the guests get into a flap 'cause you're not there yet, until everybody's assumed that you'll not come. Birds grab their bags and mumble how this party's shite, and of course it's shite! You're not there, right?

"Jesus have mercy, you finally show." Henry raised both hands evangelically. "The door opens—gasp! Gratitude hits you like a blast furnace. The room hops, turns into a real knees-up; girls bundle to the loo to comb their hair. Oh, and remember, Edgar: nice gear. Since this is a casual bash, a dinner jacket could hint that you came from some other posh do. With one word to the wise, soon the lot know you're also headed somewhere else. So the crowd's in a lather about how long they've got you to themselves. And it's a dead cert that the wingding you left *and* the one you'll leave for are well more fun than the one they're at, right? Following me so far?

"Now, thanks to Advanced Arsehole lessons, you've knotted some nifty tangles into the *social fabric*. Like those tufts that crop up in Nicky's knitting. Need me to lay it out plain, like? You're bonking more than one bird at the do. They slag each other off, wallow in the awkwardness of it all—your brand of slapstick.

"Meanwhile, *spread yourself thin*. Divide your time between the center ring and the sideshow downstairs, where you're conducting hugger-mugger journo business to make everybody else's dinky socializing seem crap in comparison. But whatever you're up to, *keep the punters in the dark*. Since you've left this number on four, five machines around town, every fifteen minutes you'll be called to the blower, just when our little soiree's in full swing. And when you heave off to the horn, you'll leave a crater behind you the size of a meteor landing."

"I get the picture," said Edgar testily, more than a little put out by this harangue.

"While you chat up one skirt, googly-eye her best friend," Henry carried on. "Keep all relationships as fucked up as possible. Never let anyone know where they stand. Don't let the bastards take you for granted. And no matter how many bims throw themselves at your feet, make a beeline for forbidden fruit. *Try getting your mitts on the one, the only plum in the room that you're not supposed to pick.*"

"Henry's right on one point," said Nicola tolerantly. "Barrington trained people not to count on him, to be grateful for what they could get. Barrington might ring; he might not. A kind of abuse, really."

"Skip it, Nicky. You know, that was the first sign something had gone funny?" Henry told Edgar. "She started slagging him off—and Nicky's the sort thinks up excuses for Hitler. It used to be, *ooh, isn't Barrington switched on,* and suddenly she starts picking at the bloke, right? Wasn't he a bit wicked, was he up to something dodgy with the Sobs, why'd he think airline sabotage was a wheeze instead of tragic, where was his heart . . . Interesting red flag, you reckon?"

"I have to warn you, Edgar," said Nicola. "Some people can be unreliable, and we dislike them for it. They're late for a party, and we don't notice. They two-time women, we think they're cads. They're evasive, we lose interest. I worry that you could follow Henry's lessons to the letter, and rather than slaver at your heels the press corps would shun you instead."

"That might make me lucky," said Edgar crossly.

"Boys like you and Henry like to take contraptions to pieces and see what makes them tick. But you could autopsy Barrington Saddler and lay his organs on the slab. You'd never find what you were looking for. It's true that he had something. I'm not sure it has a name; *charisma* seems a little slight. Whatever you call it, he was a slave to it as much as his admirers were, and he didn't understand how it worked any better than you or Henry. I don't pretend to understand it, either, but I can assure you that it didn't make him happy. It did sometimes make other people happy," she added wistfully, "but Barrington wasn't a nice enough person to take much pleasure in that."

"Poor baby," Edgar scoffed. "Too many folks loved him. What a terrible problem."

"Barrington didn't believe that his hangers-on loved *him*," Nicola countered. "He thought they fell for a decoy. After all, when you love someone, what do you love? What he's good at? If a woman only loved your writing or your aptitude as a solicitor, you'd be disappointed. I think you could even make a distinction between a person and a personality. Barrington's retinue trotted after what he had. Not who he was."

Henry sagged. "You mean Barrington had something I don't."

"Of course he did," said Nicola gently.

"And no matter what I do, I won't ever have it." Henry pressed his hands between his knees.

"That's right," said Nicola, "and maybe that makes you fortunate."

"Bollocks," said Henry.

"I'm with him," Edgar agreed. "What you're describing doesn't sound like a drag to me."

"Whether you'd like it for yourselves is of no consequence, since you can hardly pick it off a shelf at Marks & Spencer's," said Nicola, uncurling from her chair. "I have to finish dinner. Henry, have you had enough now?"

Henry did look wrung out. He uncapped another White Diamond, but his wife hadn't been referring to drink. He swigged, flopped back, and mopped his forehead. "Yeah."

Nicola padded from the room. She might as well have been carting away a pile of towels ten feet high.

CHAPTER 15
Any Slob Can Buy Shit

EDGAR LEAPT AFTER the scant little black dress to help in the kitchen. He dreaded being left alone with Henry.

Nicola's kitchen was littered with strings of garlic bulbs and bunches of bright, lethal-looking chilies. Put-up pickles, flavored oils, fresh herbs in the window box: the whole culinary nine yards. Grated lemon zest lay drying on the windowsill; God forbid that the independently wealthy should throw a squeezed-out half-lemon away.

"You do all the cooking? Sure got Henry spoiled," said Edgar.

"It used to be the other way around," Nicola said quietly, dotting butter on roasted potatoes. "In the old days, he'd have beaten you in here, begging to be put to work. For years it was, *Honey, do you need anything at the shop, don't lift that by yourself, here let me* . . . And the presents, so many, so endless, we've had to give most of them away. But it was more than things. *You've a headache, sweetheart, let me fetch you aspirin, you stay put. Would you like a video, never mind what I want to watch. Are you cold, I'll get your jumper, are you hot.* It was a tyranny, really!" She stopped buttering to press the heel of her hand to an eye. "I could hardly get anything done, he was so intent on doing for me, and he was always in the way. At last I had to ask him to stop." The other heel, the other eye. "So he did."

"Recently," Edgar intuited, having finally realized she was crying.

She bit her lower lip and nodded.

"Do you two often . . . like tonight?"

"Oh, we go through purges. They clear the air for a while. Henry's convinced that if we're not talking about *it*, then we're lying. But talking doesn't do any good! I know what he really wants explained: *What did he do to deserve this?* Of course the answer is nothing. Or, *How could I?* And the answer is I don't know. Maybe I'd been happy for so long that I was bored with it."

"Couples stray," said Edgar. "Part of the breaking-in process."

"Not breaking in, *breaking*," Nicola differed sharply. "You can glue people together again. But then your relationship's like any other repaired object, with cracks, blobs of epoxy, a little askew. It's never the same. I can see you haven't a notion what I'm on about, so you'll have to take my word for it."

"Christ, you're the babe in the woods." Edgar stopped slicing tomatoes. "You got it ass-backward. A marriage perched like porcelain on the mantelpiece is doomed. Sooner or later grown-ups treat each other like shit. You gotta be able to kick the thing around, less like china than an old shoe—*bam*, under the bed, or walk it through some puddles. No love's gonna last if it can't take abuse."

"You sound like Barrington," Nicola mourned.

"Thanks," said Edgar, taking out the salad. He meant it.

Those two did seem to have laid something to rest for the time being, and at dinner Edgar asked how they met.

"Dad raked it in with his bagel caper," Henry began. "But I never touched him for much. Truth is, I used to be a bit of a waster."

"Henry was Melissa Goldberg's toy boy," Nicola teased.

"Melissa had few financial cares," Henry allowed. "She bought me stuff, I hung about. I guess she was busy. Banking."

"The stocking," Nicola prodded.

"Christmas morning, I unload my stocking, right? And I notice, Melissa seems more curious than me to see what's in it. She keeps peering over, picking bits up and going, *Brilliant!*"

"I used to work for Selfridges in London," Nicola explained. "One of the services they offer is 'personal shoppers,' who buy customers' Christmas presents for them."

"So Melissa and I had a row," Henry proceeded. "If she couldn't buy me presents herself I didn't want them. Sorry, but I thought a personal shopper was so—"

"Crass," Edgar supplied.

"Spot on. So I walk out. After Boxing Day I go to Selfridges and demand to talk to the poor sod who really bought my presents. I'd this idea I'd bring them back. On the other hand, the presents were class . . . Since Nicky has, you know—"

"The touch," said Edgar.

"Besides, Nicky turned out to be—"

"Gorgeous," said Edgar.

"So we went out, like, every night, and had a cracking time. We had fuck-all, but we was happy as Larry. And now. . .

"Nicky says she told you about BA-321," he veered. "But you know what's real ironic? One of my pet peeves when I met Nicky was Lotto. The Tories brought in this Camelot-run national lottery, and suddenly it took twenty minutes to buy a Kit Kat at the newsstand. You had to queue up with a dozen tossers all hopped up over a 'double roll-over.' I thought they were daft. And lucky, like, when they *didn't* hit the jackpot."

"You lost me," said Edgar.

"No one in his right head would want to win a lottery if he knew what was good for him. Me, I never bought those poxy tickets. I was dead sure a pile of dosh would ruin my life. And wasn't I right."

"I thought the main problem was your money seeming tainted." Edgar followed his hostess's lead and forked a fried sardine whole, bones and all. "Maybe if you'd come by it some other way, like through a real lottery, you could enjoy it more."

Henry sighed. "Fair enough, that'd be part of it. And it didn't help I'd had a wicked set-to with my parents before they got killed, about when was I going to make something of myself. But even without 321, I knew I'd come into a fair whack of quid down the line from those freaking bagels, and I was dreading it. I never wanted to be stinking rich."

"You could have declined the jury's award," Edgar supposed. "And the inheritance. You must have some cousin who'd have relieved you of the awful burden."

Henry plunked his knife upright on the table. "Would *you* heave a trunkful of notes into the Thames?"

"Of course not," said Edgar.

"Then why would I, mate? I look superhuman to you?"

"Still, I'm sorry to seem dense," said Edgar, taking a sip of the *astoundingly* good cabernet. "And I can see how benefiting from catastrophe would be uncomfortable. But why's an instant fortune effectively a second disaster?"

Henry's eyes lit. "Not only can money not buy *happiness*. Money buys sweet F.A.! Especially when you didn't earn it. It doesn't make people like you. It makes them want to use you. Nobody thinks you're smart or sexy or talented, and though they will laugh at your jokes you can never be sure why. Oh, and you're not to have any more problems. You can't complain. Far as everybody else's concerned, I been paid off, like. I miss my sister like fury, but money's meant to stop me whingeing. In fact, I'm supposed to sort out other people now, even the ones who call me a prat behind my back. Look at the hacks in Cinzeiro. Oh, they all wanted to be my best mate when I picked up their dinner checks. Well, I stopped. They pay their own bar tabs now. And how do they talk about me at the Rat when I'm not there?"

Edgar paused. "Really want to know?"

"I already know. They think I'm a poser. But if I'd decided to shift to Barba with no more than a fiver in my pocket, trying to make a go of journalism on my wits? They'd think I was real self-starter. Or at least they'd give me a chance."

Perhaps having detected a hint of scorn peeking through Edgar's poker face, Nicola was eyeing him askance.

"I've got an idea. Why don't we all go to Mauritius?" she proposed. "Tomorrow. No need to pack; we can pick up what we need there. Last-minute tickets are expensive, but Henry and I can afford them. Are you on board, Edgar?"

"You buying?" Edgar asked gamely, stalling.

"Henry just told you: we don't do that anymore, and he's quite right, too. We'd never be certain if you enjoyed our company or just wanted a free lunch."

"The *Record* pays me dick, Nick," said Edgar, sinking back in his chair as his shoulders dropped two inches. "Have to pass on the piña coladas."

"She's having you on, Edgar," said Henry.

"But did you see his face?" she asked Henry victoriously. "When Edgar realized he couldn't wend off to an island paradise at the drop of a hat, he was relieved."

" 'Relieved' is a little strong," said Edgar. "I couldn't even consider the idea is all."

"Maybe Henry and I don't want to go to Mauritius, either," said Nicola. "Or the Seychelles, or Majorca. But we're forced to stare down fanciful schemes like that every day. You're not. Who's lucky?"

"Freedom is a curse?" said Edgar with incredulity.

"Freedom to do what?" Henry shot back.

"Maybe Mauritius is nice this time of year."

"And you could lie on the beach and drink and eat and sleep," said Henry. "Not bad for a break. But for a life?"

"Henry, come clean," said Nicola. "That's not far from the way you spent your time when we met."

"In those days, being a dosser was an accomplishment," said Henry. "Skiving is an art. Any slob can buy shit."

"Henry wasn't always a layabout. He used to drive a London minicab. And working, you meet people, see places. Now Henry and I aren't obliged to do anything. With deliveries, we needn't leave the house."

"Either of you could still drive a minicab," Edgar submitted.

"Wise up!" said Henry. "Bad air, crap traffic, rude old bags, poleaxed lager-louts spewing in your backseat? You work because you have to. Work for fun isn't work. Not to you, and not to anybody else."

"Listen, what are we talking here, thirty, forty million pounds?" Edgar asked squarely.

Nicola looked embarrassed. "In that area . . ."

"Have you two ever had a good time with it?"

"Depends on your definition." Henry shrugged. "Sure, we ate out and that. Nicky's cooking is better. And we drank. Try buying yourself out of a hangover. We went places—Italy, Greece—where we ate out and drank. Hardly put a dent in the fucking money. And I started to get fat."

"It was cute," said Nicola. "This little bloop . . ."

"So why not install a home gym?"

"I did," said Henry glumly. "Couldn't stick it. No locker-room banter, no bawdy jokes. Even missed the smell."

"How about philanthropy?"

"Thought about it," said Henry. "Nicky warned me off the starving Africans bit. She said Zambia's a horlicks partly because aid messes up the local economy. I don't totally understand it. Except for a while I dandered around Brixton, dishing out tenners. Got myself jumped once. Another time, one of the junkies I 'helped'? ODed on my charity. The junkie croaked, for fuck's sake. I start figuring, if money for nothing's shite for me, why'd it not be shite for other blokes, too?

"I could start a foundation. But for what? Education? I never went to university; I'd feel a hypocrite. Cancer research? People have to die of something; cure cancer, another disease takes its place. Or something appropriate, like. I could sponsor a 'conflict resolution' outfit. But most of that academic crowd are SOB apologists, like Ansel Henwood; and those profs only blather at conferences, which are a big wank. Maybe I don't know what I think is important. And I'm ticked off having to think about it. I'm no good at it, ask Nicky. God's honest truth, I'd rather be a dosser again."

"You obviously think a packet is wasted on us, Edgar," said Nicola. "What would you do with it?"

Edgar's mind washed blank. Even in his imagination, as soon as he made the world infinitely available it went flat.

"Go skiing?" Edgar put forward in desperation. Actually, he'd burned out on skiing five years ago, weary of the fuss, the drives, the lodges, the assholes, and the gear.

"All year?" asked Henry with a grin.

"Hang-gliding, then," said Edgar. "Or I could join an expedition up Everest."

"See?" Henry leered. "You're already killing time."

"There's always cars and stereos," Edgar supposed lamely.

"Boats and private planes," said Nicola, refilling Edgar's wine glass. "When I taught remedial English in the East End, I had my students compose their own best- and worst-case scenarios for ten years later. The nightmares were fabulous: lush with fantastic fears, hilarious with misadventure. The pipedreams were all the same: a string of products and brand names. They read like mail-order catalogs. My students' visions of the Good Life were so vapid and depressing that you could have got the two assignments confused."

"Forty million pounds," Edgar marveled, "and it goes to Mr. and Mrs. Gandhi."

"We did need a place to live," said Nicola, "and in that department we overdid it. At first we'd no idea where we wanted to settle, so wherever we camped for a few weeks, well, we bought the house. But otherwise? We picked up a few new CDs, but my sound system worked fine. Henry bought me a new bicycle. We didn't want much else."

"If I were rich, I could do favors," said Edgar. "I could give Henry here a ticket to Barba to drag him away from Melissa Goldberg and start him in journalism."

"I wouldn't be grateful," said Henry. "I'd be cheesed off you didn't cough up better than one filthy ticket. *Economy! You'd think Moneybags could spring for First Class.*"

At last it arrived: what Edgar would do with loads of cash, enough to do nothing for the rest of his life.

Everest, schmeverest. He'd do nothing for the rest of his life.

"Okay, honestly?" Edgar admitted. "With a wad that thick, I'd ice down a case of Pete's Wicked Ale, order in whole roast pheasants from Dean & DeLuca, and spend from now to eternity watching TV."

Nicola laughed. "How much does it cost to be saved from yourself?"

"You're starting to twig," said Henry. "Why the money's a curse. Because you're lazy. Everyone's lazy. Types like Win Pyre think I got it easy. But it's bloody hard writing an article, to wordage, when you don't have to. The irony of this dosh making my life 'easy' is that everything I drag myself off my bum to do is harder than ever. Meanwhile, I can't buy friends, a reputation, a career, or my own wife's heart."

Despite his attempt to be flip, Henry choked a little on the last phrase, and tossed back a glass of that splendid cabernet as if it were cherry Coke.

CHAPTER 16
A Whiff of the Old Bastard Himself

BY THE TIME he careened home to Abrab Manor Edgar was pretty plastered. Not ready to call it a night, he slipped one of Barrington's R&B compilations into the CD player and poured himself a finger of bourbon that came out a tad generous, since the bottle slipped. In the atrium, he mounded the pillows rimming the pool into a nest. Spurning the modern fluorescent lights overhead, he lit the paraffin lanterns lining the walls in sconces. Edgar was kidding himself if he expected to plow through more than three paragraphs of *Beneath de Cabelos: Women of Cinzeiro.* Edgar could only think about one woman of Cinzeiro.

At least this low-print-run rip-off from an academic press—130 pages for $55!—gave his eyes something to rest on to keep the mosaic floor from spinning. As the print danced, Edgar was torn between imagining what he might do with forty million pounds and what he might do with Nicola Tremaine. In fact, as the lanterns threw deceptive shadows, the pillows lining the other side of the pool seemed to depress, as if Edgar's leggy fantasy had extended along the opposite rim.

Yet when Edgar next looked up, those pillows didn't look dented but mashed flat. The lantern flames wafted; the *vento* whistled through the skylight seams; wind flutes on the patio huffed in a mocking minor key.

Ridiculous. Reflections off the fountain, weird night, *definitely* too much cabernet. Edgar moved his highball glass sternly out of his own reach. He scowled intently into the monograph, even when he detected out of the corner of his eye that one of those pillows had been rearranged.

"Notice how slyly Henry co-opts you."

Edgar's eyes shot up. The space over the pillows had grown milky, opaque; he could no longer make out the pattern on the drapes behind them.

"It's not easy to get people to feel sorry for you because you've shouldered forty million quid," a teasingly familiar voice continued. "The lad's resourceful, don't you agree?"

The echo, and there was one, didn't seem to reverberate off the hall's arched ceiling so much as under the crown of Edgar's skull. But if this was merely the voice of his own thoughts, Edgar didn't pronounce his Ts so precisely, nor elide his Rs so aristocratically. While he often used slang like *C-note* or *ten-spot*, Edgar wasn't in the habit of pretentiously tossing off British colloquialisms like *quid*, even in his head.

"Though he can be a bit obvious," the baritone reverberated. "By plying the newcomer with wine and confidences, Henry protects his delectable wife from the stranger's depredations. Eddie puts a hand on her knee now, and he's betrayed his trusting and tragically well-heeled new chum."

The milky cloud over the pillows had solidified somewhat. If Edgar concentrated, he could detect the birds-of-paradise stitched on the vast cream kimono from the upstairs closet. Smoke rose above the ivory expanse, exuding the faint aroma of a fine Cuban cigar.

"So Henry's *obvious*," said Edgar, recalling Nicola's explanation for why a certain reporter preferred his Yankee employers. "Like Americans."

"Took offense at that, did you Eddie? Quite the patriot."

"Don't call me Eddie."

At last a face cohered above the kimono. It was a clever face, an animated face. Edgar couldn't quite pin it down, fix the image, its planes forever flickering like butterflies in sunlight. It was the kind of face that never photographed well; a snapshot froze the animation, stabbed the monarchs to pressboard. Still, even in the study's unflattering portrait, the face was big. *Big, big, big.*

"I've been meaning to speak to you about this hostility of yours."

"Why shouldn't I be hostile?" Edgar charged. "I'm supposed to be covering a terrorist insurgency, and all anybody in Barba wants to talk about is you."

"Never fear. You're right on top of the story, Eddie."

"How would you like it if I called you *Barry*?"

"A few have tried," said Barrington dryly, tapping his cigar ash into the fountain. "But names are queer; you can't call people anything you fancy. Some names won't stick."

Of course, Barrington was right. *Barry* simply wasn't Barrington's name.

"I was trying to warn you," said Barrington tolerantly. "You've your eye on Nicola. Respectable taste, if not especially original. But you're already falling into the friend-of-the-family trap."

"What was I supposed to say?" Edgar grumbled. "*No, I won't come to dinner, I don't want to get too pally with your husband in case I slip my hand up your dress?* Besides, you fell into the friend-of-the-family trap big-time. You didn't find it too restrictive."

"You and I aren't quite peas in a pod."

"So everyone seems intent on telling me."

"You'd feel bad!" Barrington scoffed. *"I can't roger Henry's wife, he's my friend!"*

"Typical, from what I've heard—" Edgar retrieved his highball glass—"that you'd think loyalty is for suckers."

Barrington tsked. "Lotta calories in that Noah's Mill, Eddie. Watch yourself."

"Fuck you." Glaring, Edgar drained the glass.

"Ooh," Barrington purred. "Scary."

"Scarier than you. You're not even real."

"I'd say that puts me at a considerable advantage."

It did.

"I did all the hard work for you, Eddie." Barrington piddled his fingers into the pool. "You should have seen those two lovebirds when they first came here. It was sickening. Never took their bloody eyes off each other. Always holding hands, if you can credit it. And they'd crafted some cutesy private goo-goo language that was unendurable."

"You took care of that."

"Entirely. Now she's ripe enough to drop to hand. You simply have to keep from tripping over those scruples of yours. Worse than marbles on the stairs."

"What makes you think I'm such a choir boy?"

"You've got it written all over your earnest, well-meaning face. *Gawd*," said Barrington. "And you're supposed to be my replacement."

"I've served my time as a degenerate!"

"At Yardley," Barrington reminded him. "You're thirty-seven. And still clinging to public school pranks to prove how naughty you are. Even then, you merely followed Falconer's lead. What have you done since? Snorted the odd line of coke. I couldn't name a solicitor who hasn't. You've not even taken a swing at a chap since you were twenty-nine. I know your sort. Your idea of chancing your arm is to skip out on your Visa minimum for a month and have to pay the late-fee. But when was the last time you did something *wrong*? You think you're irreverent, caustic—slick, downtown, and better-not-cross-me. In truth, you're an easily injured former fat boy looking for love." Barrington's mini-bio was breezy and paternalistically affectionate.

Cheeks stinging from Saddler's geeky portrait, Edgar tried a different tack. "If I haven't betrayed every friend within arm's reach or 'rogered' all their wives, what's so shameful about decency?"

"I wouldn't waste any shame on it. You used up your lifetime's quota of shame by the time you were fourteen. But as for decency? It's a matter of taste. Decency has never much engaged me."

"I don't see morality as an optional leisure activity, like water skiing."

"I'll let you in on a secret, Eddie." Barrington rolled into an intimate loll. "Since you're so keen on getting people to like you. Remember *inversion*? Benevolence of any description bellies up like a top-heavy bath toy. Righteousness flips to sanctimony, the good to the goody-goody. Virtue, Eddie, is *not very attractive*."

"Yeah, well neither are complete pricks."

Barrington's laughter boomed through the hall. "Life would be so much simpler if that were so."

Edgar dragged himself upright. The blood drained from his head, and the room swam. "You'll think I'm a stick in the mud, but it's four a.m. and I'm going to bed. I'd appreciate it if before you hit the sack, or whatever it is you people do who aren't really there, you blew out the lanterns. And stop using the pool as an ashtray, would you?"

"Eddie, Eddie," Barrington called at Edgar's back. "You're disappointing me."

"You've made that abundantly clear."

"Your curiosity," Barrington goaded. "Where'd it go?"

"At this point, I don't give two shits what happened to you," said Edgar defiantly.

"There are more wonders in this world than my whereabouts. Scratch beneath the surface, Eddie. Why are there rubber gloves in the tower?"

"Something warped, I assume," Edgar said aloofly. "None of my business."

"You need more business," Barrington cooed. "Why don't you talk to Verdade?"

"I've tried," said Edgar sullenly. "Can't get past the flacks."

"O Creme runs a small, grotty office. Anything you say—

anything salient—will get back to Tomás. I'd advise you to feed his ego, but that would be like plying the winner of a pie-eating contest with an apple tart."

While Edgar was reluctant to solicit a nonentity's counsel, an interview with Verdade would yield mucho brownie points at the Barking Rat, and it wouldn't do any harm to hear Saddler out. Warily, he asked, "What else can I do besides suck up to the guy?"

"Play on his insecurities instead," Barrington purred. "Tomás has more than a few. Announce that the *National Record* is planning to scrap its Barban bureau in a matter of weeks. You believe that your editor is making a tragic mistake, but it's out of your hands unless Verdade makes a convincing case that the SOB is still alive and kicking."

"So I threaten to pull up stakes. Why should Verdade get bent out of shape?"

"You're not quite clued up about journalism yet, are you, Eddie?" Barrington chided, as if trying to get Dorothy to notice her shoes. "*You have the power.* You create the world, Eddie, and that's what makes a journalist an artist. Verdade merely influences the course of events in Barba. You control events on paper, in comparison to which reality is mere bagatelle. You may seem to need Verdade for now, but verbose demagogues are common as dirt; you can always plug another petty tyrant into your copy instead. By contrast, Verdade desperately needs *you*. If the headlines don't imply that he's important—he isn't. Don't ever forget, Eddie, who calls the shots, who keeps the most dangerous arsenal at his disposal. *You*. And one of the most considerable of those weapons is your neglect."

"I don't leave call-backs," Edgar sorted out haltingly. "I say, I'll call him. That is, 'when I can find the time.' Then I—don't call him. For days."

"At which point, he'll ring you." Barrington beamed, as if one of his least promising students was finally catching up with the rest of the class. "And when you get your interview, ask Verdade—just for me. Why *hasn't* the SOB claimed a single atrocity since April? Has he gone soft on us, is he a poofter? While you're at it, you might ask yourself the same question."

Edgar was no longer having any of it. "Bye," he said coolly, marching from the atrium and up the stairs with as minimal an alcoholic weave as he could muster.

Edgar refused to feel nuts. He'd merely been visited by a Frankensteinian assemblage of walking, talking gossip. Still, Edgar wished Abrab's phantom weren't so fucking rude. *Former fat boy looking for love*, indeed. Edgar slammed the bedroom door. And locked it.

CHAPTER 17
Playing Hard to Get with a British Accent

WITH A PRETENSE of casualness whose theater was for his own benefit, Edgar rummaged through Barrington's closet the next morning. There it was, the ivory kimono embroidered with birds-of-paradise, roughly where he remembered the garment hanging before. Yet the satin was crumpled. When Edgar brushed an ashy smudge on the front panel, the gray flecks came off easily, as if fresh.

Edgar snorted, and chose a shirt. He'd taken to pinching Barrington's ludicrous wardrobe with regularity. The oversize shirts had a pleasantly parodic, Charlie Chaplin flap about them; Nicola could wear them as dresses. Just then the image came unbidden, Nicola sidling to the round, black bath in this smashing rayon print, the short sleeves reaching her tiny wrists. "Please, Bear," he implored aloud. "Don't torture me."

No response. His lordship must sleep during the day. Edgar resorted to his own jeans. Likewise he was obliged to leave the magnificent black leather riding boots, natty wingtips, and luminous Italian cordovans where they lay. Alas, they were size-fourteen, reminding Edgar yet again that he couldn't fill Barrington's shoes.

Downstairs, he found the lanterns extinguished, the paraffin depleted but not spent. The pillows were scattered, on both sides of the pool. Despite the circulation of the fountain, in patches the water had developed a filthy skim.

"Pig," Edgar muttered, and took his coffee up to the study to immerse himself once again in Barban politics.

A dozen *national self-determinations* later he couldn't help but wonder whether this journo gig was so far proving any more stimulating than corporate law. Anyway, you could bet none of those lightweights at the Rat bothered to slog through the likes of Ansel P. Henwood. Clearly you could wing this beat by memorizing the last five most recent SOB atrocities and the names of a few victims. But while rote, up-to-date recitation seemed to pass for insight with this crowd, Edgar was determined to distinguish himself as a cut above. As he underlined another turgid passage about rates of legal versus illegal Barban immigration, the word *earnest* came tauntingly to mind.

In truth, he was dodging a certain phone call. Anything to do with O Creme de Barbear made him anxious, tempted to procrastinate. Though he didn't like to think of himself as prim and moralistic, much less violence-averse, there was something tainted about these SOB shills, something unsavory that felt, irrationally, contagious.

Fidgeting, he forced himself to dial. He tried to sound hurried, perfunctory and abrupt, which wasn't a strain. His eagerness to get off the phone with the haughty, self-impressed twit who ran interference for Tomás Verdade was genuine enough.

"No, I'd really prefer he didn't ring back later," Edgar concluded, clipping his consonants crisply. "Things are moving fast on this end, and I may have to be closing down the entire bureau *tout de suite.* It's possible that the idea for this interview is quite past its sell-by. With no bombs bursting in air for months, your Mr. Verdade is passé. The SOB has turned out rather a damp squib, I'm afraid. Let's leave it that I'll get back to him, shall we?" Edgar hung up first.

And laughed. The *bureau*—what "bureau"? And where'd he pick up "damp squib"? Brit-speak. That's when Edgar realized that he'd conducted the whole exchange in an *Earl Grey* accent.

As a reward for getting that distasteful task dispatched, Edgar took a break from Henwood, tucked his laptop under his arm, and scooted up the circular staircase to the tower.

Seated at the schoolboy desk, as ever he was unnervingly nagged by the hotel stationery stacked on its corner, as well as by the curious pipe contraption and rubber gloves lurking in the drawers. Attempting to turn a blind eye to this detritus of a bygone resident's life, he began another ritual letter to Angela that would never be posted. Indeed, "Dear Angela" had already evolved into a "Dear Diary" format, and was really just an excuse for teaching himself to touch-type. Hunt-and-peck seemed unprofessional, and Edgar was attached to a black-and-white film noir vision of a hot story coming in, his fingers flying at the keyboard in a blurred, blind fury.

It was magic. The flak had left messages, eight of them, in a supercilious voice that grew whiny, then pleading, at length obsequious. By the last message the silken-toned Verdade himself called, saying that he was "at the *National Record*'s disposal." Maybe Saddler was right, that for a journalist open arms were not nearly so effective as a turned back. Edgar phoned his editor with the good news.

Guy answered with a gruff, get-to-the-point, "Wallasek," that always made Edgar feel like a pest.

"Guy, Kellogg here. Listen, a great opportunity's come up. I've got Tomás Verdade to agree to an interview."

"So?" said Wallasek flatly. (The editor had grown chilly since his probationary stringer filed the Saddler piece, which had insufficiently inflated the beloved Barrington's mystique. *Whatever happened to my reporter,* Wallasek had snarled in their last call, *it wasn't ordinary.*)

"I hear tell it can be as hard to get at Verdade as J. D. Salinger," Edgar spieled, having expected the profile to sell itself. "Most hacks here have rarely got a foot in his door. Even Saddler." *Christ,* he thought, *I'm turning into one more sycophantic schmuck.*

"You know why you can't usually get at him?" Wallasek

returned. "Because he's giving other *interviews*. Which translates into hundreds of features on Verdade already."

"Maybe in *Le Monde*," Edgar argued. "The *Record* hasn't run a profile for over a year. I figured this was the time to make my move. With the SOB dormant, he's less in demand."

"He's available because there's no peg," said Wallasek impatiently. "Besides, on paper Verdade is a wet noodle. It's on camera that he's spellbinding. Gross, maybe, but when he ogles soulfully into the lens, women wet themselves. In print, he's *bor-ring*."

"Leave it to me. I've read some of those interviews. Nobody challenges the guy. They let him get away with murder—literally. I'm thinking, tough questions, hard-hitting, right? Don't let him spout propaganda, weasel out from under. Force him to face what the SOB campaign has cost innocent people. Make him uncomfortable."

"Good luck!" Wallasek jeered. "I'll look at what you come up with, but no promises. And Kellogg? Don't burn your bridges."

"How's that?"

"Some incident goes down, you're gonna need that man to talk to you—when there *is* a peg. You make him mad, you're not gonna get another appointment. In which case, I would be personally put out."

Ah. Hanging up, Edgar grasped why all the interviews he'd dug up on the Internet had been so infuriatingly polite. Never mind Verdade's gate-keeping for the SOB. For a correspondent's purposes, Verdade controlled an even more vital resource: access to himself. Despite Saddler's alluring prattle about who-really-needs-whom and how journalists "have the power," no reporter could competently cover Barba without Verdade, which meant tiptoeing in print to keep O Creme de Barbear's president on-side. So Edgar was permanently snookered. He wanted to excoriate the guy, but to preserve a capacity to excoriate him in the future Edgar was obliged to make nice.

Grabbing his microcassette recorder, Edgar bustled out the door, wondering what it would take for Wallasek to be glad to hear from him. He lunged into the Saab, tuned the radio to the World Service, and prayed desperately that something, somewhere, would blow up.

CHAPTER 18
Couscous and Balaclava

THE HEADQUARTERS OF O Creme de Barbear was located in the heart of Terra do Cão (literally, "Dog Land") above the Creamie gift shop on the ground floor, into whose gaily bunted window Edgar peered before heading for the upstairs' side entrance. He could see why Roland Ordway was a regular customer. Any healthily warped young lad would be tempted by "I'm an SOB" gimme caps, ceramic ashtrays brightly glazed with bullets and detonators, and those classy gold AK-47 tie pins like the one the barman wore at the Rat. But Edgar wasn't about to interview *o presidente* clutching a Tomás Verdade coffee mug.

The door to headquarters was heavily fortified, with a mirror instead of a window—probably two-way. Edgar buzzed, waving at the closed-circuit camera. The intercom crackled with static, but no one spoke. Edgar mobilized the skeletal Portuguese he'd been practicing in the car: *entrevista*, *jornalista*.

After a full five minutes, the door creaked open. A massive plug of flesh stopped up the whole stairwell. Edgar shit-eatingly reiterated his business—*Entrevista! Jornalista!* But Bebê Serio's face remained stolidly blank while the vibrations in his ear were transported to his brain one letter at a time by carrier pigeon. Finally the paramilitary Pillsbury Doughboy grunted, "You go," and jerked his head toward the stairs.

The upstairs office was ostentatiously proletarian. Curling linoleum was patterned with a rusty spatter, as if pulled up from an inner-city emergency room. Aluminum baseboards bent off the wall. Merciless fluorescent tubes recalled police stations, and

Edgar's own juvenile indiscretions. One desk leg rested on painstakingly folded cardboard, while metal straight-backs were upholstered in diarrheal vinyl; the seat Edgar took was ripped. As Bebê Serio stood guard with menacing idiocy, Edgar's thigh sweat and the rip made his leg itch. He felt dirty, out of his element.

As in the Barking Rat, the walls were thumbtacked with potato-heads in balaclavas blithely poking assault rifles about, as if no one had ever warned them that those things could hurt somebody. Over the desk hung a batik of the Barban flag, an invention of the last five years: local patriots had reversed the red and green panels of the Portuguese flag, and replaced the crest with the noble *pera peluda*. Its hairy tendrils swept to the right, as if the fruit withstood an easterly gale.

On the opposite wall splayed a map of Iberia. Gazing into the Atlantic as if still searching for returning ships from the Age of Discovery, Portugal formed the aquiline profile of a patriarch, over which Spain coifed a leonine head of hair. Lisbon nestled into the nostril, O Porto dented the brow, and the Barban peninsula trailed off the chin like a wispy beard. Now that Edgar had seen the country as a face, he couldn't stop seeing it, and as time ticked on the severe-looking profile made Edgar feel watched.

"*Senhor* Kellogg? João Pacheco, *Presidente* Verdade's press officer." A scrawny tough in a black turtleneck had swept in from the back room after *forty-five minutes* to shake Edgar's hand. Fucking prima donnas. The smarm had been back there the whole time. "I am sorry that *o presidente* is delayed on important party business, *esta bem*? Of course, we are most grateful to your newspaper for helping us spread the word of our struggle. You like coffee?"

"*Não, obrigado.*" Edgar instantly regretted the Portuguese. A gesture of goodwill in touristy circumstances, here it sounded fawning. What he really wanted to say was *get your hands off me.* After slapping Edgar's shoulder, the flack had left his hand there, squeezing the jacket sleeve in a gesture of oozy Latinate camaraderie.

"O Creme has many supporters in your country," said João, perching on the desk. "And many American journalists take up the cause of our people. You see *Presidente* Verdade in February's *Vanity Fair*?" He grinned.

"I don't read *Vanity Fair*," said Edgar stonily.

"*O presidente* has many letters and visitors from America. Some ladies, they propose marriage! Of course, Tomás is only married to our struggle. One American lady now writes a book. A bigo—what is this word?"

"An *authorized biography*. Oh, it's sure to sell. Ask Oliver Stone: Americans are suckers for serial killers."

João stiffened. But Edgar preferred João's fish-eyed glare to his fellow-freedom-fighter buddy-buddyism. The operative assumption when you walked into this office obviously ran that you were in these scumbags' pocket. Besides, if they clapped your shoulder and offered you coffee, and their president took time from his busy schedule to pour out his heart, and then you went off and wrote nasty, ungrateful things about their hardworking terrorist friends, why, you had clearly gained entrance to this inner sanctum and inveigled yourself into the confidence of their leadership under false pretenses.

Skipping up the stairs, at last Verdade burst in the office door, followed by a chunky goon who was puffing to keep up. Verdade was an energetic man, and seemed in better shape than most Portuguese, their diet greasy, their schedule stuporous with siestas. "Edgar, how very good to meet you!" He pumped Edgar's hand, though refrained from apologizing for being over an hour late. "Please sit down, Edgar. Fernando," he said to the goon. *"Serio esta aqui, sim?"*

The musclebound bodyguard eyed Edgar up and down before leaving; presumably the reporter didn't look like much of a threat. Edgar was stung.

"E tu, João," added the avuncular president to his press officer.

"Edgar and I have much to talk about. Please have your dinner."

João muttered something surly in Portuguese, flicking his eyes at Edgar.

Verdade chuckled. "I'm not so concerned," he said in English. "Edgar has much to learn, as I have much to learn about him. That is why we spend time together."

So thug #2 departed as well, leaving Bebê Serio standing propped against the wall. Unblinking, immobile, and expressionless, he no more constituted a third party than a cigar-store Indian.

Verdade glided into the desk chair while Edgar tested the level on his recorder. Boy, this guy was a piece of work. He was forty or so but well-kept; thick black hair swept back from his brow. The push-broom mustache was distinguished, but his chin was clean-shaven. His garb struck a calculated compromise of social class: he wore a tie and navy suit trousers, but a workingman's windbreaker over the crisp white shirt. Verdade's posture was straight though not stiff, and for a renowned orator he was surprisingly soft-spoken. His enormous brown eyes always looked slightly pained. Exuding a reserve, even urbanity, he'd earned a doctorate in political science from Harvard and his English was superb.

What made this character oily, then, wasn't so much style as intent. He aimed below the belt. Verdade's appeal—even to men—was fundamentally sexual. Those huge tawny eyes fixed a TV camera with seductive restraint, as if the secrets he kept were burdensome to him and he yearned to confess. By combining his own phrase-book Portuguese and the girls' patchily recalled school English, Edgar had tried to draw out numerous grocery checkout clerks in Cinzeiro, several of whom professed to find Verdade's support for the SOB offensive and his obsession with an independent Barba a big snore. Yet every local woman Edgar had met so far was dying to be the one lucky *senhora* to whom Verdade could finally, fully bare his breast.

"You must be very tired, Edgar," said Verdade, "of colleagues warning you how hard it will be to follow in Mr. Saddler's footsteps."

"Are you warning me, too?"

"I doubt you will find it so difficult. You strike me as a capable young man. Mr. Saddler—" He paused. "There are those who know more than they say. Others say more than they know. Your predecessor impressed me as the latter. In poker, how do you say? A bluffer."

The *how do you say?* seemed an affectation; a Harvard PhD knew the word without having to grope. Likewise, Verdade laid on the accent a little thick.

"You must be pretty tired of my first question yourself," Edgar ventured. "But I have to ask it. Is O Creme merely a flag of convenience for the SOB?"

"O Creme de Barbear is a legal political party," Verdade asserted, looking hurt that Edgar would assume anything unseemly about his brethren. "Our representatives sit on Cinzeiro's city council, and they are democratically elected. We command a sufficient mandate to also have numerous representatives in a regional assembly, but Barba doesn't have one—much to my despair. Nor of course do we have the government of our own that my people ache for. A few of my supporters believe that I myself might assume the presidency of our new country, though of course," he demurred, "I would only accept the honor of such an office were it awarded by the ballot box."

Edgar couldn't say he hadn't been warned. Ask Verdade a direct question, get back unruffled, perfectly pat, and exquisitely evasive twaddle. "Are you telling me that O Creme has no connection to the SOB?"

"O Creme and Os Soldados Ousados de Barba share the common aim of an independent Barban state. My constituency is most thankful for the sacrifice that SOB volunteers have made for their country."

"Seems to me that it's mostly SOB victims who've sacrificed for your country. The terrorists have sacrificed zip."

"Terrorist," said Verdade, "is merely an ugly label. It is what you call soldiers whom you do not like, who oppose you. It is a depersonalizing term, and I avoid it."

"I can see why," said Edgar. "Since it's what we call people who use innocent civilians for wallpaper."

"Noncombatants killed in other wars are usually guilty of something?" Verdade countered calmly. "Deserve their fate? Because I cannot cite a war that has had no civilian casualties, or in which every individual death was just. War contemplates a larger justice."

Edgar made one more approach, like a plane in bad weather that was running out of fuel. "So you have nothing to do with the SOB. Journalists who ask you for statements about SOB strategy are barking up the wrong tree. Where'd they get that idea?"

"O Creme is a legal political party," Verdade repeated fluidly. But his eyes glittered, and one corner of his mouth curled ever so slightly. The bastard did everything but wink. He wanted it both ways. And got it.

"So if I asked you to arrange for me to interview an SOB 'volunteer,' even with his anonymity guaranteed, you'd insist that you couldn't do it."

"If you're intent on such a mission, you should track down your colleague Mr. Saddler, who claimed excellent connections with so-called *terrorists*. Myself," said Verdade, looking Edgar unflinchingly in the eye, "I can honestly say that I do not wittingly know a single member of the SOB."

Incredible. If he was lying, the man was sociopathic.

"But you do support SOB methods?" Edgar pressed.

"Each casualty of this conflict has filled me with a powerful and very personal grief. I deeply regret any loss of life that has resulted from our fight for freedom. Yet the solution must be to resolve the core political problem itself, much as a doctor must cure the disease and not simply treat the symptoms."

Stagily (this was on tape), Edgar scribbled on his pad. "So I'll record your answer as *yes*." Brooking no argument, he plowed on. "Next, you must be aware that a lot of people regard your party's obsession with stemming North African immigration—in fact, I gather that you plan, on 'liberation,' to send most of them back—that tolerantly-minded onlookers regard this platform as racist?"

"Under international law—" Verdade leaned back with his hands clasped behind his head—"one legitimate reason to go to war is to defend your borders. Look at Kuwait, whose invasion by Iraqi forces was at least the ostensible reason for the Gulf War. We'll leave aside America's protection of oil interests in the region; the formal pretext for taking up arms was the violation of a sovereign domain by another state. The wholesale invasion of Barba by illegal Muslim immigrants is little different from the attack of a foreign army. It's increasingly difficult to find a traditional *carne de porco à alentejana* or *torta de uvas peludas* in Cinzeiro. Yet local restaurants serve plenty of couscous and balaclava—"

Edgar laughed. "Sorry. I think you mean baklava."

For the first time in the interview, Verdade looked rattled. "Yes, of course." He blushed. "As I was saying, our country is living proof that you needn't wear a uniform to usurp territory—"

"That's not what I asked. To repeat—"

"Bear with me, Edgar," Verdade overrode, reasserting paternal authority. "At current rates of immigration, Muslims will constitute a majority of the Barban population within ten years. In that instance, because we are a democratic country, these new arrivals could nudge indigenous Barbans out of office and vote their own people in. They could take responsibility for immigration enforcement—or lack of it. The more powerful and numerous our North African visitors, the more readily they can assist their friends and family in occupying my nation."

"But the Lisbon government—"

"Is doing *nada*. Most of our uninvited southern guests do not make it as far north as Lisboa, and so don't take Lisboan jobs. Barba has a distinct and distinguished history that by itself calls out for nationhood. We are a separate 'people' entitled to self-determination under the UN charter. Yet this unchecked African tide raises the stakes. Your own country may be on its way to becoming majority Spanish-speaking. Once that, yes, racial ratio inverts, will the congressmen this new majority elects—other Spanish-speakers, you can be sure—will they limit immigration from Mexico? Couldn't these congressmen, if they wished, change your national language from English to Spanish? And if you don't want this to happen, does that make you a racist?"

"We don't have a national language," said Edgar, irritated because he saw Verdade's point.

"In practice, you do—and in practice it is being overthrown. You see, I am sympathetic with white Americans, though I myself am Latino. Once Portuguese explorers set out to master the globe. Were we to do so now, armed with millions of fertile women, your country could justifiably repel our advances, even if we came as 'immigrants' and not as soldiers."

"But this paranoia about Muslims, as if they're mongrel hordes—it doesn't sound good, Mr. Verdade. Like, you've got to keep your bloodlines pure. What's the difference between O Creme and the Michigan Militia, the National Front, the BNP, or neo-Nazis?"

Verdade shook his head sorrowfully. "In the United States, it's never considered racist to protect the ethnic integrity of minorities, is it? Your universities now have special departments for African-American, or Native-American studies—"

"New college courses are a far cry from nerve gas on subways!"

Verdade was accustomed to shrill interruptions, and continued undeterred. "Even Jews, since you called me a 'Nazi,' are distressed that their race is dwindling. To counteract low birthrates, intermarriage, and secularization, observing Jews are campaigning to keep their culture alive, to raise more Jews as Jews. As well they should. Any people's most primitive drive is to endure. Israel has understandably refrained from fully enfranchising the West Bank, lest Jews be outnumbered by Palestinians in a conceptually Jewish state. Must indigenous Barbans wait to become a minority in their own country before they can justifiably defend their Catholic culture? Do majorities have no rights? Must a heritage be endangered before we come to its aid? Must we be prevented from taking action until it's too late?"

Verdade's rhythmic rhetorical questions were mesmerizing. Locked in the politician's fervid gaze, Edgar found the man's arguments unsettlingly sensible. He had to shake himself, to force himself to recall photos from that grisly dime-store paperback, *Forced Landing!*—of the unsuspecting passengers of BA-321, including Henry's family: arms missing, faces frozen in bewilderment, clothing snagged on the branches of trees.

"I can't help but find it ironic that you identify with Jews," said Edgar, paging his notes. "Especially since you describe Barba's history as so 'distinguished.' Oh, and 'distinctive,' which it is, though the Poles give you a run for your money. Portugal proper has a patchy record on the Semitic front. But Barba's is appalling!"

Victoriously, Edgar found the right page. "During the Spanish Inquisition, Ferdinand and Isabella expelled sixty thousand Jews to Portugal, but the hapless handful that headed for Barba were all sent back. To Torquemada! During the Portuguese Inquisition, even more enthusiastic than Spain's if that's possible, fifteen hundred Jews were garroted or burned at the stake, a full third of them in Barba. This province persecuted its Jews with such industry that for the duration of the seventeenth century Barbans shook off their stereotype as lazy. During World War Two, despite Salazar's refusal to accept Jews fleeing Hitler into Portugal, a sympathetic consul general in Bordeaux issued a thousand Portuguese visas to Jews; the three-hundred-some who ended up in Barba were all hunted down and turned in. To *Nazis*. Oh, and as for Africans, Barba did 'distinguish' itself in the slave trade, by selling and shipping millions of African captives to Brazil. Seems to me that one of the central indigenous traditions you're so all-fired keen to preserve is bigotry."

Edgar was breathing hard. He glanced edgily at Bebê Serio, who had taken one giant step forward from the wall as if playing Simon Says. With his Tarzan English ("You go"), Serio couldn't have been offended by Edgar's history lesson, though he mustn't have cared for Edgar's tone.

Yet Verdade's expression was kindly. "You've been doing your homework, Edgar. I'm pleased the *National Record* has at last hired a reporter who's so diligent."

Though he no more relished Verdade's tag of *diligent* than Barrington's scornful stamp of *earnest*, Edgar wasn't finished. "And I've been doing some cross-checking between your sympathizers' literature and the work of nonpartisan historians. Creams claim that a ragtag army led by Duarte o Estupendo rebuffed the legions of the Roman Empire. In truth, the Romans never invaded Barba. They stopped short in Algarve, which is one reason civic development was retarded here. In fact, classical historians believe the very word *Barba* isn't derived from the Middle English meaning 'beard,' since accurate maps of Portugal on which the peninsula appears beard-like weren't drafted when the region's name first appears. Instead it's probably rooted in the Latin *balbus*, meaning 'stammering.' Romans thought foreigners talked funny. Later *balbus* gave rise to *barbarian*, which specifically meant," Edgar read from his notes, "*pertaining to those outside the Roman Empire—*"

"I'm so sorry to interrupt *your* interview of *me*," Verdade intervened. "But our detractors are attached to the Latin derivation of *Barba* because the word *barbarian*, conveniently, means a great deal else."

"Yeah," said Edgar, running his finger across the pad, "*uncivilized, uncultured.* Later, *savage, rude, cruel,* and *inhuman*—OED. Or should I say, QED?"

"You see? In Barba, even etymology is political." Verdade seemed amused.

"Hey, if the shoe fits." Edgar glared.

"But I interrupted!" Verdade apologized facetiously, nodding at Edgar's fat notes.

"Napoleon, same story." This was overkill, but a guy who shoveled shit at everyone else deserved a few turds tossed in his own yard. "Your proponents maintain that Teodósso o Terrível overcame French troops and Napoleon turned tail. But according to Bonaparte's diaries, he only set foot in Barba once. He found the land barren, the people one evolutionary inch from sand fleas, and *o vento insano* 'an insufferable affliction.' The emperor never even tried to annex this peninsula. I found the same disparity in accounts of the reign of Salazar: Creamies boast that O Creme itself began as an underground resistance to Salazar's ruthless dictatorship. But I can't find a trace of this secret organization outside books with your people's fingerprints on them. To the contrary, Cinzeiro city councilors had an ongoing competition over who could rat out the highest number of their friends to the Gestapo-trained national police force.

"Mr. Verdade—or can I call you Tom? Even the *Gulf Stream* avoids this place! If SOB thugs would stop bombing the bejesus out of strangers, I bet you'd win Barba independence in a heartbeat. Because nobody wants it! In fact, you should find North African immigration flattering. You've finally found someone else who wants to live here. The only reason Lisbon hangs on to this peninsula is that they don't want to cave to terrorist blackmail in front of the rest of the world, it's too humiliating. But they sure don't keep it for selfish reasons. The province is an economic liability. It sucks up more social welfare than any other region of the country. It produces nothing but fruit it can't export and cheap souvenir ashtrays. Hell, even in the Age of Discovery Barba was notorious for constructing ships that sank. I'm sorry if I sound insulting, but people are being murdered over your patriotism, and as far as I can tell the 'culture' you're protecting comes down to bitter beer and bad wind—neither of which strikes me as endangered."

Verdade had smiled patiently through this monologue as if listening to a passionate if misguided student whose thesis was cockeyed but brassy.

"No country's record," he began, "is spotless. Your United States—"

"Please let's not get into the Indians," Edgar cut him off. "Or Vietnam, or slavery, or police brutality in Los Angeles, okay? You just said yourself that everyone's dirty. So a pot has to be able to call the kettle black, or we all surrender the right to make moral judgments of anyone, anywhere, ever."

"In a polarized society, there are no 'nonpartisan historians,'" Verdade regrouped. "You have been reading the slander of revisionists. Barbans have long been treated as second-class citizens in Portugal. We're dismissed as stupid and, as you noted yourself, shiftless. Well, we shall see how stupid, how shiftless. I believe O Creme's drive for freedom demonstrates both acuity and enterprise. Yet many northern Portuguese seek to discredit my people. Smear campaigns come and go, and I would expect an intelligent man like yourself to recognize propaganda for what it is. To accept it at face value is intellectually torpid, as well as disrespectful of the fallen heroes who have died for the glory of Barba."

"You don't seem too respectful of the foreigners who've died for the glory of Barba. Though you could hardly call them *volunteers.*"

"War is hell," Verdade returned flippantly. "Have many Americans lost sleep over the hundred thousand Iraqi civilians killed—or murdered, to use your word—in the Gulf War? Any liberty has its price. Sometimes you pay that price yourself; sometimes others pay it for you."

Drooping from exhaustion, Edgar couldn't be bothered to take issue with that hundred-thousand-casualty figure—informed estimates ran more like two thousand—which had been bandied about by the American left wing often enough to substantiate that sheer repetition could make anything true. Dolefully, he noted that he hadn't got halfway through his list of questions. "Of course the Cream and the SOB are totally separate," he resumed with fatigued sardonicism. "But any theories as to why the SOB has lain low since April?"

"Oh, I might hypothesize that Os Soldados are providing O Creme a window—an unofficial ceasefire, if you will—to pursue a political resolution with Lisboa. Perhaps this is a test, to see if we might win our freedom through peaceful means."

"Why couldn't you negotiate a settlement without any violence at all?"

"I fear that, as ever, diplomacy is only effective—" Verdade shot a wry glance at Bebê Serio—"if backed by a credible threat of physical force. Would you be conducting this interview, Edgar, if the SOB were a meek and unsung political movement in a part of Europe you'd never heard of? Before the rise of the SOB, the Cinzeiro city council sent a delegation to the Lisboan government to address our concerns about unchecked immigration and to demand stricter border controls on the southern coast. The delegation was ignored. We could not even secure an appointment with a minister, after coming so far with hats in hand. Now, Edgar, if

I phone?" Verdade smiled. "I am assured of cabinet-level contact in a matter of minutes."

By the time Edgar slumped into the Turbo's bucket seat, he was weary enough that his mind had loosened into a quirky, associative freefall. He sat stupefied for a moment, staring at the dashboard. *Saab.* The *Sobs.* The SOB. Barrington was famously sloppy, but only apropos of his obligations to other people. In matters of style, his personal effects, Abrab Manor betrayed the man as meticulous. The homonym Sob-Saab wouldn't be an inadvertent coincidence but a droll allusion.

To confirm as much, Edgar rifled the papers in the glove compartment to check when the car had been purchased. Oddly, Barrington had bought his coupe shortly after assignment to Barba, and two months previous to the first atrocity claimed by the SOB, when existence of the organization initially emerged. SOB. Hmm.

On arrival back home, Edgar was wiped out, but his brain revved into overdrive. Had he got Verdade to admit anything, to stick his foot in it once besides that telling malapropism "balaclava"? Damn, Edgar had meant to press the guy on the fact that independence didn't even have majority support in Barba itself. But then, after swallowing so much Creamie bilge, Edgar could cough up the answer himself: *My people are waking from a great sleep, and shaking off the apathy of oppression takes time* . . . That old Marxist dodge of false consciousness.

Restlessly, Edgar reached for the study phone.

"Nicola? . . . Yeah, it went fine. I guess. Gotta give the guy this. He may be an unprincipled sack of shit, but he's fucking good at his job. Hardly a hiccough. In fact, I hate to admit it, but I kinda liked the son of a bitch. He's quick, he's articulate, and he's dangerously convincing. It's a bitch to catch him out. But listen, that's not why I called. Just wanted to ask you one question. *What's Barrington's middle name?*"

Nicola laughed. "Now I know you're hooked. What was the second name of your public school idol?"

"Gimme a break. That interview lasted forever, and I'm shot. You know it, or not?"

"Why—Owen, I think. Yes. Owen."

Edgar assured her they'd get together soon, and hung up. *Barrington Owen Saddler*. BOS. Jesus.

CHAPTER 19
Saab Stories

BARRINGTON HAD DRESSED for dinner. Having stormed downstairs, Edgar found the baron of Abrab Manor in a stylishly retro cutaway and white tie sipping pink gin in the sunken living room, where he'd expropriated the emerald velveteen wingchair. His legs were crossed, black cordovans shined for the occasion, elbows resting regally on the scrolled arms.

"Okay, lardass," Edgar barked. "Time to come clean."

Barrington peered over his paper-thin martini glass. "Whatever are you on about?"

"Saab-as-in-car, Sob-as-in-'freedom fighter.' S-O-B is your own initials in reverse. I don't find much Dickensian coincidence in real life."

"My dear boy. Perhaps I would buy a *Saab* Turbo tongue-in-cheek. But the purchase date's too early. As for the initials, the birth of Barrington O. Saddler precedes SOB terrorism by decades."

"That's exactly the point. You could only have arranged these dopey, self-congratulatory little in-jokes if you were in on the formation of the outfit from the ground up. I'm sure commanding your own private army's a hoot. But I've seen enough pictures—of dismembered victims, stricken mothers, orphaned kids . . ."

Barrington despaired, "All those manly press-ups every morning, and still another member of the hankie set."

"Saddler," Edgar challenged, arms akimbo. "Are you a terrorist?"

Barrington waved his free hand modestly over his person. "Do I look like one?"

"Meaning your head isn't stuffed in a sock and you're not waving an Uzi? I'm not sure I know what a real terrorist looks like. Maybe outside of posters they wear tuxes and mix martinis. You'll have to tell me."

"Eddie, I don't *have* to tell you anything," Barrington exhaled wearily. "Heavens, I'd hoped you'd show more get-up-and-go."

"Fine, there's some dispute about the nuances of the term 'terrorist,' according to your pal Tommy Truthful. Bottom line, then. You ever murder anybody, Saddler? Even indirectly, by making *arrangements*. Are you a killer?"

Barrington smiled genially. "Eddie, you've the distinction of being the first to ask me such a thing. Have you ever been grilled point-blank on whether you're a murderer? Gives a chap pause. The mind roils with withering digs and unreturned phone messages—the thousand myriad ways in which we slay one another every day."

"I knew it," Edgar declared with disgust. "You and Verdade are kissing cousins."

"Well, if you insist on being pedantic," said Barrington distastefully, "no."

"No, what?"

"Perhaps I misinterpreted your frustration, but I gathered you craved a simple answer to a direct question—which the wily Tomás may never have provided in his life. I picture him as a small boy, responding to his mother's query about whether he cut down the cherry tree with a three-page treatise on modern innovations in horticulture. Although here, of course, it would be a *pera peluda* tree. In which case any boy who cut one down should be given a medal."

Edgar locked eyes with his landlord. Barrington appeared to have no trouble meeting Edgar's gaze, though he did seem bored by the exercise.

"No-you've-never-killed-anyone," Edgar spelled out distinctly.

"No-you've-never-blown-anyone-up. No-you've-not-helped-some-other-lowlife-blow-anyone-up."

"No, no, and no," Barrington recited, making a face. "Satisfied?"

Edgar had no cause to believe the man. Still, the evidence for the prosecution was scant.

"Scout's honor?" Edgar asked in a squeezed voice.

Barrington crooked his little finger. "Pinkie swear."

Edgar sank onto the ottoman. He was relieved.

Which surprised him. There sat Cinzeiro's social darling, everything that Edgar was not. What a vindication, should Saddler have proved a homicidal brute. So Edgar wasn't a laugh riot at parties? At least he wasn't pond scum. Maybe Dudley Do-Right rectitude was indeed a turn-off, and maybe he cherished his own delinquent side, but he drew the line at seriously bad shit. Had Barrington been a killer, they could never be friends.

"Then what's with the Saab-Sob stuff?" asked Edgar uncertainly. "The initials?"

"Must I lead you by the hand like a child?" Barrington parted with his drink for emphasis, sliding the glass onto the trunk. "I needn't have dropped any crumbs behind, you know. That was sportsmanlike on my part. Show some initiative on yours."

"What, like you?" Edgar muttered, rising to toss some logs on cold coals. "You've got squat to do all day. You could've at least built a fire."

"What for? No one ever calls by. In fact, unless I've been napping inopportunely, you haven't got laid since you arrived."

"Your dyke friend at the *Times* claims you don't care about sex."

"Shagging itself? Perhaps not. But then, the same might be said of ingestion, *itself.* I adore the way Nicola arranges whatnots on a plate, and the little *pop* of caviar eggs between my teeth. But I'm not fussed about their travel down my gullet, or about the juices of digestion. Most pleasures are window-dressing, Eddie, and that goes doubly for the delights of love. Yet we were talking about you, my boy. And doesn't your sort set a great deal of store by the old in-out?"

"What's 'my sort'?" asked Edgar, painstakingly constructing a teepee of kindling.

"You laddish chaps. Football. Mafia films. Hairy-pear beer."

"Damned if I understand why everyone thinks you're so hail-fellow-well-met when all you do is give people a hard time," Edgar grumbled, poking at a ball of damp newspaper. Its flame trembled to an unpromising purple.

"I'm chuffed you thought I was a proper terrorist. Flattering, really."

"That skank Hulbert said you were too lazy to be a terrorist. Had a ring of truth to it. Though nobody's described you as too benign." The teepee collapsed; the flame expired.

"For God's sake, man, must you do everything like a Girl Guide?" Barrington lumbered to a stand, treating himself to the rest of his gin as reward for his effort. He craned for a bottle from the bar, and splashed it into the fireplace. When he tossed a match, the fire ignited with a small explosion.

"That's my Noah's Mill!" Edgar wailed, leaping back. "Hundred proof!"

"*My* Noah's Mill is wasted on you—trickling dribs, glancing furtively about as if someone is watching—"

"Apparently, someone *is*," said Edgar hotly.

"You just don't get it, do you Eddie? Take the scullery. I find *rice cakes*. Fat-free cheese food and Weight Watchers lasagna. And you want to be a Great Character."

"Great as in estimable, not great as in fat."

"Best you gained a few stone." Barrington wiggled his eyebrows. "Anything to start you thinking on a *larger scale*."

"Enough already," Edgar snapped, tired of being taunted. "I

endured a girlfriend for two years who thought being enigmatic was sexy."

"*You* thought it was sexy, that was the whole problem. Think, Eddie," Barrington prodded. "You pick up clues, only to toss them to the carpet. Why *is* the SOB an inversion of my initials?"

"You said you never killed anybody. I'm doing you the courtesy of taking your word for it. In return, I don't expect to be trashed for my credulity." Edgar uncapped a warm Choque to spite his host.

"How did you find Verdade?" Barrington inquired conversationally.

"Smooth operator," said Edgar tersely.

"Is he a liar?"

"He's the type who gets seduced by his own rhetoric. Buys his own shtick. I doubt he'd know the truth if it bit him on the ass."

"He's an opportunist," Barrington provided. "But opportunists require opportunities."

Edgar kneaded his temples, closing his eyes to banish this officious poltergeist, who once conjured came and went as he pleased. Maybe a little imagination was a dangerous thing. Apparently just because you could think someone up didn't mean you could think him away again. Edgar squeezed his eyes and visualized a vacant wingchair. But once he looked up, all that had changed was that Barrington's martini glass was brimming with pink gin again, without his having risen for a refill. In Edgar's head, then, Saddler simply came with a full glass, like a rental car with a topped-up tank.

"I've had a very long day," Edgar objected.

"Sometimes being knackered is an assist. You make leaps, lucky mistakes. That's how the telephone was invented. Eddie, you're so close. And it's so simple."

"Get off my case!" Edgar trudged toward the kitchen. "I'm gonna warm up that lasagna."

"Eddie!" Barrington cried from the living room as Edgar pried off the cardboard top. "How's the touch-typing coming?"

"I stink," Edgar called.

"Go practice."

"I'm famished!"

"Doesn't hunger always make you feel safe?"

With nothing better to do while the lasagna warmed, Edgar shuffled upstairs to his computer. *Don't look at the keys.*

Edgar rewound his Verdade interview, which he needed to transcribe. To force himself to make his way by feel, Edgar closed his eyes and transcribed blind, *My constituency is most thankful for the sacrifice that SOB volunteers have made for their country.*

Yet when he checked the screen, he read, *<u vpmdyoyirmvu od ,pdy yjsmlgi; gpt yjr dsvtgovr yjsy DPN bp;imyrrtd jsbr ,sfr gpt yjrot vpimytu/.*

After laboring at touch-typing nightly, he couldn't be that hopeless. Edgar tried the line once more, eyes shut: *My constituendy is most thankful for the sarccritfice that SOB volunterrs made for their countru.*

Okay, not perfect. But not gobbledygook, either.

Resituating his hands, Edgar realized that on that botched effort he must have displaced his fingers' ready position one key to the right. His motions were roughly correct, but the corresponding letters were not.

As Edgar kept transcribing, *<u vpmdyoyirmvu od ,pdy yjsmlgi;* higher up on the screen nagged his eye. The wind shrilled through the window cracks like a distant alarm. The patio's wind flutes soughed like Saddler's baritone chuckle. There was something about the look of that blither. Something familiar.

In fact, he could visualize pages and pages of an identical sort of drivel.

Rooting in the upper right-hand drawer, Edgar located "SOB

STORIES" and inserted the microfloppy in his computer. He selected the directory's first file, titled:

2" Er;vp,r Yp Yjr <pmlru Jpidr

The text was no more edifying:

Vpmhtsyi;syopmd@ Nu mpe upi ,idy jsbr dryy;rf om/
O fp jp[r upi gomf yjr svvp,pfsyopmd dioysn;r/ . . .

Placing the cursor below the first clump of rubbish, Edgar followed *Vpmhtsyi;syopmd@* and hunted down each nonsense letter, striking the key to its adjacent left on the keyboard. Slowly beneath Barrington's balderdash emerged, *C-o-n-g-r-a-t-u-l-a-t-i-o-n-s!*

CHAPTER 20
Edgar Earns His Savvy

WHEN EDGAR TORE downstairs again, he found Barrington snoozing in front of the smoldering fire, hands clasped on his crimson cummerbund. Edgar kicked Saddler in the shin. "Rise and shine," Edgar snarled. "We have to *talk*."

Barrington looked fuzzy and perplexed, as if for a moment honest nonexistence had beckoned.

"What do you mean, there's *no SOB*?" Edgar demanded.

"Oh, that." Barrington rubbed an eye, prizing out a speck of sleep. "If from this rude awakening I can construe that you've finally cracked my first-former's cryptology, what's to prevent you from decoding your heart out? My journal entries are sufficiently explicit to more than sate your thus far paltry curiosity." He lolled aside. "Meantime, I could get a few minutes' kip."

Edgar grabbed a lapel and wrenched the laggard upright. "I can't believe this! The international media has been covering this story for years! Reuters, the *New York Times*, the *Washington Post*, and the *Guardian* have permanent bureaus here!"

"As I anticipated." Barrington smoothed his released lapel. "It's hardly unreasonable for me to have organized a spot of company." As he sat up, disarranged hair flopped fecklessly into his eyes. It was endearing, and Edgar was in no mood to be disarmed.

"Special reports on *Sixty Minutes*!" Edgar railed, hands thrashing. "Regular updates on *MacNeil/Lehrer*, photo features in *Esquire*! Visits to Cinzeiro from Mary Robinson and Boutros Boutros-Ghali, Jimmy Carter and Richard Holbrooke!"

"You needn't tell me," said Barrington, fishing out a fresh

cigar. "I interviewed those pious twats. Made for bloody po-faced features as well."

"Tom Clancy has plotted his new novel around the SOB, William H. McNeill has plunged into a definitive history of southern Portugal, and the villains in the latest James Bond film are from Barba! The University of Texas Conflict Studies Department has started a doctoral extension program in Cinzeiro, the U.S. State Department is sending a peace envoy to Lisbon, the Rockefeller Foundation is sponsoring a weeklong conference called 'Unity from Division' here next month!"

"I do keep up," said Barrington, lighting up.

"I've been sent to cover a hoax!" In his rage, Edgar tore the cigar from Barrington's hand and threw it in the fire, though doubtless the apparition would effortlessly generate another, as it did pink gin. "My first assignment is a joke! I finally publish a piece in a national broadsheet, all about the 'SOB' and whether they whacked you or not, and now you've made me look like a jerk, a fall guy, a dupe, a—what do you limeys say—a *prat*!"

"Only if you squeal," Barrington admonished.

"I am—floored!" Edgar raved, pacing the Oriental carpet. "What got into you? You just heard about a bomb on the radio and thought, gosh, I don't have anything else on the docket today, maybe I'll call in and say I did it?"

Barrington shrugged. "That first bomb, at Filene's Basement? I waited a couple of days. But not a peep from the usual suspects. Nothing from the Palestinian Whose-its, the Irish Bog-Standard Army, or the Islamic Globo-Omni-Panto-Front. No one claimed it! Such a waste, Eddie. All those Boston shoppers done in, not to mention a first-chop selection of discount tweeds—just for common, shite-happens badness. To what indignation could relatives cling, to what Peace Fund could they send donations? Whom could survivors *forgive*?"

"You did them a favor," Edgar proposed incredulously.

"Entirely," Barrington protested. "I gave them a bull's-eye for their darts, an acronym to sling on *Washington Week*. Besides, I've never understood the logic of unclaimed terrorism. Why not get credit for a job well done? And aren't your targets meant to be afraid of someone in particular, and not just the dark, bad karma, or the bogeyman? Of course, since I don't know any proper terrorists, I've never been able to ask."

"So you just—dialed, what. A newspaper. And they believed you?"

"Not at first. Eddie, after all that reading, you should know your SOB history. For months the Sobs were written off as kooks. No forensic evidence connected Barbans to a single atrocity. But in the end, the world rewards stick-to-itiveness. I always used the same code phrase, and these little furnishing touches can be persuasive. After about a year—there was a providently sturdy crop of anonymous incidents at the time—the FBI baptized the SOB as the genuine article. The reasoning went—surely you remember—that no trail linked bombs to Barba not because these claims were spurious, but because we were dealing with a new brand of truly professional terrorists who covered their tracks. Hence the fact that the coppers couldn't find a trace of the organization became veritable proof of its existence. Clearly, the culprits were too ingenious to get caught. I recall being struck by the admirable modesty of the agents on the case, though at the same time a little worried about your country's security. In all, a compelling experiment, don't you think?" Barrington had opened a jar of beluga from the pyramid of jars in the pantry, and mounded a cracker so gluttonously that caviar tumbled onto the trunk.

"So all those SOB 'statements'—you made them up."

"Quite." Barrington dabbed his mouth with monogrammed linen. "A challenging creative writing assignment. All journalists weary of nonfiction. After a time, reality seems so undefendedly on offer, so available, that in merely reiterating it you don't feel you're doing your part. The urge to make a contribution becomes a matter of civic pride."

"What about the Creams, are they on the payroll? When I walked out of Verdade's office today, did he bust a gut? Is that why Serio's so expressionless, because he's literally trying to keep a straight face?"

"Eddie, Eddie, you're taking this all wrong!" Barrington made a peace offering of a loaded cracker and held it out, but Edgar refused to accept. "Why so offended? The joke's not on you, for pity's sake. It's on Tomás."

"What are you saying—that O Creme is for real?"

"They seem to think so."

"But before your so-called SOB there was no Creme de Barbear—"

"Correct." Barrington made a project of tidying the trunk, dabbing egg by egg with his fingertip.

"And the only reason O Creme snags a column inch is its implied alliance with—"

"Correct."

An hour earlier Edgar had been nodding off. Now he was revved, feverishly decoding his recent past, much as he'd translated Barrington's microfloppy—only instead of converting gibberish to intelligible English he was converting the intelligible to gibberish.

"What about all that *national self-determination* bunk?"

"My idea," Barrington admitted.

"Jesus, you could have done better."

"You're new to the fourth estate. Once you've been around the houses a few times, you'll twig that originality would have marked my fictive terrorists as suspicious. Same stuporific cause, all over the world. I was obliged to opt for verisimilitude over flourish."

"The immigration gambit, that's your invention, too?"

Barrington raised his fishy hands humbly. "Not a-tall. Why should I do all the work? When I arrived there was more than enough prejudice against the towel-heads in Barba to power a small political party. Attaching the SOB to immigration was Verdade's idea." Saddler added appreciatively, "Thought it showed spunk."

"Verdade thinks there is an SOB," Edgar worked out, and Barrington nodded encouragingly. "He just can't find it. In the meantime, he makes political hay—"

"When you finally get round to putting a few pieces together, Eddie, at least you work the puzzle pronto."

"No, there's a piece missing. Why? What was the point?"

Barrington sighed. "Presently, would you consider this peninsula stimulating?"

"I wouldn't call it an amusement park," Edgar grunted. A proud New Yorker, he was too embarrassed to confess that so far in this bumpkin burg he'd had a wonderful time.

"In comparison to the Barba to which I was exiled, modern-day Barba is Euro Disney. At least this is now a province where something is believed to have happened once and where most residents suppose something may happen again. No such great expectations colored popular visions of the future when I stepped off the bus. The *bus*. Without the SOB, Cinzeiro didn't even have a sodding airport."

"You claimed atrocities for a fictitious insurgency because you were bored?"

"I'm a journalist, and journalists need news. Deprive them of it, and they go a bit barking. Deprive them of news long enough, and they'll make their own—much the way the starving will eventually turn to cannibalism."

"Shit." Edgar plopped on the ottoman. "This will make an incredible story."

"Or stories," Barrington advised slyly. "That's up to you."

"Man, at least Wallasek won't treat me like a telephone solicitor for once. The chump's gonna have a fucking heart attack when he hears."

"Perhaps," said Barrington noncommittally. "Though of course the *Record* will look rather shabby. We've led this story from the start. And his own reporter . . ."

"You're not my fault."

"No; though the bearer of bad tidings . . . And of course you'll be recalled. There won't necessarily be another slot open. Besides, if I don't miss my guess Wallasek won't be too keen to see your face. As a reminder of the egg on his. That is, if Wallasek isn't sacked himself, or, having compromised its authority, the *Record* doesn't go to the wall. Yes, I dare say that after breaking your big scoop, you'll be out of a job."

"I'll get another one," said Edgar irritably.

"But naturally you will. Unless, well—"

"Unless what?"

"Unless your tall tale is dismissed as cock-and-bull. After all, the gullible public, the FBI, the Barban police, Interpol: no one ends up looking very clever."

"Except you," Edgar supposed sourly.

"There's not much in it for anybody, this turn of the wheel, is there? The hoax, as you said yourself, is incredible. And your evidence is thin. The gloves, the stationery—"

"Hold on. What were they all about?"

Barrington whinnied. "I've gone to such pains to concoct a bit of diversion for us both. You could at least give my clues the old school try."

Edgar was in no mood to play games, but Saddler appeared adamant that his pupil add his two plus two. ". . . The SOB statements," Edgar groped. "You printed them on local hotel stationery—suggesting authenticity, without giving your whereabouts away. The rubber gloves . . . They kept your fingerprints off the page. But that stupid pipe, with the wax paper?" He glowered. "I don't get it."

"Two out of three gives you a score of sixty-seven percent, a passing mark only in our era of plummeting educational standards. You never tried talking into the pipe's open end, did you? It gives you a buzz, so to speak. It's a kazoo."

"For calling in atrocity claims," Edgar filled in, annoyed he hadn't figured it out by himself. "Voice distortion."

"A crude yet surprisingly effective device, so long as the call is not professionally recorded. Still, you see my point. Your evidence is trifling, circumstantial."

"You forgot. Mr. Preening Twit kept a journal of the whole farce."

"Yes, the disk! But you could have written those entries, couldn't you? There's no handwriting to verify. The keyboard code, well, that might have been your idea, to make the files appear genuine."

"There's the minor matter of the truth," Edgar retorted. "Like, there is no SOB, no one has ever met a real Sob, and their atrocity claims have stopped."

"Yes, for now," Barrington said doubtfully, rubbing his chin. "But then, there being no SOB hasn't prevented anyone from assuming there is one up till now. And you don't really know where *I* am, do you? As you are constantly reminding yourself, my current manifestation is confabulated; I'm a hologram of hearsay. What if I'm alive elsewhere? I mightn't care for your having peed on my parade. I'm in possession of my own code phrase. Should there be another bombing, I could ring in a statement. After you've charged that the SOB was bogus, you'd appear caught out. Perhaps I'm dead, or I've had it up to my oxters with the whole affair, but that may not be a risk you want to take.

"Then there's the matter of all your new little friends," Barrington ruminated sorrowfully. "Henry would have to shift to

Bosnia, and his faithful wife would follow. Honestly, I'm not sure when you three would meet again."

This warning hit home. No more triangular dinners with exorbitant cabernet. No more handwringing visits from the guileless Nicola. No more brow-furrowed powwows over her mangled marriage, all leading up to a tragic shake of the head, in reluctant agreement that what's broken will never be good as new . . .

"What are you driving at?" asked Edgar warily.

"Blow the whistle, and you're certain to make headlines, but in the same papers that swallowed the original story hook, line, and sinker. They'll not dwell on the scandal for long. You might flog your yarn to the tabloids, though popular culture is so ravenous lately, no flavor of the month lasts thirty days. You could write your memoirs, but they'll be short. In sum, ring Wallasek, and the party's over."

"What's the alternative?" Edgar grumbled. "Keep the scam under my hat? With no more *Sob stories*, Wallasek is sure to scrap this bureau by the end of the year. At least once I pull the plug I can capitalize on my fifteen minutes, maybe snag a job with another rag."

"That wouldn't keep Nicola in your backyard."

"I'll get posted to Bosnia, then!"

"A gamble. One other course is surefire." Barrington snapped a Bremner wafer neatly in two. "And far more diverting."

"You lost me," said Edgar stubbornly.

"Lord, we don't go to the head of the class today. You did find the code phrase?"

"Aw, get out!" Edgar stood up. "You're not proposing I use it!"

"You'll have to bide your time. But nowadays there's always one petulant group or another ready to throw a wobbly. It wouldn't have to be a seven-forty-seven. A letter bomb?" Barrington mused, nibbling, "You know, even a bomb *scare* would do."

"Don't be ridiculous!" Edgar began to fidget, fixing himself a caviar cracker. And another. There was something a touch contrived about his own disgust. In fact, he had to keep stuffing his mouth with crackers to keep from smiling. "This is your brand of fun," he charged through crumbs. "You and I aren't cut from the same—"

"Yet when people find the contrast between us too stark, you're offended."

"The main difference between us is that I have a conscience! And only a total degenerate would carry on this asinine stunt." But Edgar couldn't muster convincing indignation any more than he could keep his mouth from tugging into a grin.

"Who suffers who wouldn't suffer anyway, or who doesn't deserve it?" Barrington proposed, as Edgar knew he would. "All those bombs and gas canisters, they'd have gone off without the SOB. What does it matter which daft acronym gets credit? As for the miscreants who did plant Semtex in Filene's Basement, they failed to advance their purpose a jot, and only raised the profile of a phantom. So a few self-important journalists are sent to cover a dust bowl where nothing happens. So a tosser like Tomás keeps searching the Barban underbrush for borrowers in balaclavas. Where's the harm?"

Barrington leaned forward, his voice grown so deep and quiet that it rumbled in Edgar's gut. "Meanwhile, you'll be the *only hack who's sussed.* Remember Falconer and 'Special K,' Angela and Jamesie? You're always the shat-upon git kept in the dark. Turn the tables! A *seasoned reporter* like Win Pyre or a hotshot *insider* like Roland Ordway could never pull rank on you again. Ordway stamps out of the Barking Rat once more, because you're insufficiently in awe of Big Bad Barba, whose laugh would be last? Eddie, Eddie. You've always wanted to be the social center of some brown-nosing rabble. But how preferable to rise above one!

"Degenerate?" Barrington purred, cigar smoke snaking about his head. "For a casual agnostic, your categories are frightfully

Protestant. But there's a whole world outside heaven and hell. My SOB fiddle falls into much the same camp as I do myself: not especially wicked. Just not especially *good*."

"Nuts!" A dark haze wafted from the foyer. "My lasagna!"

Edgar didn't really care about his lasagna, though he did rush to the kitchen and shut the door. Barrington was so classically understated, so pip-pip-here-here, so *British*. Edgar didn't want the dry Yorkshireman to hear him whoop.

CHAPTER 21

One Less Ugly Landmark

THIS TIME WHEN the zomboid Bebê Serio stood blocking the doorway, Edgar launched straight into the slab of super-ball flab, knocking the Cream backward. Serio staggered into the Rat with his elbows lifted and arms dangling, like the robot on *Lost in Space* flailing its coiled limbs and droning, *Danger! Danger!* Deep in the tar pits of Serio's eyes stirred the beginnings of surprise. No one had slammed into that gut for a while.

"Desculpe-me, amigo," said Edgar in a wide, careless Yankee drawl. He was chewing gum. "Thought for a minute there you were gonna get outta my fucking way."

Jingling the keys to the kingdom on Rua da Evaporação in his pocket, and figuratively the keys to a great deal else, Edgar sauntered directly to the bar. He wasn't about to be roped into another full round for that table. "Choque," he ordered tersely, skipping his practiced, *Quero uma cerveja de pera peluda, por favor.* Still, Edgar left a generous two-hundred-escudo tip. All those SOB bumper stickers plastered around the register could as well have been decals scored from special-offer boxes of Cocoa Puffs. Edgar felt a funny flush of sympathy for the politically infatuated barkeep, much as he could be touched by the credulous enthusiasm of little boys for the A-Team.

To Edgar, the Barking Rat had overnight lost its edge. Glaring sullenly over bitter beers, murmuring in a mishmash of Slavic-sounding consonant blends, those thick-necked, shadowy Barbans lurking in corners had originally made Edgar uneasy. He couldn't decipher their palatal mumble, and he'd had every reason to view the morose local patrons as shady characters. Yet now the *zhuh-shuh-chuh* shuffled with no more menace than an old man in slippers. Potato-heads no longer gooned from their posters with sinister stupidity, nor wielded ordnance with forbidding nonchalance; on examination, the automatics in photos looked distinctly plastic. The political ephemera scattered about the premises—LIBERTA A BARBA OCUPADA teaspoons, SOB ashtrays, and cherry-bomb spangled coffee mugs—winked with the bald artifice of tinfoil swords in community theater. In fact, the deformed plastic souvenirs over the booze exuded more integrity than the publican's SUPORTE NOSSOS SOLDADOS OUSADOS tea towel. At least, if not half-melted, there really was an Eiffel Tower.

Approaching the foreign correspondents' regular round table, Edgar forded another wave of unexpected compassion. After one more week absent SOB "violence," the press corps emitted an air of impending dissolution, like a staff meeting in the last week of summer camp. Now that the fun and games appeared nearly done, they gazed at one another with a rash sentimentality safe only in moribund relationships. A fuzzy halo of nostalgia hovered over the gathering, that peculiar harkening back to the days you're still living, a nostalgia for the present. Hell, this bunch might as well reminisce fondly now, since later they'd remember Barba and wince. Poor schmucks. Every last journalist in Cinzeiro had been suckered.

Trudy Sisson would never have seized on Tomás Verdade as a pinup heartthrob if she'd realized that the dingy office atop the Terra do Cão gift shop constituted the extent of his influence, or that the arsenal at his disposal contained not a fiendish array of Semtex and Gelignite but the lone stun gun of his monotonous rhetoric. Martha Hulbert cherished having baddies to deplore, since antipathy is a form of romance, and enemies are no less luscious than lovers. Abandoned by her bête noire, the old maid would feel desolate, left at the altar. Win Pyre was bound to be less bereft than embarrassed—the wizened old hand who'd dodged mortars from Beirut to Mogadishu, reduced to tilting at windmills. Likewise Alexis Collier, Dame Truth in Journalism, would be obliged to exchange her starchy pants suits for sackcloth. Henry would be put further behind in his quest for respect; no hack who'd taken the bait in Barba would hold his head high for a while. Aside from its depressive effects on her husband, Nicola would be the least disheartened by the revelation that the SOB was Barrington's idea of a knee-slapper. In fact, she alone would be delighted: one less acronym up to no good. By contrast, after stalking from the Rat affronted that a witless greenhorn was endangering his life with loose talk, Roland Ordway had put himself in the way of poetic comeuppance.

"Heard you interviewed Verdade," said Ordway, as Edgar slid into a seat at the *Guardian* reporter's elbow. "Edifying?"

"Stultifying," Edgar corrected breezily. He took a swig of his Choque and recited, "Some folks know more than they say. Other folks say more than they know. Verdade impressed me as the latter."

"Verdade knows plenty, I assure you," Ordway scoffed.

"About the SOB? Verdade knows beans."

"I assume he fed you the old *O Creme is a legal political party.* Don't tell me you swallowed it whole."

"Oh, but I did," said Edgar cheerfully. "I think *o presidente* is totally above board. To his own dismay."

Ordway snorted get-a-load-of-this-guy toward Win Pyre. "Right. Tomás Verdade, humble populist, fighting for justice through proper political channels. There just happens to be a lethal paramilitary army bombing the trousers off three continents for the same cause. Convenient, to say the least."

"Verdade isn't humble; he's not even populist," Edgar countered amiably. "He's not fighting for justice, but for his own day in the sun. That's not illegal anywhere, last I checked. When it is, you and I are both in trouble."

At a loss for retort, Ordway disgustedly turned his back.

"Sorry we won't have got to know each other better," said Alexis, leaning from Edgar's other side. Her smile was tight and perfunctory. "Marching orders arrived this morning. I'm being transferred to Jerusalem. The Barban story seems dead as a doornail, and the Middle East is heating up."

"Mazel tov," Edgar toasted.

"Such a shame." Alexis patted his hand. "Your arriving right when this story dries up. You must have been looking forward to cutting your teeth on it."

"I've found the odd irony to chew on."

"I'm afraid self-preservation may be kicking in. Beginner insurgents crave martyrdom. Seasoned guerrillas save their own skins. The Sobs have got away scot-free so far. According to my sources, the leadership has decided to quit while they're ahead."

"Oh?" said Edgar. "What sources are those?"

"I may be leaving soon," said Alexis coyly, "but I haven't turned into Santa Claus."

"It's just, *my* sources suspect that the SOB may be planning a new offensive."

"What sources?" pressed Alexis. Her mouth assholed.

"Am I wearing a white beard and going *ho-ho-ho*?"

"Well, of course," she said, flustered, "I don't expect . . . But I haven't heard that rumor at all—"

"Oh, my sources are impeccable," Edgar assured her brightly, signaling the bartender for another Choque. "Then, since you're off for Jerusalem . . ."

"Naturally, if the situation changed, I'd—"

"Nicola!" Edgar called across the table. "Do you know how to prepare *bacalhau*?"

"Did Verdade say something?" Alexis panicked, tugging Edgar's sleeve. "Did Verdade let a hint slip?"

"See, I bought a pound of salt cod the other day," Edgar

continued, "and I can't figure out anything to do with it besides resole my shoes."

Nicola shouted across the table about soaking and the importance of parsley while Alexis cried, "Did Barrington leave behind his contact book? . . . Edgar? . . . *Edgar!*"

"What's *happened* to you?" Nicola pressed quietly once he escaped to negotiate a seat beside her. "Your posture—you're not slumping. Your face—you're not scowling. Have you got good news? Because so have I!"

"Let's just say I've decided not to take Cinzeiro too seriously," he telegraphed in all sincerity. "What's your good news?"

"Sh-sh-sh!" Roland hissed.

"I've sometimes wondered if you're right," Trudy was telling Martha. "If Barrington ever, like, totally fell in love, you know?"

"Stuff it, Trude!" said Ordway, gesturing over the bar to the TV, whose volume the publican had just turned up. *"There's been another bomb."*

The newscast was in Portuguese. Ordway raised a hand for quiet; the rest, though uncomprehending, grew respectfully silent. The Rat's local patrons were also fixed on the TV, mum and immobile. Edgar had never seen Barbans so attentive, so awake. Even Bebê Serio had rotated in the direction of the tube. Though you couldn't call his eyes focused, they did seem to have picked up something in their sights besides the wall.

At last pictures were telecast. Over the camera's meaningless pan of granite rubble, Roland translated. "Grant's Tomb. Ten injured, two critical. Japanese tourists. And the landmark itself's been completely demolished."

"Is it—is it for us?" Martha ventured nervously, like a ravenous restaurant patron when an enticing platter emerges from the kitchen.

"No claim," said Ordway. "Yet."

Barrington had said that they'd have to "bide their time,"

which Edgar had assumed meant weeks or months, giving him a chance to think this out, to get a grip, maybe even come to his senses. But the next day? And Barrington had said that it wouldn't have to be a 747, that maybe they could settle for a scare or some minor postal mischief. But Grant's Tomb? This wasn't a letter bomb.

Edgar's metabolism was sedate from churning on stationary bicycles by the hour in New York health clubs. Yet in the last two minutes his heartbeat at rest had accelerated to at least 120. The racing pulse thumped in his teeth. A muscle spasmed around his left eye.

"Please, please, make it a Sob job!" implored Henry, whom the *Independent* hadn't published in months.

"A delayed claim is par for the course," said Ordway, whose perch on the round table was making the whole thing tilt; Edgar rescued his beer. Ordway clumped a cowboy boot on a chair. "Sobs like suspense. Always keep the authorities sweating a day or two."

"It builds tension," Pyre agreed, having gimped to Ordway's side with an I've-been-the-victim-of-terrorism-myself limp that seemed a tad pronounced. "Delay means the story breaks twice: first the bomb, then who did it. Extends the operation's shelf life. Smart."

"We'll have to sit tight. Ring some Creams in the meantime, get the usual denials on the record—if we're lucky, something none too apologetic from Verdade." The Briton's terse business-as-usual failed to mask his excitement. The table top wavered; twice Ordway reached to shove his blazer above his elbows, where its sleeves were already jammed.

Speak of the devil; the newscast had switched to an interview with Tomás Verdade, who tacked on a statement in English for the benefit of his foreign fans.

"Naturally O 'Creme de Barbear has no knowledge of this

unfortunate incident," said Verdade, looking sorrowfully into the camera. "Hence we can neither confirm nor deny if this is the work of Os Soldados Ousados de Barba. Our hearts are with the injured and their families. Yet I would be remiss if I did not take this opportunity to remind the international community of my people's fight for national self-determination. Should this prove to be an action of SOB volunteers, let us resolve that those injured today will not have suffered in vain. Once Barba is free and in control of her own borders, tragedies like the bombing of Grant's Tomb will no longer be necessary. I pray fervently for that day. *Obrigado.*"

Most patrons ignored this part of the broadcast—they'd seen the performance a hundred times—but Edgar was riveted. What elegant hypocrisy: to pretend to be lying.

"Edgar," Nicola whispered. "What is 'Grant's Tomb'?"

The question endeared Edgar entirely. Brits like Roland Ordway might not know that hulking eyesore on Manhattan's Upper West Side from Mount Rushmore, but they'd never in a million years ask the likes of Edgar what it was, if only because as a New Yorker he was bound to know.

"It's a chunky architectural atrocity on the edge of Harlem," Edgar explained, "where a Civil War general and one of the worst U.S. presidents of all time isn't even buried. The monument has no redeeming aesthetic or historical value, and has become the nearly exclusive preserve of Asian sightseers. They're very dutiful."

Nicola played with a tress of her hair intently. "What does the American Civil War have to do with illegal North African immigration to Portugal?"

"What did holidaymakers headed home to Heathrow have to do with Barba?" Edgar posed. "Or two kids in a DC shopping mall? Commuters in a Paris metro?"

"Sorry." She pulled the hair in front of her face. "You must think I'm slow."

"No, no!" Edgar tucked the strand behind her ear, fingers lingering as he made the trivial but tender mental note that Nicola's lobes were detached. He dropped his voice. "Those are good questions. Nicola, you're the only one in town who's ever mentioned that the emperor might not be dressed to the nines. Your journo friends here operate like Visa card outfits: no matter how impoverished the losers look, keep giving Sobs more credit. It seems all you have to do to be classed as a mastermind is to kill people." The habit of speaking of the SOB as extant was hard to break.

"Oh, I know I'm in a minority," Nicola conceded, twisting a wisp at her temple. "All the hacks think I'm wet. Most historically 'great' men have been killers, I expect."

Edgar smiled, and forgot himself. "Barrington claims people aren't attracted to virtue. That sainthood's all very well in theory, but in practice it's a drag."

Nicola tilted her head. "Barrington? But you never—"

"You said you had good news," he interrupted hastily.

Nicola lowered her voice. "Oh, Edgar! I got a postcard!"

"Uh-huh?"

"It was blank, you see, with only our address. Edgar, he's all right!"

"Who's all right?" asked Edgar, a little wickedly.

"Oh, you know who, stop being so—"

"How can you be sure?"

"The card, it's a picture of the Kremlin. Maybe he means that he's back in Moscow, or maybe the card was old; it was postmarked in Vietnam, of all places. But who else could it be from? Because of Henry, he couldn't . . . I hadn't realized how worried I'd been . . . Oh, with this awful bombing, I feel like such a heel. I know I shouldn't be happy."

"This operation has Sob fingerprints all over it." Martha had sidled up to Edgar, carrying a fresh *vinho do porto*. A little drunk, she kept her balance with moral gravity. Her voice was solemn, her brow furiously furrowed. "High-profile landmark, no warning, total disregard for casualties. We've been lucky; this could have been a lot worse. But mark my words, if it's not the SOB, it's an organization that's studied their methods."

"BA-321 wasn't a 'landmark,'" Edgar observed contentiously. "And any terrorist operation has 'total disregard' for casualties, since if you're really concerned about not hurting people you don't blow things up. So I'm curious, Hulbert. Could anything explode anywhere that wouldn't, in your view, display 'Sob fingerprints'?"

"The *Daring Soldiers* have deployed a variety of strategies," said Martha archly. She ticked off on her fingers, "Operations designed to kill, to maim, or to warn. Bombs, shootings, nuisance scares, and thank Christ the chemical weaponry was a brief experiment. American targets, European targets, that foray into Japan. Exasperating, yes, but it's cunning to vary your tactics. Predictability would make those reprobates easier to apprehend."

"If the pattern keeps changing, there is no pattern." Hulbert would never understand that Edgar was trying to do her a favor. "Strategy? What strategy? You've just detailed yourself that Sob targets are completely random."

"Randomness is a strategy!" Martha insisted, her face beet-red.

"Man!" Edgar shook his head and laughed, rubbing his eyes. "You people deserve this."

"I'm not sure I like his attitude," Martha stage-whispered to Trudy as Edgar picked up his coat. "Those poor tourists in the hospital, and he doesn't seem the least upset. Barba is bound to be implicated. But Kellogg started chuckling! As if the SOB is some kind of joke. Sometimes he reminds me of Barrington, in the worst way."

Before he slipped out the door, Edgar paused to listen to the hubbub behind him. Theories and consternations blended to crowd hum. Yet a crowd hits a pitch distinctive to the occasion, and this wasn't the deep, funereal rumble of an assembly coming to terms with loss. Pierced with shrieks of hastily stifled laughter, English and Portuguese alike bubbled into a shrill, trippy buzz, less like the mumble at a wake than the excited pre-curtain chatter before a cracking good show.

CHAPTER 22
Taken for SAPSS

WHEN EDGAR WAS in high school, a popular if cumbersome method of fund-raising for charity was to collect per-mile pledges for athletic events. Though direct donations would have accomplished the same benevolence with a fraction of the fuss, Yardley students had learned the drill from raising money for the school's construction of three extra tennis courts during Edgar's sophomore year. The walk-athon involved door-to-dooring with a clipboard and getting the odd pledge of ten cents a mile promised largely to get rid of you; then pairing up with some pimply cretin assigned to be your "buddy" and trudging about the lake with your sandwich decomposing in your daypack; then doing the rounds with the clipboard again, when pledge-makers would often be short of cash or conveniently out. Still, anything beat freshman year, when Edgar house-to-housed in Stonington selling chocolate bars for the Debate Club. Kindly June Cleavers at screen doors never failed to remark on how much of his product Edgar appeared to have sampled himself.

February of junior year, Toby Falconer proposed a fresh fund-raising approach to his doting inner circle. This time the noble cause would be the group's private community chest. Thus, with much hilarity late night in the dorm, Falconer and his merry men, of whom Edgar had only recently counted himself a member, concocted *phoquefartic shytosis*—"a wasting disease of young adults"—along with the Society in Aid of P.S. Sufferers (SAPSS).

Edgar gave Falconer a hand in the print shop, drafting a letter of introduction and lined pledge sheets, in whose logo a gaunt teenage boy was fainting off the last S. That afternoon the printing instructor barged in unexpectedly, and Falconer didn't turn a hair. *Oh Mr. Galveston, we're so happy you turned up. We were having a little trouble centering this letterhead. See, we're running a charity marathon for the Society in Aid of P.S. Sufferers—What's that? Oh, Mr. Galveston, my brother has it, which is why I got involved. It's really debilitating and everything and he can't play football anymore—*

Galveston offered to help out. As a consequence, the SAPSS three-color stationery looked spectacularly official.

For soliciting pledges, Falconer coached his crew on the pitch. He insisted they practice saying *phoquefartic shytosis* without cracking up, and be able to rattle off a portentous pathology. Falconer claimed that the average adult vocabulary shrank by 6 percent a year; considering what he got away with reciting on Stonington's front stoops, he was probably right. Young men stricken with PS in their prime suffered from *priapism*, *ultimogeniture* (inheritance by the youngest son), and *helminthophobia* (fear of worms). House to house, Falconer improvised juvenile disorders as he went along: *rectal infarction*, *nasal globulus*, and *cerebral smegmatism*.

Doubtless contributing to a reputation for being "clingy," Edgar had lobbied to accompany Falconer himself as he rang doorbells in the suburban neighborhoods bordering the school. Toby's pledges were always twice the amount of anyone else's. The guy could really work a mark. Never oily, but often touching. The kid brother with PS became a regular feature in Falconer's rap, a brave little fellow who never cried when his legs hurt or he couldn't play Frisbee with his friends. When Falconer described the feisty, good-natured twelve-year-old who was now confined to bed, even Edgar began to believe in the wretched squirt. Falconer, of course, didn't have a brother at all.

It seemed uncanny at the time that Falconer could say *rectal infarction* to middle-aged housewives and not get chased off the porch with a broom. In retrospect, Falconer's success was less mysterious. All those women apprehended was that an angelic apparition with chiseled cheekbones had miraculously materialized on their doorstep. Though it was winter, Falconer always wore his greatcoat agape and his shirt unbuttoned to the sternum, alabaster pectorals swelling at his open collar. Winter suited those glacial green eyes, splintering like ice and glistening with the very mischief these women indulged by pledging three dollars for every fictitious mile.

The SAPSS scam flowered during Edgar's honeymoon with Falconer, a period Edgar liked to recall as an uncomplicated, typically terminal infatuation. But when Edgar pressed himself, he remembered the experience as discomfiting. The more Edgar revered the flawless Falconer, the more he resented the enslavement, and fantasized about being on the receiving end of his own devotion. Humiliatingly at another boy's beck, Edgar struggled as he would later struggle against his love for women.

One afternoon in the Yardley locker room Edgar battled his adoration more viciously than usual. They'd nearly finished canvassing the immediate Stonington neighborhoods, and Falconer announced it was time to stop. Best not to push their luck by getting greedy, and besides the joke had worn thin. If even half the pledges came across, the sting would net over $2,500. After they fabricated a few convincing anecdotes from the "marathon," collection would commence the following week.

"Shit, Falconer," Edgar slurred, back flat on the bench, "this is supposed to be for kicks, and I feel like some hunchbacked old bag volunteering for the United Way."

"No sweat, Kellogg," said Falconer coolly. "Quit. But if you don't help collect, you don't share the pot."

"Just a little sick of your calling all the shots, Falconer," Edgar griped. "Time to do this, time to do that. Yes, sir, no, sir.

Reporting for duty, sir. Yes, I've cleaned the latrines, sir. Will that be all, sir. Certainly I'll kiss your ass, sir. Requesting permission to yank my tongue out of your butt, sir. Christ."

One of Falconer's secrets was he didn't rattle. Maybe over his father's death senior year, but not over boy stuff. His other minions stood in his defense, muscles stiffening, but Falconer waved a hand to call off the dogs. "Oh-kay!" he announced musically, bouncing gracefully off the tall tennis umpire's stool, kept inside off-season. "We've got two hours before dinner. We'll do what *you* say, Kellogg. Go ahead."

"Go ahead and what?" asked Edgar warily, raising his head off the bench.

"Come up with some diversion to keep us entertained. Think I *like* having to keep the program moving? Think it isn't a little irritating that you slobs just lie there and expect me to call another fucking 'shot'? Go ahead. We're at your disposal. Anything you say."

As his neck strained, Edgar's mind went blank. Offered the initiative he'd always craved, Edgar considered that maybe he deserved no better than lieutenancy. He needed Falconer. They all did. Falconer got ideas.

Later as an attorney Edgar had a similar epiphany. Ruled by precedent, a lawyer's job was to ensure that the past recurred in the present, and an attorney's only fleeting originality was to disguise the new as the same. It was Edgar's realization that he was perfectly suited to this task that disenchanted him with the profession.

Edgar thumped his crown back on the bench with finality. "Let's run it."

"Come again?" snarled a henchman.

"The marathon," said Edgar. "Let's actually run it. It'll take some training, delay cashing in for two or three weeks. But you said yourself, Falconer, we need diversion. And what better way to convince those ladies we're legit than to really run the course?"

Following a hailstorm of *Come on!* and *Give us a break!* Falconer announced dryly, "I think a marathon sounds fab." And that was that.

Thereon, Edgar took over. He led cross-country runs every afternoon for a fortnight, the course a little longer each day. Privately he luxuriated in his new body, fleet and featherweight. All through elementary school Edgar had lumbered after classmates, trailing a hundred yards behind as they streaked the playground's perimeter. For years, he'd submitted to shrieks of laughter when a relay baton was palmed into his moist, sausage fingers. So Edgar was powered for the first couple of miles by sheer amazement. His athletic equals, the others may have lagged behind because they regarded the ability to run as ordinary.

When they ran the marathon itself on a Saturday afternoon, most of the SAPSS team dropped out after about five miles. Only Falconer himself stayed in the race and kept pace. Edgar had measured out the distance with the odometer on his bike—a good workout in itself. They hadn't trained nearly hard enough for this distance, and around mile ten Edgar hit a wall; Falconer faltered on his heels. They stumbled on at a geriatric jog, in too much distress to find each other funny. At around mile thirteen, both bent over double, their eyes met. Heaving, they keeled under a tree. Minutes passed before they could speak.

Though they'd quit well shy of twenty-six miles, Edgar always treasured the memory of that run. The SAPSS marathon constituted the acme of their short, electric friendship: a rare fortnight of chugging shoulder-to-shoulder in a relationship otherwise narrowed into the single-file formation of an idol and his pursuant disciple.

As it happened, the choice to run the marathon for real was propitious. One of the marks—signed up by Gerald, a kid with both an unfortunate smirk and a distinguishing red afro that made him easy to finger—called Yardley's administration to check if the appeal was aboveboard. When collared by the headmaster, Gerald was able to claim that the marathon had indeed been run, and a teacher confirmed sighting Edgar Kellogg and Toby Falconer limping back to the parking lot in drenched sweats on Saturday at dusk. Falconer soft-soaped as usual that yeah, they had made up the organization and the disease just for laughs, but that they were definitely donating the money to a proper nonprofit, honest. The headmaster was skeptical, and they were required not only to collect on the pledges but to show him all the paperwork and a receipt from the Multiple Sclerosis Society for the total, or face expulsion. Not one of the boys made a dime.

The upshot? They cynically fake a marathon for charity, and at the end of the day what do they do but run a fucking marathon for charity. Like Edgar's later invocation of Saddler's pestilent company, the moral seemed to run: be careful what you make up.

CHAPTER 23
Impostor Syndrome

THE SAPSS CAPER scrolled through Edgar's mind as he chugged down Rua da Evaporação the day after the bombing of Grant's Tomb, though he hadn't thought about the would-be swindle in ages. After all these years he could still run, though without the buoyant tirelessness of his late teens. He'd developed a middle-age affection for the indoor treadmill, with its reassuring readout of calories burned. But health clubs weren't on offer in Cinzeiro, and Barrington sure as hell hadn't installed a gym. There was no alternative to braving the elements outside.

That meant loping off with the massive front-door key in his shorts pocket, the key to the tower jingling against it, the heavy brass shaft hitting his thigh on every stride. He might have left the set behind and counted on Saddler to let him in, but he remembered Nicola's caution: that Barrington was "unreliable on purpose." Edgar always took the keys.

Besides, a rhythmic thump against his quadriceps was the least of his problems, and on the slog westward he sure couldn't hear any jingling. White-noise *whaaa* roared in Edgar's ears, though at least the blare obliterated the rasp of his own wheeze. Pounded into every yard across the scrubby plain, wooden *flautas ventosas* whooshed in the unified alarm of an oncoming-train whistle. The atmosphere bore down on Edgar's chest as if Bebê Serio were blocking the way. Whipping down his nostrils, the gale dried his throat, while tears streaked his temples like rain on the side window of a speeding car.

There, that stumpy *pera peluda* tree up ahead, rotten fruit sliming the ground on its leeward side: his regular turn-around. Splatting a Nike in the purplish guck, Edgar held his breath to avoid the smell and slapped the rough bark of the tree in official acknowledgment that the hard bit was over.

Edgar pivoted, and suddenly his ears went quiet. Only the moan of the wind flutes remained, the countryside's panpipes differentiating into separate notes a quarter tone apart and striking bittersweet minor chords. The return journey was almost effortless, his stride long and high. The tailwind made Edgar feel sixteen again, and newly freed from a hundred pounds of Entenmann's raspberry coffee cake. Mentally, too, he was looser, lighter, and more prone to leaps as he skipped over violet pools of *pera peluda* goop to keep from slipping. On the slog westward, the sere landscape had looked ominous, branches scraggling like witch's fingers, the flutes deep and dire, his quandary over whether to claim Grant's Tomb for the SOB weighty and torturous. On the homeward leg, Barba's hokey horror-movie theatrics seemed burlesque, and so did Edgar's agonizing.

Funny, his destitution in Yardley's locker room in the face of Falconer's gauntlet, "anything you say!"—it bothered him only to a degree. The truly original mind was a rarity, perhaps a burden. So, however disappointing, your own limitations also let you off the hook. If Edgar wasn't creative, ingenuity wasn't his job. The notion to run the marathon for real, for example: Edgar had simply taken Falconer's initial concept an extra step. Edgar was a natural executor. He didn't come up with great ideas himself, but he knew one when he saw one, and he could bring an inspiration to life.

Once he collapsed, dripping, onto the pillows by the fountain, Edgar was a little offended when he failed to draw a single disparaging word from Abrab's resident hedonist. Saddler looked coldly indifferent.

"Man, running toward the coast is like jogging in petroleum jelly," said Edgar, smearing his sweaty cheek with a sleeve.

Listlessly, Barrington browsed an *Economist*, pinching the pages with distaste. Rather than lounge amid the pillows in a convivial sprawl, he sat remotely upright in the atrium's only chair, legs crossed, one silk slipper lifted at a finicky tilt. In the context of Barrington's flamboyant wardrobe, the maroon smoking jacket was subdued. The hazy sunset filtering through skylights had grown too dim for reading, but Barrington hadn't lit a lantern or switched on the overhead, as if to deliberately make the room dingy. Oozing misanthropic malaise, Saddler looked as he might have in pre-SOB exile, week after uneventful week sifting by like so much sand.

"Nick seems to think you're alive," Edgar prodded. "Some postcard arrived, blank. She couldn't have been more over the moon at the declaration of world peace."

Flap, flap.

Often as Edgar had coached himself that the best thing with cranky prima donnas is to leave them alone, he compulsively beseeched Barrington for attention. "Heard about Grant's Tomb?" he asked, his voice high and tentative. Pathetic. He might as well have dropped to his knees and blubbered, *Don't you like me anymore?*

Barrington grunted a churlish affirmative.

"You should have seen the hacks go berserk at the Rat last night," Edgar nattered, unable to check this shameless appeal. "Hulbert full of stratagems, Collier frantically punching that flashy cellular phone . . . If the SOB doesn't claim it, they'll be crushed."

A sigh whinnied through Saddler's substantial nose. Not glancing up, he turned another page.

A little camaraderie was the least Edgar could expect, wasn't it? "I was *thinking* of claiming it," said Edgar irritably.

"Then do."

"I was under the impression you were keen for me to carry on your pioneering work," said Edgar aloofly, though the scale of his relief that Saddler was at last speaking to him at all was humiliating. Gathering his threadbare T-shirt like the shreds of his dignity, he wiped his face. "Now you don't seem to care."

Barrington closed the magazine in his lap. "Why do you care if I care? Suit yourself, Eddie. I couldn't be arsed either way." With a flick of his wrist, Barrington tossed the *Economist* in the pool.

As the magazine sogged and submerged, Edgar's enthusiasm for paramilitary farce sank disconcertingly with it. He knelt and scooped the periodical from the pool, as if to rescue his prospective project from suddenly seeming all wet.

"Have you any idea what it's like when your every acquaintance is desperate to please?" Saddler volunteered flatly. "It's living hell."

"Then you can't know much about hell," Edgar returned readily.

"You think Picasso really relished the fact that in his heyday he could play tic-tac-toe on a napkin and sell it for thousands of francs? I doubt it very much. A market that blindly elevates your every sneeze to genius invites disdain for your own enterprise."

"I thought you got off on disdain."

"I didn't used to be disdainful. I once had respect for any number of people, before they developed too much respect for me. Or whatever it was." Barrington stood and craned his chin toward the ceiling, rubbing the back of his neck.

"You know, it's not true—" though he spoke quietly, Barrington's rich, round baritone filled the marble hall as he paced measuredly by the pool—"as Trudy Sisson is fond of promoting, that I 'hate myself' or feel 'unlovable.' I find my own company tolerable enough. But everywhere I go, my company is sought above anyone else's. That is not a boast, Eddie. It is a fact. So I ask you: whose company can *I* covet? Whom am *I* meant to revere,

Eddie? You? You already lionize me; we can't turn the tables at this late date. For whom do *I* wait to walk in the door? Who do *I* hope will come to the party? Who's to be *my* idol, if I'm perpetually doomed to be yours?"

This was the first time Saddler had ever confided in him personally, and Edgar was touched. He felt frantic not to blow it, to break the spell.

"Ever hear of the 'impostor syndrome'?" Edgar asked diffidently. "It's a problem especially for professionals—doctors, lawyers. You work and study and aspire away and suddenly someone hands you a piece of paper that says, okay, you're a lawyer. A lawyer! And you don't feel any different. You know you're still that kid with a Spyder bike who shoplifted Ho-Hos. You think you're a fraud. It can get pretty bad, this terror of being discovered. Happened to me, I think—and I dealt with it by debunking the whole profession instead of just myself. If a *former fat boy looking for love* could be an attorney, bar membership wasn't worth much. I figure the impostor syndrome applies to adulthood in general. After all, being a grown-up is disillusioning. I guess being a fetishized grown-up is disillusioning in spades."

"Quite," Barrington agreed dolorously. "Apparently, I'm as compelling as people get." The assertion was steeped in disappointment.

Edgar wanted to reassure Saddler that he seemed a likable enough fellow, except it was Saddler's very likableness that depressed the man. Edgar considered a variation, about how Saddler seemed a stand-up guy, but that was a lie. Saddler was a selfish, unprincipled, untrustworthy troublemaker. (Consequently, the man was impervious to *inversion*—since how do you upend faithlessness and nihilism into qualities that are any less appealing?) Edgar gave up. Nicola was right. Enough voyeurs had anguished over the nature of Barrington's soul.

"So what's the verdict?" Edgar asked instead. "Think I should claim Grant's Tomb for the Sobs?"

"I told you, I don't give a toss!" This time, Barrington kicked a whole pillow into the pool.

That pillow would take forever to dry out, and would mildew in the meantime, but the Saddlers of this world never considered the workaday consequences of their theatrical impulses. Edgar didn't carp—Bear would call him a Girl Guide again—though in holding his tongue Edgar appreciated how Barrington tyrannized acquaintances with the threat of his disapproval. However the Big B might disparage it, that unshakable likableness protected Saddler from ever staying up nights dithering over whether Eddie disapproved of him. If Edgar Kellogg or Win Pyre got difficult, there were plenty more sycophants in the sea.

"I was only asking what you thought," said Edgar stiffly. "Making conversation."

"Bollocks," Barrington boomed. "You want my palsy-walsy complicity. Bear and Eddie against the world. You're only considering the claim in the first place to prove to me you've got the bottle—to make me happy. Well, I don't wish to be obliged to be happy to make you happy. Do what you want, Eddie. I am sick to death of being abjured that because I'm in a filthy humor, or because I don't feel like coming out to play today, I have crushed the tender petals of some nonentity's bloody *feelings. Why do you think I vanished?* Maybe I was *tired of mattering so much*."

Truthfully, Edgar had never exactly sat himself down and dwelled on what he thought of claiming Grant's Tomb for the SOB, irrespective of Saddler's opinion. "Well," he supposed out loud, "I do wonder if, when you take fraudulent credit for a terrorist attack, you're suggesting that, even if you didn't do it, you sort of wish you had."

"Right over my head." It wasn't. Barrington meant that hand-wringing of any description bored him silly.

"And I also worry," said Edgar, "about getting caught."

"My innocuous prank, illegal?" Barrington scoffed.

"Oh, nobody could do you for murder or conspiracy. But at

the very least, you could be prosecuted for obstruction of justice. Wasting police time. The FBI's involved; bingo, federal offense. Frankly, I don't understand why you've never been arrested."

"Low tech," Barrington advised. "That's the secret. In all those film thrillers, it's getting fancy that trips the culprits up. All you need for this gambit is a telephone. Even the SOB statements, which are optional—bit of stationery, a stamp."

"The risk still isn't zero."

"The escapade wouldn't be much fun with no risk at all."

Granted; the adrenal rush of the last twenty-four hours had been intoxicating.

"On the other hand," Edgar reckoned, "I don't feel like going back to New York."

"Better," Barrington commended. "Solid self-serving argument."

"And as you've said, there'd be no harm done that hasn't been done already."

"Not so far," said Saddler brightly.

"What do you mean?"

Saddler faced his palms up in coy innocence. "As I said. Not so far."

Edgar eyed Barrington warily. "And if the hoax is neither good nor bad, well. It's more interesting to keep the SOB alive a while longer, isn't it?"

"Now you're talking. But what about your King for a Day option? That would be 'interesting': turning me in."

Edgar averted his face, abashed. "That might feel, um—traitorous, at this point."

"*You* feel loyal to *me*? We've never even met."

"I know you're sick of folks liking you. And I haven't quite decided if I like you, frankly. But I do feel a warped kinship with you. Maybe that makes me loyal, by way of being loyal to myself."

"I don't see how we're the least bit similar," said Barrington cuttingly.

"The main thing we have in common is we both bore easily."

Edgar stood to strip off his soggy T-shirt and wipe down his chest. "And I'm bored. I'm even bored with blabbing to you. I didn't become a journalist to sample the world's suck-ass beers."

With that, Edgar marched into the living room and picked up the phone.

"Are you insane?" Barrington shouted at his back.

"Probably." Edgar dialed.

Barrington pressed the button to disconnect. "The secret is low tech, not low IQ. Take minimal precautions, please. I thought you read the files. There's a pay phone in Terra do Cão whose location is apt."

Edgar did feel stupid. A call to a newspaper was unlikely to be traced, but there was no need to run that risk. Red-faced, he trooped upstairs, grabbed a fistful of escudos from atop the jar in the study, tripped quickly up the tower's spiral staircase to snap on some rubber gloves, and ducked into the bedroom to pull on some jeans. After running, he should have washed up first, but this impulse was so wild and patently foolhardy that he was reluctant to test it with a contemplative bath.

Downstairs, Edgar paused at the front door. "You think I'm a copycat."

"Of course," said Barrington cheerfully.

"Well, I'm not *arsed* if you do."

"That's the spirit! Oh, and before you go. May I assume that you're taking full responsibility for this decision?"

"Why?" asked Edgar suspiciously.

"We agree that if anything regrettable happens as a consequence, it's not my fault."

"What could happen?" asked Edgar brusquely. "The bomb's gone off already."

"Oh, nothing, nothing at all. I simply don't . . ." Barrington fluttered his fingers.

"What?"

"I don't want to hear about it, is all."

"What's to hear about?"

Barrington smiled with a bashful shrug. Escudos clinking in one pocket and the other bulging with Saddler's goofy homemade kazoo, Edgar lunged out the door. *Foom,* the *vento* slapped him in the face with the sure knowledge that in crossing that threshold he had also crossed a line that could prove difficult to sneak back over.

CHAPTER 24
Barba Is No Longer Boring

IF BOREDOM PUSHED him over that threshold, Edgar had a gift for it. A knack for boredom was a knack for spoliation, like being good at ransacking bars, tearing up rose beds, or vandalizing subway cars.

As a kid in Wilmington, Edgar had taped pennies to the railroad tracks near his house. Once run over by a freight train a copper was ruined, but the penny had also been appropriated. No longer legal tender that could be traded for a one-cent fireball, the squashed oblong disc had been wrested from the clutches of the U.S. government to become entirely Edgar's. When he grew a bit older, he graduated to dimes and quarters. Older still, Edgar had placed lovers, hobbies, whole cities on the tracks, flattening what was formerly precious. Anything tamed into the thoroughly dull had been as thoroughly dominated, as thoroughly possessed. Boredom, like penny-mashing, was a form of ownership.

Case in point: Edgar had taken an expensive holiday to southern France four years earlier. As he scuffled around Arles, the town's aloof antiquity was so enchanting that he grew resentful. Narrow passageways twisting from the crumbled coliseum, the Rhône coursing out of reach, knotty branches of apple trees reaching skyward like the arms of candelabras: the scenes might as well have been crummy postcard reproductions of late van Goghs. Edgar couldn't get into the place; rather, he couldn't get the place into him. In fact, he wondered if the bloated American tourists bulging at café tables were suffering from the same frustration, and kept ordering more courses because *coq au vin* and *coquilles*

Saint-Jacques were the only elements of the bafflingly picturesque landscape they could *take in*.

After two days of squinting down dusty, infuriatingly fetching ins and outs, Edgar returned fire and got *bored* with it. Profane, maybe, but ennui was his only hope of participating in his own holiday. He'd been traveling with a girl then, and vengefully he got bored with her, too. The last night of the sagging trip she cried. Helpless, Edgar got bored with having to console her.

Edgar learned to scuba dive; he got bored with it. He learned to ski; he got bored with it. He got bored with Angela and *Jamesie*, he got bored with New York. He got bored with being a lawyer, and with half a chance he could get good and bored with journalism, too. Captivation was slavery. Boredom *macht frei*.

Insidiously, Edgar had been growing bored with Barba. Already he'd deadened the drive into Cinzeiro until the austere vista inspired only, *Oh, that*. The wither in his mouth after a swig of Choque no longer took him aback. His colleagues Edgar now liked to regard as Known Quantities. He took the absurdly palatial Abrab Manor aggressively for granted. He accepted dinner dates with Henry and Nicola as his due, if he hadn't quite perfected a blasé carelessness about what to wear. Running, Edgar plowed through the *vento insano* with the prow of his refusal to be impressed. Though at first Edgar had been privately enthralled by access to a local journo watering hole, a welcome reprieve from *NYPD Blue* reruns dubbed over in Portuguese every evening, nowadays he shuffled off to his regular bar with a worldly sigh: *Christ, another night at the Rat*.

The exceptions to Edgar's swashbuckling nonchalance were two: Barrington, and Nicola. One was imaginary; the other was married.

Deep down, Edgar realized that deliberately making your life dull was criminal. It was an irrational defacement, like scraping obscenities into the finish of your own car. The aim of changing careers had been not to be bored, so to leap at the opportunity to find his new profession passé was perverse. There was precious little point to adventuring abroad if the first mission he undertook once washed on a faraway shore was to busy about finding the odd ordinary and the foreign familiar. Yet he couldn't stop himself. If boredom didn't make him happy, it did make him comfortable, and like most people he preferred comfort most of the time. Happiness, by contrast, was hard work.

But then, abruptly, Edgar was moved to industry anyway. Abruptly, there was no danger that Guy Wallasek would snarl and put him on hold until the line disconnected, that Edgar would have to trim his wordage down to a squib lest he get squeezed out of the *Record* all week, or that his fledgling career as a journalist would hurtle from the nest and *ker-splat* on the pavement. Abruptly—like it or not—Edgar wasn't bored.

For promptly after Edgar puttered off to the pay phone in Terra do Cão, poured escudos into the slot, reached a frightened girl at the *New York Times* foreign desk, growled the magic code phrase left on Barrington's last floppy through the kazoo ("last laugh," which seemed gratuitously provocative), and announced in a thickly accented Portuguese lisp that the SOB had bombed Grant's Tomb, Barba transformed.

Sullen local patrons at the Rat became louder, drunker, and more garrulous. Portuguese newscasters delivered the day's tidings in urgent gasps. When the Lisbon news was over, the barkeep switched to CNN, and Rat regulars pricked their ears for mention of their very own shit hole from the glassy towers of Atlanta. Anxious to strike just the right note between emotive shame and shy pride, shop assistants practiced rusty school English on Edgar as he laid in another stack of Weight Watchers lasagna. Tomás Verdade's schedule was purportedly packed, and his slimeball press officer João Pacheco no longer returned phone calls. Even the wind picked up.

Edgar soon came to appreciate that Cinzeiro's core hack pack had long been dependent on not only Saddler but a steady stream of visiting journalists whom regulars could show up, lure capriciously to bed, ply slyly with their first Choques, and poke fun at once they'd left. After Grant's Tomb, the generous expense accounts of transient TV crews leveraged up the general level of nightly entertainment by an average of two drinks per head. Better still, full-time Barban correspondents could tag along to lavish dinners at Moroccan hash houses, where the couscous and *balaclava* were actually edible and the ambiance was spiced with political risk. On boozy, soup-to-nuts evenings out, *Nightline* crews welcomed even Trudy Sisson as an informed source.

Of course, compared to these scavengers, the dizzy Floridian qualified as a shrewd pundit. Blow-ins varied in their political predispositions, from burn-'em-at-the-stake authoritarians to liberal hankie-twisters frantic to *understand*, but their ignorance was universal. These professional information-mongers hadn't the sketchiest notion of Portuguese history ("Who's Salazar?"—deposed in 1974, the fascistic dictator had only tyrannized the country for fifty years), much less had they mastered Barban politics. While after twelve hundred years of North African invasion, settlement, and intermarriage the veins of every Barban coursed with Moorish blood, visiting journalists still aped Creamie references to Barba's "indigenous culture," when neither its ethnicity nor its traditions were distinct from the *Barba*-ry Coast. Hacks turned a blind eye to polls repeatedly documenting that regional support for Barban independence ran to a mere 25 percent, a figure that undermined the drama of a province overrun by illegal aliens in spontaneous, unified revolt. Every instant expert accepted Tomás Verdade's inflated immigration figures as gospel. (Verdade's projections assumed not simply that the current rate of immigration remained constant, but that the latest rate of *increase* remained constant—a cunning if statistically underhanded method of sending any rising trend into the near vertical within two inches of graph paper.)

Moreover, if one hack ever put a mistake into print, it was reiterated all over the world. A small but telling example: the *Chicago Tribune* ran a long, widely reprinted exposé about the Creams, citing their home neighborhood as "El Terra do Cão" (which the author mistranslated "dock land," not "dog land," although the slum was nowhere near the water). But Terra do Cão was never named with an article by the people who lived there. Worse, *el* was masculine, *terra* feminine. Worst, *el* was Spanish. Portuguese for "the" was *o* or *a*.

Picky? Maybe. Nevertheless, following on that *Tribune* erratum, Terra do Cão became "El Terra do Cão" in every article about Barba henceforth. In fact, Edgar discovered that his own copy was being doctored at the *Record* with the inserted "El," presumably for enhanced verisimilitude. The *El* epidemic betrayed the fact that, although journalists were supposedly sent out into the field to harvest fresh data, their primary source of information was one another.

To give his colleagues credit, after Grant's Tomb the hierarchy of the Cinzeiro hack pack subtly reordered, and Edgar's eminence ratcheted up farther than his few months on this beat should have merited. With Barrington hovering over his shoulder as he typed, Edgar developed virtuosity in Barba-speak, and his copy soon exuded the confidence of a seasoned hand. Wallasek was sufficiently impressed to assign him a couple of news analyses—one of which laid bare Verdade's statistical fallacies, to the embarrassment of other hacks too suggestible to have examined the figures.

In person, Edgar gave off a nebulous air of *knowingness*, which while off-putting as a style was magnetic as a genuine condition. His colleagues couldn't have had any idea what Edgar knew, nor could they have identified what tipped them off that he was onto something. He'd stopped asking questions, but the early onset of complacency was a common side effect of their occupation. It was unlikely that any of his colleagues had ever articulated, "That Edgar Kellogg knows something we don't." Yet despite being the most junior correspondent posted here, Edgar was the one to whom a freshly arrived *GQ* writer instinctively turned, and if Martha wanted to float another theory about SOB "strategy" she tried it out on Edgar first. He became the arbiter of the probable, and rumors circled back to him that he had inherited Barrington's brilliant paramilitary connections—which he had, rather.

More than once when Edgar was kicking back at the Rat, a pimply nineteen-year-old local would whisper an agitated request for a private chat. After insisting on buying Edgar another drink and formally asking after the health of Edgar's family in set-phrase school English, the boy would refer nervously to the reporter's notorious "contacts." The supplicant reliably wanted to be a man, to defend his people, to sacrifice for his country's *liberdade*. He couldn't bear sitting at home with *Mamãe* and shelling fava beans into a pail while his heroic brothers-in-arms risked their lives in bold operations abroad. The terrorist wannabe had reliably called by O Creme first and been turned away, on the preposterous pretense that the leadership knew no *soldados ousados*! The boy was desperate to join up, to stand shoulder-to-shoulder with his noble SOB comrades. Could Edgar put the kid in touch? Edgar's blanket mandate to protect his sources rescued him from coming across, and he always sent these poor bastards packing with the hackneyed advice that they get themselves an education—which was precisely what they were after.

As for Barrington, Edgar saw somewhat less of his host, often coming home late and hurrying off to bed rather than lingering by the fountain for a jaw. Exultantly, Edgar was coming into his own. Yet his enhanced prestige, his authority, his *knowingness* weren't the result of any hard-earned self-realization, but were the natural outgrowth of having been handed the punch line when the rest of the crowd was still listening with earnest expectancy to the joke. The ghost of Abrab Manor was an unwelcome reminder that Edgar owed his elevated station to the warped ingenuity of Barrington Saddler.

Edgar did keep his end up, however, and in the maintenance of any tradition the latest standard-bearer took some modest credit on his own account. Edgar's articles—interpreting SOB "statements" anonymously posted from Cinzeiro, describing moves afoot in Lisbon to offer Barba regional autonomy—were all composed with the textual equivalent of a straight face.

In retrospect, Edgar couldn't castigate himself for having done anything malevolent. True, one of those Japanese tourists in intensive care had died, but that wasn't Edgar's fault. He was genuinely sorry, and the creepy afterthought that mortality would increase the political impact of the bombing for the SOB he shoved hastily aside. In the plus column: Edgar was having a wonderful time, Edgar was rapidly becoming man of the hour, Edgar was getting his articles published, and Edgar wasn't bored.

Having enlisted himself as a good little soldier, naturally when another story broke a few weeks down the line that a bomb had been placed outside the Moroccan embassy in DC, Edgar could only consider the event heaven-sent. The embassy had been evacuated, the bomb defused. No especial opprobrium would be conferred even on the incompetent terrorists who had left their toys behind, and by a staggering stroke of luck the SOB bombing a North African embassy would make an iota of political sense. When no other acronym took credit, after dark Edgar gunned the Saab off to *El* Terra do Cão, fed the phone the escudos he'd been stockpiling since Grant's Tomb, and asked for Cindy.

In late October, a fellow prankster claimed to have planted a bomb at the final game of the World Series, forcing the crowd to decamp and the game to be delayed by two days while sniffer dogs snuffled through the stadium. No device was found. The whole country was subsequently in such an uproar that Edgar was a bit sorry to miss the hoo-ha. Nothing melted barriers between strangers like shared indignation, and it would have been open season on chatting up attractive women in supermarkets for a week.

As a baseball fan, Edgar was admittedly torn. The most venerated of American institutions had been defiled. On the other hand, one more year and the fucking Orioles hadn't made the Series . . . Besides, how better to punish the real culprit than to steal his thunder? Edgar's gas tank was full, his pockets jingling. Thereafter, his compatriots leapt at the chance to blame the un-American scare on foreign riffraff.

Edgar gave the strafing of the Indianapolis Planned Parenthood a miss (too much of a political stretch). Likewise, though philosophically sympathetic, he passed on a dud fertilizer car bomb outside the Holtsville IRS. Officers at the scene had derided the detonator wiring as inept, and Edgar was averse to association with the unprofessional.

By contrast, the explosion at Sea World was irresistible. Permanently establishing the SOB's reputation as cutthroat, the Orlando bomb produced nationwide outrage—indeed, a far more abiding public outcry than the foofaraw following BA-321. Though the Sea World device only injured a few tourists, it did kill "Bubbard" and three of his adorable dolphin friends. (Much was made of dolphins' reputed intelligence, which raised the question of how highly Americans rated the average IQ of airline passengers.) All through November, CNN reporters announced gloomily that the FBI had made no progress in the "Bubbard Bombing," but that a fund established to ensure the survival of Bubbard's traumatized offspring had swelled to $1.5 million.

The Orlando device *was* professional, efficiently obliterating any forensic evidence linking its designers to the blast. Successful anonymity was crucial, since bunglers who left clues imperiled the credibility of the SOB. Were a trail to lead to the real agents, subsequent SOB "atrocities" were bound to be greeted with dubiety. Why, choosing which incidents to claim was far more complex than it had first appeared, and Edgar surfed the Internet for hours before committing Os Soldados Ousados to anything rash.

Edgar did patriotically incline toward appropriating ructions on U.S. soil, whereas Barrington had displayed a natural European preference for "the" Continent. A fresh proliferation of U.S. targets translated into a much-remarked shift in SOB *strategy*. But Edgar's Yankee predilections proved surprisingly unrestrictive. Owing to the spread of mischief-making pages on the Web, any boil-faced teen could access recipes for homemade explosives, many of which could be concocted from ingredients in his mom's kitchen.

Consequently, domestic bombings in the States had tripled in the last decade to over three thousand a year. (Using Tomás Verdade's percentage-of-increase linear projection, in ten years that figure would necessarily multiply to nine thousand, in a hundred years to about 180 million, or half a million criminal explosions every day.) While Edgar disdained piddly stuff (pipe bombs, nail bombs) and tried to avoid isolated rural communities (where everyone would know that *'course, Crazy Bob Rafter did it*), the number of incidents on offer was sumptuous. Best of all, U.S. authorities seemed grateful to write off a few craters around City Hall as the evil doings of foreign agitators, since the notion of such a large proportion of America's citizenry festively blowing up their own backyards was far more unsettling.

Barrington had a point. To a degree, Edgar was performing a service. Unclaimed, all these incidents had a bereftness about them, as if they were wandering friendless in the wilderness, or left in baskets on his doorstep waiting to be adopted. Their sheer arbitrariness cried out for redress. Edgar was in league with the forces of meaning against the forces of chaos. Fine, best if bad things never happened. But once they had, better they did so for a reason, even an inane reason like Barban independence, than for no reason at all. Hence Edgar was conscientious and kept the claims coming, until he came to regard his lisping phone calls not as elective entertainment but as his job.

Yet despite the teleological benevolence of giving purpose to what was otherwise witless anarchy, Edgar had encountered one difficulty that, were his paramilitary doppelgänger to continue to be taken seriously, he would need to overcome. Irrationally, he shied from claiming atrocities with fatalities that, unlike Bubbard, once stood on two legs. When that Japanese tourist died, Edgar felt funny. Rotten-funny. Over and over he assured himself that the hapless fellow would have taken a dirt nap even if Edgar had never reached for the *El* Terra do Cão pay phone, but his very repetition of these assurances revealed that they didn't work. Meantime, the SOB was reluctantly applauded for its recent resort to "nonlethal pressure tactics." Barrington had started wheedling as Edgar rushed in and out, "Weak stomach, have we?" And maybe the honest answer was: *Hell, yes.*

CHAPTER 25

Portugal Denies Immigration Overhaul Is SOB Appeasement

EDGAR KELLOGG, BARBA CORRESPONDENT

LISBON—After six years, the Lisbon government is running short of fresh obloquy to denounce the international atrocities claimed by Os Soldados Ousados de Barba, intent on an independent Barban peninsula. Stock adjectives like "imoral," "diabólico," or "escandaloso" having depreciated, Lisbon legislators vilify the SOB with increasing flamboyance. One MP's recent press statement began, "The SOB has once again plunged into the fetid cesspool of mindless animals . . . ." A goulash of subsequent mixed metaphors made for queasy reading.

Yet while one set of Lisbon functionaries decries Tomás Verdade, President of O Creme de Barbear, the reputed political wing of the SOB, as base-minded, blackmailing, and blood-thirsty, another set is ordering tea sandwiches for tête-à-têtes with the man.

Officially, negotiations between O Creme and Lisbon cabinet ministers have been covert. Yet Portugal is as small a country as Mr. Verdade's Latinate braggadocio is sizable. Between government leaks and O Creme boasting, the frequent hush-hush meetings have become an open secret.

Talk is cheap. Should concessions at effective gunpoint have stopped at dialogue, Lisbon's implicit capitulation to terrorism would remain nominal. Indeed, many argue that the tantalizing prospect of negotiating an SOB cease-fire is well worth the indignity of engaging with so-called "thugs in suits," whom most lawful northern Portuguese consider beneath contempt.

Moreover, Lisbon is under severe American pressure to resolve the dispute. In the last year, the United States has borne the brunt of SOB terrorism.

But concessions to O Creme demands have gone far beyond tea service. Despite a recent Iberia Trust poll documenting that 73% of Barbans have no interest in home-rule, Lisbon is now tendering the province more devolved autonomy than any other sector of Portugal.

Thus far Mr. Verdade has ridiculed the proposals, deriding the regional powers on offer as little more than granting Barbans the privilege to "collect their own trash and bury their own dead." O Creme continues to hold out for a fully independent Barban state.

To date, Lisbon has resisted outright accedence to the fringe group's primary agenda of statehood. However, each of the government's denunciatory rhetorical salvos at O Creme has heralded another package of "confidence-building measures"—known in the Barban vernacular as "Creamie-pleasers."

In addition to seeking the sovereignty that Barban nationalists claim is the only answer to the peninsula's racial and religious tensions, O Creme is fighting to stem largely Muslim immigration from North Africa. The party maintains that Moroccans and Algerians are migrating to the province in such numbers that they will soon overwhelm Barba's dominant Catholic culture.

Previous to the rise of the SOB, Barban objections to unchecked immigration went unheeded. Since the mobilization of the SOB's armed campaign, Portuguese immigration laws have been drastically overhauled:

- Portugal's annual ceiling on newcomers has been halved;
- In three separate, widely publicized asylum cases this last year, Algerian villagers fleeing Islamic fundamentalist murder gangs were all deported, though such political refugees' admission to Portugal would have been assured six years ago;
- The residency period for citizenship has been extended from five to ten years;
- Tourist visas have been reduced from six to three months;
- Work permits have grown scarce, and Barban Muslims charge that the Portuguese equivalent of the American green card is now routinely denied all North African applicants;
- As of last month, the required documentation for all foreigners working legally in Portugal has become oppressively Byzantine.

Portuguese Prime Minister Otelo Delgado flatly denies that any of his government's initiatives are concessions to SOB violence. Mr. Delgado insists that immigration laws have been tightened in the interests of Portugal as a whole—to protect jobs nationwide, and to assert administrative autonomy in the post-Maastricht European Union.

Official denials betray official embarrassment. The dogs in the street in Portugal see recent moves as more than coincidental. A lethal insurgency demands closed borders. Simultaneously, this sparsely populated Iberian nation erects more barriers to foreign residents than Switzerland. Though underdeveloped Portugal rates as one of the least attractive destinations for immigrants in all of Europe, its naturalization policy is now nearly as prohibitive as that of Japan.

In its most aggressive accommodation of O Creme demands so far, Lisbon has tripled its spending on immigration enforcement, beefing up a formerly underfunded, languid arm of the national police dedicated to checking ships for stowaways, riffling passports at airports, and running to ground delinquent guests with expired visas. Though the peninsula constitutes only 18% of the country's land mass and contains only 11% of Portugal's people, three-quarters of the expanded and revamped sting force has been deployed to Barba.

Its uniforms having been redesigned in loud cardinal red, the immigration contingent of the police force has been reincarnated as a Brigada Encarnada da Imigração Portuguesa (BEIP).

Liberal Lisboners decry the BEIP as a recrudescence of the much-hated Polícia Internacional e de Defensa do Estado (PIDE), the goose-stepping militia of António Salazar, the widely despised dictator deposed in 1974. Consumed with seizing communists and dissidents, consciously modeled on and initially trained by Germany's

Gestapo, the PIDE tyrannized Portugal's citizenry into informing on one another.

Similarly, posses of BEIP officers troop conspicuously around Barba's provincial capital of Cinzeiro, occupy the airport, and patrol Barban beaches. Naval BEIP squadrons cruise the Atlantic scanning for boats smuggling immigrants from Tangier.

The force is offering a 5,000 escudo ($300) reward to citizens who report illegal aliens. More, any illegal immigrant who turns in three of his fellows earns immunity from prosecution and deportation. Such incentives encourage the widespread fearfulness, distrust, and painful personal betrayals common to the Salazar era.

Yet Mr. Verdade has charged that BEIP sweeps for illegal aliens are all show. He asserts that the BEIP has deported only a handful of North Africans, most of whom would immigrate successfully to Barba on a second attempt.

As gestures of appeasement from Lisbon accumulate, O Creme's rhetoric has grown only more belligerent. "The pallid nature of these placations," Mr. Verdade objects, "is a slap in the face." Without serious moves toward full independence, warns Mr. Verdade, there is "no telling what the SOB might do."

In response to such vague but ominous threats, the Delgado administration has called for more rigorous enforcement techniques from the BEIP. Heads rolled last month when the local Lisbon press caught the State Department inflating its figures for returned illegals.

Opinions about Mr. Delgado's "confidence-building measures" among northern Portuguese are deeply split. Some see "Creamie-pleasers" as an insult to democracy, the direct rewards of airline sabotage, like the infamous bombing of British Airways Flight 321 five years ago.

Embarrassed by the reputation for *barbarity* that the SOB is building for the Portuguese internationally, others maintain that tightening immigration regulations and enforcing these laws more strictly is a small price to pay for the violence to stop.

Unfortunately, Mr. Delgado's carrots seem to whet more than sate the O Creme leadership's appetite for concessions. All fat cats are alike, in politics and commerce. The more Mr. Verdade gains, the more he wants.

Though once it was finished Edgar was pleased with the article, drafting the very first paragraph he'd hit a wall. Fingers frozen over the keys, Edgar realized that if he had to type "Os Soldados Ousados de Barba, intent on an independent Barban peninsula" or "Tomás Verdade, President of O Creme de Barbear, the reputed political wing of the SOB" one more time he was going to shoot himself. Though anyone in the U.S. unfamiliar with the SOB and its president by now clearly lived in a survivalist underground bunker eating canned Spaghetti-Os and rereading curling *Time* magazines from the 1960s, the *Record* style guidelines required that this information be repeated in every piece Edgar filed. Only when he had programmed the phrases into his computer as two-keystroke macros could Edgar finish the piece, normal blood pressure restored.

The article's inspiration was Edgar's own inconvenience. The most recent "Creamie-pleaser" required Edgar, himself a legal alien, to furnish paycheck stubs, a full bio going back to high school, original paste-ups of his journalism, a letter from Wallasek confirming his employment, a copy of his birth certificate posted from Wilmington, three passport-size photos, a *police background check* both in Delaware and Cinzeiro, a medical report covering everything from hemorrhoids to HIV, a thirty-five-page application form demanding the names, postal and e-mail addresses, telephone numbers, and titles of his every acquaintance in Portugal, and twenty thousand fucking escudos in order to justify his remaining in Cinzeiro. Running around collecting this absurd stack of nuisance documents, Edgar felt as if Tomás Verdade had personally sent him on a scavenger hunt.

Otherwise, Edgar's private reaction to Lisbon's groveling before his own fantasy acronym was schizoid. It was gratifying to dick around a whole country like that, to dictate its headlines, to alter its laws, and to recontour its political landscape with a few prank phone calls. But as much as Edgar was tickled, he was disquieted. Not because the SOB didn't exist, but because as far as the rest of the world was concerned it did. That conversation with Ansel P. Henwood on the plane kept coming back to him, about how "the assholes had always won and the assholes were still winning." Much as Edgar cherished his own cynicism, it also depressed him. Watching Lisbon contort itself to satisfy the "SOB" was a hoot, but at the end of the day the fact that appearing to blow people up meant you got your way wasn't altogether funny.

"I'm shit-canning your piece."

"Why?" Edgar wailed into the receiver. "I worked—"

"It's too long by a factor of two," Wallasek snarled. "I don't have the time to edit it down to the three paragraphs it deserves. You buried the lead up to your knees. That is, if there was one. And since when are the *dogs in the street* cited as an informed source?"

"That's just an expression!"

"A moronic expression. No reader has to strain his brain to figure out that our perceptive dog goes by the name of Kellogg. You're a reporter. This copy is baldly editorial."

"Get out! The whole paper—any paper—is manipulative. You only invoke that old saw about objective reporting when it suits you. You and I both know there's no such thing."

"Are you in secret cahoots with Saddler, Kellogg? Because I've heard this line before, and believe you me, I don't like it. It's hard to be objective, you betcha. That it's difficult makes it that much more important to try. Nobody gives a shit what you think, Kellogg. They only want to read what you know."

Edgar decided this was not the time to get into a philosophical discussion about whether what you think and what you know amount to roughly the same thing. "You just disagree with my angle on the story," Edgar charged.

"What story? The trouble isn't that I disagree with your 'story,' I don't care about it. The whole approach is too inside, Kellogg."

"I know the nitty-gritty's a little tedious, but the devil's in the details!" Okay, Edgar was spoiled. Other *Record* stringers—even *super*-stringers—had their work spiked all the time. But SOB stories enjoyed high priority, and every article he'd written for months had run. Day-rate checks were piling up nicely, more than compensating for Edgar's derisory retainer.

"Damn straight it's tedious! Our readers are titillated by

terrorist saber-rattling, maybe. The bombs, they eat up. But small-print readjustments of wetback policy in some European jerkwater are a big yawn. Stick to the big picture, got it?" Wallasek hung up.

The dial tone blaring, Edgar wouldn't be able to make his editor understand that in the complex mosaic of Portugal's hastily revised immigration law was a motherfucking big picture, and a dark one.

CHAPTER 26

Every Former Fat Boy's Dream

THE NATIONAL RECORD correspondent was provided an office in the center of town, though for his first few weeks with so little to do there—like, nothing—Edgar had mostly puttered at his computer in the tower, writing unposted letters to Angela, whom nowadays he gave no more thought than a returned library book that he hadn't bothered to finish. Once the SOB's *campanha militar* resumed, however, Edgar needed to protect Abrab Manor as a haven from the badgering imprecations of visiting journalists (could he pretty-please-with-sugar-on-top introduce them to a real live Sob?), so he'd begun to conduct business from the office.

The *Record* bureau was on the third floor of another flimsily constructed savings-and-loan-style chunk of brown-painted aluminum called Casa Naufragada (inexplicably, "Shipwreck House"). At least Barrington had copped the largest and least drafty suite along the hall, its speckled lino blanketed in Persian carpet, the prosaic metal and wood-grain-appliqué furnishings provided by the management replaced with sandalwood antiques, and the walls boastfully decorated with Nicola's pen-and-inks, over which Edgar was prone to moon.

His favorite was an exterior of Abrab Manor niggled in rapidographs of various thicknesses, some no wider than a hair. Each roof tile and walkway slate was painstakingly detailed, their hues hinted at with a tracery of colored pencil. The drawing must have taken her a week, though a pleasant week, making the end product that much more entrancing. Himself, Edgar would never have drafted such a delectable little landscape and then parted with it, but would have clung to it eternally as proof of what a clever fellow he was.

Yet Nicola's version of completing a project was to give it away. Edgar had already benefited from this compulsion in the form of a hand-knit watch cap stitched with the *National Record* logo, a pinwheel (Cinzeiro youth craze) covered in harlequin silks, and a regular deluge of cod balls, pizza rusticas, and tray cakes that Nicola persisted in calling "leftovers." No one had ever made him feel so stingy in comparison.

The *Record* bureau shared its hall with the offices of the *Guardian*, the *New York Times*, the *Independent*, *Le Monde*, the *Washington Post*, the *Tokyo Times*, Reuters, and Trudy Sisson's one-woman photographic agency—the sort of clannish line-up from which the term "hack pack" derived. Certainly for journalists covering the same beat to be concentrated on a single floor of Casa Naufragada increased the likelihood that they'd all tumble off to catch the same events, like kids carousing from the classroom for a school trip.

Too, once arrived at a newsworthy spectacle en masse, these world travelers, like travelers everywhere, tended to cling to one another, in preference to dispersing into funny-smelling crowds. Before filing, Edgar's cohorts often dropped by adjoining offices nervously to compare notes. Since an editor's primary sources of information about their patch were other newspapers and wire services, it was far less crucial to square their copy with the truth than with other copy.

Theoretically, Edgar abhorred this clubby office arrangement. He deplored consensus journalism as bland, packs of any sort as insecure. News gatherers roving together in throngs narrowed coverage, diminished its dynamism, and encouraged a timid, tidy company line. Besides, Edgar thought of himself as a loner, if he'd never been thoroughly sure that this was a role he'd chosen and not one he'd been stuck with, of which he'd learned to make the best.

In practice, however, Edgar adored cruising down Hack Hall of Casa Naufragada and poking his head into succeeding doors. He loved lingering by the coffee machine to trade insider tittle-tattle. He secretly relished covering Creamie rallies flanked by garrulous cohorts, to whom he could make caustic asides while they aggregated aloofly at the back. After teeming north in a convoy, Edgar flushed with a warm, safe glow seated between his fellow Known Quantities at Lisbon press conferences, scrawling messages on his pad, like "That's the fourth time he's used the word *fiendish*," and passing them to Win.

Edgar's pleasure at being ensconced snugly in a collegial covey didn't reduce to so wholesome a matter as an embracing affection for his colleagues. He wasn't sure he liked them that much, as individuals, and as a group they were ludicrous. But he liked knowing their names. He liked that they knew his. He liked it that, little by little, some of them seemed to like *him*. Oh, wallowing in this cozy clique was weak, it was frail, it was intellectually bankrupt and professionally suspect and probably even pathetic, but it was also every former fat boy's dream.

So when Edgar got word that in the North African ghetto of Novo Marrakech a BEIP house-to-house sweep for illegal immigrants was turning nasty, he happily mustered the troops down the hall. It was that dickhead João Pacheco who'd tipped him off. Creamies were keen for publicity about "Beep" raids, for while never satisfied that the new get-tough immigration policy was adequate, and reluctant to cede their professional-victim status to competing unfortunates, they gleefully reaped credit for making Lisbon dance.

Serendipitously, Nicola had just stopped by to dispense a basket of date-nut squares, and Edgar entreated her to join their joyride. While for denizens of Casa Naufragada the premium enticement to any excursion was its potential for violence, Nicola was one of those obtuse creatures who regarded the fact that someone might get hurt as reason to steer clear. Edgar was obliged to assure her that Cinzeiro "riots" were akin to impromptu street fairs, replete with vendors hawking fresh *tortas de uvas peludas* and opportunistic minstrels.

Henry greatly assisted Edgar's case by pontificating stiffly that a riot was no place for a girl, and that Henry himself "only risked his life for journalism" in order to "get to the bottom of what happened to his family and why," not in the capacity of a "conflict voyeur," after which Nicola flung her basket of goodies on the desk and said she "wouldn't miss their silly riot for the world." In all, she seemed to be growing impatient with her husband's icy histrionics (for which, to his credit, Henry displayed little flair)—although not, to Edgar's despair, quite impatient enough.

Meanwhile, from the exuberance along Hack Hall you'd have thought they were preparing for a picnic. Trudy tied a pink ribbon around her straw hat, checking for stray blond hairs with her compact while stuffing her Real Photo-Journalist's Vest with extra film. Roland donned a pair of Barba's traditional plastic goggles, ostensibly to shield his eyes from wind-borne grit but more probably because he'd concluded they looked cool. Martha wrapped up a packet of date-nut squares for a snack she might better have skipped. Win shrugged into his coat-of-many-countries, its zipper shot and leather worn soft, while whinnying a weary *here-we-go, another-fucking-riot* sigh; Pyre had mastered the ownership-through-boredom gambit before Edgar was born.

Her plans to shift to Jerusalem put on indefinite hold, Alexis yanked her cellular phone from its recharger and lunged for the elevator, but Edgar beat her to the button. Now that Barrington had relinquished his role as class bathroom monitor, Alexis was ever anxious to assert her a priori leadership just because she worked for the *Times*. Edgar had grown equally anxious to deny her that authority by the pettiest means possible. Maybe no one would ever replace Barrington quite, but if anyone stepped into the breach it wasn't going to be that officious, sexless prune.

The Jap, the Frog, and a collection of visiting leeches from Fleet Street and the *Wall Street Journal Europe* brought up the rear, and the field trip commenced. Gloriously, Nicola was still pissed off at her husband and shared Edgar's Turbo. Yet once settled in the adjacent bucket seat she went quiet, running her finger dolorously along the dashboard and taking deep lungfuls with her nose lifted. Edgar didn't get it until she murmured, "That smell." Right. She was bent out of shape because this was Barrington's car.

It was all Edgar could do to stop himself from exploding, yeah, we're in Saddler's Saab, and I'm wearing Saddler's shirt, and Saddler's musky fuck-me cologne as well, and we're on our way to a hullabaloo that probably wouldn't even be happening if it weren't for Saddler's twisted notion of a good laugh. We've got everything, honey, except Saddler himself, who left you without so much as a fare-thee-well, though not before bolting a chip on your husband's shoulder the size of a two-by-four. So how about turning that pretty face in this direction, sister? I may be a powerful disappointment in comparison, as you said yourself *lost*, *hostile*, and hunkered into the paranoid posture of a rope-a-doped boxer. I may be a *former fat boy just looking for love*, in the words of our mutual friend whose very absence talks. But the one thing I've got going for me is that I'm not a myth or an icon or a void in all of Cinzeiro's social life but a man with the standard equipment who's actually here.

"I should obviously buy," was all Edgar said aloud, "one of those cardboard pine trees."

After several minutes of laden silence, Nicola said softly, "I'm sorry about Henry's behavior, back in the office. I know he sounded—"

Edgar provided, "Like a *prat*," a Britishism for which he was finding multiple applications.

"This morning." She sighed. "He found the postcard."

Since Edgar's whole, total, entire life was not consumed with Barrington Saddler—quite—it took him a moment to remember postcard-from-supposedly-whom. "Big deal. You said it was blank."

"Well, that's suspicious, isn't it? Addressed, with no message? Better he'd written some innocuous wish-you-were-here, and signed someone else's name. I swear, that is *typical* of Barrington: to go through the motions of discretion, without thinking it all the way through and being genuinely considerate!"

Given that Saddler had walked out cold on his every friend, relative, and responsibility without explanation, complaining that the composition of his alleged postcard was inconsiderate was rather like objecting that Son of Sam didn't pay his gas bill. Yet instead of emphasizing this absurdity, Edgar found himself indulging Nicola's desperate fantasy that the card could only have been posted by Himself.

"Do you wish he'd never sent it?"

Nicola snapped, "Don't be stupid." Henry wasn't the only one in a bad mood.

"If you thought the sender was recognizable, why didn't you throw it away?"

She threw up her hands, and glared out the side window. "I don't have—! I don't have much. Physically. To remember him by. Bin it? I simply couldn't. But I'm not very good at hiding things."

"Where'd you put it?"

"My top dresser drawer."

"You're right," said Edgar. "You suck."

"Henry said, it came the day Grant's Tomb was bombed, didn't it? He said I'd been too 'giddy' when news of the bomb came in, and he knew something was up. Perverse, isn't it, when happiness is a sin?"

"I assume you denied all this."

"To what end? He'd know I was lying."

Edgar hit the steering wheel. "Woman, you're hopeless. You lie to allow them to lie to themselves. It doesn't matter if they believe you. Not at first. Just stick to your story and don't budge. Eventually you'll talk them into it, because they'll talk themselves into it, and you'll talk yourself into it, too. Say anything enough times and it starts to sound true, since most people don't know the difference between the true and the merely familiar."

"I won't lie," said Nicola stolidly.

"Don't do the crime if you can't do the time."

"But I didn't—"

"Save it for Henry," he cut her off. "You got nothin' to explain to me."

Edgar's portrayal of Barban civil strife as one long Ninth Avenue Food Fair was exaggerated, though the last "riot" he'd covered in Cinzeiro amounted to little more than a shouting match between some unemployed Creams and an Algerian construction crew. An enterprising vendor had indeed materialized to sell the journalists, who outnumbered the antagonists by half a dozen, soupy cups of pistachio *gelado*. This time, however, as Edgar approached Novo Marrakech the melee was audible from farther away, and he was already considering parking the Saab safe from projectiles when the choice was made for him: a Beep van had blocked the road and was turning all traffic around. Edgar flipped his *Record* ID—a gesture of instant access that still brought him boundless joy—then swung the car up on the curb, pulled the pouting Nicola from her seat, and proceeded on foot.

Being dirt-poor, Novo Marrakech was one of Cinzeiro's few neighborhoods whose eighteenth-century housing stock hadn't been leveled, and was consequently one of Edgar's favorite haunts. The row houses were faced with painted tile, the lanes paved with slippery cobble, the air sharp with garlic and chili oil. The area had an animated, chaotic feel, flashing with opalescent scarves, tingling with obscure spices, lively with tongue-lashing vendetta and tearful reconciliation—like a real foreign country. Oh, lately when Edgar ventured into this maze for a lamb kabob the residents seemed more closed, their smiles less ready, their service brisker in an apparent anxiousness to be done with him, but Edgar hadn't been sure if the Moroccans had really changed or if he'd merely become more alert to his own status as an intruder.

This afternoon, the chaos wasn't rambunctious but forbidding, and the hostility toward anyone not a card-carrying raghead went well beyond normal wariness of strangers in an ethnic enclave. As Edgar took Nicola's hand and threaded toward the dull *poom* of rubber bullets, householders slammed shutters and locked front doors. Garbage rained from overhead, and Edgar nimbly dodged potato peelings and soft tomatoes. Since the narrow passages doubled as wind tunnels, the refuse assumed a horizontal trajectory in gusts, and followed them down the road.

When the duo arrived at the small commercial square where the commotion appeared to be centered, Edgar pulled Nicola into the entryway of an optometrist's that seemed safe enough, since its every window was already smashed. A red Beep van was parked across the square, full of arrested locals presumably, since it boomed with a rhythmic pound of protest from inside. Pistols at least still holstered, Beeps in riot gear ringed the middle of the plaza waving wide-barreled rubber-bullet rifles in aimless, jerky circles. Masked by hard plastic visors, any expressions of alarm or confusion would be obfuscated by glare, but full-blown riots had been hitherto unheard of in this town, and the rookies couldn't have had the faintest idea what they were doing. Which was dangerous. Most of these immigration cops were likely to panic by running away, but there was another sort of panic you got from people with guns, and it was the stuff of tribunals.

By contrast, the Moroccans did seem to know what they were doing, since the cardinal rule of rioting is that you foul your own nest. That is, you concentrate wreckage in the area where you, your family, and your friends live; you put your own well-being at risk far more than the health of anyone trying to contain you; and you vent most of your anger not on its real object but on your own kind.

Illustrating that Novo Marrakech dwellers had graduated from Riot School with honors, the square was strewn with oranges, eggplants, and squashed pumpkins from nearby fruit-and-veg stands, glopped with broken eggs, rolling with burst sacks of dried chickpeas, and fragrant with toppled tubs of coriander seeds. Frames from the optometrist's behind him crunched under Edgar's feet and mangled across the front walk. The display case of the electrical appliance shop opposite was empty, its window smashed, like most of the glass in sight on ground level and several residential panes on upper floors. A Ford Cortina on the corner was on fire, and chances were good that it belonged to someone in the neighborhood. Though the vicinity was hardly blanketed with fallen bodies, half a dozen Moroccan youths glowered from entryways, cradling arms or pressing T-shirts to bloodied foreheads; brandishing three-foot shields and padded like cricket players, the Beeps had suffered no serious injuries that Edgar could see. Magnificent if only for its voluptuous irrationality, rioting is a carnival of self-destruction.

Yet since they'd previously been prepackaged into three-minute TV news segments, before this journo gig Edgar had missed certain essentials about riots. A well-edited broadcast splices together several pitched sequences to evoke nonstop tooth-and-nail pandemonium. Fine entertainment. Not remotely true to life. A respectable riot goes on for hours, and even experienced, ultra-fit troublemakers cannot sustain full-tilt havoc for more than a few minutes at a go. Violence is exhausting, it's hazardous, and it demands a surprising degree of ingenuity. Rabble-rousers need continuously to light upon new objects to hurl, new vehicles to burn, new abuse to scream, new premises to loot, and new stashes in which to hide microwaves.

Accordingly, bouts of ferocity were fitful, and the abiding atmosphere in the square was desultory. A group of young men would charge the Beeps in the middle, pitching stones, flinging fistfuls of hard chickpeas, thumping the plastic shields with their tennis shoes and scampering back again as if playing a civil-disobedience version of kick-the-can. Or a chorus would rise from an alleyway, reminiscent of the "Hell, no, we won't go!" chants from the Vietnam era, albeit whatever they were shouting was completely wasted, since Arabic flew right over the heads of most Portuguese cops. Alternatively, veiled women in djellabas leaning out upper windows would mobilize a hailstorm of old shoes. Though at one point another sedan went up in flames, all these instants of unruliness punctuated an uneasy stalemate, as gangs regrouped and Beeps propped shields on the ground because their arms were tired.

Another curiosity about riots in the round is that they're not that loud. Yelling, sure; the odd *poom* of rubber bullets (cast in a fleshy pink, the thick, snub-nosed cylinders scattered the square like discarded marital aids); the rattle of hurtled cans bumping across the cobbles to a standstill; Martha Hulbert's cries of "Edgar! Over here!" from beneath an awning where his colleagues had all congregated—cries he ignored, not wanting to seem prey to the herd mentality in front of Nicola. But Edgar had arrived too late for the smashing of glass; the gas tank in the sedan refused to explode, and for stretches the only cacophony within earshot emitted from seagulls.

Yet the silence, in its relentless demand to be filled, was ominous. And so was the occasion's perfect lack of structure, which called out for an imposed climax. The Moroccans were running out of both impromptu ammunition and ideas. Beeps did not know what to do or where to go or whether to fire their weapons or at whom. Neither the cops nor the immigrants had a plan. The fracas had no leaders and frankly no purpose, and neither party to the stand-off seemed clear on how to bring the impasse to an end.

With the rumpus so sporadic and dispersed, Edgar was hard-pressed to decipher what exactly was going on. In his latter days as a lawyer, when he'd been pining to become a foreign correspondent, he'd imagined that in the thick of world events eyewitnesses were granted absolute access to the truth, which those forced to consume news secondhand would at best piece together in hearsay dribs. An attractive fiction. A news *story* was a postmortem construct. Those *We Were There* books were full of lies, since when you're *there* you've rarely the tiniest notion of what's happening. Odds are if you were "there" at Pearl Harbor you didn't know the Japanese had bombed any ships, any more than grassy-knoll rubberneckers grasped in the very moment what those cracking sounds meant in Dallas. Nevertheless, We-Were-There Edgar was now professionally responsible for putting all those eggplants and chickpeas into credible narrative order for his readership.

"Edgar, we should leave," Nicola whispered. "Without any journalists watching, everyone might just go home. With all these television cameras, Trudy snapping away . . . Look: those kids are showing off for her. You scribbling on your pad . . . You're inciting them. If you keep waiting for a story, they might just give you one."

"Nick, this is no time to discuss the 'Observer Paradox.' I've got a job to do." Edgar trod carefully, skirting wide of *risking his life for journalism* like her posturing husband.

"Nothing good can come of this. These people, they used to be so kind, so decent and warm! God, something terrible is happening to this country. If anything awful goes down here, Edgar, it's going to be partly your fault."

Edgar started. In point of fact, he had been feeling hauntingly culpable. No anonymous phone calls from Terra do Cão, no renewed SOB campaign. No renewed SOB campaign, no need to appease O Creme de Barbear. No appeasement, no BEIP. No BEIP, no sweeps of Novo Marrakech for illegals. No Beep sweeps, no riot. Edgar told himself that this chain of cause-and-effect was overextended—like the tenuously linked sequences through which kingdoms fell for want of a nail, or weather patterns in North America traced to butterflies over Tokyo. But he also told himself that *telling yourself* anything instead of plain old thinking it is the red flag of self-deception.

Unsettled, Edgar begged Nicola's indulgence, and dodged into the adjoining entryway, where he canvassed the group huddled there with, "English? English?" One mustachioed hothead stuttered in a mix of English and Portuguese that over a hundred illegal immigrants had been rounded up for deportation that afternoon. His friend asserted the numbers were much higher—two hundred, three! A third claimed that five Morrocans had been killed, while his companion said more like twelve; the number of officers in the Brigada Encarnada slain in retaliation numbered either zero, three, or twenty-seven. Great. More "eyewitnesses."

Just then, two patrols of Beeps entered the square from opposite roads, each corralling handcuffed captives. The crowd howled in outrage. Meanwhile, one Moroccan contingent had stockpiled crates of oozy missiles to rain on the police, positioning themselves cannily upwind so that the glutinous blobs carried a distance and landed with force. The *pera peluda* season was nearly at an end; the hairy pears left on the market were formless and corrupt, good only for beer or fertilizer. A cloying stench rose in the square.

Recruited from Lisbon and O Porto, Beeps were unfamiliar with the hairy pear. When handfuls of reeking purplish slop plopped on their helmets and stained their riot shields, the officers gagged and clawed goo from extruding hair. The BEIP had kept its cool admirably through cannoned lemons and eggplants, stoically submitting to fusillades of dried fava beans, but this new assault of noxious local napalm was apparently the limit. Revulsion rapidly transformed to rage.

At once, Beeps unholstered pistols and advanced on the crowd, firing in the air. Women ululated from overhead windows. Moroccans crumpled to their knees, arms raised against baton blows. Another car burst into flames. The sedan's gas tank finally exploded. As echoes of shattering plate glass radiated off the plaza, Portuguese and Arabic merged into an Esperanto roar. At last the pitched battle takes were spliced one to another, the silence fed, the nagging narrative need for climax met. If it had been difficult to know what was happening before, it was impossible now, and sticking around to reconcile conflicting versions was out of the question. Having promised warm tarts and mandolins, Edgar had a responsibility to more than his apathetic readership. He had to get Nicola out of here.

CHAPTER 27
Friend of the Fucking Family

"OBRIGADO . . . SIM. You're sure? *Definido, categórico*? *Sem mortes*? Fantastic. *Muito, muito obrigado. Adeus.*" Edgar hung up, patting his moist forehead with the tail of Barrington's flowing rayon shirt. His hands were unsteady, and he had to sit down.

"The Chicken Littles in the next doorway were full of shit." Edgar collapsed on the ottoman. "The hospital confirms Lieutenant Carvalho's version. Nobody killed. A few injuries. Bones'll mend."

Nicola stooped and touched his cheek. "Your face is clammy! You're relieved. *Really* relieved."

"Those immigrants aren't my pen pals, but I've no reason to wish them tough luck," said Edgar brusquely. "Why shouldn't I be relieved?" The fact was, he felt a bit sick.

Nicola cocked her head. "I've never seen a journalist who's entirely pleased when no one gets killed. No deaths, and your story slips below the fold."

"No byline's worth somebody's life," Edgar said airily.

He sat up and took a deep breath. Light-headedness subsiding, Edgar detected impending high spirits. The riot in Novo Marrakech had resulted in no fatalities about which to feel nauseously culpable; he'd persuaded Nicola to accompany him back to Rua da Evaporação instead of groveling home to her snit-prone husband; and after eating nothing today but one date-nut square, Edgar could contemplate a substantial dinner with the fearless righteousness of the underfed.

"The injuries," Nicola asked, "are there many, are they serious?"

The adrenal buzz of making those phone calls had left Edgar jittery. Rubbing his thighs, he jumped up again. "How should I know?"

"You're a journalist, and you just rang the hospital."

"Fifty, sixty, something like that," he said impatiently. "But no blindings that they mentioned, nothing permanent, all right?"

"Why so prickly, so—?"

Edgar blurted, "Barba suffered from plenty of racial and religious tension before the SOB!"

"I've gathered—" Nicola licked her lips, tolerating his non sequitur—"that the rise of the SOB has made friction between Catholics and Muslims much, much worse."

Edgar assured her briskly, "The Sobs just tapped poisonous groundwater."

"Why absolve the SOB of responsibility for what happened this afternoon?" Nicola puzzled. "A brutal round-up of law-abiding immigrants, some here for twenty years, paying taxes? I can't see why that would be happening, if the Portuguese government weren't trying to golden-handshake your little terrorist friends into early retirement."

For an apolitical naïf, she fingered the salient dynamic pretty quick. "Immigration would still be an issue," Edgar dug in, "Sobs or no Sobs."

"You wrote yourself how the bloodlines of Moors and Barbans are intermingled!"

"But don't forget the religious divide." Edgar settled on the ottoman at a professorial slant. "And you can understand Barban territorial paranoia just a little, can't you? With all that jihad jingoism coming out of hard-line Islam—"

"Most North Africans are progressive Muslims, and Edgar, I don't understand you! When you arrived here, you'd no time for those SOB scoundrels, and had contempt for their intolerance. Now you seem to be coming round to their way—"

"Nick, don't put words in my mouth. I don't approve of

blowing up airplanes. I'm just saying that you can't blame the SOB for everything that's wrong with Barba."

"I'm sorry." Her voice softened. "I shouldn't, if you will, read you the Riot Act. At least you seem to care." Nicola perched next to him and placed a hand shyly on Edgar's knee, which occasioned another amphetamine rush. "Your colleagues can be so callous that to see you anguished about total strangers . . . Ringing the police, you were shaking! You're sure to turn into another jaded crocodile like Win Pyre, but while it lasts, your compassion—well, it's lovely."

Edgar wished she wouldn't go on like that. Yes, he was relieved, but only because headline fatalities could have been all his fault.

"I don't suppose you got Barrington," Edgar milked it a bit, "bawling his eyes out over the vicissitudes of the world's sad sacks."

"No." Nicola straightened and collected her hands in her lap.

Idiot! He actually had her talking about *Edgar* and what *he* was like, never mind that he wasn't really like that, and then he had to go and ruin it by mentioning *Saddler*.

"You've still not found anything peculiar here, have you?" she asked forlornly.

"Very weird shampoos, why?"

She rose and paced a few steps, fiddling with the strings of her lacy black blouse like a rosary. "This may sound far-fetched, but I've sometimes wondered if Barrington was—if he might have been *involved*."

"In what?"

"In this—in the SOB somehow. That sounds unlike him in a way. He was a cynic. Still, if you don't believe in anything, then I expect you can play at believing whatever you like. It seems improbable that he'd put himself on the line for any cause. But it seems positively preposterous that Barrington of all people would share a town with a notorious terrorist outfit and have nothing to do with it."

"So if Saddler covered the Russian mafia, he must have been a made guy?"

"Funny you should mention that, because he was up to his neck in Moscow. He ran a smuggling ring. These silk pillows, this villa—you can't imagine that he afforded all this on a correspondent's salary. Barrington was an operator. For every finger, a pie."

It bugged Edgar that he hadn't clued up to the Slavic swindle, as if being the repository for Saddler's final secret he was the rightful vessel for them all. Besides, he'd had enough of being told what Barrington was like, and his lover's blithe presumption of greater intimacy rankled. Edgar didn't have to take it up the ass from the guy to know a thing or two about Saddler.

"What made you suspicious that he was in cahoots with the SOB?" Edgar taunted, if only to remind himself who had the inside track here.

"Enigmatic asides, and the fact that he found Barban politics altogether too enthralling. I don't mean prissily that death oughtn't to be entertainment. Only that I think the issue of immigration bored him senseless. Or should have. And he'd an air. How do I explain it? Of keeping something in. Of being about to burst."

She didn't have to explain it. An air of combustible smugness. An air of rattling a skeleton in your closet with the door ajar and wheedling, *Guess what I've got!* An air of aching to whisper sweet-somethings to Nicola Tremaine in particular, to enfold her sharp shoulders into the damp, dark embrace of your confidence. An air of hearing your own voice begin, *Nick, you'll think I'm pulling your leg, but . . .* , or, *Nick, I think I may have done something incredibly stupid and I've no one else to turn to . . .* , until your head is so cluttered with elliptic ice-breakers that you trip over them like pick handles in a tool shed. Except Barrington wouldn't have felt watched by Barrington himself, who disdained a weak-willed stoolie unable to keep his trap shut.

"Did you suspect he was *involved* before he disappeared?" Edgar asked neutrally.

"For a while, yes." Absently, she sank into the emerald velveteen wingchair.

"And that bothered you? You didn't like the idea?"

"Of course I didn't like the idea," she snapped. "But I still liked Barrington." Glancing down, she seemed suddenly to realize where she was, and sprang up again, as if she'd sat in someone's lap.

"He could be a murderer and you'd still—*like* him."

"More than like him," she admitted.

"And if he were actively involved in the SOB, that could implicate him in the massacre of Henry's whole family."

She nodded, eyes downcast.

"So this suspicion of yours, it makes you feel like a jerk."

Nicola's eyes rolled, like, *Duh.*

Edgar took pity on her. "Saddler was no terrorist," he said carefully, "strictly speaking."

"Oh, how do you know?" she snapped. "But whether Barrington was a terrorist is academic. He's not here. The point is, I'd not have gone off him if he were!"

"Does Henry know that?"

"I hope not. And I wish I didn't know that about myself, either. But self-knowledge is like any knowledge: you can't take it back." Nicola perched on the trunk, as if she didn't deserve a real chair. "I'm a fine one to be high and mighty with you, Edgar. You've never done anything dodgy, while I, I'll fall for a murderer, I'll sell my own husband downriver, for, for—"

"For what?"

She threw a hand at the empty wingchair. "For *nothing*, apparently!"

"So," Edgar pried quietly, "do you wish you'd never met him?"

"You must know the answer to that question." She dropped to the ottoman, limp.

Edgar gazed into her attractively harrowed face, drawn and wan like that of a nineteenth-century heroine perishing from consumption. He couldn't remember when he'd ever felt this jealous. "You think about him all the time, don't you?" he said blackly. "Saddler's having vanished, it's tearing you up. Not a day goes by—"

"Not a day. Not an hour. Which, without his being told, Henry knows very well. And every time I brood about Barrington, I betray my husband."

"Thought-crime?"

"There is such a thing. Cheating in your head may be more treacherous than cheating in bed. It's cowardly, and cheap; you can almost always get away with it. Lately I feel duplicitous even with strangers. When you introduce someone as your 'husband,' you're not meant to be saying, 'Hello, I'd like you to meet the second-most important man in my life.' "

"You said once that people chased after something Saddler had—a facility, a façade—and not who he was. What about you? Did you go for the decoy, or the real McCoy?"

"Oh, I've wondered. Whenever I try to get my hands on the distinction, Barrington goes to gossamer. Maybe you can't separate the 'real' person from the illusion they create—from the way they turn a phrase, light their cigarillo."

"I thought Saddler smoked Cubans."

"Heavens no, he smoked those foul-smelling Café Crèmes that come in tins."

"But to you," Edgar filled in dryly, "they smelled like lilies-of-the-valley."

Nicola half-smiled. "Not quite."

"Sorry, I interrupted. You were about to explain how only you understood *the real Barrington*. How you alone recognized that in his heart he was a wounded little boy—"

"Edgar! If you're going to be unkind to me, I wish you'd have the decency to sneer at me behind my back, the way you're unkind to everyone else."

Chastened, Edgar apologized, and begged her to go on.

"It's true," she resumed warily, "that Barrington had a B-side—not flashy and booming, but torn, reflective. For a time that did seem like the Queen's shilling. But I came to doubt if quiet-confiding-Barrington was any more authentic than big-booming-Barrington. I wondered if this introspective variation might be another illusion he was terribly good at. Oh, maybe I had started to fancy that only I knew *the real Barrington*. But this conviction that only you knew *the real Barrington*, you're right, Edgar, it was the form. I can't tell you how many of his acquaintances told me, 'What most people misunderstand about Bear . . .' It was like continually running into claimants waving competing deeds for the same property. Because this sensation of ownership, of special insight—I'm convinced that Barrington deliberately induced it. For him, intimacy was one more deception. Did I love Barrington for who he was? I told you when we met, Edgar: I'm an aesthete. I'm superficial. I'm sure I loved what Barrington appeared to be, like everyone else."

"I never heard you say that before," Edgar grunted. "That you loved him."

"Sorry. I didn't mean to embarrass you."

"Embarrass me! Hell, Nick." Edgar covered his own stupidly hurt feelings by tossing off, "All of Cinzeiro and half of New York knows about your affair."

Nicola bristled. "I never said we had an *affair*."

"Not in so many words, but we're adults here—"

"Even adults spend evenings playing Parcheesi."

"Right, Nick, and pigs fly." As her expression remained constipated, Edgar raised his hands. "But hey—I'm the one who advised: take a line and stick to your story."

"It's not a story."

"What, are you trying to tell me that you two *never*—?"

"We never."

"Are you shitting me?!" Like Barrington who-me?-ing that he'd never blown anyone up, Nicola met his gaze with serenity. "Man, I don't believe this!"

"Neither does Henry. Interestingly, it's been every bit as destructive for me to tell the truth and be disbelieved as had I lied. The emotional algebra is so neat that Barrington must have worked it out in advance. Besides which, my faithfulness to Henry was a technicality. I should have liked to sleep with Barrington, all things being equal. That I didn't constituted a by-the-book loyalty that hasn't, in retrospect, made much difference. It did, however, make our threesome possible. I expect Barrington worked that out as well."

"You make him out as so conniving. But didn't you yank his chain yourself? A womanizer like that, who can help himself to any broad he wants? Saddler rose to a challenge. You were shrewd, with his type, to hold out."

"I didn't 'hold out,'" said Nicola with distaste. "Barrington held out on me."

"Jesus," Edgar mumbled. "Maybe Saddler *was* a fudge-packer."

"I think not," Nicola submitted. "But he was fiendishly clever."

Edgar rose to run his fingers through his remaining hair, a stagy gesture that he might as well make the most of before he went bald. Somehow Saddler's implausibly chaste relations with Nicola were infuriating. Maybe the ultimate possession of any woman was to turn her down. Besides, an age of easy sexual access had devalued physical conquest, lowered the tone. Now commonplace, doing the extramarital nasty merely dragged every romancer down to the same coarse literalism, making sex, as much as death, the great leveler. Edgar's prurient mental flashes of Barrington and Nicola thrashing on the canopied four-poster upstairs had always evinced a pleasantly incongruous aspect. As

Alexis had observed, Barrington's "soul was clad," and Barrington in the buff couldn't gift-wrap his round pink-gin tummy with a cummerbund. Consequently, these fleshy notional centerfolds were prone to stimulate less Edgar's jealousy than his sense of humor. Besides, Edgar had done *that*, Edgar knew all about *that*. Since there are limited variations on what-sticks-where, Edgar felt relative confidence that, whatever those two got up to, he'd got the T-shirt.

But this! This—sickening chivalry, this—titillating repression, this—archaic, otherworldly restraint! *Oh, honey we shouldn't! Darling, we mustn't! Please, I can't stand it, stop!* The whole montage would have to be reshot in soft-focus. Unconsummated yearning elevated Barrington's courtship of Nicola Tremaine from daytime TV to Edith Wharton: a wrenching tale of thwarted passion, wasteful self-denial, and cruel social convention. While we sordid mortals were porking each other blind, the lofty Mr. Saddler and his winsome lass were exchanging fiery glances across a tea tray and doubtless packing more of a sexual wallop into an inadvertent grazing of fingers than Edgar experienced with coke on his cock.

But does the same gambit work for drones? *Edgar* hadn't jumped Nicola's bones. *Edgar* hadn't disrespected her marriage. *Edgar* walked around with a hard-on for the woman all day, but does Edgar get credit for being "fiendishly clever"? No, look at her: spread over the ottoman, drowsily relaxed, legs extended, ankles crossed but knees canted to expose a trustingly undefended shadow beneath her miniskirt. She wasn't averting her eyes, lest Edgar glimpse the desire with which they smoldered. She wasn't self-consciously tugging her lacy blouse to cover the swells at her collar, or begging to use the phone and assure Henry that she was fine, she'd be right home, no need to worry. Who was worried? However forewarned, Edgar had been beaten out of the role of leading man before he stepped off the plane in Lisbon. Left only bit parts, he'd joined the nameless supporting cast: Friend of the Fucking Family.

So Edgar was hard pressed to keep his lip buttoned as well as his fly. The thing was, Nicola thought he was a nice guy. She thought he was an ingenuous journalist who wrote his earnest copy about those dreadful terrorists and turned it in on time. He wrote sturdy topic sentences; he spell-checked. He wasn't, presumably, an "operator," and she didn't toss nights anguishing over whether that shifty, mercurial Edgar Kellogg was really a terrorist Godfather. No, white-bread Ed didn't engage her imagination one little bit. Unlike the ever-elusive, potentially nefarious, disturbingly cynical Barrington Saddler, with his bits on the side and fingers in pies. Well, big surprise, Nicky Tremaine, meet Son of Saddler. If you figure Barrington was a shady wheeler-dealer while I'm drowning in my own sincerity, that just means that of the two I'm the better actor. *Nick, you'll think I'm pulling your leg, but . . .*

Edgar chewed on his cheek. Barrington, no doubt, loitered in the wings—or wingchair, whose cushion was depressed. Were Edgar ever to spill the beans about the SOB, he wouldn't do so under the disapproving eye of its mastermind. So there was no alternative to remaining a what-you-see-is-what-you-get drudge in Nicola's view for the time being.

"The key!" Edgar grasped at one last straw, determined that Nicola confess to the groping, unseemly snuffling of earthly relations. "The night I arrived in Cinzeiro. You gave me the key to this joint. You're not the next-door neighbor. Only lovers have keys."

"Commonly, Sherlock, you're right. But Barrington only gave me that key the day he disappeared."

"What for?"

"I wasn't too clear, at the time. But later I concluded—he left it for you."

Edgar did a double take. "I don't get it."

"Perhaps not you personally. But he clearly intended his successor to assume this villa. I imagine he hoped to make the transition graceful, and that you'd make yourself at home."

What Saddler planned was for some loser with time on his hands to decipher those floppies. "Why were you so secretive, then? About having the key?"

"Obviously, since Barrington made preparations for his departure, it's unlikely he was cold-cocked in the dark of night. But if Henry assumed that Barrington was, well—dead—my life would be easier. Selfish on my part. And fruitless—because for some reason, I don't know why, Henry has never once supposed that Barrington was assassinated or felled by a lethal misadventure. At least that key kept me sane, even if it was only when the postcard arrived that I could be sure my assumptions were sound. For that first arid month or so, when Henry wasn't home, I'd clutch the key in my fist until the brass grew warm. Feeling it was real, so that Barrington must have been safe, because he'd given me a signal, if no substitute for a proper good-bye. Relinquishing it to you was a sacrifice. I was tempted to deny having it. But that would have put you to such inconvenience for my silly keepsake that I couldn't play dumb."

Sometimes the plain physical world provides a welcome reprieve from the tortuous mental mangle people make of it. "I'm starved," Edgar announced vigorously, as if calling a time-out. "It's time I fixed some grub."

"Can I—?"

"You stay here. In fact, you could do me a favor. I need to know how this ruckus in Novo Marrakech is being spun on CNN." Edgar switched on the TV, and left to hunt down Barrington's last jar of beluga.

Returning with an open bottle of wine and some messy appetizers, he checked his watch. "Shit. To get anything in the *Record* about that riot, I've gotta file in less than an hour." Typically, publishing in a national newspaper had slipped from privilege to pain in the butt. "Do you mind hanging around while I bang something out? After dragging you to that free-for-all, I at least owe you dinner."

"Oh, I don't think so, Edgar. I should leave you to your work. Though you might keep your word count down. If the report I just watched is anything to go by, a garden-variety riot is bound to be sidelined by Madrid."

Edgar's eyes narrowed jealously. "What about Madrid?"

"A big car bomb just went off, near the Prado. It killed one MP, for whom they think the device was intended, and four bystanders. The schoolteacher was eight months pregnant." Nicola added deadpan, "Beat that."

"No claim?" Meaning, did duty call? Must he finally face down his superstitious scruples about not claiming fatalities? Did the jar in the study have enough change?

"Yes, for once. ETA. Barba doesn't have a monopoly on hideousness, even in Iberia. Your SOB friends have competition."

"There might be a way," Edgar muttered, stroking his chin, "of pulling the rug out from under those Basque bastards."

"Sorry?"

"Nothing."

"That's exactly what I was talking about," said Nicola, helping herself to a cracker.

"Come again?"

"Just that sort of opaque, throwaway remark. Barrington dropped them all the time. They're most annoying."

So distracted that he only implored her to stay a time or two, Edgar fetched her coat.

CHAPTER 28

Barrington Has Feelings

EDGAR E-MAILED THE *Record* a hastily written story on which a few months ago he himself would have promptly turned the page. An article about some trifling riot by a bunch of foreign nobodies over deportations from one slag-heap to another would have belonged in the who-cares pile along with reports from Bosnia-Herzegovina and any other country he couldn't spell. He might have felt sheepish, grinding out text he wouldn't want to read himself, except that, eclipsed by Madrid, this copy would never see daylight.

Once Edgar tripped back downstairs, the caviar crackers had been dispatched (barring the crumbs all over the carpet), and the wine bottle was empty.

"Saddler!" Edgar shouted. "Get in here! If you're not too ashamed to show your face, you fucking fraud!"

The figure seemed to fold out of the pale green drapes, wearing the officer's uniform from the bedroom closet, with the scarlet Nehru collar and cuffs. While the khaki was starched and cornered, he wore the jacket unbuttoned, his shirt collar open—combining the residual discipline and off-duty languor of the soldier on R&R. Leaning against the wall at a jaunty tilt, Saddler appeared at once dashing top brass and costume ball jape. In short, he looked every bit the part of SOB Chief of Staff.

"Fraud," Barrington repeated critically, straightening the medals he hadn't earned on his breast pocket. "I get impatient with that accusation, in case you think it's fresh. I don't, surprisingly, pretend to much. Other people are perpetually making claims on my behalf. When I fail this contrived reputation, I'm a poser."

"Don't act all offended." Edgar sucked the last few drips from the wine bottle. "I couldn't hurt your feelings with a pile driver."

"A prevailing theory runs that I have none," Barrington volunteered brightly.

"What you don't have is an honest bone in your body." Edgar thumped the bottle on the seaman's chest with force. "You never told me that you and Nick just held hands."

"I don't recall your asking."

"But you were glad for me to make assumptions."

"Eddie, lad, what I have and haven't done preoccupies so many people so much of the time that I could spend all day doing nothing but rectify their misconceptions."

"What's with the iron will? You could have slipped Nick the snake if you'd made an effort."

"A vulgar sensibility blinds you to life's more refined pleasures." At the bar, Barrington trembled four delicate drops of bitters into two fingers of gin. "You regard Henry Durham, for example, as an impediment to your happiness. To the contrary, he fertilizes the garden of earthly delights. No Henry, and you meet the single most ravishing woman in Cinzeiro on your first night. You ask her to dinner, have your way with her, and part company. You're still stuck in Cinzeiro, the only enticement in town exhausted, and before you know it you've stooped to Trudy Sisson."

"But I heard that you—"

"*Don't* make the same mistake." Saddler turned heel, and Edgar trooped behind him to the atrium like a dutiful private. "After that one rash evening, I was obliged to keep the answerphone on for a month."

"Diversions like Trudy must have got back to Nick. In this town, you could as well have put *Saddler just fucked Trudy Sisson* in skywriting."

"She was hurt. But how could Nicola object, shacked up with another fellow herself? I'd endured so much jealous hair-tear over the years. Imagine my relief when the tenant of my affections was obliged to keep a lid on it."

Saddler settled onto his favorite pillows by the pool and lit up a *cigarillo*—a detail Edgar disliked having got wrong as much as having been left in the dark about Moscow.

"Consider the advantages of the triangle." Saddler stabbed his Café Crème, which smelled like one of Edgar's scurfy running shoes set on fire. "The lady is married, still likes her chap; she has qualms. In fact, qualms provide a constant conversational fall-back. Likewise the do-you-think-Henry-suspects-anything palaver, or the wistful spinning of mutual futures whose realization, relaxingly, never threatens. Eddie, our three-way suppers were fabulous! The nuances, the double entendres, the eyes, the hands on thighs under a serviette! And the gobsmacking, jaw-dropping innocence of Henry Durham was enough to bring tears to one's eyes. Furthermore, inhibition can be far more delicious than your standard thrust-and-parry. Public school memories tend to be erotically charged because you *didn't* get shagged."

"Go ahead and call me vulgar, then, since coming up on forty I find abstinence a pretty second-rate thrill." Sullenly, Edgar refused to collapse into his usual nest by the fountain, but scuffled restlessly over the marble parquet. "I don't notice Nick breaking out in a dizzy sweat because I haven't tackled her to the sack. It seems I'm insufficiently fascinating. This notion you might be a real live terrorist has got her all hot to trot. Your basic foreign correspondent doing his dumpy bit at the keyboard doesn't make her moist."

"Please don't tell me," said Barrington, pained, "that you've only been visiting my Terra do Cão phone box to impress the girl."

"I've kept my yap shut, thank you. Most guys would've already been dining out on your microfloppy for months."

"Our little secret is burning a hole in your pocket like an

unspent fiver." Barrington had removed his shoes and socks, and was diddling his toes in the pool. "But were Nicola to twig that you moonlight as paramilitary prankster, would that matter a jot?"

"Oh, I'm sure you'd still seem exciting-evil, and I'd just seem ignoble-evil," Edgar despaired. "The trouble is I can't compete with you, Saddler."

"Then stop trying," he advised kindly.

"You said the way was paved! That you'd done all the hard work, that she was ready to drop like a ripe peach! Or whatever." Edgar deepened his voice, which had grown whiny. "Something corny."

"I've done what I can," said Barrington sympathetically. "When Nicola arrived, her fortress of a marriage was unassailable. I bridged the moat. But I did not, it's true, shove my battering ram through her gates. I'm sorry if that means in your terms that, like Operation Desert Storm stopping shy of Baghdad, I didn't finish the job."

"It might help if you sent her a funeral notice or something. Shit, that fucking blank postcard will keep her panting by the mailbox for the next ten years. How can I ever get anywhere with that woman if she's still hung up on you?" Edgar added malignantly, "I sometimes think you want to keep her on a short leash, too."

Instead of protesting, Barrington padded to the glass door, leaving wet footprints on the marble, and gazed out at the dark patio. With the man's back turned Edgar couldn't tell if the *vento* was shrieking through the cracks or if Saddler was whistling lightly through his teeth. "I do miss her, funnily enough. The woman always says what she's feeling. You wouldn't think that rare, but it is. I do enjoy it when she stops by."

"Good God. *Feelings*."

"Charming, wasn't it, the way she worried about Moroccan casualties this afternoon? And she was trying to act sophisticated for your sake, but she was clearly quite distressed by that business in Madrid."

"She's sentimental."

"She has sentiments. People like us don't know the difference. By the way, did I detect that you're contemplating some atrocity-poaching?"

"It's an option," Edgar allowed guardedly. Even warmed by the uncommon compliment of "people like us," he felt protective of his autonomy. Barrington had delegated, and claims were Edgar's end of the operation now.

"Dicey," Barrington cautioned, tapping the glass. "If you don't succeed in winning credit over ETA, our Soldados Ousados look greedy. And ETA's got the edge on you. Madrid's their patch."

"I might risk it," Edgar determined, hands in pockets, businesslike. "Timing's good. We're perceived as strong, escalating, on a roll. Could prove an interesting test of SOB power and credibility. There's a solid political logic to Sobs hitting Madrid. Lisbon has an investment in keeping on good terms with Spain, since their historical relations are so fractious. And it's not a bad idea to expand our theater of operations to include Europe again. I was getting Yankee-centric for a while. Better to keep our options open. Something juicy comes along on the Continent, gift horse—don't want to have to look it in the mouth."

"What about your weak stomach?"

"Sick fucks who blew up a pregnant woman deserve to have their wretched bomb hijacked. Your reasoning, right? And," Edgar appended reluctantly, "if we don't claim fatalities pretty soon, nobody's gonna take us seriously anymore."

"True," Saddler granted. "But if you start filching meticulously planned, expensive festivities from established organizations who want their names in lights, they'll get pissy."

"That crossed my mind. But I'm already in up to my eyeballs, and if even the FBI can't trace the claims to me, ETA sure can't."

"You've watched too much Efrem Zimbalist Jr. Don't overrate the feds."

"After this gig, I don't rate terrorists. So between the two of us, we're not afraid of anybody." A stretch. Now routinely collecting abominations as philatelists did First Day Covers, and as habitually discoursing with a Mary Shelley monster of stitched-together gossip, Edgar was increasingly afraid of himself.

"To return to that problem in your trousers." Barrington stopped drawing pictures in condensation and turned around. "I wouldn't dismiss a move on Nicola as futile." Saddler's encouragement rang with the believe-in-yourself condescension of a high school guidance counselor urging Edgar to apply to a better grade of college than he'd a snowball's chance of getting into. "She feels so guilty already that she might find it a relief to have something of substance to feel ashamed of. And the marriage is moribund. A coup de grace would be merciful."

"Save the big brother advice," said Edgar. "If you can find keeping your fly zipped so electrifying, I can at least live with it."

Even fucking, if Barrington didn't do it, seemed uncool.

CHAPTER 29
Stealing Shit from Shitheads

"KELLOGG?" WALLASEK'S VOICE was grainy; Portugal's lousy overseas phone connections were a crucial assist to this enterprise.

Calling his own editor was pushing his luck, but what else was luck for? Edgar poured on the accent more thickly. "I am zhe Cinzeiro Brigade Commander of Os Soldados Ousados de Barba."

"This some kind of crank—?"

Edgar was accustomed to Doubting Thomases when he broke in a new contact, and proceeded unperturbed. "Ve veesh you to know zhat vile ve much support our fellow freedom fighters een *España*—"

"Christ, you really from the SOB? Hold your horses, man, let me get a pencil!"

"Zhe car *bomba* een Madreed," Edgar barreled on, "eesh not zhe brave work of our comrades een ETA. Eesh SOB *bomba*. Zhees attacks veel continue unteel Barba veen her freedom, and *Norte Africanos filhos da putas* invading our homeland go beck vere zhey belong."

"Please slow down, sir!" Wallasek cried. "That's *files de putsies*—?"

"Inglês?" Edgar furnished, pleased to have at last insinuated his schoolboy Portuguese into one of these calls, "Sans of hoors. Zhat you may know zhees eesh *legítimo* SOB, I geev you code phraze, *sim*?" Lowering his voice into the conspiratorial stage whisper his editor was bound to expect—it paid to stick to cliché—Edgar delivered the magic words.

"Thank you," Wallasek blubbered. Catching himself, since

gratitude for the explosion of pregnant civilians was less than apt, he revised, "I mean, I copy, right?"

"Sim."

"Seem?" Wallasek repeated helplessly. Having no previous experience with accepting a terrorist bomb claim, Wallasek mustn't have been up on the etiquette of bringing such conversations to graceful conclusion. "Anything else you wanna add to that statement, mister?"

"Ve sorry for loss of life. Ve *muito* sorry about zhe lady and her unborn *bebê*. Ven Barba veen her independence, zhees regrettable meestakes veel not occur."

"Mistake!" Wallasek returned to the blustery hard-nose Edgar knew. "You filthy—!"

"Liberdade! Vitória!" Edgar hung up. That was the etiquette.

Edgar folded up his cloth handkerchief, wet from the spittle of rolled Rs. He'd come to prefer the classic hankie-over-the-receiver to Saddler's awkward homemade kazoo, which distorted his voice a bit too well. It was tiresome enough reciting all that go-Barba rah-rah once a call without having to repeat each hackneyed patriotic buzz phrase three times. Edgar had no idea how Tomás Verdade could stand it.

Ducking out of the phone booth, Edgar glanced around edgily, like Clark Kent readjusting his tie. As ever, it wasn't inconceivable that he'd make a phone call from Terra do Cão, but he could skip the explanations. Gunning off in the faithful Bear-mobile, Edgar reflected on the callowness of clarifying after murdering five people that, like dropped digits in a column of figures, certain casualties were *mistakes*. The admission translated roughly, "The PR backlash was somewhat more severe than we anticipated." After all, bad press was the only reason a terrorist was ever "sorry," since if you weren't prepared for *mistakes* you didn't set off car bombs but pasted posters on bus shelters instead. Edgar's smarmy apology had been hypocritical and insulting, worse than no apology at all. Which must have been why it felt just right.

That afternoon Edgar jawed with Lieutenant Carlos de Carvalho, Cinzeiro's chief of police and a Latino Barney Fife; ever since Edgar had allowed he was bosom buddies with The Bear (*O Urso*), Carlos had been garrulously cooperative. They commiserated over the Madrid operation, whose forensics Interpol had sent out to police services all over Europe. Cops everywhere loved waxing eloquent on that D-48K-Yellow-Jacket-single-fuse-detonator-from-the-Czech-Republic technical stuff, so that Edgar was able to tease out any number of "off the record" details about the device that weren't distributed to the press.

These details contributed an invaluable sense of authenticity to the SOB statement Edgar drafted when he got home from Terra do Cão. You could pick up responsibility for most orphaned incidents without much documentation, but to beat out ETA he'd need to exhibit thoroughgoing acquaintance with their ordnance. Edgar cited the nature of the explosive and its origins, the type of detonator, the tripping method, and the timing of the fuse. After that brothers-in-struggle what-have-you on the phone to Wallasek, he typed that ETA and the SOB had simply experienced a "communication breakdown"—as if all terrorists worked under the same multinational umbrella and there'd been a bureaucratic foul-up, the way payment for a contract fulfilled by one company could sometimes be deposited in the wrong subsidiary's account.

Edgar had already sealed the envelope and tucked it in his baseball jacket when he realized in horror that his hands were bare. Leaving fingerprints all over the stationery, he might as well have signed his name. After scurrying back up the tower, snapping on a pair of surgical gloves, and printing another copy, Edgar burned the original statement in the fireplace. He might have just thrown it out—no one was here besides you-know-who—but Edgar could just as soon skip Saddler's lambaste for having got so sloppy.

Impatient, the next morning he mailed the envelope *em correio expresso*. He was careful at the post office to wear leather gloves, which made handling bills awkward and exasperated the clerk that he wouldn't take them off. His change spilled over the floor. Edgar fled, flustered at having attracted attention to himself, though leaving the escudos behind on the parquet attracted more.

At Casa Naufragada, he logged onto the *Record*'s Web page, where an article casting doubt on ETA's responsibility for Madrid was prominently posted. There was nothing left for Edgar to do but sit tight, like watching the metal ball bounce about a roulette wheel with a C-note riding on red.

ETA must have been mystified, but the truthful rarely see the need for the substantiating evidence incumbent on good liars; it was unlikely that the Basque separatists' claim included the SOB's meticulous corroboration. Besides, since even scumbags preserve their own concept of scumbagginess, the Basques may have leapt at the chance to evade the onus of rudely terminating an eight-month pregnancy in a devoutly Catholic country. At any rate, ETA didn't raise a stink. Five days after Edgar's postal mission, "security sources" announced that the judges had carefully considered both applications and the SOB took the prize.

Naturally they didn't put it that way, but for Edgar his imaginary bad boys winning credit for Madrid over more traditional (not to mention more extant) terrorists marked the fiction's coming of age. Award of such official recognition conferred the political equivalent of cash: clout he could spend like money.

The Prado car bomb attribution was big. Affronted op-eds foamed on every editorial page. The Sobs had *fallen off the edge of the civilized world*, shown their *cowardice and moral bankruptcy* and *tipped their empty hand*. Words like *scurrilous*, *calumnious*, and *unspeakable* were a dime a dozen. Edgar was reminded of his favorite storybook as a kid, *The Velveteen Rabbit*, about a bedraggled stuffed bunny that was loved real. Maybe you could be despised real as well. Amid hailstorms of opprobrium, the letters of Barrington's concocted acronym rose off newsprint with a hard, violent clarity. Loathing made the SOB stronger, the way a sow grows stout on garbage.

In successfully adding Madrid to his team's scoreboard, Edgar was naturally jubilant, as if the Orioles had finally made the Series after all. Yet post-Prado he did begin talking to himself rather a lot—mumbling at the wheel, muttering down the halls of Casa Naufragada, or declaiming to Saddler while ranging Abrab Manor. In these private soliloquies, Edgar often articulated the vital distinction between the *im*moral and the *a*moral. Having himself supposed that if Nicola got wind of the hoax she'd be sure to find Barrington "exciting-evil" and Edgar "ignoble-evil," he now rejected both reproachful labels. Who'd been killed who wouldn't have been killed anyway? Sure, there'd been a few skinned knees at that Novo Marrakech deportation scuffle, but every immigration enforcement arm was obliged to conduct the odd shakedown for illegals, right? And there'd been plenty of racial and religious tension in Barba before the SOB, Barrington said! Saddler was right. Perpetuating the myth of the SOB wasn't evil at all. It just wasn't especially *good.* Nevertheless, a tiny, peevish voice whispered that the distinction between *a*moral and *im*moral wasn't a hard line but a smudge, and that the former prefix slid easily to the latter when you weren't looking.

For there may indeed have been, as Saddler maintained, "a world outside heaven and hell," where the likes of Barrington felt at home. But while Edgar had played the renegade in his shoplifting youth, his choice of law in adulthood suggested a conservative bent, a thirst for order, structure, and direction. In the ethical nether region where he'd recently dwelt, whose signposts pointed toward neither vice nor virtue, Edgar felt disoriented. Constitutionally, even if the *a*moral didn't slip insidiously to something more sinister, Edgar wasn't cut out for it.

Atrocity poaching became Edgar's salvation. Edgar convinced himself—strike that. Edgar *was convinced* that pilfering mainstream guerrilla operations on behalf of some no-account, backwater phantasm was the ideal punishment for blowing pregnant women to kingdom come. Imagine, so much preparation: hush-hush palavers in some smelly garret; you-nitwit! exhortations to *never mention operations over the phone*; edgy negotiations with unsavory arms dealers; sweat-drenched drives with volatile cargo; aerobic tangling with alarm-clock timers in your own mother's basement, since many poorly paid terrorists would still live at home: *let's see—does the detonator connect to the blue or the yellow wire . . . ?*

All to advance *Barban independence*? The resultant sense of misappropriation would be akin to that of donating thousands of dollars to the Africa program of Save the Children, only to discover that you had really funded Iowans for Tax Relief. Surely, Edgar reasoned, if so much effort in the name of Palestine, Islamic fundamentalism, or the Aryan Brotherhood only jacked up the notoriety of larcenous cretins in Portugal, the motivation of orthodox terrorists to assemble still more wayward science-fair projects ratcheted down a peg. Throwing off the ill-fitting mantle of the *a*moral apostate to whom ordinary rules of right and wrong did not apply, Edgar recast himself as the Robin Hood of the paramilitary underworld. Instead of stealing riches from the rich, he stole shit from shitheads.

Edgar swiped a Delhi suicide bus bombing from a Kashmiri rebel who, being indisposed, could no longer object. He snatched credit for decimating an entire wing of London's Victoria and Albert from the 32-County Sovereignty Committee, a breakaway faction of the IRA. He whisked responsibility for a slice-and-dice melee near the Sphinx out from under the Islamic Jihad; desperate to preserve tourism by belying homegrown cutthroats, the Egyptian government hastily endorsed the SOB claim. Edgar nosed in on one cyber-terrorism job, though the computer hackers who cut off electricity to Milwaukee for three days were first suspected of belonging to the Michigan Militia. Edgar even filched the burning of three black churches in Georgia from the Klan.

How was this possible? True, Edgar continued to access full Interpol dossiers, while bringing to police station tête-à-têtes such journalistic swagger that it was Lieutenant de Carvalho who imagined he was getting the inside dope. But the ease with which the SOB accrued abominations could not be put down to Edgar's A-plus technical homework alone.

The more the SOB was blamed for, the more the world was dying to blame the SOB for everything else. The monotheistic West was monodemonic as well. The Evil Empire having bitten the dust, Edgar's contemporaries were hungry for another all-purpose enemy, in preference to a dissatisfying dispersion of small-fry scoundrels. As MI6, Interpol, and the FBI threw infamies at Edgar's feet like alms, the SOB filled a psychological, even religious void.

Alas, Robin Hood Ed had no Merry Men with whom to toast his successes. While his paramilitary kleptomania gave rise to countless boisterous booze-ups at the Rat, for Edgar the rollicking round tables were theater, and actors know that artifice is work. Though Barrington's initial promise that, in assuming the helm of the SOB, Edgar would "rise above" his fellow hacks had been offered as enticement, Saddler might also have portrayed elevation as a price. Superiority was a form of distance, secrecy a quarantine. Edgar had never been so social, and he'd no one to talk to. He sympathized fleetingly with real terrorists, who, however despicable, were probably lonesome. Even Nicola had accused Edgar of becoming remote. She'd no idea what lay between them, yet once went so far as to mourn that she'd thought at first they'd become great friends and now, well—never mind.

In private, Edgar punched the air in righteous triumph when he wrested one more act of malice from the clutches of reprobates. Yet that same petulant little voice whispered the unwelcome wisdom that only minor mischief issued from the parochial or small-minded; in politics, the pursuit of pygmy-size self-interest was relatively safe. History's wholesale horror shows were staged by crusaders. But that little voice was unadventurous, boring, lawyer-Edgar, unpopular, party-pooping fat-Edgar, and Edgar told the little voice to shove it.

CHAPTER 30
Supporting the Peace Process

LIFE IN BARBA was looking up.

Under the guise of bringing the primitive peninsula up to economic speed, the European Union was shoveling money at Barba as if trying to smother a brush fire. Thanks to agricultural subsidies, crop selection had diversified beyond the unmarketable *pera peluda* (the glut of which an enterprising Brussels bureaucrat arranged to export to Guinea-Bissau, where no one had ever tasted one). That spring, local stands in Cinzeiro sold red currants and pomegranates. The EU funded working women's child-care, adult literacy, AIDS awareness, and water fluoridation. In the pipeline: a new city hospital, a dozen new schools, and a classical concert hall with state-of-the-art acoustics that locals quietly planned to convert to a venue for arm-wrestling contests when the continental longhairs went home. Despite the average Barban's sixth-grade education, there was even promise of constructing a University of Barba, to offer accredited doctoral degrees. Meantime, a grant fund for artists was going begging. Barba didn't have any.

Under the aegis of the EU Special Support Program for Peace and Reconciliation, the European Commission announced a string of "community relations" initiatives, all intended to "reinforce progress toward a stable society." Casa Naufragada's upper floors were now occupied by the Cross-Community Rural Regeneration Council, the Committee for Cultural Exchange and International Cooperation, and the Iberian Social Inclusion Coalition. All these bodies did the same thing, of course. They plied every Barban they could get their hands on with cash.

The export souvenir industry drew a sizable subvention to update its technology, though to EU's dismay one result of this financial infusion was a whole new array of Creme de Barbear knickknacks in the party's ground-floor shop. In the spirit of flowering civic pride, Barba began to mass-produce souvenirs of itself: a hairy-pear squeaky toy for pets, a GI Joe-style SOB guerrilla doll with balaclava, dark glasses, and automatic, and a model DC-10 whose fusillade, tail, and wings pulled apart to scatter a confetti of tiny plastic passengers.

What's more, the trinkets sold. The traditional holidaymaker, of course, wouldn't go near badass Barba with a barge pole. But Cinzeiro became a Mecca for the political tourist: the bespectacled day-packer who bought radical paperbacks, asked directions to *El* Terra do Cão on his first walkabout, took notes on graffiti, photographed racist murals, attended Creme rallies in the hopes of violence, and greedily collected all five Tomás Verdade coffee mugs.

Inevitably, Edgar's hijinks benefited Creamies in particular. Verdade's controversially star-struck biography topped the *New York Times* bestseller list for nineteen weeks, and an unauthorized biography in the works from a competing publisher, expected to be scathing, was bound to further improve his PR profile by a yard. Though the State Department had refused him a visa for years, the administration reversed itself in the interests of "encouraging dialogue," and Verdade had become a much sought-after guest speaker for outré luncheons in New York. At length eager to support "the peace process," the White House invited Tomás to attend its formal Independence Day dinner, where he presented the president with one of Cinzeiro's misshapen souvenir ashtrays with crossed Barban and American flags. His reputation laundered by no less than the highest executive in the land, Verdade's standard honorarium went up to $10,000.

The release of an inflammatory American Enterprise Institute study in Washington gave the Creams another shot in the arm. The DC think tank had commissioned a detailed analysis of American immigration and its effect on the future ethnic makeup of the United States. According to the widely publicized report, by 2050 whites would no longer constitute a majority in the U.S., just as whites were already outnumbered in California, Hawaii, and New Mexico; Nevada, Texas, Maryland, and New Jersey were also on the cusp of "minority majorities," the fastest growing group of which would consistently be Hispanic. Trudy Sisson seized upon the study's revelation that three-quarters of her fellow residents in Miami spoke a language other than English at home, and 67 percent conceded that they were not fluent in English ("Translate," said Trudy, "don't know the word for *airport.*").

The AEI report galvanized an American "white rights" movement, for whom O Creme's platform was politically expedient. Members of What's Wrong With White People (or WWWWP, to the annoyance of the World Wildlife Program) sported bumper stickers urging, HONK IF YOU LOVE HONKIES, DON'T TAKE VANILLA FOR GRANTED, and I SCREAM FOR O KREME! [sic]. *Look,* campaigned WWWWP lobbyists, *in their own countries, even Latinos resent being overrun!* Consequently, a foreign freedom-fighting movement whose rhetoric was revolutionary found itself rabidly supported by a bunch of right-wing gun nuts.

Not that Verdade was complaining. A shit-storm of contributions from reactionary Texas tycoons deluged O Creme. Headquarters got a facelift. Even Bebê Serio started to dress better.

With the incursion of journos, EU functionaries, groveling governmental delegations from Lisbon, academics on conflict-resolution junkets, kibitzing Congressmen on fact-finding missions, Amnesty International busybodies snooping for BEIP human rights violations, and celebs like *Sir* Elton John holding Peace Concerts whose grand finales always involved releasing hundreds of white doves—encrusting Cinzeiro's bullfighting stadium with a stucco of bird shit—Cinzeiro sprouted two garish high-rise hotels that competed with one another over which could charge more. Though the rooms were cramped, the beds hard, and the minibars extortionate, a night's fitful rest in the provincial capital could not be had for less than $350 and rising.

Upscale beaneries were fruitful and multiplied. At last Edgar could hit the town with a visiting crew from *60 Minutes* and choose between an Italian trattoria, a Szechuan tearoom, a Swedish smorgasbord, an Indian curry house, a Mongolian barbecue, a French bistro, an Indonesian *rijsttafel*, or a full Japanese sushi bar that, though run by Algerians, had only made Edgar projectile-vomit once.

Yet the grandest manifestation of Europe's sudden concern for Barban development was the peninsula's proliferation of public leisure centers. No more was Edgar forced to battle the elements in long, odious slogs down Rua da Evaporação, wind *wah*ing in his ears and *peras peludas* gooping the treads of his Nikes. The new fitness multiplex in Terra do Cão contained five squash courts, two indoor tennis courts, and an Olympic-size swimming pool. Alternatively, the vaulting cathedral to physical suffering three blocks from his office was equipped with an array of Stairmasters, LifeCycles, and Concept II Ergometers, all measuring heartbeat, caloric output, and kilometers per hour in red digital readouts. Even better, given that most Barbans' idea of exercise was— Actually, Barbans had no idea of exercise. Edgar pretty much had the cavernous downtown facility to himself.

But then, the speedball rush that revved his metabolism in the Rat when Grant's Tomb was bombed had never quite abated. Ever since that evening, standing on a street corner thinking, or waking up in the morning and remembering where he was, had doubled as ad-hoc aerobic exercise. Edgar had now jittered away ten pounds by accident. If anything he looked gaunt, and for the first time in his life watching weight shiver off his frame was unnerving. Still, the blessedly mindless pedaling at the gym with his eyes trained on Portuguese-dubbed *ER* evoked his old routine in New York and made him feel normal. It made him feel safe.

Increasingly, safe was just what Edgar failed to feel on the streets of Cinzeiro. These days on a cruise through Terra do Cão (which its residents had now taken to calling "*El* Terra do Cão") Edgar's urban alarm bells did go off. Which was queer, since the neighborhood's slick new public housing looked almost middle-class. On the other hand, the tidy brick bungalows with double-glazing were soulless, and a little affluence can often be just enough to give people a taste for whatever else they haven't got.

The photogenic brat who'd first fleeced Edgar for five hundred escudos was now charging two thousand escudos a snap. No longer conscientiously stenciled and overwritten to correct misspellings, graffiti had grown slashing and careless, trailing thick, bloody drips of red spray paint. Its language didn't run to the cheerfully civilized ADEUS, NORTE AFRICANOS! either, but to the cruder MARROQUINOS CHUPAM O PENIS DO BURROS! or the grisly mortality score-keeping of SOB—3,945/TOALHAS-CABEÇAS—0. In one playground wall mural, the endearingly moronic smile painted on Teodósso o Terrível's black charger had been cross-hatched over with bared white teeth.

Clumps of young men now skulked on corners with passable menace. For wind guards, clear plastic goggles were passé, full jade-green welding masks the rage: industrial, opaque, and occlusive of the entire face. Edgar missed the innocent uncool of high-water bell-bottoms and canary-yellow knee socks. Now they'd opted instead for timeless tough: abused leather and dirty denim. None of the boys played with pinwheels anymore.

The kids' transformation wasn't all style. The last time Edgar claimed a bomb from his Terra do Cão phone booth, the finish on the passenger door of the Saab was keyed, more suitably than the juvies could have known, with the jagged letters SOB fifteen inches high.

In Edgar's reading, the Portuguese were repeatedly described as great-hearts, if suffering from a certain fatalism, dourness, and distinctive *saudade*—defined in Marian Kaplan's *The Portuguese* as "an emotional, fathomless yearning," perhaps for the Age of Discovery when the Iberian boonies were the center of the world. As descendants of an empire that had hit the skids centuries before and had merely flicked them crumbs when its table was groaning, Barbans had some reason to grouse. Nevertheless, when Edgar first got here, they'd displayed traces of an easygoing and philosophically self-effacing nature. Yet with villainies from embassy bombings to dead dolphins notched on their collective belt, Barbans were rebuilding an empire of a kind, and had become accordingly high and mighty. In recent vox pops, Edgar found natives haughty, touchy, coy, detached, and stuck-up. Having himself goosed them to life, he had a pretty good handle on Barban politics, but local yahoos refused to believe that any outsider could possibly understand their terrible, complicated problems. Not that they felt obliged to understand anyone else's. If he ever ventured off the subject of their beloved immigration spat and its attendant badness, their eyes glazed like those of *vento* junkies propped against a deafening wind.

Likewise shopkeepers had originally been good-humored about Edgar's poor-to-absent Portuguese, and flattered by the few words he'd mastered. Now his regular merchants for frozen lasagna and special-order small-batch bourbon bristled at grammatical errors, and refused to volunteer their patchy school English. Her own Portuguese exquisite, Nicola had remarked that these days locals seemed to get sniffy when she *didn't* make mistakes.

Nevertheless, Edgar wasn't about to take the rap for so abstract a business as a shift in provincial character. If Barbans preened under the eye of CNN cameras, a buried vanity had merely been enticed to the surface. Escalating savagery was harder to finesse.

A dozen Moroccans and Algerians had been tarred and feathered. A whole row of houses in Novo Marrakech was burned to the ground. Lewd graffiti wasn't restricted to Terra do Cão but was smeared defiantly through immigrant neighborhoods, no matter how many times shame-hunched women in djellabas scrubbed it away. Street-gang clashes between dog-landers and towel-heads now routinely involved knives, and one Terra do Cão teenager who was dating the wrong sort had her waist-long hair hacked to the scalp. Pitched riots between Muslims and Beeps or Cinzeiro cops were no longer news.

In the early stages of this escapade, just after Grant's Tomb, Edgar had exulted in his newfound power to dial up headlines at will. Even once he settled into a blasé routine of calling in bomb claims as part of his job description, he could sometimes fully inhabit Barrington's moral Switzerland and be flushed with not horror but awe—an electrifying recognition of his own sway that raised hairs on the nape of his neck. Like most well-off Americans, who were swaddled in a cotton wool of comfort that made everything they read about seem muffled and far away, in his lawyer days Edgar had begun to lose faith that anything ever happened really, much less that he could make anything happen himself. In Barba, Edgar had discovered the miracle of his own agency, and in truth he was still grateful for that.

But he'd initially been exhilarated by the sensation of control. He could pick that incident, reject another. He was not in the mood for one more atrocity; he was in the mood, rather. Doubtless the same thrill of efficacy engorged genuine terrorists, and in this respect Edgar Kellogg was as real as the best of them. Yet as the streets of Cinzeiro reverberated with obscene chants and crowded with bigoted placards, homes were torched, and pretty girls lost their hair, while governments fell over themselves to appease an enemy that wasn't there, Edgar felt anything but in control.

CHAPTER 31
The Tooth Fairy Gives an Interview

FEELING OUT OF control could make you giddy; it could make you rash. The graver matters grew in Cinzeiro, the more Edgar inclined toward camp. The SOB had started as a joke, and Edgar was going to force it to remain one if it killed him.

Thus when one more journalist washed up on his threshold at Casa Naufragada begging for an interview with a Real Live Sob, Edgar flippantly said yes. Maybe he was actually getting bored with claiming atrocities. Why else take such a risk?

Well, for several reasons. Tiddling nails on his door, though it was open, Jasmine Petronella arrived self-consciously overdressed—replete with a doublet of artificial pearls—and as a rule journalists showed off by dressing like slobs. Fragile and uncertain, Jasmine first introduced herself as an essayist for the highbrow quarterly *Granta*, but couldn't keep her game face. Within thirty seconds, the young woman had confessed to writing on spec; for now, *Granta* "didn't know her from corned beef hash." Unlike most of the add-water-and-stir experts who lounged into Edgar's office, Jasmine had read every book about Barba she could lay her hands on, including Ansel P. Henwood's, for which she deserved a medal. The fact that a girl just out of Northwestern's journalism school had forked over her own meager funds to fly to this dung-heap where nothing ever happened (or never used to) made Edgar feel responsible—yet more evidence that across the board Edgar's Dexedrine omnipotence was subsiding to a phenobarbital wooze of self-reproach.

Although Edgar himself contrived to appear tough, assured,

and jejune, he found Jasmine's tentative, hair-messing underconfidence refreshing. Her features a little outsized and asymmetrical, Jasmine had those marginal, "interesting" looks that improved with a few beers. Most winningly of all, Jasmine had never met—had *never even heard of*—Barrington Owen Saddler, and so couldn't find Edgar Kellogg a soul-destroying disappointment in comparison.

As for this self-starter's prospective interview with *o soldado*, Edgar laid down ironclad rules. Only Jasmine could attend. No photographs. No viewing or direct contact, not even shaking hands. No real names. No recording devices; she'd have to take notes. No questions that might lead to the identity of his source. Half an hour max; Edgar wasn't sure he could keep up the accent for longer than that.

He arranged to meet the girl outside Casa Naufragada at two a.m., by which time the rest of the hack pack would be safely asleep or stinking drunk. Heartbreakingly, she was still wearing the pearls. He ushered her hugger-mugger into his office, where he'd tacked up a white sheet that partitioned the cubicle in half. Apologizing, Edgar patted her down gingerly for a microcassette—nice build. She was shaking.

"Excited?" asked Edgar.

"Nervous," Jasmine corrected. "These people . . ."

"You'd be surprised. One-on-one, homicidal sorts can be almost exasperatingly likable. I expect you'll get on with *O Borbulha* like a house on fire."

"*O Bore*—?"

"*O Borbulha*. Just a handle."

She printed meticulously. "What does it mean, like, The Butcher, or something?"

"The Zit. With a face like that, you'd give interviews behind a sheet, too." Winking, he settled her in his desk chair and headed for the door.

Jasmine grabbed Edgar's sleeve. "You're not going!"

"You'll develop a better rapport just the two of you." Edgar patted her hand.

"But—with all they've done—how do I know—alone in a room . . . ?"

As its puppeteer, of course Edgar couldn't take the SOB seriously; the numerous other blasé journalists who'd sashayed into this office—for whom a killer was no more than a rent-a-quote with exceptional cachet—had no such excuse. Jasmine, by contrast, thought a killer was scary. That was astute.

"I personally vouch for boil-face," Edgar promised. "Three's a crowd. Stay here, I'll bring him in the back. Half an hour. Don't worry, I won't be far away." Quite.

Edgar scuttled around the hallways, hooking on a pair of Groucho glasses, and ducked into his office through the fire door, all the while picking at a pestersome whitehead on his chin that had inspired his *nom de guerre.*

The instant he switched on the light to cast his bulbous profile on the sheet in silhouette, Edgar felt like a heel. Jasmine was a nice kid, frightened out of her wits, and she thought this was real. Freshly chagrined, Edgar shit-canned the satirical narrative he'd planned, going for a somber, confessional tone instead. His story of an impoverished childhood and crushing low self-esteem, his desperate efforts to find respectable work as a tradesman that were continually undermined by Algerian illegals who would work off the books, his parents' loss of their modest house to a Moroccan arsonist because they once dared to invite the noble Tomás Verdade to their home, and his grateful discovery of dignity and purpose when he embraced the cause of his people's freedom finally built to such heartfelt patriotic fervor that by the time he was through lisping his consonants, shushing his Ss, and trilling his Rs Edgar himself was ready to sacrifice a few hapless, incidental civilians for the high-flown romance of Barban independence.

When Edgar ventured into the Rat the next night, he came upon Jasmine being interrogated by Alexis. Of course, it was no surprise that the kid's news nose had led her to this bar. Every animal on earth instinctively sniffed out its own kind.

Be that as it may, Edgar had been ready for a night off from babysitting the uninitiated, hoping for a quiet drink with a few cronies who would all get each other's allusive wisecracks. Besides, he was anxious to be spared the resident hacks' historically irresistible impulse to dazzle any newcomer with their pyrotechnic command of Barban politics. Having taken on the role of Jasmine's minder, Edgar felt a little put upon, wondering if he was now duty-bound to protect her from the press corps' predatory sarcasm. To emphasize that the fledgling was on her own tonight, he sat instead beside Martha Hulbert, who shot him a wobbly smile of gratitude. Clearly his choice of chair meant horribly much to Martha; he hadn't thought ahead. In fact, as the conversation in progress attested, his foresight was lacking in every respect.

"What exactly did he say?" Alexis was demanding. Regarding any information snatched from her turf as stolen from the *New York Times*, Alexis rapped the round table, as if insisting that the young lady, caught red-handed, surrender a shoplifted candy bar. Like many an older feminist, Alexis had beaten by joining, and universally treated other ambitious women like impertinent children.

"He talked about his upbringing," said Jasmine cautiously. "How barren it was, and poor. How kids here absorb without being told that Barbans are dirt."

Just out of grad school, Jasmine could hardly be expected to keep her only scoop under wraps. Edgar hadn't precisely sworn her to silence, since he hadn't quite articulated to himself the dangers of the interview story leaking. He tried to catch Jasmine's eye. But she was busy fending off Alexis Collier, and there was no use crying over spilled beans.

"You buy that?" Alexis snapped.

"I bought *that*," said Jasmine deliberately. "Although it's a big leap from feeling underprivileged, even despised, to planting car bombs."

"I've had it up to my eyes with the hard-done-by natives and their snot-nosed whining," Win snarled. "The more Europe pours payola into this sewer, the worse the bellyaching gets. The Sobs are sure to blow a dozen more pregnant schoolteachers off the map because Dogshit Land's three-million-dollar leisure center doesn't have an ice rink."

Jasmine was clearly taken aback. Win looked anything but contrite. He may have despised Tomás Verdade first and foremost, but his sticky black antipathy had oozed like an oil pipeline leak across the entire peninsula. It wasn't fair, it wasn't *attractive*, but for years he'd watched pettiness, petulance, and, by all appearances, blind murderousness pay off in spades, and Win Pyre's vituperation was understandable. All the same, the screwed-up mangle of his face testified to the fact that acid was eating him hollow. The more he sputtered with impotent contempt, the more any casual observer could see plainly that Barba was winning.

"Still . . ." Taking a preparatory breath, Jasmine seemed to realize that she was about to say something Pyre wouldn't like. "Why not give Barbans independence, if they want it?"

The girl had guts.

"They *don't* want it!" Win exploded. "Independence has thirty-five percent support tops!"

"It used to be ten percent." Jasmine's body had contracted into a small, dense ball.

"Sure enough, that Creamie fan club keeps adding members," Martha wedged in. "It's the damnedest thing. The more people they kill, the more popular they get. Whenever I've tried to ingratiate myself, I've obviously gone about the project all wrong.

I should have skipped the Godiva gift assortments and bought a machine gun."

"Maybe Barbans don't all want independence," said Jasmine, "but most could probably abide it. Meanwhile, nobody else gets killed. Isn't that all that matters?"

"*Is* it?" Win's cheeks bloomed with apoplectic blotches. "So why not hold the world to ransom for whatever you want? If it works? You said you want to publish your essay in *Granta*. What if they say no? Tell that quarterly that you'll keep blowing up shopping malls until they publish your piece. It's a little thing to ask. One lousy essay in one lousy journal, to save all those people's lives? Isn't that all that matters?"

"That's already happened," said Jasmine. "The *New York Times* published the Unabomber's manifesto at his insistence, in full."

"News," said Alexis primly, "but a questionable precedent." By which she meant that the letter-bomber's pretentious pseudo-intellectualizing about the corruptions of industrialism took up a whole page of *her* paper and wasn't her story.

"We've been through this before, Win," said Martha, cutting her eyes toward Edgar as if to enlist his support. "I started out on your side, totally. Reward terrorist temper tantrums, and you're asking for more of the same. But I'm starting to question—"

"Hulbert, not you, too!" Win took any passing sympathy with the SOB as a personal betrayal.

"The Sobs have killed almost four thousand people," Martha persevered. "That's a lot to pay for principle. What would it cost to give rinky-dink Barba independence? A little face. If we could trade a Barban state for a complete Sob cessation, maybe we'd get the better end of the deal. Maybe it's a shrewd enough bargain to be worth the embarrassment of caving to creeps. I sure wouldn't want to die to keep this penis of a peninsula part of Portugal."

Finished with her recital, Martha turned to Edgar like a little girl curtsying at a school assembly. She want a blue ribbon, or what? Saddler was right. Having your sleeve continually tugged for approval was a nuisance.

"Hard-nosed practicality is the essence of *realpolitik*," announced Alexis. "Purism has no place in politics, where you make deals with the devil every day. How many casualties would you sacrifice for your insistence that crime not pay, Win? You must draw the line somewhere."

"I draw the line," Win growled irascibly, "at bending over for pig swill. At proposing a separate parliament for halfwits whose first political 'statement' is sure to be blowing up the legislature building. At revising a whole canon of immigration law to suit kitty litter. At sending some gimcrack Gestapo rousting wetbacks house-to-house just to placate animate garbage. *That's* where I draw the line."

"So theoretically," said Alexis, "you'd see every last man on earth blown to smithereens before this crummy hinterland was given its independence."

Win's eyes narrowed to slits. "Fuck, yeah."

"The Creams sure got some awful good ideas about immigration," Trudy intruded. The non sequitur was deliberate. Trudy was afraid of Win. The only way she could get in her two cents without being brutally cut down was to contribute her thoughts when they were beside the point.

"With *community relations* in the gutter," Win snarled at Trudy, "give this dump independence and forget that 'repatriation' plan. Next day, you'll have doggy-doo-landers slaughtering rag-heads like sheep. Lining 'em up in front of ditches, just you wait."

"Win, I know how you feel," said Roland. "You don't want to negotiate with Creams, you don't want Lisbon to meet with them or make any deals—no concessions, no favors, no attention. But that's like asking Lisbon to overlook the elephant in the living room—"

"I didn't say elephant. I said *garbage.*"

"I've more respect for these blokes than you, I mean they're dead sussed," Ordway proceeded. "This campaign's been brilliant, like—bordering on genius. All right, Sobs are wankers. But you want to pretend the SOB don't exist. That's worse than purism, Pyre; it's wishful thinking." Ordway clomped his cowboy boots on the table. "Like having some hood burst into your off-license and hold a pistol to your head and then saying to yourself, 'There's no pistol to my head,' and going about your business. Sorry, mate, but you're gonna get done."

Jasmine began, "In resolving any conflict—"

"Peace at any price, is that what you people want?" Win barked. "Chamberlain thought the same way. What did Sudetenland matter?"

"You have to negotiate with combatants," Jasmine persisted. "Even if they're distasteful—"

"Hitler was a 'combatant,' wasn't he?" Win wheeled to their guest with video-arcade reflexes. "Distasteful, too! But what the hell, give the guy half of Europe—"

"For pity's sake, Win!" cried Martha. "We're talking raggedy-ass Portuguese thugs, not Hitler. Nothing flags losing your intellectual grip like dragging in World War Two!"

"Martha," Nicola entered in slowly, drawing idle pictures in poured salt. "You said that the 'only' thing capitulation to Barban independence would cost is principle." She looked up. "Is principle that cheap?"

"Principle is a commodity, which can be swapped along with pork bellies and coffee futures," said Ordway. "It isn't priceless, Nicky. Nothing is."

"That's a depressing perspective," said Nicola quietly.

"Well, what would *you* do about the Sobs, Nicky?" Ordway despaired. "Let them bomb their little hearts out, while you stick to your bleeding principles?"

"You'll say I'm gormless," said Nicola mournfully. "But instead of rewarding them, you might have them arrested."

Trudy got few chances at savvy, and pounced. "Honey, you can't be serious!"

"How can you arrest the buggers if you can't flipping find one?" Ordway sneered in Edgar's direction. "Oh, except our resident Sob-diviner—whose precocious gift for journalism seems to extend to nicking Bear's contact book."

Edgar smiled pleasantly. Ordway's uncanny incapacity to wound his rival must have driven the little snake insane.

Jasmine began, "Military defeat of indigenous guerrillas has proved almost impossible since the Revolutionary War—"

"Or look at Vietnam!" railed Ordway. "You can't win against these people, Nicky, they're too sharp. Having gone this long without getting lifted, if anything they'll just get better at scarpering. Besides, it's easy for you to cling to that old we-shall-not-be-moved, mustn't-give-in-to-terrorism waffle. You haven't had to pay the price of your convictions. But what about your husband? His whole family's been blown off the frigging planet. How about you, Durham? Want to see more planes incinerated, more families be-fucked, just so sorts like Win and your wife here can keep their hands clean, unsullied by compromising with rubbish?"

Henry looked uncomfortable. During most of this discussion, he hadn't seemed riveted, and Edgar suspected that, despite his history, questions like the one Ordway posed didn't engage Durham on a profound level. The likes of Henry were made for lager-drinking contests and darts. His story and his feckless character were a gross mismatch.

"Aw, I don't know." Henry's mop of brown hair flopped in his eyes. "At first I'd have been with Pyre. Not wanting the wankers to win, doing what they done. But—" Henry glanced apologetically at his wife—"it just goes on and bleedin' on, and I'd not want any more sons and brothers to go through what I done. Maybe at the end of the day I don't give a monkey's. Maybe give them what they want and get the whole balls-up over with. I'm knackered. I'm about ready to go home, and when I do, I don't want the plane to blow up."

"That's just what they're counting on!" Win declared fervently. "Exhaustion! Zealots have the advantage! Fanatics never get tired!"

"But don't you?" asked Edgar.

Funny—abruptly, Win sagged. Rather than look rugged, he just looked haggard. In fact, Win may have been sicker of this conflict than anyone else at the table. But he was hooked, just as he'd been hooked on despising Saddler. Loathing was an addictive emotion, and though Pyre was wildly, claustrophobically bored with the SOB, he was also *passionately* bored. And all passion was a trap.

Edgar slipped off to the bar, where someone hissed, "Edgar!" behind him. He swiveled with dread. Alexis Collier's shoulders were thrust back, her hard little nipples pointing like accusatory arrows. Her uplifted chin exposed a neck that, to his mean satisfaction, was just beginning to wattle.

"It's not easy to cover a beat where the main story is *invisible*, would you accept that?" Alexis whispered harshly. "Being a foreign correspondent is challenging in the best of circumstances. But in Barba we're all especially hobbled, because the SOB is so secretive. And these are the very sources our editors most want to hear from—"

"Alesbo, how about you cut to the chase?" said Edgar, elbows on the bar.

"I think you owe this entire journalistic community an explanation!" she huffed, discarding any pretense of speaking softly. "Some of us have been here for years, and we're under a lot of pressure to produce groundbreaking copy. We try to support each other—"

"Gimme a break!" said Edgar, glancing over his shoulder.

"Yes, we're in competition, but we're also in the same boat. Loose cooperation is in order, don't you think? So one day some flibbertigibbet who's never published so much as her phone number flies into town unannounced—a kid, a *freelancer*—"

Edgar murmured, "Alex, I'd be willing to talk this out—"

"And you save your favors for this zero? For a wannabe?"

"Some other time," Edgar urged sotto voce. "Right now, *keep a lid on it.*"

"For God's sake, if you're going to be that way," Alexis was shrieking, "I could see, maybe, keeping a source like that to yourself—a rare, cooperative source, who's willing to interface with the media. I wouldn't like it, but I might understand it, especially since you're new to journalism and you don't know the unwritten code. But this—this beggars belief! Even for a greenhorn! What, were you trying to impress her? To get her into bed? A leg up for a leg over, is that it? And the only way you could think to give her goose pimples was to say, 'You know, I've got this terrorist friend'?"

"Alex, would you shut the fuck up?"

"What about us? If you're going to parcel out Barrington's contacts, you might have started with serious journalists who publish in mainstream newspapers. This is a headline, international story! *So why didn't you arrange an interview with a member of the SOB for the* New York Times?"

The most indifferent bystander at the Rat that night would have registered Alexis Collier's outrage. At first, Edgar had feared that Jasmine Petronella would overhear the tirade, and her feelings would be hurt. But by the time Alexis was through broadcasting his business to the whole world, Edgar's nervous glances had shifted from the hacks' round table to the silent hulk looming by the door. He'd never been sure just how much English Bebê Serio understood.

CHAPTER 32

Renowned International Terrorist Brakes for Pussycat

JOÃO PACHECO BUZZED the next morning to grant Edgar a rare second audience with Verdade. Though Wallasek had nagged for an updated profile, Edgar courted a reputation as unsympathetic with Verdade's cause, and had expected his pro forma request to re-interview the great man, put in months ago, to be regally ignored.

The now-or-never interview was for this very afternoon, when Edgar had planned to give Jasmine Petronella the Terror Tour around Cinzeiro. Fair enough, his Terror Tour was lame—an expedition to the Creme gift shop, a hasty careen through Terra do Cão (where he was disinclined to linger since repairing the Saab's gouged finish), and a wend about the dreary countryside for an ooh-ah over the landscape's weirdo wind flutes. Still, with Nicola's infernally platonic friendship wearing thin, celibate Eddie was getting desperate, even if through the fug of a daylight hangover Jasmine's looks would inevitably revert to *interesting*. Anyway, forget it. As a reporter of current events, naturally he had to go haggle over the heroic exploits of Teodósso o Terrível in 1794.

At headquarters, no Serio. Pity; kiss all that sparkling repartee good-bye. Instead, Pacheco hooked Edgar's thumb into a yo-brother clasp with a smirk. Ferret-face now wore a dark mafioso three-piece with a turned-up collar and wraparound shades indoors. His patronizing collegiality implied that the office was plenty up to speed on the *National Record*'s hostile coverage, but that Creams sucked the poison from pens like Edgar's for breakfast.

Seated sullenly in O Creme's outer office for over an hour, Edgar had ample time to assess improvements to the premises: closed-circuit cameras, IBM computers, fax and photocopier, five phone lines. They'd swapped populist grunge for swank: grass wallpaper, carpet thick as a zoysia lawn, obese armchairs nubbled in raw linen, lined brocade drapes; this roach nest was done up classier than the Wall Street digs of Lee & Thole. As if to offset the Creams' murderous rep, the reception room was now swaddled in passive, mauvey pastels, which clashed painfully with the wall's red-and-green Barban flag, no longer silk-screened but professionally stitched.

This time Verdade didn't bound up the stairs, but casually opened the inner office door, unabashedly present the entire time. Having bagged the working-stiff windbreaker for an Armani suit, Verdade had gone for the debonair statesman look, and was as crisply cornered as an army bunk. His red-and-green silk tie was dotted with tiny hairy pears.

During their first encounter Verdade's verbiage had slithered with the insinuation that he fronted for truly evil fucks. Now that Edgar had peeked behind the curtain to discover Barba's Wizard of Oz was a common shyster, Verdade's propaganda should have lacked subtext. Strangely, the man's wide brown eyes continued to glitter, and a sibilant hidden agenda still hissed beneath his academic banalities.

As time wore on Edgar grew perplexed. Verdade made such a flap about his tight schedule, his precious time. Yet Edgar had to flip his ninety-minute tape to fill the B-side and then start a second cassette. What's more, this was all pat national-self-determination soft-shoe that he could have downloaded from O Creme's Web site. A wicked smile playing on his lips, *o presidente* seemed to be torturing his interviewer on purpose.

By the end of the interview, Edgar's chest had tightened and his throat felt constricted as if to warn of an oncoming asthma attack, and Edgar didn't have asthma. When he was finally allowed out the door it was pitch-dark, and for once the slap of the wind was exhilarating. *Liberdade!*

Edgar surveyed the Turbo for abuse, but his cardboard sign on the dashboard, CONVIVADO DO CREME, had protected the coupe. Chances were that kids kept their hands off a guest of the party's car not out of respect, but from fear—which might be justified. For no reason that Edgar cared to formulate, he glanced under the car. Christ, you're getting paranoid, he mused—ducking in and central-locking the doors.

Edgar pulled out with relief. He'd come to dislike Terra do Cão, which always made him feel unclean, a sensation he'd usually blame on the neighborhood's unhealthy political quarantine. The area had an Orwellian feel, as if all its residents had been through reeducation camp; you never heard a word against the Creams. Yet whizzing past his regular red wooden phone booth, Edgar wondered if the ghetto's association in his mind with his own SOB atrocity claims might be contributing to its foulness. Because after he drove out of Terra do Cão, that unclean sensation? It didn't go away.

Maybe he was tired, but for once Edgar *couldn't be arsed*, as Bear would say, to contrive distinctions between the *a*moral and the *im*moral, or to sail into congratulatory flights about having hijacked the car bombs of truly warped individuals for a mortifyingly nerdy cause. Fair enough, Edgar was sick of his conscience wheedling that glory might be fleeting but infamy sticks around like gum in your hair. At this point he was even sicker of the callow huckster who continuously rattled off, to no one in particular, pompous excuses for a project at best dubious, at worst repugnant. For once he didn't mean Barrington, but himself. For Edgar no sooner flicked on the radio to the World Service than his ears reflexively pricked for a calumny that might require another hustle from Barba's own Fast Eddie.

He switched off the report, and suddenly a black cat scuttled through the beams of his brights. Edgar hit the brakes. Though he'd missed it, his heart was whomping. Catching himself, Edgar grinned. **RENOWNED INTERNATIONAL TERRORIST BRAKES FOR PUSSYCAT.**

Then, wouldn't he. Not long ago, after Edgar had lit into another lacerating riff about his colleagues, Nicola collapsed into peals of laughter. Finally she'd explained in a teary-eyed wheeze, "Edgar, give up! You're a lovely man!" Maybe it was the memory of Nicola cracking up at his unconvincing tough-guy pose that did the trick, because right then a resolution mushroomed in his head.

Edgar wanted out.

He'd flirted with the proposition before, of throwing in the towel on the SOB while he was still ahead of the game, if that's what he was. Certainly Edgar was a damned sight more anxious than he let on to his notional landlord that any day now Interpol could plow up Abrab Manor's drive to bark on their loudspeaker that they had the house surrounded. Anyone with a lawyer's faith in order believed that sooner or later everyone's brought to book. That he'd got away scot-free so far was miraculous, and the close shave with the fingerprints had brought Edgar up short.

What had kept him claiming bad business this long wasn't duty, much less mischief, the spirit of which he'd lost some time ago, but more narrative panic. If Edgar plain stopped—simply didn't call in any more bomb claims—what kind of closure was that? And from then on the SOB is never heard from again, no one knows why, until one by one the Reuters, *Guardian*, and *Times* Cinzeiro bureaus shut . . . An enervating, listless ellipsis, is that how this *Sob story* should end? Edgar had never cared for songs that faded on the refrain.

Yet slumping behind the wheel, Edgar faced the ugly truth. He had a suck-ass imagination. He couldn't contrive an inspired climax for this farce any more than he could invent innovative diversions for Yardley's after-school playgroup. Edgar was an able imitator, the *clingy* sidekick of a man he'd never even met, and this SOB sport was just a run with Barrington's ball. Half plagiarist, half errand boy, Edgar didn't have a creative bone in his body. He was like one of those hacks hired to write sequels to a classic like *Peter Pan*—travesties of the original on which critics heap opprobrium, with endings crafted purely to allow for yet more second-rate sequels.

Chastened, humbled, and chagrined, by the time Edgar arrived home, he'd made a vow. Okay, it made for a punk story: Edgar picks up where Barrington left off and then calls it quits. It was a tale with no moral, no irony, no final chapter twist. But he couldn't turn state's evidence now without incriminating himself, and probably doing some serious time. No narrative orgasm was worth five years in the slammer. So there was nothing to do but resign as quartermaster of the SOB. He wouldn't call in any more claims. The commitment had a hollow feeling, but all regimens felt bogus at the start. What was it AA people said? One day at a time. Maybe he could start a chapter of Terrorists Anonymous right here in Cinzeiro.

With an Interpol manhunt fresh in his head, finding the front door ajar fortified Edgar's determination to skip his evening's ritual Choque and dive straight for the Noah's Mill. On entering the living room, Edgar considered that in that case he would have to find the bottle, a task that could prove formidable.

The room had been ransacked. Cushions were flung about, and coughed feathers. The seaman's chest gaped open, the quilts it stored snarled in far corners. Chairs were upended, antique end tables smashed. Charred logs littered the hearth, and coals had been ground into carpets. The liquor cabinet was toppled, its cut-glass snifters in bits. Since it was the only whole bottle in sight, tonight this bourbon drinker would have to settle for gin. Lots and lots of gin.

"Saddler!" Edgar hated to admit it, but at the moment he could use a friend.

Only the emerald velveteen wingchair remained upright. Plumped with unmolested pillows on either arm, it formed the room's sole island of repose. Barrington obligingly materialized in the chair, sipping his usual pink gin from that improbably thin martini glass.

"We've had visitors," Barrington advised usefully.

"*Thanks*. I'd never have noticed." Scanning the detritus on the floor, Edgar spotted a silver cigarillo case, an ornately faceted crystal candy dish, and a solid-gold snuffbox. "This can't be a run-of-the-mill burglary."

Barrington laid a finger on his chin. "I think not."

"Why didn't you stop them?" Edgar cried, even as he recognized that depending on imaginary-Barrington to protect the property was like keeping a stuffed Rottweiler. "We're overrun by barbarians, and you rescue the Beefeater and bitters!"

"Naturally I—what's that linguistic abortion you Americans use? *Prioritized*." Barrington's brow dimpled. "But Eddie. I'm a bit concerned about the study."

Edgar groaned. Before trudging upstairs, he took a slug of Barrington's gin.

It was the study on which the twister had planted its most passionate kiss. The jar of international coins was cracked open like a piñata, and change plinked under Edgar's feet as he waded through ankle-deep tossed paper. Barrington's three-ringed clip files were pulled from the shelves and splayed. Since their brain-surgeon guests apparently couldn't work the fiddly clasps on the glassed-in bookcases, the panes were smashed and the woodwork splintered. The pitching to corners of Barrington's melted bicycle pump, hairy skull, and rare demagogic button collection confirmed that one man's memorabilia was another man's junk.

In the tumult of tossed objects, it took Edgar a few minutes to sort out what *wasn't* there: his own computer. After scrounging on all fours for fifteen minutes, he resigned himself that the floppies were gone, too.

Edgar numbly retired to the atrium to allow these absences to sink in.

"Did you," Barrington began with an air of diplomacy, "save your translations?"

"What translations?" Edgar snapped.

"Of my SOB STORIES. Did you save the decoded files to disk, or store them on your hard drive? Or might you have hit that most magical of keys, D-E-L?"

"I saved them," Edgar admitted glumly.

"Ah," said Barrington. "And you've been switching the code phrase every so often? It's terribly important, like changing your underdrawers."

"Of course!" said Edgar impatiently.

"But you don't keep a record. You keep them in your head."

"No," Edgar moaned. "I keep a list. At first I relied on memory, but after two or three replacements I was afraid I'd forget."

"A handwritten list," Barrington proposed hopefully, "that you store on your person, perhaps?"

"I don't even write my grocery list by hand."

"So." Barrington sighed. "This list of code phrases is on your computer?" Hangdog, Edgar nodded. "And it is up to date." Edgar's answers had proved so consistently unfortunate that this last query Barrington didn't bother to phrase as a question. "Then I suggest," he continued, "that you go ring a newspaper."

"I decided to quit!"

"You've no choice. Unless you want our visitors to ring them for you."

"What good is that code phrase to anyone but me? Christ, it's not even any good to me, really—except to carry on with a joke that's got pretty fucking old."

"We've spent so much agreeable time together," Barrington

despaired. "Please don't force me to conclude that you're an idiot."

"But why would anyone tear this place apart? What were they looking for?"

"Anyone," Barrington scoffed, "was more or less looking for what they took."

"Nobody would search for evidence of our racket unless they'd already caught on. How could someone have found us out?"

"Now it's *us*, is it? I've noticed that we're only in this together when something goes wrong. But I really can't accept responsibility here. You called attention to yourself with that cabaret act for Jasmine Petronella. Oh, I grant you it was cute. Too cute, by half."

"Reckless, yeah. So? The whole world thinks Cinzeiro's crawling with Sobs. My 'interview' fed local superstitions is all. Like sighting a leprechaun."

Barrington settled by the pool, dipping the belt of his smoking jacket into the water. "Never mind our humble home. You realize that Tomás Verdade has been metaphorically turning this whole town upside-down for years?"

"Looking for what?"

"*Soldados Ousados*, you halfwit!" Barrington got *shirty* when Edgar was slow on the uptake.

Edgar shrugged. "Why has he bothered? The make-believe kind work swell."

"Think of matters from Verdade's perspective," Barrington chided. "He leads a movement whose paramilitary arm provides him all the power he's got. But he's no notion who these people are. He's no more prescient about SOB operations than any old punter. Tomás has to stay light on his feet, and though he plays a good game and looks in control, he isn't. You've talked to our friend a time or two. Think he enjoys being buffeted by the winds of fortune? You set up an interview with a leprechaun. He got word you knew a Sob, Eddie. Tomás has never located a Sob, Eddie. As of this afternoon? He's found one."

Having poured himself a tall straight gin, Edgar lay flat on the marble floor. The cold stone's evocation of a morgue slab seemed apt.

"Will he blow the whistle on me?" Edgar mewled.

"That's the one fate you're safe from. It's less in his interests to expose the SOB than it is in yours. If the SOB's a joke, it's on Tomás. He'd become a laughingstock."

"Then maybe it doesn't matter." Edgar brightened. "Maybe he'll keep playing along. Meantime, I don't call in any more claims. The whole debacle peters out."

"No, Eddie," Barrington cautioned with a rare note of seriousness. "It matters."

"Leave me alone!" Edgar implored. "I'm shot!"

"If you don't listen, you very well may be. Aside from myself, you're the only soul in the world who's twigged that the SOB's closest corollaries aren't Hamas and the Tamil Tigers, but the Tooth Fairy and the Easter Bunny. Tomás won't want that information in anyone's hands but his own. You're a threat to his future presidency of an independent Barban state. Equally, to his cushy honoraria in America, his *Vanity Fair* profiles, and the stretch limos sent to escort him to the Lisbon parliament. Now, I doubt that Tomás has ever done anything dire, actually. But not because he's such a good Catholic. He's kept his goons in check because he's afraid of the SOB. He won't be afraid of the bugaboos from now on."

Edgar hoped that Barrington would stop there, but not wishing his point to be lost Saddler spelled it out forcefully: "As of tonight, your existence, Eddie—is *inconvenient*."

CHAPTER 33

Little Jack Coroner Sits on a Foreigner

BARRINGTON HAD THE gall to urge a return to Terra do Cão that very night, but Edgar refused—first by railing, then by whimpering, finally by conking out cold by the fountain. Only when Barrington roused him before first light—meaning Barrington himself arose before noon—did Edgar register how soberly his conventionally indifferent mentor apprehended the situation.

Bumbling and bleary, Edgar plopped into the Saab's bucket seat, failing to see the necessity for this expedition. Hadn't he sworn off this drill, and if so why was he heading once more to that filthy phone booth?

He opted to call his contact at the *New York Times*, where at midnight they'd still be putting the paper to bed. The night staff secretary on the foreign desk had grown so genial that, in more conducive circumstances, he might have asked her out.

"Ceendy?" Edgar was so exhausted he probably sounded drunk; in fact, maybe he was still drunk. "Thees ees Os Soldados Ousados de Barba, *sim?* . . . No, no *bomba*. Just, we change zhe code phrase, *sim*?"

She interjected something puzzled like, "Again?" but Edgar let it go. He wanted to get this over with and hit the sack.

"You ready? You have pencil? . . . That's right, *lápis! Muito bom!*" (Edgar's regular calls had inspired Cindy to take an introductory course in Portuguese at the New School.) "Last code we decide go, 'Jack Splat was once too fat, his wife could be so mean.' *Esta bem?* New code: 'Leettle Jack Coroner sat on a foreigner, eating his words and clay.' " Edgar's latest fad in code phrases was fractured nursery rhymes, and usually Cindy would repeat the couplet to confirm. Instead he heard crackling silence, so Edgar decided to make this one long and racy: "'He stuck in his cock, and pulled out a sock—'"

"Mister, Mister SOB man," Cindy interrupted, as she wouldn't usually dare. "There's no call to use that language."

Impudent! "You want our new code phrase or *not*?"

"Not," she snipped.

"Run that past me again?" Edgar forgot the accent.

"No, I don't want your new code phrase," she said primly. "One of you people called this afternoon and changed the Jack Splat to something else, which has already been distributed to staff. You're not up to date."

Edgar's cheeks tingled. The last time he felt this chagrined was after a few months of "freelancing" and his platinum American Express card was declined at Tavern on the Green. "What, if I call up and claim a bomb with my Little-Jack-Coroner-sat-on-a-foreigner tag, the SOB doesn't get credit?"

"Your responsibility would be reviewed, yes," she explained, as if his account were overdrawn and he'd be considered for another card after a period of probation.

Edgar was enraged. Not only had those Creamie yahoos ransacked his house, but they'd filched his clout—the hard-earned clout of an organization whose reputation, like that of any respected family business, had taken years to build. This was a hostile takeover! At least now Edgar grasped why Barrington was so exercised about changing the code. As of last night, Edgar had been cut out of the loop. Without the current code phrase, the authority of any SOB statements he issued would be called into question.

"There's—there's been a split!" he sputtered.

"I'll inform the editor," Cindy said stiffly, and then softened. "And—I didn't like the dirty stuff. But the first part—the coroner-foreigner thing—that was cute. Better than the other guy's. His was kinda boring."

Edgar said defeatedly, "I can imagine."

Edgar did go to bed for a few feverish hours, during which he enfolded the entire SOB hoax into a dream from which he'd shortly awaken, just as the B-movie director escaped the sticky cinematic cul-de-sac with a hackneyed squiggly screen. Slitting his eyes open, he half-expected to glimpse his old blond-wooded bedstead on West Eighty-Ninth Street.

When he confronted Barrington's bordello-red canopy instead, the last twenty-four hours restored themselves as belligerently real. Fair enough, Edgar concluded, burrowing further in his satinate cocoon, if the Creams had taken over the SOB, he'd effectively been bought out. They were welcome to it. The burdens of management had been lifted from his achy shoulders. Like any retired CEO, he could sleep late, eat well, and spend the rest of his days fishing.

But once fully, obnoxiously awake, Edgar glared over the duvets to accept that the SOB may have been Barrington's ball, but he *had* run with it. Without being pumped up by Edgar's faithfully frequent phone calls, that ball would have deflated into puckered historical oddity. If the Creams did anything untoward with that acronym, anything at all, it was his fault. But what could he do? There was nothing worse than feeling culpable, and powerless.

Hungry and hungover, Edgar dragged on his jeans and drowned himself in one of Bear's oversize military jackets, which made him look suitably absurd. He felt so bewildered that no sit-down with Saddler would do—Saddler whose enticements to don his own demigod mantle had lured him into this fiasco to start with. No, Edgar was frantic to talk to someone who was actually there.

"Special K!" Nicola exclaimed fondly. She'd laundered the boarding school epithet into an endearment with the same thrifty ingenuity that converted her old Raleigh bicycle seat into a stool. "You look ridiculous!" she cried, taking in his get-up. "You also look dreadful. Do come in."

"Listen, is Henry here?"

"No, he's off covering the big story. I'm surprised you're not as well."

Edgar didn't ask what story. He didn't want to know. "Gotta talk. Better it's just us."

He nestled into her bunchy hand-upholstered couch, propping his head against the pillow lumpily crocheted with the Barking Rat logo, while Nicola rustled up coffee. A stained-glass mobile poppled sun blobs onto the throw rugs' strange off-center stripes. Since it was Nicola's "mistakes" that made her handiwork loveable, Edgar prayed that the same could be said of people.

"I heard on the radio there was a split!" Nicola shouted from the kitchen. "In the SOB! According to one pundit, a splinter group may want to call a ceasefire!"

"Yeah," Edgar slurred, head back. "There's an element in the SOB that's had enough alright." All the way here he'd rehearsed what he planned to say, but hadn't come up with quite the optimal, well, *transitional phrase.*

Coffee arrived. The steamed milk was sprinkled with cocoa, the mugs glazed in celadon with salamanders scampering the handles. Right now Edgar wished he could spend the rest of his life sipping this fortifying brew while Nicola Tremaine massaged his feet.

"What was so urgent?" she asked cheerfully.

That fantasy with the feet would only wash if Nicola were still speaking to him.

"I, uh, owe you an apology." Edgar rubbed his forehead and

avoided Nicola's gaze. "In a way, I've been lying to you. I never meant for things to get so far out of hand. But it's too late now, and I have to get this off my chest." He smeared his hands down his cheeks to inspect the palms as if they belonged to somebody else.

When he glanced up, Nicola was leaning forward, considering his face intently. "It's Barrington, isn't it," she intuited. "You know where he is."

Rattled, Edgar broke stride. "Um, no. I haven't the faintest idea where he is, or if he's alive or dead. If I had, I'd have said so."

Her eyes drilled him another long beat before Nicola sank back in her chair. "Sorry," she said wiltedly. "Of course you would."

"Christ, you still jump when the phone rings, don't you?" Edgar asked, peering at her sunken expression with incredulity. "But it's been—"

"I know. Gave myself away there, didn't I?" She smiled. "And I was terribly rude. Here you came to confide in me, and I leap right into my own neurosis."

"I've got a few quirks myself."

"Let's see, what else could it be?" Nicola mused. "Angela's begged you to come back. You're tempted, but she's still 'friends' with Jamesie, and even considering it makes you feel ashamed of yourself."

"I've a whole file of old letters to Angela on my hard drive, but not one of them got sent. Or I used to have a file," he mumbled. Shit—those letters, which had morphed into his journal . . . Verdade could now scroll through Edgar's personal life at will. "That's not it."

Nicola leaned forward again, and if Edgar didn't know any better he'd think she was coming on to him. "You're in the CIA?" she teased.

As she bent so far across the tray that her hair trailed into her steamed milk, Edgar realized with horror that she knew very well he'd got over Angela ages ago; that she was expecting a declaration of love. He'd have liked nothing better than to fall on bended knee, but now was not the time. Jesus, this was embarrassing.

"Nick, the SOB—" he began.

At this unexpected detour to politics, Nicola drew back, wiping the milk from her split ends with hasty self-consciousness. He gave her a moment to rearrange both her hair and her expectations.

"The SOB isn't real," said Edgar bluntly. "It doesn't exist. It was just Barrington's idea of a ha-ha."

Her face remained unchanged. "Edgar, check your calendar," she said evenly. "It's not April first."

"Heard of that American tourist trap called 'Santa's Workshop,' where it's *Christmas all year long*? Well, in Barba—" Edgar's eyes met hers—"every day is April first."

"I'm not going to like this, am I?" Her voice was calm.

"Well, it sounds more dastardly than it is, or was, at least at first . . ."

"Start at the beginning," she urged neutrally. Though her body language remained languid, inviting, her temperature was dropping. Edgar had to talk fast, before her demeanor cooled from tepid to icy.

Edgar told her everything—or almost. About the statements, the surgical gloves, the phone booth. The accent, the atrocity poaching, even the interview with Jasmine and the Groucho glasses. He did save the Creamie break-in at Abrab Manor for later, to give her a chance to accustom herself to the core concept. And the other bit he tactfully omitted was that he'd become inseparable pals with Barrington Saddler—whom he'd never met. She only interrupted to ask simple, practical questions.

When he finished, Edgar fell back onto the couch, weak with relief. He'd had no idea that keeping his eccentric hobby to himself had taken such a toll. He hadn't felt so liberated since submitting his resignation at Lee & Thole.

However, that untethered sensation on quitting the firm had proved grievously short-lived. It was the briefest of windows: when you were released from one life, but weren't yet forced to face the life that followed. As Edgar had recognized lifting off from Kennedy, you could never perfectly leave. You were always arriving somewhere else. And Edgar arrived somewhere else the next time Nicola opened her mouth.

"That," she said slowly, "is the most juvenile story I have ever heard."

"You don't believe me? But I—"

"Oh, I believe you," she cut him off briskly. "It's the very juvenility of your story that makes it credible. Is this what I've heard about all my life, 'boys being boys'? Do you really think people are *toys*?"

Edgar realized that he might never have seen Nicola angry.

"Tell me," she went on, and somehow the fact that she kept her voice low and steady instead of screaming made the drubbing harder to take. "Are there any limits? If someone released smallpox on the New York subway, would you claim that? Or if bubonic plague were dropped from airplanes all over Europe, would you claim that?"

"The SOB was supposed to be harmless!" he protested. "No one would get killed who—"

"Yes, you explained all that—several times. But you're aware that two Muslims were murdered in Novo Marrakech last night? In an anti-immigration riot?"

Edgar bundled the crocheted pillow against his stomach like a teddy bear. So that was the "big story." "No," he said forlornly. "I switched off the BBC last night. Lately the news makes me ill."

"I can see why. It's hard to imagine those immigrants would have been lynched if your 'harmless' prank hadn't got, as you say, 'out of hand.' And is it surprising? In fact, isn't an incident like that positively overdue?"

"How was I to know!"

"Oh, you mightn't have been able to determine what, exactly, would come of those phone calls. But you should have known for certain that if anything came of them it would be bad!"

Edgar groped to reconstruct all those copacetic justifications his tempter had supplied. "It does a favor for victims' families . . ." (How did that go?) "It's better to have some object . . . somebody to blame, you know, instead of it just being, like, a drag . . ." Barrington's phrasing had evidenced more flash.

"My husband is better off having his family's tragedy turned into a 'ha-ha'?"

"He'd only feel lousy if, you know, he found out, and, in the meantime, he's got, like, an enemy, to, you know, hang on to—"

"The world suffers from a scarcity of enemies. In your view."

"Well, I was trying, especially since, you know, Madrid, to make these guys who really do this shit, well, pissed off. I figured, if those bombs and all didn't boost their own pet causes . . . maybe they'd give up." If anyone was going to give up soon, it was Edgar. This wasn't going over well, as Barrington would say, *a-tall, a-tall.*

"Your terrorist affiliates have handed in their notice? Out of frustration, your colleagues in the FARC have formed a book club instead."

"No, but—"

"To the contrary, haven't there been more bombings in the last few years than ever?"

"Well, maybe—"

"And wouldn't watching Tomás Verdade incrementally get everything he wants inspire other groups to use the same disgusting tactics?"

Edgar retreated. "The SOB was Barrington's idea!"

"Maybe, but no one forced you to keep making his 'ha-ha' phone calls, did they?"

"He left instructions! The code phrase! The gloves!"

"So in your version of Genesis, Eve eats the apple at gunpoint."

Edgar didn't care for her girly metaphor. "It was an interesting experiment, right? A social, I don't know, psychology thing. I thought it was worth finding out what happens next."

"I see. We're not toys. We're lab rats. Well, you've found out what happens. And you'll keep finding out."

"Nick, I said I was sorry. And if I had it all to do over again I'd . . ." Edgar pulled up short. He didn't want to lie to her anymore, not even in the hypothetical.

"You'd what?"

"Oh, I'm not sure. For a little while," Edgar confessed sheepishly, "it was fun."

"Yes, it was Barrington's brand of fun, but I am floored it was yours!" She could no longer sit, and paced. "When you first got here, you must have noticed how screwed up this place had become. How Barbans had fallen in love with the idea of themselves as dangerous. How a whole new political party had started here that would never have got off the ground without your SOB 'ha-ha'—a party that does nothing but goad its followers to glory in their own murderousness! Wasn't that enough evidence to demonstrate that what you found on Barrington's floppy disks was poison?"

"Maybe I didn't think it through," said Edgar morosely. "When I first got here, nobody had been hurt, really—"

"People were badly hurt in that riot you and I got caught up in. Though now I see why you were so extravagantly glad no one was killed. Their blood would have been on your hands, wouldn't it?"

Chin dropped, Edgar nodded.

Nicola flapped her hands in the air with uncharacteristic jerkiness. "I—I don't understand. You have to help me out here. I don't get it. I cannot for the life of me grasp why you would do such a thing. Can you explain? Please?" She really did appear to be begging, if only for some small scrap to hang on to that could keep her from detesting him.

But then, maybe she was doing Edgar a favor, since this was a question he'd never answered to his own satisfaction. As a stopgap theory, he could have bowed to Saddler's charge that, in perpetuating the SOB, Edgar was planning to wow Nicola with his unsuspected dark side. But frankly, her recoil was no surprise. He'd known she'd go ballistic. Edgar hadn't been trying to impress Nicola. He'd been trying to impress Barrington.

CHAPTER 34

The Tooth Fairy Leaves Behind a Bigger Surprise than a Quarter

EDGAR BEGAN HALTINGLY, stroking the salamander on his mug. "When I was fat . . ." He hadn't expected to get into this area, but instinct dictated that he eschew a grandiose rationale, à la Sadler, for an explanation that was maximally pathetic. "Sorry. This is roundabout."

"I have time." Nicola sat back down, scissoring her legs to the side in a pose of grim tolerance. The froth on her cold coffee had died; the cocoa looked like dirt.

"Anyway, I thought, if I lost the weight, I'd be like everybody else. Or, strike that. Not like everybody else, since that's not what I've ever wanted. I told you about that kid, Toby Falconer? He was like, from another planet. I was pretty sure I wasn't a fag, since all the other guys seemed to think Falconer was, you know, anointed, too. They couldn't keep their eyes off him. He was surrounded by a force field, a glow. And everything he did was perfect."

Edgar sighed. "So I ate almost nothing but celery for six months. After which, Edgar the frog was supposed to turn into a prince." He checked for signs of impatience, but this was a gracious woman. She'd hear him out.

"Except I only shrunk into a scrawnier frog. Oh, I'd clambered a few rungs on the social ladder. But I was still craning my neck at the top until it gave me a crick. Ditto in college, in law school, at the firm. There was always someone else who was the bee's knees. All my life I've wondered what it was like to be extraordinary. Not to be the second-in-command, the trusty adjutant, but the Big Man, the *ne plus ultra*. The guy who leaves regular people slack-jawed, who slays them with his throwaway one-liners, who never wishes he could be somebody else because everyone else he knows wishes they could be him.

"Then I ship here—and I land smack in the middle of another fucking cult of personality. Except that Saddler himself has vamoosed. And he's left everything behind, like a do-it-yourself kit. His clothes, his house, his car, his friends, his woman—which you were, even if you never sealed the deal. He's even left me his idea of amusing himself. Maybe that amusement involved dicking people around—his readers, his editor, his colleagues, his for-all-practical-purposes lover. But I figured that ignoring the rules that apply to proles, abiding by different principles or maybe by no principles at all, had to be part of the kit. A little shady business obviously came with the territory. In fact, an awesome obliviousness to consequences seemed like the very source of Saddler's genius."

"Having tried on this 'genius,'" asked Nicola, "you're finally a prince? A free spirit? You shrug off whatever mess you leave behind as a squalid matter for the little people to clean up."

"I don't seem to have the knack," said Edgar glumly. "I get anxious. I'm afraid Saddler thinks—I mean, if he were here, Saddler would think—that I'm a candy-ass."

"And are you?" she asked point-blank. "A candy-ass?"

Edgar didn't hesitate. "Yup."

"Good." Apparently, his first right answer of the afternoon. "Barrington couldn't leave behind what you really wanted."

"I know. Though that do-it-yourself kit? It did work, for moments. I've had glimpses. Of another life."

"You saw a wonderland. A paradise."

"I don't know. I've never gawked into Saddler's garden long enough to tell. Still, if Saddler had confessed, about the SOB, would you be this irate? Would you despise him?"

"Barrington did all sorts of dreadful things that I did know about, Edgar. But I'm determined to believe that I loved him, not because of, but in spite of the way he was always testing people—who liked him so much more powerfully than he thought they ought to."

"That's just another way of saying that different rules apply to Saddler," Edgar grumbled. "Barrington initiates a con of international proportions, and it's, *Isn't he a sly dog.* Alternatively, *Isn't Bear misunderstood, isn't he tortured, look at what he's been driven to, isn't it tragic that everybody LIKES him so much.* Smitten lackeys buzzing about his head like flies around a cow."

Edgar lurched up and ranged the room. "But Kellogg picks up where Saddler left off? Does a bang-up job, keeps his mouth shut, makes the SOB bigger and more notorious, and even tries—whether or not you think it backfired—tries to rearrange the grand shell game into something beneficial by sticking it to cretins. Is Kellogg a sly dog? Or is Kellogg misunderstood, a heartbreaker? No, he's just a terrible person! Some kind of scurrilous, immoral—loser!"

"Edgar, you're being incredibly self-indulgent." Despite the sternness of her tone, when Nicola turned away it was to hide the fact that he was making her laugh.

Encouraged, he hammed it up. "Not only is he a despicable cur, the lowest of the low—" Edgar pitched the Barking Rat pillow *thwap* into the couch—"but he's a phony! An off-brand knock-off! A mediocre understudy for the Great Barrington—"

"Edgar, stop it!" Nicola pleaded, seeming to recognize that on some level he was serious. "Yes, I think you're misguided, that you've made a dreadful mistake—I don't get the impression you appreciate yet how dreadful. But I don't despise you."

"You sure?"

"I'm sure."

"Anyway." Edgar thumped to the couch. "I've resigned from the SOB. No more claims."

"This is like listening to an alcoholic promise he'll never take another drink when he's still stewed." When Edgar looked blank, Nicola prodded, "This afternoon. You must have claimed it shortly before you came here. So you'll forgive me if I'm underwhelmed."

Edgar squinted. "Claimed what?"

Nicola tilted her head. "The news said they used a recognized code phrase. Didn't you bother to get the details before you leapt to take 'credit' for it? Fertilizer—not too big; and crude, the radio said. It only partially exploded. A few people hurt, no one killed. At a peace rally, of all things. But after what you've told me . . . It doesn't make sense." Her gaze went middle-distance.

"Why?"

"That's why it's a big story. Not because the device was so large. But because the fertilizer, it was for *peras peludas*. For the first time, a bomb's gone off in Barba."

The hairs rose on Edgar's arms in a domino ripple. He'd vowed to come clean with Nicola, to be honest to a fault. But Edgar had assured her there was no such thing as the SOB, and once more, if unwittingly, he'd lied. There didn't used to be an SOB.

There was now.

The next few minutes tested the limits of Nicola's political acuity. It took too long for Edgar to connect the dots for her, though maybe Nick just didn't like the looks of the picture.

Hurriedly, Edgar described yesterday's break-in, his rebuff at the *Times* foreign desk early this morning. So the Creams had the code phrase, and were in on the ruse. They were no longer afraid of leprechauns. They'd done their market research, so they could be sure of a sizable constituency with a stomach for armed revolt. More than stomach. Appetite. If neither Edgar nor Barrington had ever claimed bombs he actually planted, nothing prevented the company's new owners from diversifying. Thousands of column inches may have been wasted on distinguishing the two, but for all practical purposes there'd been a merger, and O Creme de Barbear and Os Soldados Ousados de Barba were now one and the same. As of the last eighteen hours, the Creamie-Sob alliance was actually dangerous.

"Well, why—why don't you declare a ceasefire?" Nicola proposed desperately.

"For one thing, I don't have the current code phrase."

"You could get it. You're a journalist. Ring Guy Wallasek. Say that since there are now bombs going off in Barba—" she was already using the plural—"you need to know the SOB's code, in case they ring your office to deliver a warning."

"Nick, who cares if some renegade Sob announces a ceasefire if it's not observed?"

"I don't understand the point of blowing up your own turf anyway! If Verdade wants to stem immigration because he loves his own country so much, why plant bombs in it?"

The kid *was* naive. This was Terrorism 101. "Because for all his seeming cosmopolitanism, Verdade is provincial. He's been to the States, but it's only Barba that counts. This is the only place he can blow up and feel the earth move under his feet.

"Why do you think the SOB was given credit for being so smart? Because they didn't shit in their own bed. Because they appeared to exploit larger geopolitics: they unnerved the G-8, not just no-account Portugal. Sobs defied the ironclad law that *all politics are local.* As an abstraction, the SOB displayed a rationality that real terrorists almost never do. Real terrorists are lunatics, Nick. They don't care about killing their own people, because it's the folks nearest to hand whom they most want to control. What Verdade has started may be broadly self-destructive, but it's not bizarre. It's totally normal."

"Then you've no choice, Edgar, you'll have to discredit Verdade by—" Nicola's jaw clapped shut.

"Henry!" Edgar hailed weakly.

Durham looked from one to the other. "Don't let me interrupt. You were saying?"

"Nothing," said Nicola. "It wasn't important."

"Didn't mean to break up the party!"

Nicola risked a beseeching look at Edgar. Edgar shook his head, just. He didn't know how to get out of this hole with the Creams yet, but as for spreading his secret further afield, Edgar's butt was on the line, and Henry was hardly the soul of discretion.

"We were just talking about the bomb at the peace rally," Edgar said heartily. "Why the Sobs would switch the campaign to Barba itself." Which was indeed what they'd been talking about, but which felt like a cover-up, since it sounded like one. What were the chances that Henry's arrival had poured cold water on a conversation about politics?

"That so?" said Henry, smacking gum. "What about it?"

"Self-destruction," Edgar condensed lamely. "Never mind, Henry, it would bore you."

"But Nicky here. She wasn't bored, was she?"

Henry having developed a keen nose for conspiracy, Edgar was now treated to the triangulation that Barrington had found so intoxicating: the jumpy glances, double meanings, and over-obvious gropes for any feeble excuse to get off alone with Nicola.

Well, Saddler could have it. Begging off dinner, Edgar fled.

Edgar puttered toward Abrab Manor, in no great hurry to return to the ruin of his violated hideaway. Yet despite the day's aura of urgency, there was nothing else to do but head home and pray there was still a lasagna left in the freezer.

Looming on his tail, a chunky, top-heavy truck filled Edgar's rearview mirror—one of those rickety, wooden-slatted haulers brimming with crates of *peras peludas*, and probably headed for the port, where the noxious crop would be forklifted onto ships bound for unsuspecting Guinea-Bissau. The truck was gaining on him, and Edgar motioned out his window for the vehicle to pass. For this wind, it was perilously overloaded, and he wanted the weaving hulk safely out of his vicinity.

The truck pulled to his bumper, but didn't overtake. Edgar motioned again, his wave impatient. The fucking thing reeked. Bad enough that it was billowing black exhaust; where the hell did all that EU money go, anyway? But you couldn't even smell the fumes for the overpowering stench of the hairy pears themselves.

Pointedly, Edgar touched the brake. At last, gears groaning, the truck drew alongside. Edgar looked over to make grateful eye contact, but the driver was wearing one of those newly popular full-face welding masks. The road was only two-lane, and those trucks had lousy acceleration. In consideration, Edgar eased up on the gas.

But the truck didn't pass. It hovered right next to the Saab, slowing as Edgar slowed. What's more, the truck had pressed over the yellow meridian, nudging the Turbo over to the extreme right until its tires traced the road's perimeter. Edgar blasted his horn. In response, the truck edged over another foot. To avoid being sideswiped, Edgar had to steer the Turbo onto the rocky shoulder.

"You fucking maniac!" Edgar screamed, as his left-hand tires, too, juddered onto rubble. "Are you trying to *kill* me?"

As if in answer, the thick trunk of a roadside *pera peluda* tree hurtled toward his windshield. Yanking the steering wheel hard right, Edgar missed the tree by inches. The Saab bumped down a slope to plow into a *flauta ventosa* in a Barban's front yard. The stout wooden pole breathed *hoo* as it went down.

Edgar mopped his forehead as the truck chugged past. *Now, don't be silly*, he told himself. *You're prone to fanciful thinking right now, because you're jittery, you're hungry, you're overwrought. Barbans are terrible drivers. Those trucks are hard to control. The guy could have hit a diagonal headwind—couldn't pull forward, and the wind bore him into the Saab. Right? That could be it. Right?* But as Edgar craned his neck out the window, he could see the back of the driver's head as the truck barreled away—suddenly, no problem, the vehicle keeping to its lane. That head: it was massive. It was round. And it looked really, really *stupid*.

CHAPTER 35

Bubbardizing Humberto

THE FACT THAT he was still an on-the-job stringer for the *National Record* may have become farcical to Edgar, but not to Wallasek, who'd left an irascible message on Abrab's answering machine, demanding a detailed account of Barba's first bombing for the morning edition. As a fresh-faced cub, Edgar would have scurried off to the stadium to personally check out the damage and vox-pop eyewitnesses. As an old hand, he wasn't such a sap, especially if nipping into town meant presenting himself as potential sport for passing *pera peluda* trucks.

Armchair journalism was much more efficient. Edgar dialed Martha Hulbert at the *Post* for the lowdown. The quotes he could invent; like General Syedlo's, they'd be sharper, smarter, and livelier than authentic er-uhs. Overall, covering a complete fabrication had helped Edgar to relax about his work, and for months now he'd concocted statements from nonexistent government underlings, faked statistics he couldn't be *arsed* to look up, and contrived sociological studies. Owing to the profusion of fellow armchair hacks, Edgar's creative factoids had infected copy all over the world. It was so satisfying to spot quotes from "Dr. Anselmo Bitterbottom" on the *Sydney Morning Herald* Web page that he finally understood the hitherto unfathomable allure of authoring the computer virus.

Hulbert's thumbnail: Since breast-beating peace rallies were regularly held in the *praça dos touros*, the noontime fertilizer bomb had been hidden in a trailer delivering one of the bulls for that night's fight. The swaying assembly of lunchtime do-gooders had still been crooning *"Aonde foram todas as flores?"*—a Peter, Paul, and Mary standard that was interminable in any language. The event hadn't yet climaxed in its traditional flap of white doves, whose cages were still stacked by the trailer. To wit, many Barban gentlefolk were dining on squab this evening.

Other than pigeons, *o touro* was the only fatality. When Edgar phoned Trudy, she guaranteed a bathetic close-up of the dead bull's bewildered face, replete with flies. So Edgar decided to *Bubbardize* the story, as the animal-shtick was now known in the terror trade. Opting for the poor-old-bull angle was intellectually bankrupt if the SOB had shifted its "strategy" to blowing up its own patch, but Edgar was eager to divert attention from the tactics of an organization that, overnight, actually had tactics, thanks to him.

Edgar had appealed to Barrington to please put the study in some kind of order, but figments of your imagination just weren't very helpful around the house. His computer having been filched, Edgar subsequently set up shop in the atrium with a *pen and paper*, which felt no more practical than chiseling out the story on a stone tablet. Concentrating his exasperation on this crude chicken-scratching process, for a full hour Edgar blocked out the suspicion that being run off the road this afternoon was no accident.

Yet once Edgar had laboriously dictated the article down the line instead of e-mailing it like a civilized person, even one of those nefarious pink gins couldn't forestall a deepening funk. Had that device fully exploded, the bullring bomb could have whacked any number of innocuous peaceniks. Edgar had been lucky, but this was the kind of luck that ran out.

The Creams had a ready-made constituency inured to political violence, both in-country and abroad. Creams had more cash than they knew what to do with and a huge pool of footloose juvies on tap—those pimply kids desperate to get their hands on a detonator instead of a colander. The technology for Easy-Bake terrorism lay a few keystrokes away on the Internet. Verdade would have his army of downy-cheeked losers improvising recipes with sugar and ammonia in no time, and sooner or later those bombs would work swell.

Inevitably, too, after practicing small beer on home turf, Verdade was bound to turn on Lisbon—a politically logical target that any real SOB would have been blitzing all along. Edgar liked Lisbon, and he was sickened by visions of the majestic marble arch of the Praça do Comércio or that nifty iron elevator-to-nowhere designed by Eiffel being sent skyward for the asinine cause of Barban independence.

Still trudging numbly through the paces of a good little scribbler, Edgar had no choice but to attend O Creme's press conference at the new Hilton the next afternoon. Walking from his car to the hotel, Edgar had to negotiate around countless broken Choque bottles and acrid pools of puke; a bomb in Cinzeiro at last had goosed the whole city into an all-night booze-up. Hitherto, locals had felt a little left out. Here Barbans had apparently provided the rationale, matériel, and know-how, and the party was held perpetually somewhere else. Cinzeiro had a hell-raising side, and its residents far preferred an impromptu fertilizer fest to staid events like the pitifully undersubscribed opening of their classical concert hall, featuring flautist Jean-Pierre Rampal. Had the Creams hawked tickets to yesterday's bullring bomb, they'd have sold out.

In the Hilton's lobby, Edgar battled through jumped-up pubescent Creamie-boppers, girls who shrieked and flopped about in a frenzy at every false sighting of Tomás Verdade. You'd think that blasting holes in your own town would be a bit of a black eye, but no. Sponsoring one cut-rate fireworks display had already jacked Verdade to the status of Van the Man.

The Creams' press conference was held in the banquet room. Reflecting an arbitrary theme-park vulgarity perfectly calibrated to Barba's hick tastes, the hall's motif was unaccountably designed around colonial India; murals depicted pith-helmeted British officers astride elephants in little red hats. Tentacled flowers in bulbous bowls poked reporters in the eye, and a rancid reek from the tropical blooms lent a literal cast to O Creme's leadership having a bad smell. The taint only drew jackals, and the hall was jammed.

The dais was arranged with individual mineral waters by each party official, Pacheco among them, Serio not—an absence Edgar took obscurely as bad news; he felt safer with Creamie muscle in plain view. Half a dozen young Turks stood guard behind the table, one of whom had once pressed Edgar for an SOB referral at the Rat. Repressing grins, these proud new deputies stood erect, chests out, shoulders back, like freshly pinned Eagle Scouts.

Verdade's late entrance drew applause. Good-humored, personable, and dashing, Tomás was popular with the press.

"Yesterday was a heavy day for my country," Verdade boomed into the mic, as the crowd hushed. "Perhaps the rest of the world can appreciate that Barba herself is not immune to the violence that injustice invites. Even if that violence is not always vented on those who most deserve it—like our friend Humberto." A chuckle rippled through the media; Humberto was the name of the bull. "I understand that the correspondent for the esteemed *National Record*," Verdade continued, eyes seeking Edgar, "was especially moved by Humberto's poor fortune." Another chuckle, at Edgar's expense; Bubbardizing might work a treat with readers, but had a tacky tabloid rep.

"Others of the press," Verdade continued in a more serious vein, "have made much of the irony that yesterday's SOB operation took place at a peace rally. Though I would not presume to speak for our brothers in the SOB, I would hazard that this irony was intended. Those good citizens gathered in *a praça dos touros* wanted peace. But the SOB also wants peace. We all want peace. No one aches for peace more than I.

"But there are different types of peace. There is the peace of oppression—the peace of silence, of fear, of those unwilling or unable to speak up. This is an unsettled peace, a thin peace, a whitewashed peace, like a single coat of paint over a cracked wall. Most of all, this is a peace that cannot last, and in this sense it is no peace at all.

"I yearn for another sort of peace," Verdade intoned as the audience jotted and an ABC cameraman frantically fiddled with a silver reflective shield aimed at the president's face. "The peace of justice. The peace of freedom. Yet the road to true tranquility—ironically, as many of you have written—is not always peaceful. It is all very well for my people to cry, *Enough! We must have peace for our children!* Yet our children must also be allowed to grow up with self-respect, in a nation they can call their own, where they can speak their own language and be understood, where they are not marginalized or overrun. Our children have a right to deep-seated peace, not the peace of inertia, of embarrassment, of gloom—the peace of abdication, of colonization, of defeat.

"However well-meaning my countrymen at that bullring rally yesterday, I must charge them with wanting a cheap and easy peace. We in O Creme de Barbear and our noble comrades in Os Soldados Ousados de Barba are willing to pay the price for a profound peace, a lasting peace. We must therefore redress the grievances that have given rise to this conflict. If we do not treat the germinal causes of violence—if we only suture infection into a gaping wound—that wound is sure to fester, and the violence will resurge with all the terrible recrudescence of gangrene."

As Verdade began accepting questions, Edgar added up the tally-marks on his notepad appreciatively. In justifying a bomb that might have killed two dozen people had it worked properly, O Creme's president had managed to use the word *peace* twenty-four times.

"Mr. Verdade!" cried Martha Hulbert. "Can we put you on record, then, as refusing to condemn yesterday's attack?"

A ritual question demanded a ritual reply. "Condemnation is an empty formality, Senhorita Hulbert. Of course I am regretful about the incident, and relieved that no one was killed. But I wish to excavate the taproot of this violence, not recite platitudes. Roland?"

"Does your refusal to condemn extend to the Novo Marrakech lynchings two nights ago?" Verdade never turned a hair, but Ordway flattered himself that he was putting Tomás on the spot. What a pill.

"Those 'lynchings,' as you call them, were tragic." Verdade's head canted at a mournful angle, achieving an attractive three-quarters profile for the ABC camera. "But those unfortunate Moroccans were in the wrong place at the wrong time—that is, they were in the wrong country. I fear that unless we get unwelcome migrants back where they belong there are bound to be repetitions of this week's outburst of frustration."

"Mr. Verdade, are you inciting your people to commit more murders—?"

Meantime, Edgar was transfixed. Two days ago Verdade discovers his whole political movement is founded on a sham, and the guy doesn't miss a beat. The man was unflappable. Verdade could as well have been a tycoon just informed that his stock portfolio was worthless, and his reaction was to write more checks.

"Mr. Verdade!" Edgar waved his hand. "Was the bullring bombing an aberration, or is Barba likely to suffer more of the same? And now that the SOB has gone local, do you anticipate that the armed campaign could move to Lisbon?" It was humiliating to be inquiring after the intentions of his own acronym, like having to quiz the neighbors about the whereabouts of your own wayward kid.

"Edgar," Verdade chided familiarly. "I couldn't possibly have any idea."

Edgar pressed on as Nicola's proxy, "And what's the logic of blowing up your own country?"

"You would have to ask the SOB." Verdade's capacity to look Edgar smack in the eye was unnerving.

"I *am*, apparently." Edgar glared with the impotent indignation of the dispossessed. Meanwhile, with nine-tenths of the law on his side, the thief toys in plain view with what he's stolen, with no intention of giving it back.

"If I were to venture a theory," Verdade posited coyly, "I might suppose that when you are being held hostage against your will, it is in your interests to make your company as disagreeable as possible. If Barba becomes a sharp enough thorn in Lisbon's side, perhaps the government will eventually do the sensible thing, and detach the thorn."

"Lisbon is a very old, venerable city," Edgar appealed. "Full of irreplaceable castles, plazas, and artifacts. It wouldn't just be bad PR, but a tragic waste—"

"You *are* a man of broad passions," Verdade commended, eyes twinkling. "I'm sure the SOB will take your architectural attachments into account. Win?"

That twinkle: it wasn't simply the glimmer of having caught on about the Terra do Cão phone booth. Rather, Verdade's gaze sparkled with intelligence about Edgar's late-night weakness for the faithless Angela, his unmanly two-year tolerance of *Jamesie*, his high school prostration before the platinum blond icon of Toby Falconer, his dead-end infatuation with Nicola Tremaine, and his secret indenturement to the immortal Barrington Saddler, a windbag whom Edgar publicly disparaged but privately resurrected as the best friend he'd never had. Far from being the flinty, clinical records of a thick-skinned cynic, the journal entries on Edgar's hard drive were the outpourings of a puppy dog. The exposure was unendurable. Edgar slipped from the banquet room early, and fled to his car.

Fleeing *to* his car was quite another matter from fleeing *in* it. After peering under the chassis for any alarming lumps or wires—a procedure already as routine as a woman's check in the mirror for blemishes or stray hairs when exiting a restroom—Edgar nosed into a nearly immobile tailback. Owing to the arrival of copious foreign do-gooders, local radio now broadcast the news in English, to which Edgar tuned in. According to the lead story, this traffic jam wasn't restricted to downtown. Most of Cinzeiro was paralyzed by bomb threats.

Unless Verdade had been sitting on an arsenal that was primed and ready to go, the threats were empty, though scares worked every bit as well as the real thing in the inconvenience department. Had Edgar called in the scares himself, he might have hunkered into his upholstery with sly satisfaction, but being dicked around turned out to be substantially less amusing than doing the dicking. Road after road was cordoned off with yellow security tape, and Edgar's usual route to Abrab Manor was blocked. In fact, listening to which areas were affected, Edgar could almost conclude that the scares were deliberately confected to impede his personal journey home.

Three hours. In the course of which Edgar had progressed 2.6 miles, the while forced to confront the painful crumple of his glossy black hood, still dented from that encounter with the *flauta ventosa* pole. Between torturous rebroadcasts of Verdade's press conference—*I yearn for a different sort of peace; the peace of justice, the peace of freedom*—the radio announcer delivered a warning that grew increasingly stern as the sun set. For tonight the weather service was issuing a Wind Watch, cautioning Barbans to secure their homes and stay indoors. Gales that drove most nationals to storm cellars Barbans regarded as kite weather. If Radio Cinzeiro forecast the wind would be "severe," it would be deadly.

As Edgar finally struck the long road out of town and traffic began to move and thin, the atmosphere was already throwing its weight around. It was difficult to keep the Turbo in lane. The blasts were unpredictable, and this time when oncoming trucks wobbled over the meridian Edgar couldn't indulge his paranoia that the bumpers were lunging for him on purpose. The high-pitched *eee* shrieking through the ventilation system gave him a headache, and gripping the wheel ten-and-two stiffened his neck. As ever when the *vento*'s assault grew more punishing than usual, Edgar felt hounded, badgered, and bullied by forces beyond his control, and in his current besieged political circumstances the harassment took on the character of metaphor. During a Barban Wind Watch, cars had been known to roll like tumbleweed, so that simply being prevented from getting home as zero hour approached could be chalked up as a second attempt on his life.

Edgar managed to shudder into his drive by seven-thirty p.m., half an hour before the watch began, though groping from the car to the front door was a quasi-military maneuver, like scrambling through enemy flak. Abandoning all pretense of dignity, Edgar groveled this distance on hands and knees. Opening the jimmied front door was a cinch, closing it an athletic feat.

He leaned with his back against the door with relief. Though the house was haunted with thumps and creaks, in comparison with the roar outside it was blessedly quiet. From that brief journey to the porch, his cheeks felt raw and dry; his ears were ringing. Damn those miscreants to hell. He was out of Choque, Noah's Mill, and lasagna; with the whole town gridlocked, shopping had been out of the question.

Edgar shambled to the kitchen and wrenched open a bottle of Rainier cherries in kirsch, about all that was left of Barrington's ludicrous gourmet larder. The cherry glop was cloying, but in this sirocco the villa had acquired the live-by-your-wits austerity of a bomb shelter, where the finicky would perish. Edgar slurped grateful spoonfuls of the syrup with survivalist resourcefulness.

Edgar was spent. He didn't want to use his time wisely, he just wanted to slaughter it. Figuring that *Jerry Springer* could only be improved in Portuguese, Edgar picked through the pillow fluff in the living room to the TV, only to find that the *vento* was blowing reception to snow. Trailing with his silly dinner to the atrium, he plopped onto a nest of cushions by the fountain and stared vacantly at the glass double doors. He had to keep yawning to equalize the pressure in his ears. As the gale gathered, *flautas ventosas* over the countryside *whoo*-ed at a gradually higher pitch. With all the rattles and thumps resounding throughout the house, Edgar might have been on edge without the assurance that this structure had withstood similar poundings for over two hundred years. At any rate, the *vento* was coalescing into such an event in itself that he didn't much miss the tube. Funny, though, that buzzing sound from the double doors—that was new.

"*Eddie . . . ?*"

It was a quiet, cooing call that Edgar first dismissed as more wind.

"*Eddie!*" whispered more insistently, this time distinctly from the kitchen.

Rats. What now. Edgar was just beginning to enjoy the show.

Edgar stumbled up and trundled into the kitchen. "Don't tell me," he grumbled, "you've found a jar of double-chocolate truffle sauce with Cointreau for my main course."

"Get your backside in here *now*, you git!" Weird—Saddler's voice emitted from the walk-in pantry.

"What?" Disconcerted, Edgar ventured in.

The pantry door slammed. Edgar's ears popped. Outside, the deep *whoo* of wind flutes glissandoed to a shrill upper octave. At once from along the whole westward wall of the manor came an end-of-the-world crash, as if twenty loaded china cabinets had simultaneously pitched forward.

Frozen, Edgar waited in the dark as the crash subsided to tinkles. A nippy breeze began whipping under the pantry door.

"Thanks, Saddler," said Edgar soberly. The cherry-kirsch goo wasn't settling well in his stomach. Woozy, he cracked the pantry door open, and crept out.

Having written about the devices daily, Edgar assumed it was a bomb. Smashed kitchen windows seemed to confirm as much. He padded nervously to the atrium, where the glass double doors were completely blown in. The pool glinted with glass. Dagger-length splinters pinioned the pillows on which he'd just been slumping. Yet he was unable to locate an epicenter, a black mangle where a bomb had been planted.

In the living room, all the windows along the western wall were also shattered inward. The *vento* had lunged inside, and eddies of pillow stuffing fluffed in cyclones about the furniture. Newspapers flapped against the ceiling like spastic seagulls. Squinting into a gust as his eyes teared, Edgar examined a window frame. Chisel marks.

CHAPTER 36
Barringtonizing the Barking Rat

WHETHER HAM-HANDED MURDER attempt or deft threat, loosening windowpanes prior to a Barban Wind Watch went well beyond practical joke. Standing amid the shambles of his living room—the floor crumbly with loosened caulking, wind currents coursing from the shattered windows like water penetrating a flow-thru teabag—Edgar was seized with that quintessential American experience of wishing he had a gun. For a lethal projectile, he was forced to settle instead for the heavy cut-crystal candy dish, which he hoisted in assault position until his arm ached. Upstairs, he clutched its cold stem wide-eyed in bed. Edgar would have vacated the premises immediately, were it not for the Winnebago-flipping whimsies of the great outdoors.

By daybreak, the *vento* had subsided to its old steady pummel. Decidedly incurious about what other misadventures Verdade had planned, Edgar darted out to the Saab, and this time his chassis scan was as thorough as a woman's survey for spots when she's already had skin cancer. It was too early to bother Nick and his office was no safer than Abrab, so Edgar drove blindly away from town. At last sure that he hadn't been followed and surrounded by the vast desolation in which the peninsula specialized, he pulled to the side of the road and caught some narcotic shut-eye. By the time he called from a bar phone in a village on the northern coast, Nick was out.

Punctuating the aimless journey with more fruitless payphone calls to Nick and Henry's machine, Edgar drove around the monochrome Barban countryside all day, thus verifying the madness of anyone who'd kill to gain full possession of a dismal, scrubby outback that you couldn't give away. Edgar supposed that if the Creams were really trying to whack him he should hightail it to Lisbon; better yet, to Seville or Madrid. But the notion of a real off-screen hit man was so foreign to a former corporate lawyer that Edgar couldn't quite take his own plight seriously. However imprudent the return, all afternoon he knew for certain that eventually he was headed back to Cinzeiro. He had to get the hell out of Barba, but not without saying good-bye to Nick. Or maybe, he thought rashly, asking her to come with. Shit. Come with where?

So, against his better judgment, Edgar cruised back down the coast. Cinzeiro on the horizon at sunset achieved that same roseate glow of his West Eighty-Ninth Street apartment and his two-timing girlfriend once he'd decided to leave them behind. In this terminal light, even the hunky souvenir factory looked grand, the gaudy hotels glamorous. Similarly, the unsettlingly extant SOB, the backbiting Barban hack pack, and his own double life as mild-mannered reporter by day, *soldado ousado* by night were already acquiring a nostalgic halo in his head.

The screwiest sentimentality Edgar indulged was over Abrab Manor. Sure, he'd miss the satin sheets, the fragrant cedar furnishings, the nut-house padding of polychromatic pillows, but it was the impending loss of a less tangible luxury that grieved him more: the merely residual yet still intoxicating presence of Barrington Saddler.

With still no answer at Nick and Henry's, they were surely at the Rat, and a public venue might be safer than a private home at that. He disliked the predictability of his showing up at the bar, but the whole reason a man had an orbit was that it encompassed all of the places he had reason to go.

In spite of himself, Edgar smiled at the logo of the Barking Rat on his way in. Ever since he'd resolved to cut and run, Barba had seemed funkier, kookier, kinkier. Too bad he hadn't noticed what a kick he got out of Cinzeiro before he had to leave town. This time, no Bebê Serio at the door: bad sign. Every time Serio *didn't* show lately, something nasty went down.

All day, Edgar's senses had been jacked up. The *vento*'s rush widened to the obliterating *whah* of Niagara Falls; grains of sand pelted his cheeks like chickpeas; rotting roadside *peras peludas* exuded the ammoniacal shock of smelling salts, and sweat drizzling from his upper lip stung his tongue with such distilled acridity that he might have been licking a urinal. In kind, Edgar's advance on the journos' regular round table went slo-mo. So sharply was each consecutive instant exposed on his retinas that Edgar would later be able to reference the images like cinematic stills.

Trudy Sisson noticed him first. When her eyes lit on Edgar, a smorgasbord of a smile spread across the girl's face, like a table of appetizers to which he might help himself. He had sensed for a while now that she'd come across if he crooked a finger. But that would have been accepting the kewpie doll when he'd failed to win the stuffed bear, and love was one contest in which second prize could be worse than losing. Cute, yeah, but Trudy had never passed the Breakfast Test—a crude cost-benefit analysis that assessed whether X (getting his rocks off) equaled or exceeded Y: enduring the awkwardness of a mealtime whose underlying presumption ran that sex had made them intimate, when in truth they'd have got to know each other just as well had Edgar stuck his finger in her ear.

While Trudy's face brightened, Martha's sank. Since in Hulbert's life agony and love were interchangeable, Martha's dread was more touching than Trudy's come-and-get-it. Martha had a crush on him. Conveniently, no one else in the press corps had suspected that, because it's expedient to assume that the undesirable themselves lack desire, as if they should know better. More conveniently still, Martha would never declare herself. But she wouldn't have the discipline to avoid him instead, because women like Martha could no more resist tormenting themselves in romance than Angela had ever been able to refrain from squeezing messily at ingrown leg hairs.

When Alexis Collier spied her colleague from the *Record*, tiny vertical striations scored her upper lip—pleats that by her fifties would gather into a permanently disapproving pucker. She still had a bug up her ass about that Sob interview. But then, Alexis had only two categories, the folks to whom she condescended and the folks whom she resented, so Edgar had risen as high in her estimation as it was possible to ascend.

Win Pyre wrenched around to greet Edgar with uncomplicated masculine welcome, and worked his chair aside to make room. *At last,* said his improved posture, *a decent conversation.* By contrast, Roland Ordway's rolled eyes left Edgar with the satisfying confidence that his arrival had ruined Ordway's evening.

The penultimate visage in this circle should have been the most gratifying. Not so long ago, Henry Durham would meet Edgar's arrival with a casual *Hi, mate*, casting the American reporter into that undifferentiated sea of humanity that Henry, out of laziness more than naiveté, broadly construed as benign. Edgar had been a cooperative audience at which Henry could pitch his various despairs, like pennies against a curb: his embarrassing twinning of too much money and too little talent, his pernicious affection for his own romantic rival, his bleak discovery that tragedy didn't always produce profundity, and his train wreck of a marriage, in which mutual mawkishness over their own lost innocence was the main thing that still bound them together.

But the wariness now clouding Henry's pupils signaled that at last Edgar had been differentiated all right, and as a threat. Instinctively, Durham huddled closer to his wife. From a schnook as carelessly affable as Henry Durham, the leeriness was an achievement.

Oh, Edgar didn't kid himself that this life-of-the-party sensation was anything more than a momentary confluence of transitory influences, an alignment of planets. Trudy wasn't in love; she was horny. Martha was smitten precisely because Edgar would never return the compliment; Hulbert had a nose for men who could make her miserable, and sought out misery for the same reason that Edgar courted boredom: it was comfortable. Alexis would compete with a corpse if it got its name in the paper. Stuck between two broads, Win was hungry for guy-talk and had a weakness for cronies; Edgar had won his favor merely by becoming familiar. Roland detested Edgar with such flattering virulence because, in their mutual desperation to be streetwise, they were too much alike. And no amount of jealousy on Henry's part could make up for the fact that there was far too little between Edgar and his wife to be jealous of.

Even so, however fleeting, the *look who's here!* was a bona fide glimpse of the Saddleresque. Edgar had turned heads, electrified a roundtable. For just a few seconds, Edgar had Barringtonized this little gathering. And he didn't care.

He didn't care if they liked him anymore, if his arrival caused a stir. Indeed, the very fact that for the moment he didn't give a rat's ass what they thought may have generated his magnetic field—a revelation that, since he didn't care if they liked him anymore, was of no use. Maybe having someone trying to kill you was clarifying.

Whatever they felt for him, across the board what Edgar felt for them was mild. He had nothing against Trudy; she wasn't as stupid as she first appeared, but that was the end of it. He felt sorry for Martha Hulbert, and he'd turned a blind eye to her growing partiality because it was a burden. Maybe he disliked Alexis Collier, but the dislike was as scrawny and meatless as Alesbo herself. His liking for Win was equally vegetarian. He couldn't return Roland Ordway's loathing in kind, one reason Edgar drove the guy nuts; Roland was simply immaterial. The only reason he had any feelings at all about Henry Durham was that Edgar was in love with his wife. And what Edgar felt was all that mattered. Received emotion was as worthless as a fistful of escudos in New York; you couldn't spend it without first converting it into the currency of your own heart.

Only when Nicola's face lifted last of all did Edgar meet the flash of heat that he always imagined would singe his eyebrows on lighting up a bar. A simple black turtleneck set off the tendrils of her tumbling pre-Raphaelite hair. Her eyes, though troubled, were undefended. She was glad to see him, and he was glad to see her—dollar for dollar.

As Edgar threaded toward Nicola, for once he was thankful that she'd never seen him as larger-than-life. Magnification was still distortion of a kind, and as Toby Falconer had claimed so long ago, there was no such thing as larger-than-life; there was only life-size and "other people's bullshit." Formerly, Nick's frank appraisal of Edgar as a normally proportioned character had seemed insulting. But now he got it: a man built plainly on the scale of Nicola herself had surely a far greater chance at her abiding affections than the mythically immense. Lingering by the phone, Nick had been awaiting a call not from a lover but from a legend. Just now, Edgar had never been happier to be an unimposing five-foot-eight, no unflappable paragon but a ragbag tatter of mortal terrors in need of common comforting.

"Listen," said Edgar, kneeling by her chair. "Can we find a corner and talk?"

Nicola shot an inclusive glance at her husband. "Henry, do you want to—?"

Edgar sighed, rose, and slapped his thighs. "Never mind."

"No, we should talk," Nicola pleaded. "All three of us."

Great. Hey, Henry. Be a sport. I'm going back to New York. No, I'm okay for cash. But lend me your wife for a while, will ya? Like, for about fifty years.

Pointlessly, in Edgar's view, the trio relocated to a side booth. This triangular farewell was not what Edgar had planned. Maliciously, he talked about the weather. "Some wind last night, huh?"

Henry wasn't having any of it. "I want to know what's going on."

"Too much in one department," said Edgar obliquely, "not enough in another."

Nicola leaned forward. "Any secret kept from your partner is a worm in the garden. It doesn't have to be an affair. It can be what you did last Thursday—that you went to the shops instead of the park. I've had enough of that life, Edgar. I can't keep anything from Henry. I haven't told him. But I want you to. Please. For me."

Edgar sat back, annoyed. "You realize I could be arrested?"

She traced the graffiti gouged into the table, VIVE OS SOB! "Yes."

"And you still want to spread this all over town. Just so you and Henry can read each other's e-mail with impunity."

"I've thought about this, Edgar," said Nicola. "Those scares, the bullring. It's going to get worse. You've got to spanner it. You'll have to tell the truth anyway, to discredit . . ."

"I could get at least five years." Edgar kept his voice low. "Ruin my career. For this shit hole? I'm not that 'lovely' a man, Nick."

"Blame it on Barrington!" she urged in a whisper.

"Sounds like a sitcom." Edgar grinned. "Like *Leave It to Beaver.*"

"What are you two talking about?" Henry intruded petulantly.

"It may have been Saddler's idea," Edgar carried on speaking to Nicola, "but I ran with the ball, Nick. My hands are dirty."

"Say that even after he disappeared," Nicola proposed, "he was the one who called—from wherever. Say that you just now found out, and immediately rushed to report . . . Look, Edgar, I know I promised not to tell, but all this coded hugger-mugger isn't fair to Henry! You owe him an explanation."

"Oh, I do not. I have nothing to feel guilty about with you, Nick. Wish I did." Skirting the truth was risky, but it felt good.

Nicola blushed. Henry glared. And it was all Edgar could do to stop himself from leaning over the table and kissing her then and there.

"Is he gonna blab?" asked Edgar.

"Listen, mate," said Henry. "I got plenty experience keeping a secret."

Henry's assertion had an edge that was unlike him, and Edgar looked twice. At which point he also noticed Bebê Serio shamble past with a bulging plastic carrier bag and thump into the booth behind Henry's head. Funny, Serio didn't seem the type to pick up milk and pork chops for the little woman on the way home. Still, the goon's presence was an opportunity of sorts. They were in public, Edgar was probably safe for the time being, and he was sick of being pushed around.

"I could start the story at the end," said Edgar, full-voice. "Tomás Verdade is trying to have me whacked. *Assassinar-me, sim?* Too bad for Tommy that his minions are too *GORDO* and *ESTÚPIDO* to pull it off."

"Are you having us on?" asked Nicola in alarm.

"No fooling," said Edgar. "First this *elefante* tries to run me off the road in a *pera peluda* truck. But our *idiota* can't even do a proper job of driving like shit. Next, during the Wind Watch last night? Turns out the Creams have installed free air-conditioning. Bracing, but not fatally, right? I figure these lard-heads have seen too many *Batman* reruns. That always bugged me as a kid, the too-clever-by-a-yard. The villains always had to dangle Adam West over boiling oil, wire him to a ticking A-bomb. Why not just shoot the fucker?"

Having followed Edgar's line of sight to the back of Serio's head, Nicola advised, "I wouldn't give them any ideas."

"A Cream wouldn't know an idea if it sucked his weenie."

Bebê Serio pulled himself up again, and hulking past their booth he paused. It was awful: the massive moon-pie face turned to Edgar and *smiled.* The upturned lips in the expanse of his vacant features described the perfect fleshly equivalent of the "smiley face" blighting so many T-shirts in the 1970s—which, in its lobotomized cheer, had always looked to Edgar faintly evil.

As Serio ambled from the Rat, Edgar remembered who his real enemies were, and was no longer inclined to torment Henry with his silly secret. Edgar was leaving, and from the looks of this couple—which they still determinedly were—he was leaving without the girl. It was all Barrington's fault. Saddler may have loosened the bolts in that marriage. But however a machine screw wobbled in its grooves, total detachment was dependent on that one last turn, and Nick felt too guilty to do the honors. That was the one aspect of Saddler's legacy that Edgar couldn't combat. At best, Edgar represented a salvation that Nicola the flagellant might deny herself. At worst, he'd presented her a glorious opportunity to relive the errant past and right her sins. Edgar hadn't only walked into the friend-of-the-family trap; he'd been doubly hoodwinked by Nick's twangy country-western This-Time-I'll-Be-True. Maybe if Edgar were to hover in the wings another year or two . . . But life was short. Very short, if Edgar dallied much longer.

"Guys, I'm going to have to quit Cinzeiro," said Edgar.

"Oh, no!" said Nicola.

"The Creams are gunning for me for real," said Edgar, thinking, *Sure you're crestfallen, Nick. Gonna have to find some other sap to be a saint with.* "They didn't used to be dangerous, but they've taken a correspondence course."

"What's this?" Henry asked skeptically, though he didn't look too upset that Edgar was leaving town. "You dared to slag off the Creams in print, and now they want your head? I've heard this waffle once before, and it sounded dodgy the first time."

The din in the bar covered him, and Edgar proceeded in a steady murmur. "Try not to take this personally, Durham. What happened to your family sucks, and nothing could make BA-321 into a joke. Still, whoever killed your parents, your sister, and your brother-in-law? They were sons of bitches alright. But they weren't in any, quote-unquote, 'SOB.' "

Despite further prefatory assurances that Henry himself wasn't being made a fool of, Edgar couldn't help but feel as he exposed this kid's archenemy as smoke and mirrors that he was robbing the guy—of purpose, of pathos. For no good reason, Henry had apparently wasted the prime of his thirties in a wind-battered dustbowl, while a multimillionaire might at least have been drowning his sorrows with boat drinks in St. Barts. Edgar's glib assurances to the contrary, Barrington's "ha-ha" left Henry not a bold aspiring journalist who'd spurned the lap of luxury to get at the truth about his family's destruction, but a common patsy. Overnight, Henry's precious clip file was invalidated as anything but an embarrassment, evidence that he'd been had. In the course of Edgar's fifteen-minute monologue the slumped and scowling Henry Durham was demoted from Richard the Lionheart to Man of La Mancha.

"I'd a gut sense Barrington was winding me up," Henry grumbled.

"You suspected the SOB was a leg-pull?" Edgar asked in surprise.

"Not that," Henry said irritably.

Nicola cocked her head sharply. "Winding you up about what?"

"His tearjerker story about how the Sobs were after him and that," said Henry. "Since he'd been so bloody hard on them in the *Record*. He said the leadership had offered to 'spare him for a price.' Else they'd track him down wherever he went, and he'd always be looking over his shoulder. Bear said if he couldn't buy the wankers off, there was no point in scarpering at all. The SOB has ears to the ground, he says, all over the planet. Might as well face the music here, he says. Might as well enjoy the time he has left, he says. Having tea with me and *Nicky*."

"Henry," said Nicola, in the same neutral voice she'd used when Edgar broke the news that every day in Barba was April Fool's. "How much did you give him?"

"I figured—" Henry didn't look her in the eye—"best a good round number. Check's easier to write, and what do I care? We've got loads. We'd never miss it. Haven't, have we?"

"How many zeroes?" asked Nicola calmly.

"Never counted," Henry admitted. "However many in ten million pound."

"But you said," Nicola said, a subtle over-enunciation her only sign of incredulity, "you'd a 'gut sense' he wasn't telling the truth. That the story about needing to buy off the SOB's *fatwah* seemed concocted."

"He was telling the truth that he wouldn't leave Cinzeiro without the money! What did it matter to me if he was bluffing about the rest? With everything we did, Nicky, I'd hear, *Why don't we ring Barrington*? or *Is Barrington coming?* or *Let's wait till tomorrow, so Barrington can come as well.* When he was meant to call by, you'd spend all day in the kitchen, and that night you'd open a third bottle of wine and stay up till all hours . . . And if we're on our own? Bangers and beans, cup o' tea, bit o' Portuguese telly and drawing pictures for Barrington's office. Oh, and an early night! To sleep, mind you, right? I started keeping track, mate," Henry told Edgar. "Bear calls by, every bleeding time, after he leaves? She's all over me. No Bear? It's too hot, she's too knackered. Tell me that isn't fishy!"

"I promised you, Henry," said Nicola, "I never—"

"Who bloody well cares what you never did, if you wanted to?" Henry cried, loudly enough to draw glances from colleagues at the middle table. "A lousy ten million pound! I call that good value, Nicky! I'd have paid twice that! I'd have given that bloke my every last bob to clear off and leave you be!"

It was a potentially heartwarming moment, were Edgar in the mood to be moved, which he wasn't. All the same, the woman couldn't have quite had a grip on herself if Nick could lean toward her husband right then and ask breathlessly, "So do you know where he is?"

Well, there you had it. Henry's face imploded. Nicola's hungry inquiry about Barrington's whereabouts was so colossally uncool that Edgar's romantic optimism on his own account revived in a flash. So long as he left a contact address behind he had a very, very good chance of seeing Nicola, on her own, single or soon to be, and not a year or two from now, but next week.

As if to give expression to Edgar's epiphany, at that instant the air pressure in the bar altered. In concert, the background hub-bub against which this too-public discussion had been conducted went silent. For one elongated microsecond, Edgar could see the open mouths around him, emitting no sound. Then the vista washed white. That was the point at which Edgar remembered, the way your mind will seize on incidentals of daily life in dreams, that when Bebê Serio smote them with that hideous simper and lumbered from the bar, he wasn't carrying the bag.

CHAPTER 37
The Curse of Interesting Times

BLINKING DUST FROM his lashes, Edgar came to on his back. He was lying on the vinyl back of a banquette, his feet tangled up on the seat cushion. Blessedly, when he commanded his legs to lift off the cushion, they obeyed. Shaking dirt, glass, and bits of white noise-proofing tile from his hair, Edgar took a primitive inventory: a gash in his right arm and a sticky lump on his skull, but so far everything worked.

He dragged himself to a sitting position on the floor, resting his arms on his knees and blearily scanning the disheveled bar. Overhead, rough-hewn roof beams thrust jaggedly into the dusty air at the cubist angles of Picasso's brown, murky period. The banquette had sailed a good fifteen feet, its original location marked by a dropped metal steam pipe. Blasted plaster reinforced with chicken wire formed sinister, ghostlike silhouettes, reminding Edgar teasingly of the people to whom he'd last been talking—to whom or about what he couldn't quite recall.

Gradually his hearing returned.

"*In what security sources deem a discouraging indicator, this morning's SOB statement* . . ." Uncannily, the television over the bar—what had been the bar—was still yammering CNN.

"My face! Win, is it bad? Will it scar?"

"Those motherfucking fuckers! Those sick, demented peckerheads! They blew up their own fucking bar! Stupid fucking fuckwit cunts! Since when do *Sobs* hit *hacks*?"

"Clear the area! There's been structural damage here, folks, it's not safe! Let's move on out, now! No panicking, slow and orderly, but don't knock those beams!"

Dizziness returned. Edgar's face went clammy, and his peripheral vision contracted. He dropped his head to give it some blood. While his head spun, a fresh crisis seemed to ensue. A tumble of advice—*Head down! A blanket!*—was pierced by repeated cries for an ambulance. *What about CPR? . . . Hey! ANYONE HERE KNOW CPR?* Yet the uproar mysteriously dwindled as rapidly as it had arisen.

Head still buried between his knees, as his faintness began to clear Edgar realized with surprise that he did like these people, for all their foibles. As a crude tribute to this fact, he worked his way mentally around their traditional round table to make sure that all of his colleagues were accounted for. The woman who'd gashed her face must have been Alexis; at least a fit of healthy cosmetic terror beat a frantic search through the rubble for her cellular phone. The guy incensed that the baddies had broken the rules could only have been Ordway, who just then crossed Edgar's line of vision inexplicably cradling a pound of hamburger; it took a second to register that it wasn't a purchase from the butcher but his right hand. Edgar spotted Trudy pulling Martha from the rubble, while certain that the practical, head-in-a-crisis voice organizing an evacuation could only have belonged to Win Pyre.

Edgar jerked his head upright. *"Nicola!"* The bar's pandemonium having grown subdued, the loud voicing of the young woman's name had an unseemly quality. But Edgar was beyond decorum. "NICOLA!" he bellowed again, scrambling unsteadily to a stand.

Henry slammed his chest to splay Edgar on the glass-strewn linoleum. "You stay away from Nicky!"

"Henry, where's Nick? Is she all right?" When Edgar began warily to climb up again, Henry kicked him brutally back to the floor. In the days when Edgar had gone looking for trouble he'd given bar brawlers as good as he got, but he let Henry dig a boot into his ribs without coming up swinging. The pain almost felt good.

"She was *fine* before you showed up," Henry shouted, kicking, "she was *finer* before Saddler showed up, so I hope you're both happy!" In the distance, sirens wailed.

"Henry, tell me what's happened," Edgar pleaded on all fours.

"Think I didn't notice, you taking notes, like you was on a bloody course? Well, it worked, didn't it? You got your A-levels! Now you're just like Saddler—you're a *menace*!!"

"I'm sorry," said Edgar feebly, "but what—?"

"She's—!" Henry clutched his face.

In a wave, Edgar's body washed cold and damp. He could only lurch to his feet when the weakness passed. Apparently Henry couldn't be bothered to knock him down again.

"We should all, really, evacuate the premises," Win continued to urge, although his voice had lowered, as if he were in church.

The legs of the journalists' regular round table had been blown off, and the top, swept clean of detritus, sat flat on the floor. Nicola was laid on its surface. As Edgar approached, the others parted to make way. They looked embarrassed. He thought he'd kept his feelings for Henry's wife successfully private, but they all clearly knew the score, and no doubt carelessly assumed that Edgar and Nicola had been conducting a sordid little affair for the duration.

Crouching, at first Edgar exhaled in relief, because her face was unmarked, though frozen into the slight censorial frown with which she had chided him two days back, *Is this what I've heard about all my life? Boys being boys?* But her black turtleneck was blacker, as if she'd spilled something on it. Her hand was limp, and so, as he felt her neck, was Edgar.

In this small, dense instant, Edgar learned more about his ostensible expertise than he had through his whole swaggering, know-it-all Barban stint. In fact, every hack in this bar was presumably an authority on terrorism. But to understand "terrorism" you needed at least a hazy appreciation for what you were afraid of. Accordingly, you got past this idea that bombs, however *unfortunate*, were at least events—talking points, big blooming flashes of action. Many were the bored Barbans this evening who would be secretly contented that something in dumpy Cinzeiro was finally *happening.*

But beyond a single loud noise that Edgar couldn't even remember, this occasion was mostly about what wouldn't happen. He would never unwrap another painstaking pen-and-ink drawing of his villa, or a merciful portrait of his own face that looked back at him with all the kindness of the artist herself. The afternoon would never arrive when he received his promised replica of the Barking Rat logo crocheted into his very own throw pillow. He would never again open his door to the one person whom he most wanted to see, so that greeting his every visitor forever onward his expression would imperceptibly sag. He would never be allowed the Casablancan melodrama of begging this woman to fly away with him.

"Don't you touch her!" cried Henry, thrusting Edgar from his wife. Kneeling, Henry scooped Nicola's body into his arms and looked daggers at Edgar. "That was rich before, you assuring me my family's plane crash wasn't 'a joke.' You just got the woman you fancy murdered for *national self-determination* in Barba. Who's the joke on, mate?"

Though knowing better, Edgar reached a consoling hand to Henry's shoulder.

"Get out!!"

The idea recommended itself. Edgar was a lawyer, and understood that grief was an entitlement, lodged in the fine print of a marriage license. The only thing that would insult Henry more than his simply walking away was for Edgar to stay.

Backing off from his colleagues, Edgar made the grisly discovery of how brass-tacks practical the human animal could prove amid catastrophe. A discreet retreat served a double agenda. Yes, Henry deserved to escape the torment of his presence; no, he couldn't help Nicola now; no, he hadn't earned the right to join the procession as Nicola's impromptu pall-bearers carried her body out the door. But it was also about time that he bore in mind precisely for whom this bomb had been intended.

For the moment, O Creme might assume they got their man. Edgar had a tiny window of opportunity through which to squeeze his own ass, and it would close up as soon as a single Creamie caught sight of him in one piece—at which point they might well take his *Batman*-plotting advice and "just shoot the fucker." There would be ample time for scathing self-recrimination later, but in order to feel really, really sick about his house-that-Jack-built responsibility for Nick's death he would first have to stay alive himself.

Edgar quietly picked his way out a hole blasted in the Rat's side wall. Luckily, it was dark, and the Saab wasn't far. Much as he might have liked to honor Nicola's memory by fulfilling her last request of him, going to the authorities to expose the SOB as a fairy tale right after this "imaginary" organization had blown a local establishment to smithereens was bound to lowball his credibility. It was better to grab the next plane to anywhere, and plan on spilling his guts from a safe distance—like, from *Micronesia*. He checked the Turbo's chassis, then plowed back toward Abrab Manor to get his passport.

As he gunned down the main road, Edgar's mind was a miasma of terror, fury, and self-disgust. He tried to direct his rage toward Tomás Verdade, but it kept looping back to himself, the way when you flick a lit cigarette out a four-door's front window it will fly in the back and burn up the car. Anger at Verdade was like anger at a scorpion for being a scorpion. The guy was an opportunist, and, as Barrington had observed, opportunists need opportunities—which Edgar had obligingly provided. Indeed, as Edgar reeled through the past to locate exactly where he'd gone wrong—pleading with Whoever negotiated these things that he would right his mistake if only he were given a second chance and then Nicola would rise from that round table with one of those balmy smiles like an opened window—he found himself spooling all the way back to the cursed, miserable day he was born.

Desperate for distraction, Edgar wondered how Barrington would handle this. Picturing Saddler as stoic, Edgar seized on this calming vision of impassivity to keep from bawling while he drove. Saddler might be philosophical, sedately reflective . . . Or terse, remote, contained . . . Grave, but he wouldn't fall to pieces . . .

Maybe he fucking well should fall to pieces, the cocksucker.

And naturally a star-crossed romance with his friend's wife, thwarted by a terrorist bomb on the very eve the illicit lovers might have fled the country in one another's arms, would have pumped Saddler's already bloated reputation to the size of the Hindenburg. But for once Edgar didn't fume that this nauseous turn of events would never have the same inflationary effect on his own renown, because he didn't want it to. Fiercely, Edgar promised himself never, ever to lounge in a gin mill on his third drink with some standoffish fox and launch in, *You know, I've had a hard time, like, feeling anything since this thing happened, like, I've just been sort of numb . . . Oh, it's a long story. Gary, another white wine for the lady!* No longer nursing the slightest desire to be mythologized, he wished and deserved to be remembered forever after as nothing so dignified as a bounder or a scoundrel, but as a clown.

In fact, if the rubble of the Rat was the sort of ugly scene that Barrington would rise above, it was here that Edgar decisively parted company with his ambient alter ego. He didn't want to rise above. Rather, he accepted that tonight's calamity was destined to loom over his head for the rest of his life. If that meant he didn't have the goods to be a Great Character, maybe at heart he was too decent to be interesting.

In other circumstances, Edgar might have spared a sigh that his beloved Abrab Manor had turned into a wind tunnel, where the adoptive objects of his recent life swirled in a continual disassociated cyclone. But mortality put the inanimate in its place, and Edgar didn't give a damn.

Edgar was intent on making this a sixty-second operation, so his inability to lay his hands immediately on his passport sent him into a tizzy of ripping the study apart even more thoroughly than it had been ransacked by the Creams. In a blizzard of paper, Edgar shouted, "Moron! Asshole! Moron! Asshole!" at the top of his lungs. Only when he located the thing—sheepishly, in the "safe place" he had stored it—did Edgar admit to himself that he'd become hysterical.

When the doorbell rang, Edgar decided that he might just keep on being hysterical, too. Peeping down from the study window, he saw a taxi in his drive—Christ, couldn't a Creamie hit man afford his own car?

"Mistah Kellogg!" piped a high voice from the porch, and the door rapped. "Mistah Kellogg, I have somesing faw you!"

Yeah, I bet you do, Edgar thought. But as he eyed the porch—remembering, sickeningly, that the front door lock still wasn't fixed, and this assassin could sashay right in—a slight figure stepped back so he could see her. A girl?

Edgar retrieved the cut-glass candy dish from the bedroom, and crept downstairs. Crouching below one of the shattered windows, he eyed his visitor, who shone in the headlights of the cab. She was tiny, exquisite, and, of all things, Asian. For a parochial outfit like O Creme, a mind-blowingly chic contract killer.

"Mistah Kellogg!" She rapped the door again, and stabbed the doorbell. Not exactly the form for your average assassin, but Edgar wasn't taking any chances.

"I'm warning you, I've got a gun!" he shouted.

"Please, mistah. Don't shoot. I have—" She raised an envelope.

"Open it!" Edgar wasn't falling for any letter bombs.

The girl looked frightened, so Edgar ducked. Nothing went blooey. When he peeked up again, she was waving an oblong flap of paper that whipped in the wind. "Is for you! I have message, you come quick!"

Warily, Edgar sidled to the front door and cracked it. "What is it?" he grunted mistrustfully.

"Is plane ticket." She smiled, tentatively.

"I didn't order any plane ticket," said Edgar, accepting the envelope through the crack.

"We must go now. Plane leave in just sree hour."

With connections in Lisbon and Hong Kong, it was a one-way to Bangkok. "Who the fuck is this from?"

"Mistah Ballington."

Edgar almost objected that *Mistah Ballington* was a fabrication of his own diseased mind, a make-believe consort because he was lonely, until he reminded himself once again that he wasn't that original—that he did not concoct his alter ego from nothing—that somewhere out there might lurk the real thing.

CHAPTER 38
Inversion 102

NATURALLY THE TICKETS were first class, so Edgar snagged the complimentary toiletries when he deplaned. At Don Muang International, he asked his escort, Mai, to keep his place in line at immigration while he ducked into the head. Inspecting his face critically—lined from the flight's feverish half-sleep—Edgar ran a comb through his hair, brushed his teeth, and shaved. The fact that in these somber circumstances he could still worry even half-heartedly about making a presentable impression confirmed his intuition that the forthcoming encounter was the consummation of a parallel romance.

Lacking Barba's bludgeoning wind and stunted vegetation, the great blazing white house up to which their limousine drew did Abrab Manor one better. Trimming tropical blooms under an indolent sun, three slim brown women waved as Edgar climbed from the stretch. Inside the foyer, the reflective blond flooring, teardrop chandelier, and luminous banister swooping up the stairs all gleamed with the care of industrious underlings. The air was fragrant with fresh flowers, lemon oil, and floor wax. Though he was a stranger here, and might well be asked for nothing more than a cup of tea, Edgar experienced the absurd sensation of coming home.

Mai led Edgar through the house, in the course of which he glimpsed more willowy Thai women sidling down hallways, narrow hips wrapped in sarongs. Out the other side, mimosa trees framed a capacious backyard. In its center sat a convivial arrangement of wicker chairs in the shade of an umbrella. A glass patio table was arrayed with trays of tidbits, an ice bucket, and a kaleidoscope of liquor bottles. Young ladies splashed together lethal-looking concoctions or giggled with one another as they languished on towels, while one lissome brunette trained a portable electric fan on the central wicker armchair. Striding across the plush lawn, Edgar considered wryly whether the bomb at the Rat might have zapped him after all, and this was his afterlife—a slightly clichéd paradise that beat the dickens out of the hellfire he deserved.

The figure in the middle chair faced out toward the mimosas, and the broad back in the cream jacket matched the grand scale of the house itself. One hand dangled a highball, the other a cigarillo, whose stale stink reached Edgar at ten paces.

"*Mistah Ballington*, I presume," said Edgar offhandedly to the big man's back.

The figure twisted in Edgar's direction. "How very *fortunate*," he said with gusto, "that you have arrived safely, Mr. Kellogg." Barrington nestled his drink in the grass and rose to extend a hand. "I have read your copy assiduously, and feel as if we've known one another for the longest time. You won't think me presumptuous?"

The hand was vast, dry, and grainy with a hint of talc; too soft, for a man's man. Yet the clasp was firm while not irksomely hearty, held long enough to seem gracious, not so long as to seem oily: just right. And the hand was sufficiently large to wrap Edgar's own halfway around the back, enveloping him in the same home-from-the-wars sensation of when he first alit on the property.

Meeting the eyes of his host, Edgar found them surprisingly mild—both scintillating, and a little sad. The features of the face all strangely gathered in the middle were familiar from the study photo, though the cheeks had grown if anything a little fleshier, and the incipient double chin could increasingly be deemed a success.

"You're not a-tall as I imagined," said Barrington. "So disgustingly fit. And sleek as a saluki, aren't you! Silly, of course, but I fancied you'd look more like me."

"Yeah, I'm sitting on a bestseller: *The Anxiety Diet.*" Edgar didn't wait to be invited, and sauntered to the table for an empty glass. "Thanks for the plane ticket," he said casually, popping in ice cubes with bamboo tongs.

"I hoped it would be timely. May I suggest the lemon-grass vodka? With a twist."

"Speaking of twists," said Edgar, "what tipped you off that things had queered in the homeland?"

"The bull-ring bomb, of course," said Saddler, leaning back into his chair as the wicker groaned. "The only group that would bomb Barba itself was our very own SOB. You're familiar with the myth of Pygmalion—who so loved his own creation that the statue came to life. Perhaps you grew too enamored."

"Not a chance," said Edgar, sinking into an adjacent chair as a girl slipped a flaxen stalk for a swizzle into his glass. "Calling in those bomb claims got pretty fucking old."

"Yes, I found that myself," said Barrington with interest. "Didn't really *go* anywhere, did it?"

"Oh, it went somewhere all right." Edgar slumped. While hopped up over meeting Saddler Incarnate, Edgar could only sustain this buzz so long as he forgot, in those spates of seeming amnesia during which you gradually made the intolerable tolerable to yourself, the bomb at the Rat. When Nicola's pale frown on the flattened round table returned to him, the wind died in Edgar's sails, and even for-real Barrington couldn't huff and puff them to life.

"Yes, the incident was in all this morning's papers," Saddler sorrowed. "I'd never pretend that I saw it coming, precisely. But something like it. Yet for Nicola, of all people . . ." He waved his hand in fatalistic despair. "A waste."

Edgar stared at Barrington in appreciative disbelief—a little appalled, a little impressed. Barrington might easily have connected this "waste" with his own gratuitous mischief, but the impractical exercise didn't seem to entice him. Clearly self-castigation would result in no more preferable an outcome, while casting a pall over his day.

When in doubt, *Blame it on Barrington*. "If you were so concerned that the SOB would end in tears, why did you leave me a how-to manual?"

"Mawkish attachment to my own brainchild, perhaps. It was a fascinating experiment."

"Not fascinating enough."

"No," Saddler agreed readily. "On departure, I didn't miss it. And I'd no idea that you'd prove such an able apprentice. You were sure to be a journalist, in which case the chances were terribly high that you'd also be a prat."

"I was," said Edgar glumly.

Barrington patted Edgar's injured arm. "Mustn't be too tough on yourself."

Edgar flinched. "You don't seem too torn up about it."

"I am regretful," said Barrington, his intonation provocatively flat.

"You're *regretful*," Edgar snorted. "But you won't apologize, or condemn the bombing outright? I know this script. Vintage Verdade."

"A compliment of sorts. Tomás is a master—at whatever it is he does."

"He's a fascist."

Saddler smiled. "And I thought I'd been called everything. Mr. Kellogg—"

Edgar couldn't stand it; he wanted it to be like the old days. "Call me Eddie."

"Eddie," Barrington continued indulgently, if with a touch

of bafflement. "Should you be awaiting a lachrymose display of howling and gnashing of teeth, you're in for a disappointment. I don't parade my feelings for public consumption. Nor do I keen on command, like the royal family blubbing over the death of Diana, to prove that I'm not a monster. Not even for you."

By every indication, Barrington felt sorry about Nicola, but sorry as in sad, not sorry as in contrite. Missing the accountability gene, he was free to pursue no end of "fascinating experiments" with remorseless impunity. But exploit disengaged from liability wasn't very interesting, even to Barrington. All of which helped explain not only his impulsive creation of the SOB but why he was able to abandon the conceit and never look back. Besides, like W. C. Fields's blind customer heedlessly smashing jars with his cane in *It's a Gift*, Barrington was accustomed to shattering folks on either side of him with the oblivious flamboyance of his gestures, and Saddler wouldn't be Saddler if he looked before he leapt. More, people would forgive him indefinitely for what really ought to be a flaw, because he provided something else that they needed, in trace amounts like a mineral in the diet, besides responsibility.

Edgar was constructed of more earthly stuff. He'd never done a single thing wrong—from lifting a packet of LifeSavers to lifting the receiver in Terra do Cão—that he hadn't felt bad about later. Like it or not, he had what Barrington lacked, and could no more rid himself of it than cut off his own head. Nicola was dead and it was mostly his fault and he felt like a sack of shit.

"You're not an emotional exhibitionist?" Edgar muttered. "That's not what I heard."

"You must have heard a great deal. A little bird tells me it couldn't all be dead-on."

"Win Pyre said—how'd it go? *Saddler won't take a dump without someone watching.*"

"Is that so?" said Barrington politely. "Forgive my prudery, but *take a dump* is one American expression I've always found distasteful."

"Oh, and you'd like Ordway's theory. I guess when hounds are retired from fox hunting, they get a bullet through the head, right? They're pack animals. Isolated from the pack, they pine. You can't keep them as pets, because they'll tear up the house. So Ordway claimed that if you failed to find yourself another entourage pronto, you'd have to be shot."

"I may get a bit restless, but I've yet to sink my claws into the furniture." With that, Barrington shifted to one side and glanced off to the mimosas with a manufactured-looking yawn. Funny—Edgar always found what people said about him behind his back irresistible.

Edgar regrouped. It was exasperating: on the one hand he knew this man backward and forward, down to his prissy preferences in shampoo; on the other, they'd just met, and propriety dictated tact. But Edgar didn't want to talk about Barban politics; his genuine curiosities were of an intimate sort. Circling the lemon-grass swizzle through his ice cubes, he inquired with strained nonchalance, "Did you ever ask Nick to come with you? To Thailand?"

"Considered it. I refrained, in the end."

"Why?"

"I was afraid she'd say yes, of course."

It was so trite it was dull. The old only-wants-what-he-can't-have. Christ, no wonder women were always badgering men to grow up. "You'd get tired of her?" Edgar didn't conceal his scorn.

"Heavens no. She'd get tired of *me*." Saddler intently relit his Café Crème, which had never gone out.

"False modesty doesn't suit you, Saddler. You know very well that of all the folks who couldn't stop yakking about everyone's favorite missing person, Nick was the worst of the bunch. It got a little trying, if you don't mind my saying so. Mooning by the silent phone . . ."

"Yes, I'm sure my absence was an assist in this department. A flesh-and-blood paramour can interfere awfully with the smooth conduct of romance."

Come to think of it, maybe up close Nicola really would have burned out on Barrington's bluster and savoir faire. Even for a self-confessed aesthete, pure style was more durably appealing in objects. At second glance, Saddler's dolorous faith in Nicola's inexorable disaffection looked sincere. Like Tomás Verdade behind the façade of the SOB, Barrington, too, must have worried that behind his own mystique crouched a carny pulling strings. Since any mystique was part hogwash, it stood to reason that most Great Characters lived in mortal terror of being found out.

"You should have seen her when she got that postcard," said Edgar, trying to be a comfort. "She was beside herself."

"A moment of frailty on my part, I'm afraid," said Saddler. "It's simply, few of these young ladies speak intelligible English, and I was . . ." If the word *lonely* beckoned, Saddler let it go. "I had misgivings the moment I gave the card to Mai to post in Saigon. I even considered, too late, that the gesture might have been unkind. High hopes may be nutritious, but a little hope is surely debilitating."

Rashly, Edgar asked, "Did you love her?"

"I couldn't afford to, could I?" Whether Barrington was blasé or injured it was impossible to say. "I assume you two became *fast friends*."

The jealousy was unmistakable, a hint of weakness that Imaginary Barrington would never have allowed. Edgar said coolly, "We got pretty close."

"You're bluffing!"

"I guess you'll never know," Edgar tossed back with a smile. "Anyway, you don't seem to be suffering here. Like, correct me if I'm wrong—" one of the girls brought Edgar a tray of shrimp toast—"but isn't this an upscale cathouse?"

"Not precisely. Oh, you correctly surmise that our attendants are whores. And had I the entrepreneurial spirit of you enterprising Americans, I might indeed have assembled my talented workforce into a nice little earner. But while trolling Patpong for household staff, I confess that however infatuated I became with these charming young ladies, I became conversely repelled by their customers: sweaty foreign dissolutes with their zips down."

Edgar hazarded, "Men like you."

"Quite. And I really could not stick more than one of us in my house at one time."

"So this is a harem."

"What an excellent choice of words! Yes, I do like that very much. My *harem*. Don't they cheer the place up? And while I'm sure the girls turn the odd trick for pocket money, it's quite unnecessary. I have many a shortcoming, but I am generous."

"Is it called generosity when you're giving away someone else's cash?"

"Good question! Though recall that Henry Durham was frantic for something on which to spend his fortune that didn't do more harm than good. Shifting attractive women from working the street to dusting my furniture is as well as he's likely to do."

"Is there anything you can't rationalize?"

"I should hope not," Saddler purred. "Besides—" the pillowed hand swept the lawn—"at least I understand why *they* like me."

Reflectively, Edgar chewed on his swizzle with his front teeth; the fibers tasted like Lemon Pledge. "Nick said that adulation was the bane of your existence."

"Oh, self-pity on this point would be entirely inappropriate. How much more disagreeable to be universally detested. Nevertheless—" Barrington raised his pink drink into the sun and viewed the yard through its rose tint—"simply because someone fancies you doesn't mean that you fancy them back. Simply because some breathless tosser wants to visit doesn't mean that you wish to be visited. By the time I stepped from the frame, my pied-à-terre on Rua da Evaporação had become a year-round summer camp for underemployed hacks. I'd never a moment's peace. And *Eddie*—have you ever been worshipped?"

Edgar was about to guffaw, *You must be joking*, and pulled up short. Like most people, he preferred caricature to characterization, especially when depicting himself. In the terms of this cartoon, shat-upon Ed had suffered a string of entrancements from childhood, translating into a string of crushing disappointments. Edgar had fallen head-over-heels for every girl he'd ever dated, and they'd each ditched or betrayed him. Equally, he'd been held in ceaseless thrall to larger-than-lifers of his same sex who, to a man, had let him down. Little wonder, then, that Edgar was hard-bitten and cynical. It was a portable self-portrait that he was quite attached to, and that he kept in good order with some effort, since maintaining this degree of perceived consistency by almost forty was quite a job.

Exceptions were chucked in his mental Dumpster, like Mary—he couldn't remember her last name—a pretty but fragile functionary for the New York City Council, who had fallen hard for Edgar in his late twenties. While obviously aching to marry him, she officially moved in with him for a trial period. But Edgar was starting to feel his oats at the firm and didn't want to be constrained, especially by a woman so suffocatingly selfless. She seconded his every opinion, and he was forever obliged to decide on the restaurant, film, or erotic position. Her steady assault of presents put him off buying her knickknacks in return. And Mary's adoration was boring. So he'd no sooner provided a drawer for her panties than Edgar called it quits.

Mary was distraught. She sobbed. She flopped on the floor. She washed his bare feet with her tear-soaked hair. Edgar didn't change his mind; if anything, this display was the last straw. But before kicking Mary out of his apartment and his life for good, he fucked her first.

"Yeah, you could say I've been worshipped," Edgar conceded heavily.

"Remember how you felt?"

"Ashamed of myself," said Edgar, paling and wishing the memory would go away.

"Yes," said Saddler dolefully. "It seems so awfully unfair."

Since Edgar had arrived, his eyes had continually shunted between Actual Barrington and his own makeshift mock-up, with whom Edgar had shared a villa in Cinzeiro. The biggest difference between the confection and this—well, stranger, presumably—was that the stranger was confoundingly warm.

"Saddler—" Edgar leaned forward—"I've never lost any sleep over where you disappeared to. But I have wondered *why*. I know that you blackmailed Henry Durham—"

"Nonsense! *Blackmail?*"

"It's still called a ransom, whether it's forked over to get someone back or to get them to leave. Durham never bought your hokey Sob story for a minute. Paying you to make yourself scarce didn't do him any good with Nick in the end, but he was desperate. Still, you already had a nest egg from the black market in Moscow. You'd never vanish just for cash. So why'd you give everyone the slip? Were you sick of that crowd? Was that all?"

"Let me tell you a story." Barrington handed his empty glass to a handmaiden for a refill.

"I had a philosophy professor at LSE whose name was Remington Clewes," Saddler began expansively, springing his fingers against each other. "He was articulate, stylish, wickedly funny. Students loitered about to press him with contrived questions after class, and hovered in the corners of his local. When possible, they took his courses more than once, though the waiting list for each was the length of a parliamentary white paper. I should know, because I was one of the few who inveigled themselves into a second, even a third of Clewes's seminars. Have I set the table?"

"You've set the table," said Edgar.

"On a swing through London a few years back I resolved to look up the redoubtable Clewes. I harbored the usual sad little vanity that my old professor would be pleased that one of his protégés had done him proud. While bygone nondescripts would have faded, I presumed that Remington Clewes would certainly remember *me*.

"But when I ducked into his local to ask after Professor Clewes, the barkeep sniggered. When I called by the philosophy department, the secretary rolled her eyes. Odd. Informed of his schedule, I waited outside his classroom for the seminar to conclude.

"I noted through the cracked door that the few students in attendance were staring into space. The stylish mannerisms I'd so admired in Clewes as a student had become extravagant. His dress, always natty, was now foppish, and he had taken to wearing—fatally—a bow tie. From what I could hear, his ideas hadn't changed at all—which may have been what was wrong with them. They were frayed about the edges, like worn tweed."

"You're a kid, you impress easy," said Edgar. "You grow up, naturally—your idols are no big deal."

"My stories are neither so obvious, nor so clichéd," Barrington abjured. "Unsettled, I didn't approach Clewes when the class broke up, but fell in with one of his students, who seemed in a haste to be gone. It took little prompting to elicit that Remington Clewes had become the campus fool. Apparently he'd divorced, and the obeisance he had once shrugged off he had come to rely on. Throughout his second bachelorhood Clewes had been inviting students to little soirées at his home. At first a few students made appearances; they were worried about their marks. But in his eagerness to be loved, Clewes never gave anyone poor marks anymore, which soon got about. By the time I called by, he was buying cases of good wine and mountains of melba toasts at the weekend, and no one showed. Possibly the toasts went stale, but the wine didn't go to waste, since he'd developed a notorious thirst. Meantime, for ten years he'd ostensibly been 'researching' a three-volume analysis of the metaphysicists, of which no one had seen a page. Nevertheless, he had announced to each of his classes that this mythical trilogy was destined to win him a Nobel Prize."

Edgar waited for the end of the story, but that seemed to be it. "So you don't think it was you, the way you used to see him," Edgar prodded. "He'd really changed."

"Yes." Barrington sipped his new drink through a tiny straw.

"What happened to him?"

"Isn't it obvious? Perhaps I didn't tell the story properly. Remington Clewes," Barrington despaired, "had begun to believe what other people said."

"About him," Edgar inferred.

"I've seen it before, but rarely in such high relief. It's more than possible to become one of your own fanciers—to trot down the steps of the proscenium and join the squealing crowd. If an orator sits in the audience, no one remains at the lectern.

"In this instance, you spend most of your time trying feverishly to re-create your own legend. As a consequence, you ape yourself, and badly. You become your own pretender. Ironically, in this process of self-parody you're bound to lose that mysterious *desideratum* to which your acolytes were drawn—whatever that was."

"You went AWOL," said Edgar, "to keep from becoming a horse's ass."

Barrington clinked his glass against his guest's. "Touché."

"I think," Edgar ventured, "you've seen yourself as a horse's ass all along."

"Am I," Saddler returned simply, "a horse's ass?"—less as if fishing for compliments than as if he truly wanted to know.

So Edgar took a moment to consider the question in all sincerity. Saddler himself looked to be pretty rigorous in the booze department; odds were these daytime cocktails weren't a first. He was conceited. He was verbose. He was affected. To Edgar's untrained Yankee ear, Barrington's posh accent was unerring, but that didn't rule out its being, as Nick suspected, self-taught. Though Pretend Barrington may have had a point, that virtue wasn't very attractive, neither, face-to-face, was vice. Once Edgar awoke in the rubble of the Rat to apprehend a world ineffably desolate forever after, Barrington's playful *a*morality had permanently converted to the other morality with a less ambiguous prefix.

Then there was the physical plant. The cream-colored suit, like most of Saddler's wardrobe, was a bit much. In this heat the linen had wilted, while wet patches darkened the armpits, lending Saddler the seedy air of Sidney Greenstreet. The yellow ascot and matching citrine cufflinks were self-conscious. While his boosters made much of Barrington's stature, in an era of good nutrition numerous Western men grew to six-foot-four or -five. As for his measurements on the horizontal axis, there were no two ways about it now: the guy was overweight.

Lastly, given the build-up, that Edgar would find real-life Barrington a disappointment was a narrative inevitability. Little wonder that Edgar had been agitated before this meeting. No mortal biped could hope to compare with the two-headed, five-legged, one-horned, and winged: the mythical creatures of hearsay.

Be that as it may . . .

There was something endearingly undone about Barrington's person, almost woebegone, with the ice in his drink melted and the translucent pink liquid grown weak, the highball held at a careless angle off the arm of his chair, the meniscus tipped to the rim. Yes, he was pompous, but not nearly so pompous as Edgar had expected. While Saddler's paramilitary flimflam did have grim results, Edgar was equally at fault, and the man had at least seen fit to rescue Edgar sight-unseen from the lethal stupidities of Bebê Serio halfway around the globe. That—a word that hadn't cropped up often in the Cinzeiro gossip mill—was *nice*.

Moreover, any master of *inversion* might have noticed that the pastime of flipping the coinage of character from heads to tails could be played in reverse. In adjudging Saddler, Edgar was therefore free to substitute *assured* for *conceited*, *elegant* for *affected*, and *articulate* for *verbose*. He might even grant that there was an ashen cast to his host, a sag to the man's bearing in unguarded moments, suggestive that Nicola Tremaine's death had dejected Saddler more than the man cared to admit. In taking too long to answer Barrington's simple question, Edgar found himself making what he had never before regarded as a choice. Apparently the very talent that Edgar had exploited to be so hard on people could be deployed to find them marvelous instead.

Besides, much as he might try to deny it, there was something . . . something about the guy. Edgar had felt it the very instant his hand touched Saddler's and their eyes locked for the first time: an electricity, a pull, a thrum. Label it as you like, this quality produced in its audience an instantaneous desire to please. Edgar had been fighting the impulse for an hour, if only because an evident desire to please was not itself pleasing and therefore defeated its own purpose. The fact that this magnetism was subject to neither analysis nor description made it no less palpable. Whatever the quantity was called, Edgar himself did not quite have it.

What drove him to belie the magic, was it plain envy after all? For in a sweep, Edgar recognized his own life as a continual act of reduction. His willful boredom, his hunger for savvy more than wisdom, the alacrity with which he leapt to conclude that he knew all there was to know, and his repeated hoisting of great-hearts onto pedestals only to sledgehammer them off again: it was as if he were perpetually trying to make the world smaller, the better to cram it inside himself as he'd once binged on raspberry coffee cake. But none of this diminishment made him happy, and gobbling miniaturized icons like animal crackers had never filled him up. In fact, he could vividly concoct a plausible alternative future whereby Nicola survived at the Rat and agonizingly left her husband for his good self, only for Edgar to shrink her as well—to a spoiled, trivial woman whose politics were obvious and whose decency was drab. Having victoriously demoted Nicola from Isolde to Mary Tyler Moore, he would replace her with another Isolde in ten minutes.

This project of serial embitterment was a battle against his own nature: Edgar was born a fan. Having never successfully defeated his own gaga disposition, Edgar realized that he'd spent the preponderance of his life being enchanted—utterly, blindly, lavishly enchanted—and that he was good at it.

"Saddler?" said Edgar. "You're not a horse's ass to me."

"Well, then," said Barrington lightly, patting his thighs as he stood, "that's all that matters, isn't it?

"Dinner is at eight," Saddler instructed as they ambled toward the house. "I've had a room prepared for you, but let me know if you prefer another. Do take your pick."

"I won't impose for long, I hope—"

"Don't be absurd," Barrington scolded. "You will stay indefinitely."

"What'll I do with myself?" Edgar stopped on the path. "I don't see writing much journalism from Bangkok. There's no war here, and nobody cares about Thai whores."

"These young ladies," said Barrington. "I've tried to impress on them that their previous employment did not have the makings of a durable career. In the interests of expanding their options, I wonder if you might improve their English. We should both be better entertained by their company if you did. I don't know about you, but on balance I should much rather chat all day than shag. It's far less exhausting. And however fetching, my butterflies are also illiterate. Please teach them to read."

"What's all this enlightened adult education, expiation for the SOB?"

"If that's the way you choose to look at it, you may expiate away for the both of us. Might I recommend a catnap before we dine?"

"I'd rather go for a run, if you don't mind."

"Good heavens, of course I mind," said Barrington with disgust, heading again for the back door. "How barbaric."

Falling into single-file, shaded by the vast man's shadow, Edgar considered his lifelong position of second-in-command. Sure, constitutionally Edgar was a sidekick. But there was nothing disgraceful about lieutenancy should your captain be splendid. Saddler might be *only* six-foot-five, but bigness was in the eye of the beholder. For that matter, as Edgar reviewed his shortlist of idols—like his suave, super-jock older brother, the glow-in-the-dark Toby Falconer, the awesomely august Richard Stokes Thole, and now Saddler—he concluded that in every case he himself may have got the better end of the deal. Edgar was bursting with *inchoate yearnings*, like wishing to be like Barrington. But Barrington had never woken a day in his life wishing to be like Barrington, and how bleak—to have no one else to emulate. It was probably more interesting to adore than be adored, more transporting, more engrossing, and in any event much less creepy. What the hell, given a choice, Edgar might rather revere a hero than be one.

Heading up to settle into his new room, Edgar tripped nimbly behind his new landlord as Barrington's towering cream-clad figure foreshortened up the staircase.

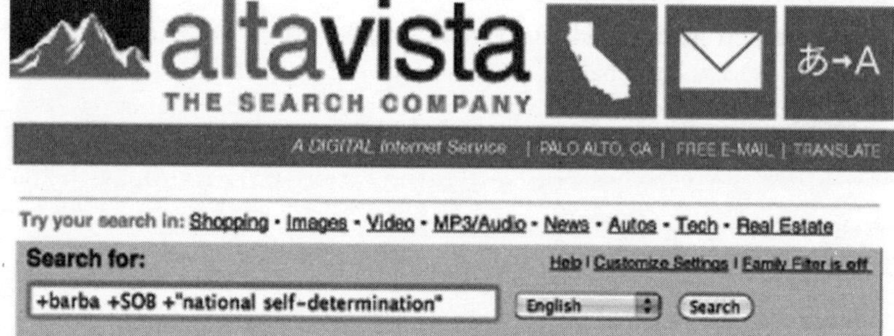

500,196 documents match your query.

Search **Amazon.com** for top-selling titles about +barba +SOB +"nationa. . .

1. Washingtonpost.com: British Journalist Charges SOB a Fake

From The Post. London Independent journalist Henry Durham asserts SOB claimed bombs it did not plant. Press skeptical. Lost whole family to terrorism. By MARTHA HULBERT in Cinzeiro. Inside "A" Section Front Page Articles . . .

http://www.washingtonpost.com/wp-srv/Wplate/2000-04/15/078l-051199-idx.html - size 11K - English - Translate

2. New Cinzeiro Concert Hall Demolished by Massive SOB Bomb

WIRE: 5:47PM New Cinzeiro Concert Hall Demolished by Massive SOB Bomb. BIRMINGHAM, England, (Reuters) - Using a recognized code phrase . . . *http://www.abcnews.com/wire/World/Reuters51489938.html - size 6K - English - Translate*

3. Verdade Claims Journalist Is Demented by Grief

Weekend Magazine. ROLAND ORDWAY's exclusive interview with Tomás Verdade on bizarre assertions of Henry Durham. Verdade suggests Durham suffering from post-traumatic stress disorder. Sidebar: "I'm No Longer Anyone's Right-Hand Man": Roland Ordway's tragic disablement by terrorism.

http://www.guardian.co.uk/magazine/cover.html - size 23K - English - Translate

4. UK News Index

Issue 1054. SOB Targets Journalists in Second Cinzeiro Pub Bombing. After a pub frequented by foreign correspondents was destroyed in August, journalists were again thought to be the intended targets in a second SOB pub bombing. After the ominous disappearances of Barrington Saddler and Edgar Kellogg . . .

http://www.telegraph.do.uk/ixnews.html - size 10K - English - Translate

5. Durham's SOB "Smear Campaign" Discredited

Terrorist expert Jonathan H. Stevenson dismisses Henry Durham's theories about the SOB as "half-baked." Even with SOB terrorism now concentrated in Portugal, Stevenson urges travelers to be vigilant. Feature, Sunday Week in Review . . .

http://www.latimes.com/lat-sr/193847-idx.html - size 29K - English - Translate

6. BBC News| International

Front Page. Eiffel Elevator Destroyed by SOB Device in Lisbon. Nine injured, four critical. Historic landmark once great tourist attraction leveled. Prime Minister fears SOB campaign is moving to the nation's capital . . .

http://www.news.bbc.co.uk/hi/english/uk/default.htm - size 11K - English - Translate

7. 37 Immigrants Killed in Cinzeiro Riots

Front Page. Editor's comment, Op-Ed, see same issue. Demonstrations against unchecked North African immigration to Barba turned violent yesterday, when . . .

http://www.nationalrecord.com/current/news.html - size 10K - English - Translate

8. From The Editor – NR

From The Editor. NATIONAL REVIEW examines how Henry Durham's career is in ruins after far-fetched accusations. "As a warning to all journalists . . .

http://www.atr.org/nationalreview/fromed.htm - size 6K - English - Translate

9. Rival Terrorist Group Arises in Barba's Muslim Community

After years of being hit, Muslims in Barba are hitting back. A series of attacks on El Terra do Cão seems to implicate the newly formed "Norte Africano Defense Associacão" (NADA). ALEXIS COLLIER explores the grievances of a leadership convinced that, without violence countering the SOB's, their people's cries will go unheard. Sunday Magazine, Cover Story . . .

http://www.nytimes.com/magazine/feature.html - size 17K - English - Translate

10. North African Defense Association Assassinates O Creme Security Chief

WIRE: 7:34PM. North African Defense Association Assassinates O Creme Security Chief. WASHINGTON, DC (AP) - Known only as "Bebê Serio," or Baby Serious, O Creme de Barbear's Security Chief was beheaded and disemboweled today . . .

http://www.newsint.com/wire/World/AP3857566.html - size 4K - English - Translate

11. Washingtonpost.com: Lisbon Sends Portuguese Army into Barba

From The Post. Continued ethnic violence brings full-scale army occupation to Barba. Troops on streets of Cinzeiro. Heavy rioting. Critics warn it is easier to move an army in than get it out again. Front Page, Comment . . .

http://www.washingtonpost.com/wp-srv/Wplate/2003-03/1/3456-2873674-idx.html - size 11K - English - Translate

12. USA Today

Lisbon Plaza Bomb Kills 5. SOB claims responsibility. Palatial Praça do Comércio in ruins. Lisbon on security alert. Checkpoints create traffic havoc. By acting Reuters Bureau Chief JASMINE PETRONELLA in Cinzeiro.

http://www.usatoday.com/uwire/mon/cobriefs.htm - size 8K - English - Translate

13. Sydney Morning Herald - Portuguese Minister in Secret Negotiations with SOB

LISBON EXPOSED IN COVERT HORSE-TRADING WITH TERRORISTS. American peace envoy expresses outrage. 'Realists' in Portugal defend talks. (Op-Ed: Barban authority ANSEL P. HENWOOD argues no harm ever comes from talking.) 'The minutes of secret negotiations were made public today . . .

http://www.smh.com.au/daily/content/world/world1.html - size 10K - English - Translate

14. O Creme de Barbear Home Page

Creme leadership denies incitement to arson in burning to the ground of Novo Marrakech. Letter from our presidente: violence will continue without stemming its root causes. Subscribe to O Creme archive for only $30/mo. Chat room, Bulletin Board, Fundraising Online, links with O Creme magazine, Liberdade!

http://www.barbanet.com/ocremedebarbear/Cinzeiro/Forum/2383/ - size 20K - Translate

15. 'Disappeared' Journalists Resurface

Former Barba correspondents Barrington Saddler and Edgar Kellogg, long presumed casualties of the conflict they covered, have emerged in Bangkok as consultants for the Thai government. Using their renowned expertise on terrorism, the incorporated duo will advise on how best to fight insurgencies based in Burma. For an undisclosed sum informed sources claim is unprecedented . . .

http://www.newsweek.com/international - size 9K - Translate

16. SOB Claims Attacks on World Trade Center and Pentagon

NEW YORK: New York Times editorial assistant Cindy Groves was contacted by an SOB representative yesterday claiming the attacks of September 11 were the work of the Barban terrorist group. As the contact's bona fides do check out, FBI and CIA sources now cast serious doubt on previous assumptions that the attacks were instigated by the Islamic extremist . . .

http://www.nytimes.com/frontpage/news.html - size 14K - English - Translate

17. Referendum on Barban Independence Scheduled for April

Front Page, by Barba Correspondent TOBIAS FALCONER. In a move Portugal's prime minister insists is not designed to capitulate to SOB violence, the Lisbon government set the date yesterday for . . .

http://www.nationalrecord.com/current/news.html - size 10K - English - Translate

18. Barban Referendum is Hobson's Choice

Op-Ed. Former Reuters Barba Bureau Chief WINSTON R. PYRE argues that the SOB has Barba over a barrel. "Presented the stark option to vote for 'peace' or 'bloodshed', I'd feel sufficiently blackmailed to choose the latter . . .

http://www.thenation.com/issue287/comment.html - size 12K - English - Translate

19. It's YES!

Cover Story by REINHOLD GLÜCK, Full Photo Essay by TRUDY SISSON. Barban Peace Referendum Passes by Resounding 91%. Wearing red carnations to symbolize sacrifice, Barbans dance in the streets to celebrate their independence from both Portugal and years of gruesome . . .

http://www.theatlantic.com/feature/387.html - size 13K - English - Translate

20. "FREE AT LAST: HOW WE WON OUR FIGHT FOR LIBERTY"

Commencement address for Harvard University by Dr. Tomás Verdade, President of the Republic of Barba.

Http://234.3.345.1/iveagh/foreignaffairs/press/827388c.htm - size 13K - English - Translate

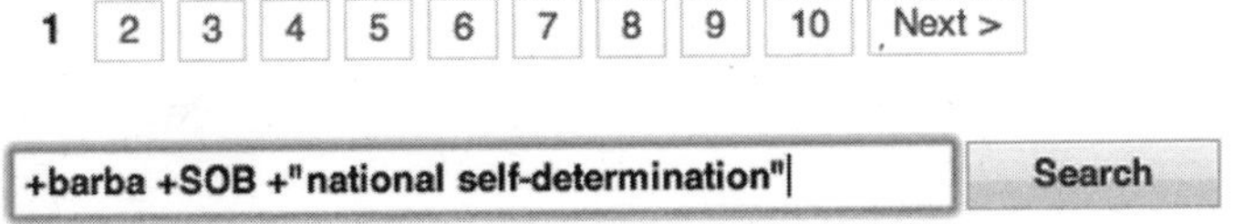

AUTHOR'S NOTE

Written between *Double Fault* and *We Need to Talk About Kevin*, *The New Republic* was completed in 1998. At that time, my sales record was poisonous. Perhaps more importantly, my American compatriots largely dismissed terrorism as Foreigners' Boring Problem. I was unable to interest an American publisher in the manuscript.

In short order, both discouragements lifted. My sales record improved. Post-9/11, Americans became if anything *too* interested in terrorism. Thus for years after the calamity in New York, I was obliged to put the novel on ice, because a book that treated this issue with a light touch would have been perceived as in poor taste.

Yet the taboo seems to have run its course. Sensibilities have grown more robust. I am hopeful that this novel—whose themes have become only more trenchant since it was written—can now see print without giving offense. Though tightened with the cold eye of distance, the book is published roughly as I first wrote it, with one small, irresistible addition in the epilogue that readers will readily recognize.

ACKNOWLEDGMENTS

WITH SPECIAL THANKS to Jonathan Burnham and Katie Espiner, who in relation to this manuscript displayed vision, intellectual independence, and appreciation for a boy-book written by a girl. You are both a joy to work with.

ABOUT THE AUTHOR

Lionel Shriver's novels include the National Book Award Finalist *So Much for That*, the *New York Times* bestseller *The Post-Birthday World*, and the international bestseller *We Need to Talk About Kevin*, which won the 2005 Orange Prize and has been adapted for a feature film. Earlier books include *Double Fault*, *A Perfectly Good Family*, and *Checker and the Derailleurs.* Her novels have been translated into twenty-six different languages. Her journalism has appeared in *The Guardian*, *The New York Times*, *The Wall Street Journal*, and many other publications. She lives in London and Brooklyn, New York.